Bernard Shaw's Irish Outlook

David Clare

palgrave
macmillan

First published 2016 by
PALGRAVE MACMILLAN

The author has asserted their right to be identified as the author of this work in accordance with the Copyright, Designs and Patents Act 1988.

Palgrave Macmillan in the UK is an imprint of Macmillan Publishers Limited, registered in England, company number 785998, of Houndmills, Basingstoke, Hampshire, RG21 6XS.

Palgrave Macmillan in the US is a division of Nature America, Inc., One New York Plaza, Suite 4500, New York, NY 10004-1562.

Palgrave Macmillan is the global academic imprint of the above companies and has companies and representatives throughout the world.

ISBN 978-1-349-55433-1
E-PDF ISBN: 978-1-137-54043-0
DOI: 10.1057/9781137540430

Library of Congress Cataloging-in-Publication Data

Clare, David, 1971–
    Bernard Shaw's Irish Outlook / by David Clare.
        pages cm.—(Bernard Shaw and his Contemporaries)
    Includes bibliographical references and index.

    1. Shaw, Bernard, 1856–1950—Criticism and interpretation.
    2. Shaw, Bernard, 1856–1950—Homes and haunts—Ireland. 3. Irish in literature. 4. Ireland—In literature. I. Title.

PR5368.I67C57 2015
822'.912—dc23   2015020035

A catalogue record for the book is available from the British Library

For Deirdre

Contents

Acknowledgments

Special thanks to:

The Irish Research Council and NUI Galway's Moore Institute (Dan Carey, Seán Ryder, Martha Shaughnessy, and Kate Thornhill) for their abundant support—financial and otherwise—during the preparation of this book.

The editors of the Palgrave Macmillan "Bernard Shaw and His Contemporaries" book series—Nelson O'Ceallaigh Ritschel and Peter Gahan—for their helpful comments on my manuscript and their belief in my work. Thanks also to my editors at Palgrave Macmillan—Shaun Vigil and Erica Buchman—for seeing this book into print.

The Society of Authors, on behalf of the Bernard Shaw estate, for permission to quote from his published works.

Those who have served as my academic advisors and mentors since my return to academia in 2007: Emilie Pine, Patrick Lonergan, Declan Kiberd, and Tony Roche. Your wise advice, astute feedback, and exceptional scholarship have assisted my development beyond measure.

Feargal Whelan, for our highly stimulating, weekly chats on Irish literature and culture: they have helped clarify my thoughts on Shaw, Irish Protestants, and so much else.

Colleagues and friends with whom I have discussed Shaw and/or issues around identity: Matt Bothner, John Brannigan, Tom and Kris Burns, Frank Byrne, Peter Byrne, Clíodhna Carney, Barry Casey, Sam Cromie, the Cutler family, Daithí de Bláca, Fionnuala Dillane, Matt Duss, Victor Fairbrother, Paul Gibson, Dave Goldberg, Miriam Haughton, the Heaton/Barch/McGovern family, Éanna Hickey, Rónán Johnston, Ken Keating, Derek Kelly, Des Lally, P. J. Mathews, Charlotte McIvor, Audrey McNamara, Trish McTighe, Archana Nagraj, Sr. Mary Eileen O'Brien, Adrian Paterson, Graham Price, Mike Roy, Sean Hunter Ryan, Sally Sharkey, Sr. Kathleen Sullivan, Brian Tavey, Eric Tiénou, Tim Ural, Ian R. Walsh, Jesse Weaver, Jon Woodhouse, and my cherished workmates from my years at the Gate Theatre. Extra thanks to Eric Tiénou for proofreading this book in manuscript.

Important teachers from my formative years, for helping to shape my mind and my socio-political outlook: Louis Antonietti, Tony Barrand, Gary Chester, Bert Hughes, Jim Maginley, Ken Mitchell, Ishwer C. Ojha, and Judy Thomas.

Chris Humphrey and Konstantinos Peslis of Cambridge Scholars Publishing; Jim Rogers of the *New Hibernia Review*; Paul Hyland, Neil Sammells, and Nicola Presley of the *Irish Studies Review*; and Taylor & Francis Ltd (the publishers of the *ISR*) for permission to republish material that has previously appeared before the public. Chapter 1 incorporates my book chapter "Bernard Shaw's Irish Characters and the Rise of Reverse Snobbery" from the essay collection *The European Avant-Garde: Text and Image*. Ed. Selena Daly and Monica Insinga. Newcastle: Cambridge Scholars, 2012. (Available from www.cambridgescholars. com.) Chapter 2 incorporates my article "Bernard Shaw, Henry Higgins, and the Irish Diaspora" from *New Hibernia Review* 18.1. (Available via ProjectMuse.) And the Conclusion incorporates portions of my article "Wilde, Shaw, and Somerville and Ross: Irish Britons, Irish Revivalists, or Both?" from *Irish Studies Review* 22.1. (This special issue on the Irish Revival was guest edited by Giulia Bruna and Catherine Wilsdon and is available from www.tandfonline.com.) A heartfelt thanks also to the editors and peer reviewers of these publications for their helpful comments regarding my work.

Finally, my family, for their invaluable love and support: my beautiful and brilliant wife, Deirdre; my mother and father (your thoughts on culture and politics were undoubtedly the most significant influence on this book); my sister, Nadia, her husband, Dan, my nephew, Holden, and my niece, Emily; my foster brothers, Nhi and Phong Tran, and their families; and my extended family in Europe, the Middle East, and North America.

Introduction

At the age of 75, Bernard Shaw told an interviewer that the happiest moment of his life was when as a child his mother informed him that his family was moving from Synge Street in the Dublin city center to a cottage on Dalkey Hill in south County Dublin.[1] The young Shaw was so excited, because he already knew (and treasured) the magnificent view that is available from Dalkey Hill: the Wicklow Mountains and Killiney Bay to the south, the Hill of Howth to the north, and Dalkey Island and the Irish Sea directly below. Throughout his career, Shaw always insisted that it was "the beauty of Ireland" that gave Irish people their distinctive perspective, and, in his own case, he believed that it was the beauty of this particular view that helped to shape him into the visionary iconoclast that he was.[2]

Indeed, upon receiving the Honorary Freedom of Dublin at the age of 89, Shaw told journalist James Whelan, "I am a product of Dalkey's outlook."[3] As Shaw approached the end of his life, he was eager to emphasize the importance of his Irish formative years to his work. In an article published three years later (and two years before his death), he declared, "Eternal is the fact that the human creature born in Ireland and brought up in its air is Irish...I have lived for twenty years in Ireland and for seventy-two in England; but the twenty came first, and in Britain I am still a foreigner and shall die one."[4]

Those who know Shaw by reputation as a writer of English society plays may be surprised to learn that he regarded himself as so thoroughly Irish, even after living in London and Hertfordshire for decades. While one might expect to see evidence of Shaw's Irishness in his three plays set in Ireland—*John Bull's Other Island* (1904), *O'Flaherty, VC* (1917), and *Tragedy of an Elderly Gentleman* (1921)—this book demonstrates that Shaw's Irish outlook is also manifest in his plays set outside of his native country.[5] In this book, I analyze Shaw's use of Irish and Irish Diasporic characters, as well as what I am calling Surrogate Irish and Stage English characters, to prove the veracity of R. F. Dietrich's recent contention that Shaw "wrote *always* as an Irishman."[6]

Chapter 1 examines all of Shaw's plays that feature Irish-born characters (including the English plays *Man and Superman* (1903), *The Doctor's Dilemma* (1906), *Press Cuttings* (1908), and *Fanny's First Play* (1911)).[7] In each of these works, Shaw uses Irish characters to express his Irish reverse snobbery; that is, he suggests through these characters that it is better to be from a marginalized background, because early struggles and external resistance from others are a better preparation for life than a childhood full of indulgence and ease. Although the reverse snobbery expressed in these works was regarded as "typical Shavian perversity" when these plays were first produced, Shaw's enduring popularity with audiences has ensured that this idea has gained purchase in the Anglophone world.[8] Today, it is often suggested that people from less-advantaged backgrounds are cannier and have more joie de vivre than those from higher class backgrounds, and, in recent decades, we have regularly seen middle- and upper-class people pretending to be from less prosperous backgrounds than they actually are. Shaw's Irish outlook—including the Irish chip on his shoulder—is at least partially responsible for this remarkable societal change.

Chapter 2 demonstrates that Shaw—like most Irish people—had conflicted feelings regarding the Irish Diaspora. On the one hand, he could be quite scathing about those born outside of Ireland who claimed to be Irish (he once called them "sham Irish").[9] On the other hand, he was also adamant that his friends of Irish descent, including the American boxer Gene Tunney and the Welsh-born freedom fighter T. E. Lawrence ("Lawrence of Arabia"), should be regarded as Irish. This ambivalence is reflected in his plays. While some characters of Irish descent in his work are treated as not Irish "at all," he suggests that others owe their strengths and weaknesses to their Irish cultural backgrounds.[10] The most notable example is Henry Higgins from *Pygmalion* (1912), but others include Fergus Crampton from *You Never Can Tell* (1898), Captain Kearney from *Captain Brassbound's Conversion* (1900), Cashel Byron from *The Admirable Bashville* (1901) (and the novel *Cashel Byron's Profession* (1885)), "Snobby" O'Brien Price from *Major Barbara* (1905), and "Boss" Mangan from *Heartbreak House* (1919).

Chapter 3 examines the plays in which Shaw uses Surrogate Irish characters to comment on Irish politics and history and to explore issues that were important to his Irish Anglican subculture. (This Irish cultural group has traditionally been called the Anglo-Irish, but I have rejected that moniker in this book; as Shaw himself rightly pointed out, calling Irish writers of British descent from Church of Ireland backgrounds "Anglo-Irish" was a convenient way for English commentators—and bigoted "Irish-Irelanders"—to imply that these artists are not really Irish.)[11] The title character from Shaw's *Saint Joan* (1923), Napoleon from *The Man of Destiny* (1897), and the long-livers from *Tragedy of an Elderly Gentleman* are all non-Irish characters who occupy an adversarial, crypto-Irish role when confronted with the English characters (or characters of English descent) included in these works. The Irish Anglican preoccupations present in these plays—and in many works by writers from Shaw's subculture—include marked ambivalence (and occasionally outright hostility) towards England, a deep familiarity with (if not always respect for) Roman Catholicism, a finely tuned sense of differences in social class, a fixation on "cross-breeding" between people from different backgrounds, and a distrust of art and artifice (and a related fear of disappearing too far into dreams and the imagination).[12] In the futuristic play *Tragedy of an Elderly Gentleman*—set in Ireland after the extinction of the Irish—Shaw explores an additional trope from Irish Anglican writing (and Irish Protestant art and letters generally): celebrating the Irish landscape while removing or ignoring the people who actually populate that landscape.

In chapter 4—this book's longest and most ambitious chapter—Shaw's use of satirical Stage English characters in his Irish plays is analyzed. A survey of Shaw's Stage English figures reveals that he retained a stubbornly Irish perspective regarding the people among whom he lived for most of his life; it also reveals the degree to which Shaw's Stage English characters are indebted to, and deliberately distinct from, satirical portraits of the English found in the work of other Irish writers. Most notably, it will be shown that there is a tendency among Irish writers to depict the English as either "racist, officious hypocrites" or "sentimental, romantic duffers." Broadbent, from *John Bull's Other Island* (1904), is an ingenious combination of the two, and Shaw's combining of these two English character types influenced important, later portraits of the English in Irish literature, including Haines from James Joyce's *Ulysses* (1922), Gerald Lesworth from Elizabeth Bowen's *The Last September* (1929), Basil Stoke and Cyril Poges from Seán O'Casey's *Purple Dust* (1940), and Leslie Williams and Monsewer from Brendan Behan's *The Hostage* (1958).

Before embarking on my analysis, I should note that my campaign to emphasize Shaw's Irishness is part of recent, growing interest in the "Irish Shaw."[13] Contemporary critics who have done important work exploring under-examined, Irish aspects of Shaw's drama include (among others) Peter Gahan, Nicholas Grene, Brad Kent, Declan Kiberd, Audrey McNamara, James Moran, Nelson O'Ceallaigh Ritschel, and Anthony Roche. The work of all of these fine critics will be drawn upon in this book. I have personally met most of these critics, and one topic that we have frequently discussed is the need to put a shape on Shaw's huge canon of work (he wrote over 50 plays). The current tendency to overlook or marginalize Shaw in scholarly works on twentieth-century drama and Irish Studies is due in large part—I believe—to the fact that critics are intimidated by the sheer size of Shaw's canon (it seems that they do not know where to start reading). Some may also have dismissed Shaw after seeing subpar productions of his frequently revived but—I would contend—dramaturgically flawed plays, such as *Mrs Warren's Profession* (1898), *Misalliance* (1910), and the revised versions of *Pygmalion*; like many Shaw critics, including Leonard Conolly, A. M. Gibbs, Arnold Silver, Diderik Roll-Hansen, and St John Irvine, I believe that the original version of *Pygmalion*— first performed in English in 1914 and first published in 1916—is superior to the later 1939 Constable and 1941 Penguin versions, which were altered to their aesthetic detriment by Shaw.[14] In this study, I focus on the plays that I believe are the center of Shaw's achievement: his masterpieces (*Saint Joan*, the original *Pygmalion*, and *Man and Superman*), his Irish plays (*John Bull's Other Island*, *O'Flaherty, VC*, and the admittedly patchy but certainly intriguing *Tragedy of an Elderly Gentleman*), and the various plays in which he tackles—however obliquely—Irish affairs, usually through inclusion of an Irish, Irish Diasporic, or Surrogate Irish character.[15] The fact that so many of Shaw's best plays are also the ones in which he engages with Irish issues is another strong indication of his enduringly Irish outlook.

1
Shaw and the Rise of Reverse Snobbery

Much has been written about Bernard Shaw's profound influence on British and Irish thought during the twentieth century. In 1977, the Irish playwright and critic Denis Johnston rightly contended that Shaw "more than anybody else is at the root of the ways of thinking that dominate the English-speaking communities of today... We live in fact in a Shavian world—with Shavian education, Shavian economics, a Shavian view of sex and marriage, and certainly a Shavian view towards religion."[1] One of Shaw's most lasting contributions to modern thought, however, is a little publicized one: the fact that he helped make reverse snobbery a commonplace of Anglophone art and public discourse during the twentieth century.

Shaw accomplished this through the careful contrast of English and Irish characters in his plays. By making the childhood poverty and struggle against prejudice endured by his Irish characters seem like an advantage in life compared to the material comfort and public school educations enjoyed by most of his English characters, Shaw helped create a new kind of underdog hero: the member of an oppressed populace having to deal with spoiled, politically unrealistic, dangerously sentimental imperial overlords or social superiors. Unlike the characters from the English novels and plays of the preceding centuries, Shaw's Irish characters are proud and not ashamed of their disadvantaged backgrounds and early material struggles. An examination of this dynamic in Shaw's plays reveals the role that socialism and his belief in the Life Force played in the formation of this view, but also the role played by the Irish intellectual tradition.

Six of the plays that Bernard Shaw wrote between 1903 and 1915 feature Irish characters who express and demonstrate the purported advantages of being Irish over being English. While Shaw's original audiences may have regarded this as typical Shavian perversity, contemporary audiences are much more inclined to accept the contention that it is desirable to be from a marginalized background. This is because, in the decades since these plays were written, the English-speaking world has seen a sharp rise in reverse snobbery—sometimes referred to as inverse or inverted snobbery. People across the English-speaking world now struggle to hide their privileged upbringings and mimic those who they see as having emerged from the kind of salt-of-the-earth backgrounds that produce greater shrewdness, joie de vivre, and physical/psychological courage. In Great Britain, for example, Michael Roper has written of a peculiar phenomenon he found in the factories he studied in the early 1990s:

> Middle-class, university-educated arts graduates occasionally showed off their technical knowledge to me, as if they were 'practical men' who had worked their way up from the shop floor...The hard masculinity associated with a working-class background...was particularly admired by the men I interviewed. Middle-class managers more often imitated their inferiors in class terms than the reverse, [attempting to]...shak[e] off the effete image of the pen-pushing professional.[2]

Likewise, journalists Antony Miall and David Milsted have observed that, in contemporary England:

> There is a...reverse snobbery about being working class. It used to be the proletarian dream to become middle class and drop all working class connections. This has gone into reverse and to be middle class is now seen as effete and conformist.[3]

Within a specifically Liverpool context, John Belcham has written of the rise in recent decades of "reverse snobbery and pride in... [being a] real Liverpudian, the true Scottie Road scouser."[4] Commentators in other Anglophone countries report the same phenomenon. In Australia, political scientists have written about the "inverse snobbery" that causes people to have pride in their "convict ancestry" as a sign that they are "resourceful and resilient" and as a way of distancing themselves from the English, who are perceived to be more uptight and classist.[5] In the United States, sociologists like Harold M. Hodges and Geoffrey Gorer have discussed the endemic "inverse snobbery" that has discouraged elitism and attempted to "cast all in the same social mold."[6] And Ihab Hassan and Terry Eagleton have successfully argued that anti-elitism is a key feature of literary postmodernism as it has manifested itself across the Western world.[7]

From a Shavian point of view—given the plotline of *Pygmalion*, in which an East End flower girl is taught to speak like an aristocrat—one extremely interesting development is the trend that has been examined by Lynda Mugglestone, John R. Reed, and Ulrike Altendorf: the fact that in England, since in the 1930s, "Ruling-class persons [have] mimicked the speech and dress of the lower classes and demonstrated a kind of inverted snobbery."[8] Along the same lines, in the United States over the past 30 years, an ever-increasing number of white suburban teenagers have been incorporating African-American slang into their speech and wearing clothing labels associated with "hip-hop."[9]

All of this is a stunning reversal from the eighteenth and nineteenth centuries when characters in countless novels and plays imitated their social betters, clung tenaciously to any claims they had to a higher social class than their present circumstances suggested, and disowned any aspect of their backgrounds that hinted at descent from "backward, superstitious, and uncivilized" foreigners.[10] Given the fact that Shaw began his playwriting career in such a cultural climate, it was astonishingly groundbreaking that he chose to place Irish characters into his plays who not only exposed "the fakery of circulating versions of Irishness" (to quote Colin Graham) but who also revealed, through their words and accomplishments, that an Irish background was superior to an English one in preparing a person for life.[11]

The first Irish-born character to appear in a Bernard Shaw play is the surly Kerryman Hector Malone, from *Man and Superman* (1903). Malone has made millions in the United States and seems to credits his success to the disciplining effects of his early sufferings (his mother was a barefooted girl who nursed him by a turf fire in a cottage and his father died in the Famine). Shortly after Malone appears on stage, he insults the Cockney chauffeur Henry Straker's intelligence by correcting his pronunciation and sarcastically calling him a "bright Britisher." A little later, we discover his clear disdain for the English middle classes through his conversations with Violet. He tells her emphatically that he "want[s] no middle class properties and no middle class women" for his son. And when he brags to her that he has "the refusal of two of the oldest family mansions in England," we see his happiness at how low the lazy, impractical, English leisure classes have fallen.[12]

In *John Bull's Other Island* (1904), the Irish lead Doyle is a cynical fact-facer due to his Irish childhood, disdaining the sentimental platitudes and confused political philosophies enunciated by his English business partner Broadbent. He and the Irish mystic Keegan see the situation in Rosscullen and the world much more clearly than the Englishman Broadbent, whose judgment is clouded by racist stereotypes of Irish people, Jews, and the Asian subjects of the British Empire, as well as by an "intellectual laziness" that Shaw says Englishmen like Broadbent are prone to.[13] (According to Shaw, that "intellectual laziness" is the tendency among Englishmen to cling to pre-formulated notions given to them by their educations and the newspapers, despite the disconnection between those notions and the realities they see every day.) Broadbent's judgment is further clouded by a ruthless efficiency that is deeply offensive to Irish sensibilities.

Doyle and Keegan also independently observe another of Broadbent's character flaws: the hypocrisy which enables him to use whatever socially approved principle comes to hand to justify whatever action will help him succeed in a given situation. He instinctively shuts out alternative, competing points of view that—in Doyle's words—"it doesn't suit [him] to understand."[14] Doyle and Keegan both agree that this tendency to "let not the right side of [his] brain know what the left side doeth" is the secret behind the success of all Englishmen.[15] But another secret behind Broadbent's success is Doyle himself, illustrating Shaw's belief— articulated in the play's preface—that "the successful Englishman of today...often turns out on investigation...to be depending on the brains, the nervous energy, the freedom from romantic illusions (often called cynicism) of...foreigners [such as Irishmen, Scots, Jews, and Italians] for the management of their sources of income."[16] Thus, Shaw is emphasizing the benefits of being raised in an impoverished or marginalized environment like Ireland.

Despite the English Broadbent's somewhat greater success in the play (winning the girl and the local parliamentary nomination), Doyle is still proud to be Irish and to see life more clearly than "God's Englishman," even when his clear-headed, lengthy analysis is repeatedly dismissed by Broadbent as "blarney," "tommy rot," and "Irish exaggeration," or mistaken for humor.[17] Doyle is proud to be friends and business partners with Broadbent, because he desires to have his Irish character refined by exposure to Broadbent's English efficiency and optimism, thus freeing himself from the sneering Irish attitude and propensity to dream that he deplores. Ultimately, it is by showing these strengths in the English character as well as the weaknesses that Shaw avoids reverse racism in the play, fulfilling his stated desire to not only "shew the Englishman his own absurdities" but also to "teach Irish people the value of an Englishman."[18]

In *The Doctor's Dilemma* (1906), the gruff Irish doctor Sir Patrick Cullen is free from the unflagging belief in medical progress of the credulous, optimistic English doctors Sir Colenso Ridgeon and Sir Bloomfield Bonnington. Cullen remains cool-headed in the face of new medical breakthroughs, pointing out that every supposedly new discovery was made decades before in a slightly altered form and subsequently disproved. He is also very cynical regarding the English medical profession in general, scornful of doctors who he believes have base financial motives. He accuses one character, Cutler Walpole, of pretending to cure people by surgically removing organs that evolution has rendered useless. In addition to this cynicism/realism, Cullen's other Shavian Irish traits are his dark sense of humor, his ability to detect spongers and blackguards like Dubedat, and the sensitive conscience that makes him remember patients that he and Ridgeon have failed, long after Ridgeon has forgotten them. These traits are the product of an Irish upbringing in which, despite being the son of a doctor, he witnessed much human suffering and a population enduring endemic financial hardship.

In 1909's *Press Cuttings*, the English General Mitchener proposes marriage to the Irish Mrs Farrell, the cleaner in the government building where they work, because he is impressed by her "practical ability and force of character."[19] Mrs Farrell, another Irish fact-facer, at first refuses because "I'd have to work for you just the same; only I shouldn't get any wages for it."[20] When Mrs Farrell does accept his offer, she is happy that her snobbish daughter (who is engaged to a duke) can be proud of her for no longer being a charwoman, but she is obviously unimpressed with the people in the social circles she will be entering. After accepting the General's proposal, Mrs Farrell (free from silly, romantic notions regarding their situation) refuses a kiss from him, saying "You'd only feel like a fool and so would I."[21] The General, meanwhile, is very happy to unite with the Irish charwoman, because he is excited to overcome the supposed disadvantages of his own background. As he says, "I am not clever at discussing public questions, because, as an English gentleman, I was not brought up to use my brains."[22] He also blushes when Mrs Farrell talks frankly about sex and childbirth, making practical conversation on these important aspects of women's role and rights (in a play about women's suffrage) impossible. Mitchener's and Prime Minister Balsquith's cynical views regarding democracy and the press show up the hypocrisy of their public rhetoric. They openly refer to the common people as "the mob," are willing to use bribery and state-sponsored violence to achieve their goals, and boast that "if we need public opinion to support us, we can get any quantity of it manufactured in our papers."[23] Both men, with their comic repetition of the phrase "Dash it all," are satirical portraits of well-to-do but ineffectual Englishmen, and are comparable to Broadbent in possessing what Shaw saw as the peculiarities and hypocrisies endemic in the English national character.[24] (As indicated in the Introduction, the negative, allegedly English traits associated with Broadbent and some of Shaw's other English characters will be the focus of further analysis in chapter 4.)

In *Fanny's First Play* (from 1911), Count O'Dowda from the epilogue and prologue is an Irishman who has lived mainly on the Continent. Thanks to these Irish and European influences, he has escaped the crassness of taste and thought demonstrated by the English critics who attend his daughter's play. Fanny O'Dowda is of Irish extraction but has lived on the Continent or in England her whole life. She seems more like some of the strong English women Shaw populated his plays with in order to demonstrate the power and admirable audacity of the New Woman. In the play itself, "Darling Dora" Delaney, while not explicitly said to be Irish, can be surmised to be so (despite her occasional use of London slang), through her surname, her reference to "Carrickmines" in County Dublin, and aspects of her character; Dora's role (like that of other Shavian Irish characters) is to make sentiment, pomposity, and useless social divides appear ridiculous and to inject vibrant life and humor into the scenes in which she appears.[25]

The play's English middle-class parents, meanwhile, are insecure regarding their place in society (having recently risen in the world) and are paralyzed by what society and the neighbors think. They are full of little hypocrisies regarding impure habits like drinking, are xenophobic against the French, and are rude to Dora because they feel they must be in order to keep up middle-class appearances. Meanwhile, Bobby and Margaret, the securely middle-class children, are attempting to explode the hypocrisies of their English, public school upbringings, because they have been inspired by the new perspectives given to them by Dora, the Frenchman Duvallet, and the suffragettes that Margaret met in prison.

In *O'Flaherty, VC* (written in 1915 but first performed and published in 1917), the soldier O'Flaherty is immune to the British patriotic sentiment espoused by the Irish Anglican gentleman Sir Pearse Madigan. O'Flaherty joined the army merely because he was bored in Ireland and wanted to get away from his overbearing mother. His perspective on World War I and the struggle between the Irish and the English is much clearer than the muddled thinking of the hybrid character Sir Pearce or the romantic idealism of Sir Pearce's English wife. O'Flaherty's girlfriend, meanwhile, is too anti-romantic and meanly practical, Shaw seems to imply, because she is overly focused on the money to be made through soldiering. To her credit, however, she—like O'Flaherty—is not remotely in danger of falling for the jingoistic propaganda that (according to Shaw's preface) the English public are swallowing whole.

O'Flaherty's mother, by contrast, is oblivious to the English propaganda, and this is because—to Shaw's way of thinking—she is too full of hate for the English. (This constant channeling of political energy into hatred of the English could destroy the Irish, Shaw warns in *Tragedy of an Elderly Gentleman*; they must learn, he implies, how to use more than just their revolutionary political muscles.)[26] Despite this fault, Mrs O'Flaherty is very practical and full of savvy compared to most of the English people in Shaw's plays, her poverty having taught her important lessons about the nature of the world. A good example is her explanation of how she swindles money out of the British government, which she feels justified in doing because they "oppress the poor."[27] She readily agrees with her son's observation that "if there was twenty ways of telling the truth and only one way of telling a lie, the Government would find it out."[28]

In all of Shaw's plays with Irish characters, the early financial hardship and prejudice endured by the Irish have helped to make them the practical, clear thinkers that they have become.[29] In the cases of the men who have emigrated, this has meant financial success (Malone, Doyle, and O'Dowda are all well-off). These men and even the Irish women who are living in relative poverty outside of Ireland (such as Mrs Farrell and Dora) are proud of their practicality and their ability to detect schemes and see through rhetoric and sentiment clearly. This results in a reverse snobbery that prizes being Irish over being English. In these plays, Shaw makes it seem (contrary to the thought of the time—judging by Punch Magazine or the newspapers) that it is an advantage in life to be Irish, as opposed to well-to-do English.[30] Undoubtedly, it is Shaw's socialism and belief in the Life Force that informs this view. His socialism told him that class consciousness was key for people to rise up in life. The Irish characters, by being continually reminded of their marginalized status by the English and the world, are made very aware of their outsider status economically. Shaw's English characters who have risen from working-class backgrounds—such as Sartorious in *Widowers' Houses*, Mrs Warren in *Mrs Warren's Profession*, and Eliza Doolittle in *Pygmalion*—are very aware of their poor backgrounds, but (for the most part) are ashamed of them and trying to cover them up, like the stereotypical heroine of a nineteenth-century English novel who hopes to marry a man of property. They also work very hard to spare their children the sufferings they endured. For their pains, their children, such as Blanche Sartorious and Vivie Warren, either "hate the poor" or cannot relate to them at all, giving their originally poor parents pause.[31] One gets the impression that the Irish parents in Shaw's work, such as Hector Malone and Mrs Farrell, wish that their children could endure some hardship, for the good of their souls and their ability to rise in life, so as not end up slaves to fashionable society and full of ennui.

Thanks to Shaw's socialism, we do, however, see the first signs of class consciousness and reverse snobbery among the English— reverse snobbery that Shaw noted to be growing slowly among the working classes. We see this dawning working-class pride in the butler from *You Never Can Tell*, who is proud of his vocation and disappointed that his son has not followed in his footsteps but chosen instead to become a lawyer. We also see this new pride in Straker, the chauffeur from *Man and Superman*. The Shavian hero Tanner notices Straker's reverse snobbery as the chauffeur talks with pride about his old school, where "they teach you to be an engineer or such like," not "a gentleman," as they do at Oxford or Cambridge, as well as Straker's pride in being able to fix things— instead of standing around in "gentlemanly helplessness"—when some practical, physical task needs to be done.[32] Another example is, of course, Doolittle from *Pygmalion*, who is very proud of having been a dustman, and upset that a big inheritance has raised him to the middle classes.

In addition to his socialism, Shaw's belief in the Life Force also contributed to his freedom from fear regarding upward social mobility. He believed that the class you were born into made no difference as to whether or not you had the requisite Life Force to succeed in life and that the parents of the Superman could come from anywhere. As he once wrote, "the objection of a countess to a navvy or of a duke to a charwoman" is abhorrent because "to cut humanity up into small cliques, and effectively limit the selection of the individual to his own clique, is to postpone [the birth of] the Superman for eons, if not forever."[33]

Bernard Shaw's personal pride in the advantages of being Irish over English also have roots outside of the political and religious beliefs that he adopted as an adult. They have roots within the Irish tradition itself. W. J. McCormack has written about the fact that

Relations between Britain and Ireland had long been discussed in terms of the classical contrast of culture and barbarism. To the Elizabethan, the Irish were barbarians, but by the eighteenth century cultivated descendents of the colonists liked to think of themselves as Greeks compared with the more practical but imaginatively limited English (Romans). Cultured slaves, perhaps.[34]

Shaw inherited this sense of the Irish as "cultured slaves" compared to their boorish English overlords from his forebears. In incorporating this perspective into his work, Shaw was "contest[ing]...colonialism's discourses, power structures and social hierarchies," fulfilling the duties—according to Helen Gilbert and Joanne Tompkins—of the postcolonial writer.[35] Later Irish writers more commonly studied in a postcolonial context, such as James Joyce and Brian Friel, followed in Shaw's footsteps in suggesting that the Irish are more cultured than the English. One thinks in particular of Friel's play *Translations* (1980)—a play in which the Irish characters discuss mythology, poetry, linguistics, and philosophy in Irish, English, Greek, and Latin, while the English characters are ignorant of all but their ultra-practical specialty subjects and speak only English (a language described in the play as "plebeian" and "peculiarly suited...[to] the purposes of commerce").[36] From a postcolonial point of view, Shaw's embrace of reverse snobbery can be seen as a manifestation of the second phase of national liberation movements, as outlined by Frantz Fanon in *The Wretched of the Earth* (1967) and applied to Ireland by Declan Kiberd in the essay "From Nationalism to Liberation" (1997).[37] In the first phase ("the colonial"), "artists mimic the occupier culture," but in the second phase ("the national"), "movements like *Négritude* assert that 'black (or green) is beautiful.'"[38] This explains the uncompromising Irish pride implicit in Shaw's use of reverse snobbery. That said, to give Shaw his proper due, his attempt in *John Bull's Other Island* to explode certain stereotypes of the Irish, while showing others to be "true in a deeper and subtler way than many suspected," indicates that he is reaching for the third and final phase ("the liberationist"), "in which binaries are exploded in a sort of Hegelian synthesis."[39]

Of course, Irish writers had explored the idea of the "culti-vated" Irish versus the "imaginatively limited" English prior to Shaw (examples include Richard Brinsley Sheridan, Maria Edgeworth, Lady Morgan, and Dion Boucicault), but Shaw was different and far more radical. Sheridan's schooling at Harrow and an adult life spent entirely in England and Edgeworth's English birth and partially English childhood meant that, when it was politically expedient, they would occasionally refer to themselves as "English."[40] Lady Morgan and Dion Boucicault, meanwhile, favored what Robert Tracy has called "the Glorvina solution" in their work, in which Anglo-Irish political difficulties are smoothed over by a marriage between an Irish colleen and an English gentleman—hardly a suggestion that the Irish are inde-pendently minded, strong, and even superior to the English.[41] Shaw was the first Irish writer from a Protestant background to explicitly state in his work that the Irish nation as a whole—from the farmer cutting turf in a bog to the landlord taking rents in a Big House—and not just certain enlightened or special indi-viduals were blessed with the unique and valuable Irish perspec-tive. This Irish perspective, he explains in the preface to *John Bull's Other Island*, was not the product of racial tendencies but came from living in the foggy Irish climate and enduring Irish hardships—be they material privations or the humiliations of living, or even attempting to lead, in a subjugated nation whose political ambitions were thwarted. His continual championing of *all* the Irish—from thinkers like Berkeley and Tyndall to writers like Swift and Wilde to "country rapscallions"—was, it seems, made possible by his broad definition of an Irish person as anyone touched by the island's climate and atmosphere.[42] This unique and groundbreakingly inclusive "climatological" view meant he was willing to face *all* anti-Irish prejudice head-on, not dismissing Irish foibles as something belonging to a lower class of Irish of which he was no part or the Catholic Irish of which he was no part.[43] Although we will discuss Shaw's ancestry in greater detail in chapter 3, it is important to note here that his refusal to believe in an "Irish race" also justified his own Irishness, making irrelevant the fact that he was a Protestant of mainly Scottish and English stock.[44]

Shaw's firm belief in the valuable Irish perspective does not mean that he had an unrealistically positive view of his fellow countrymen and women. As mentioned earlier—and as will be discussed in greater detail in chapters 3 and 4—Shaw believed that Irish people were too narrowly nationalistic, were prone to derision and "begrudgery," and, when times got tough, would often seek refuge in dreams and the imagination.[45] In Shaw's opinion, the best way for Irish people to get free of these Irish weaknesses was for them to live abroad, even for a short time (as Hector Malone, Larry Doyle, Peter Keegan, Sir Patrick Cullen, Mrs Farrell, Count O'Dowda, Dora Delaney, and Private O'Flaherty have done).[46] However, even these characters occasionally betray what Shaw saw as the Irish national weaknesses (for example, Doyle's anger and Keegan's retreat to the Round Tower at the end of *John Bull's Other Island* indicate that they are falling prey to derision and dreaming, respectively). While the Irish characters who have never left Ireland (such as the townspeople of Rosscullen and O'Flaherty's mother and sweetheart) are much more likely to be held back from worldly success by succumbing to derision and dreaming, even they possess a Shavian Irish clear-sightedness regarding sentiment and cant and have survived difficult financial circumstances through shrewdness and hard work.

As A. M. Gibbs has proven, Bernard Shaw was by far the most performed playwright in the English-speaking world during the twentieth century, after Shakespeare.[47] Therefore, it is hard not to see Shaw's plays—especially his plays featuring Irish characters—as being key components in the rise of reverse snobbery, a social change he both anticipated and predicted. His plays, when new, were a loud and insistent statement—now accepted in many circles—that the leisure classes are impractical idlers somewhat divorced from reality, while the ethnically marginalized and the poor are made practical by their experiences of

hardship and are often possessed of admirably earthy and incisive senses of humor.

Thanks, at least in part, to Bernard Shaw, life in the English-
speaking world is now far different from that depicted in works
like Fanny Burney's *Evelina* (1778), in which the reverse snobbery of the lower middle-class Branghtons is deemed unjustified
and preposterous by the author.[48] In that novel, the Branghtons
are blamed and mocked for not knowing how to behave in an
upper-class manner at the opera, and—what is worse—for not
caring. Because Shaw was concerned with proving that the British
class system was a ludicrous invention based on a set of arbitrary,
learned manners (as we shall discuss further in chapter 2), it is
impossible to imagine him judging characters like Mrs Farrell,
Dora Delaney, Mrs O'Flaherty, or even Keegan for not knowing
how to imitate English upper-class manners. It is also impossible
to imagine these proud, pragmatic characters—or their real-life,
modern-day equivalents—feeling ashamed over such ignorance.

2
Shaw and the Irish Diaspora

Ever since Bernard Shaw's *Pygmalion* premiered in London in 1914, critics and audiences have assumed that Shaw chose the name Henry Higgins for the male lead primarily for the comic effect produced by having the Cockney characters drop the letter *H* that begins his first name and surname.[1] However, such an explanation ignores the crucial fact that Higgins is an Irish surname; the name is found in all four provinces of Ireland (though primarily in Connaught) and comes from the Irish Gaelic name Ó hUigín, meaning "son of the Viking."[2] Shaw was undoubtedly aware of the name's Hibernian origins, and not simply because he was born and raised in Dublin. By his own estimation, he knew "more about Irish names than anyone outside the professions of land agency...can possibly know"; this knowledge was gained while working in an estate office in Dublin as a young man, in a job which required him to "collect...rents from tenants in every province in Ireland" and to enter their surnames on receipts and in ledgers.[3] Shaw's decision to give Higgins a name he knew to be Irish cannot be lightly dismissed, since (as many critics have pointed out) Shaw's character names frequently tell us something about the fictional figures who bear them.[4]

Shaw elected to endow his rude but winning phonetics professor with an Irish name, because he wanted to signal that Higgins is an Englishman of Irish descent. Those who watch or read *Pygmalion* are meant to understand that the professor's Englishness is somewhat altered by an outside cultural influence, which explains why he is so at odds with the society in which he lives and why he can analyze it so coldly and sharply. To strengthen this Irish, outsider aspect of Higgins's character, Shaw also imbues the professor with many of the traits that he repeatedly associates with a canny Irishness in his journalistic pieces on Ireland and in the plays discussed in chapter 1. Ultimately, the positive Diasporic Irishness of Henry Higgins helps to complicate Shaw's reputation as someone who was rudely dismissive of the Irish identities of those born in the Diaspora.[5]

The main Irish aspect of Higgins's character in *Pygmalion* is the fact that he is, like many of the Irish characters analyzed in chapter 1, a cynical fact-facer who punctures English "sentimentality" and "intellectual laziness."[6] When Higgins repeatedly makes incisive speeches in support of the dignity of the individual and the need for greater equality between social classes; when he is ruthlessly honest in telling Eliza how she looks; and when he explodes Clara's notion that life would be easier if everyone said exactly what they think, he brings to mind the clear-sighted, if unpopular, analysis enunciated by Larry Doyle and Peter Keegan in *John Bull's Other Island*, Sir Patrick Cullen in *The Doctor's Dilemma*, Mrs Farrell in *Press Cuttings*, and Private O'Flaherty in *O'Flaherty, VC*. Likewise, Higgins's ability to spot immediately that Alfred Doolittle is a blackguard recalls Sir Patrick Cullen's ability to see through "chancers" like Dubedat and corrupt surgeons like Sir Cutler Walpole in *The Doctor's Dilemma*. And perhaps the most Irish of Higgins's tirades in *Pygmalion* are the ones in which he—like the Kerryman Hector Malone from *Man and Superman*—disdains the English for not being able to "speak [their] own language properly."[7] In expressing this anger, Shaw is echoing a sentiment to be found frequently among Irish writers, who, for centuries, delighted in puncturing the linguistic pride of their English overlords. Maria Edgeworth suggests in the 1809 novel *Ennui* that the Irish Lady Geraldine speaks English more precisely than her English guests, Mrs Norton and Lady Hauton.[8] The Irish characters Major Yeates and Mrs Knox in the Somerville & Ross story, "The Aussolas Martin Cat" (1915), are bemused at the way the "grotesque 'stage Englishman,'" Mr Tebbetts, drops his *Hs*.[9] And, of course, James Joyce suggests through Stephen Dedalus in *A Portrait of the Artists as a Young Man* (1916) that the best English in the world is spoken in Lower Drumcondra on Dublin's Northside.[10]

This pride—indeed, reverse snobbery—over the Irish way with English was, of course, shared by Shaw himself, who claimed that his English was that of the Dublin-born Jonathan Swift and not the "unspeakable jargon" found in London newspapers.[11] In the 1916 preface to *Pygmalion*, Shaw even claims that "the English have no respect for their own language" and that he wishes that they spoke "the noble English of Forbes Robertson."[12] It is revealing that Shaw singles out the actor Johnston Forbes Robertson for praise, as Robertson was the English son of Scottish parents from Aberdeen; the character of Henry Higgins was originally written with Robertson in mind.[13] Therefore, from the start, Shaw seems to have been suggesting that Higgins is a man with roots in the Celtic Fringe who speaks English better than the English do.[14]

In *Pygmalion*, Higgins's anger over the poor language skills of many English people leads him to help reform the accents of his London clients, who engage Higgins to help them fulfil their social ambitions. The need to reform one's way of speaking in order to be taken seriously by the English middle and upper classes is historically a very Irish concern. In the mid-to-late eighteenth century, the Dublin-born actor Thomas Sheridan conducted popular elocution classes throughout Britain and Ireland, in which he taught Irish, Scottish, Welsh, and working-class English people how to speak "proper" English.[15] For his son, the playwright and politician Richard Brinsley Sheridan, having such an influence in his childhood home paid off handsomely; when he was in parliament, English politicians praised him for the fact that, although he spent his formative years in Dublin, he spoke with an admirably English accent. By contrast, they lamented that another

Irish politician, Edmund Burke, who was raised in Dublin, Kildare, and Cork, spoke as though "he had never quitted the banks of the Shannon."[16] In subsequent centuries, Irish people in England would face the same dilemma as these celebrated eighteenth-century Irishmen: whether or not to reform their "barbarous" tongues.[17] Shaw himself decided to adjust his accent, depending on his audience. As footage of him speaking reveals, when he was in the United States, he spoke in his normal Irish accent.[18] When speaking at formal engagements in England, Shaw's pronunciation was decidedly more RP (received pronunciation), though still clearly Irish.[19] Shaw presumably made this decision because he sincerely believed the views expressed in the preface to *Pygmalion*, in which he states that in early twentieth-century England, it is extremely ill-advised to speak in a way that will limit your social and professional opportunities. Henry Higgins, inspired by his belief in political equality—but perhaps also by the humiliations that he saw his own Irish family members endure—wants to see people speak in a way that will help them to succeed in class- and accent-obsessed England.

Of course, such conjecture is risky. Other than the Higgins surname, there are few, if any, indications in the play that Higgins's family is definitively Irish. If they are, they would appear to be from a Church of Ireland background, since Higgins's brother is a vicar.[20] If the Higgins family are indeed Irish Anglicans, it makes Henry's excessive devotion to his London-based mother interesting, for two reasons. First, a strong Irish Anglican mother in London with her artistic, bachelor son not only recalls Shaw himself, but also his contemporaries Oscar Wilde and W. B. Yeats. Second, Shaw makes clear that Henry's devotion to his mother is the reason for the man's "confirmed" bachelorhood, which is so central to the play's plot.[21] As many commentators have noted, marrying late is prevalent among Irish males.[22] Higgins was presumably born and raised in England; but the tendency toward late marriage was also common in the Irish Diaspora, as extensive anecdotal reports have suggested and as sociologists have verified.[23]

Higgins's Irish foreignness is not only signaled by his surname, his bachelorhood, and his laments over the English inability to speak their own language properly; his Irishness is also present in his disgust over the fact that the English have a class system based on a set of arbitrary, learned manners, and—what is worse—that they are not even very good at performing those manners. After the party at which Eliza passes herself off so successfully as a "toff," Higgins complains to Pickering that many of the English aristocrats were poorly mannered, concluding "the silly people don't know their own silly business."[24] Higgins himself, we might note, never bothers to behave in a mannerly way. This is partially out of conviction—that is, it is an expression of his staunch democratic principles—and partially because, in the words of Pickering, he has "never been broken in properly to the social routine," which may be another clue that Higgins's family is Irish, or, at least, not typically English.[25]

Higgins's Irish disregard for polite English manners strongly recalls the Irish character Dora Delaney, from *Fanny's First Play*. Both Higgins and Delaney exhibit flagrantly "low" manners, which not only provide comic relief in each play but also imply a criticism of the unjust English class system.[26] Both characters are determined to treat all equally; as Henry says, "I treat a duchess as if she was a flower girl" and vice versa.[27] Higgins's anti-snobbery, his sermons on equality, and his attempts to get working-class people to "pass" as middle- or upper-class are all a much more deliberate attack on the inequalities rife in English society than Dora's.[28] In fact, Higgins's campaign on behalf of equality is underwritten by what is arguably an Irish anger at the English class system: there is a subversive, destructive mischief in his suggestion that Clara should try the "new small talk" at her next three at-homes.[29]

Notably, Henry's mother—the only other Higgins in the play—generally behaves in an elegant, that is to say, an upper-class English fashion throughout *Pygmalion*. Despite this, there are two hints that Mrs Higgins comes from an Irish background, and they both relate to her manners. First, she exhibits what could be construed as an Irish fieriness of temper and "freedom of manner" when she says that she would have thrown the fire irons at Henry and not the slippers if she had been in Eliza's position.[30] (Shaw's Irish female characters, including Nora from *John Bull's Other Island*, and Teresa Driscoll and Mrs O'Flaherty from *O'Flaherty, VC*, also have such volatile tempers.) Mrs Higgins may also be betraying a possible Irish Anglican background when she expresses distaste for the English habit of talking about their "insides."[31] (An identical sentiment is voiced by the Irish Anglican Lady Naylor in a memorable scene in Elizabeth Bowen's 1929 novel *The Last September*.)[32] In spite of these impulsive outbursts, Mrs Higgins has obviously decided to conform, in the main, to London social manners.[33] By contrast, her son—like others in England from marginalized cultural backgrounds—has decided to rebel against the prevailing "artificial" manners of the English middle and upper classes.[34] Indeed, Higgins swears frequently—often with an Irish taste for alliteration.[35] He is also in small ways rather slovenly, and throws his body onto sofas informally and inelegantly. Exaggerated depictions of such "low" manners and lack of cleanliness were associated negatively with the Irish on the London stage and in the English press for centuries; since Shaw strongly indicates that Higgins's outrageous behavior is harmless, his portrayal of the English fear of such "Irish" informality suggests that the English leisure classes are unnecessarily hidebound and strict in such matters.[36] Given the possible Irish Anglican background of the Higgins family, it is noteworthy that even a member of the Irish gentry such as Elizabeth Bowen was criticized for exhibiting such unmannerly "Irish" traits by her English friends: after visiting Bowen's home in North Cork, Virginia Woolf noted in her diary, "One can see, after Bowen's Court, how ramshackle & half squalid the Irish life is."[37]

Other—arguably more concrete—pieces of evidence from the text suggest that Higgins is of Irish descent. First, throughout the play, Higgins shows that Ireland is never far from his thoughts. When describing his own ability to tell where people are from based on their speech, he contrasts it with Pickering's ability to "spot an Irishman," when he could have said, for example, a Scot or a Liverpudlian.[38] When he suggests that Freddie is beneath Eliza as a suitor, he says he wants to see her marry "the Governor-General of India or the Lord-Lieutenant of Ireland."[39] He teaches Eliza to speak of the weather "in...these islands"—a distinction an unequivocally English phonetics professor would not necessarily have made.[40] And he demonstrates a heightened awareness of fellow Celts: witness his repeated references to Doolittle's Welshness.[41]

Additionally, Higgins speaks of "the English" in the play as though he himself were not an Englishman. For example, he proclaims that "the English will keep [Eliza] in the gutter" as long as she speaks in a Cockney accent.[42] Likewise, he shows an outsider's eye for the comedy value inherent in many supposedly august English place names when he laughs at the name of the estate where Mrs Eynsford Hill grew up, Largelady Park—the mocking of posh English names being a durable tradition among Irish writers.[43] These verbal indications that Higgins is not English are probably what led—or, at least, enabled—Sir Herbert Beerbohm Tree (the first Higgins) to attempt to play him with a Scottish accent, before he was stopped from doing so by Shaw himself.[44]

A final hint from the text that Higgins is Irish is Pickering's description of one of Higgins's ideas as "very clever but not sound sense."[45] This is essentially the identical complaint made by the Englishman Broadbent in *John Bull's Other Island* about the incisive analysis provided by his Irish business partner Doyle and the mystic Keegan—analysis that, as we noted in chapter 1, the Englishman repeatedly dismisses as "blarney," "tommy rot," and "Irish exaggeration," or which he mistakes for examples of Irish humor.[46] "Very clever but not sound sense" was also a frequent (and unjust) complaint regarding the braver ideas voiced by Irish thinkers such as Wilde and Shaw. Like the characters Doyle and Keegan, they had to put up with English commentators describing their radical insights as "Irish exaggeration" or Irish comic perversity. Higgins, who desires to see England adopt a more rational alphabet and abandon its artificial manners, is likewise dismissed by English people who surround him as a monomaniacal eccentric. There is one other piece of evidence from Shaw's pen indicating that Higgins is not simply an Englishman. In a letter to the actress Ellen Terry from 1912, Shaw describes the role of Higgins as "essentially an English part of a certain type."[47] The inclusion of the qualifier "essentially" is noteworthy, and the adjective itself is appropriately ambiguous. As the Oxford English Dictionary avers, "essentially" not only means "in essence," but, since the seventeenth century, often means "substantially" or "in marked or eminent degree"—which carries the corollary of "not entirely." Shaw's remark to Terry suggests that Higgins is both truly an Englishman—that is, in his very essence—but also implies that there is another cultural influence complicating his straightforward Englishness. What keeps Higgins from being unequivocally English, Shaw suggests, is the fact that he is a member of the Irish Diaspora.

Shaw, of course, had a problematic relationship with the idea of Diasporic Irishness. As various critics have noted, Shaw often spoke negatively about the children of the Diaspora. He was regularly scathing about "American Gaels," as well as "Clan na Gael Irishmen" from Liverpool, Glasgow, and London.[48] He stated on occasion that the British and American children of Irish immigrants are not "real Irishmen," and, in one of his articles for the American press, he even calls them "sham Irish."[49] He teased devotees of the Irish-American Republican activist, John Devoy, by suggesting that Devoy's surname is not actually Irish.[50] In *John Bull's Other Island*, the Shavian mouthpiece, Larry Doyle, says that the Glasgow-born Tim Haffigan is not Irish "at all," despite being the son of Irish parents.[51] Similarly, the daughters of Mrs Farrell from *Press Cuttings* and Count O'Dowda from *Fanny's First Play* are presented as unequivocally English, and Hector Malone's son in *Man and Superman* as simply American.

Shaw's repeated dismissal of the Irishness of those born and raised outside of Ireland is clearly related to his climatological view of Irish identity. As we discussed in chapter 1, Shaw defined an Irish person as anybody touched by Ireland's unique climate. He even hinted that those who live there for a few years begin to show Irish characteristics. Shaw's climatological view was in some ways a groundbreaking and admirably inclusive concept, because it privileged residence in Ireland over exclusionary racial or ethnic considerations. However, the positive aspects of this climatological view aside, Shaw repeatedly contradicted his own seemingly watertight theory, and admitted the durability of Irishness beyond the shores of Ireland. In essays and interviews, he occasionally recognized the importance of the "Irish blood" of those born or living outside Ireland.[52] He argued for the inclusion of Eugene O'Neill and T. E. Lawrence in the Irish Academy of Letters, and he forged a strong friendship—based partially on a mutual Irishness—with the American boxer, Gene Tunney.[53] His championing of Lawrence and O'Neill is especially interesting, given his climatological theory, as neither of these men ever visited the land of their ancestors.

Other, perhaps less obvious, instances of Shaw suggesting the durability of Irishness beyond the island of Ireland can also be cited. The characters Hector Malone, Larry Doyle, Sir Patrick Cullen, and Mrs Farrell all have markedly Irish personalities, despite living outside of Ireland for many years. Likewise, in the futuristic play *Tragedy of an Elderly Gentleman*—discussed in more detail in chapters 3 and 4—the Irish leave their native land to stir up revolutions across the colonized world, and, despite remaining outside of Ireland for generations, remain (in their own eyes and in the eyes of others) Irish. The Elderly Gentleman character in the play is very recognizably a Stage Englishman, despite the fact that his countrymen have been based in "dear old British Baghdad" for hundreds of years, where—at least according to Shaw's climatological theory—the hot, arid climate would presumably have altered the English national character.[54]

The clearest expressions of Shaw's belief that Irishness persists in the Diaspora are found in his catalogue of English and American characters of Irish descent, who, he suggests, derive their power—and some of their weaknesses—from their Irish ancestry and cultural backgrounds. The prime example of this is Henry Higgins, but there are a number of other characters of this type from Shaw's oeuvre.

One is the American naval officer, Captain Kearney, from the play *Captain Brassbound's Conversion* (1900). According to Shaw's stage directions, aspects of the Captain's personality are the result of the "old world" blood coursing through his veins, including—presumably—his Kearney (Irish) blood.[55] The forcefulness of the Captain's personality is best exemplified by his wittily threatening letter to those who have taken Sir Hallam and Lady Cecily hostage. The letter recalls the darker pronouncements of Shavian Irish characters such as Keegan, Doyle, Cullen, and O'Flaherty: it is marked by realism laced with grim humor, and is free of the idealistic, sentimental cant indulged in by many of Shaw's English characters.

John Bull's Other Island and Shaw's other plays featuring Irish characters show the playwright's fondness for reversing old stereotypes of the English and the Irish. In *Captain Brassbound's Conversion*, Shaw subverts old notions of English civility versus Irish barbarism by making the Irish-American Kearney more cultured than the English sailor, Drinkwater. Kearney regards Drinkwater's reading material as exceedingly low-brow, agreeing with the chaplain that his books should be burnt and counseling the Cockney that he'd "be better without that sort of reading."[56] Social class is another factor in this contrast, but—given Kearney's use of low idioms—his class background does not appear to be much higher than Drinkwater's. Kearney's remaining Irish trait is his preference for "natural" manners over English, aristocratic reserve.[57] Kearney says he does not mind people using bad language when provoked, because it shows they have "flesh and blood"—that is, it proves that they are human.[58]

Another Shaw character who demonstrates Irish qualities, despite being born and raised outside of Ireland, is the English boxer Cashel Byron from the 1901 play, *The Admirable Bashville*, the stage version of Shaw's juvenile novel *Cashel Byron's Profession*.[59] The prizefighter's first name is clearly a reference to the Rock of Cashel in County Tipperary, and indicates the man's physical and psychological strength. As Peter Gahan has noted, the name is also an allusion to Cashel Hoey, the fiery Young Islander who married Shaw's cousin, the novelist Frances Johnston.[60]

Byron, whose Irish heritage presumably comes from the de Courcy branch of his family, possesses a number of traits that Shaw routinely associated with Irishness.[61] The boxer recalls Larry Doyle and Sir Patrick Cullen by being both learned and streetwise. He repeatedly punctures English sentimentality, scorning English romantic notions about "duty" and love of one's mother.[62] And his occasionally low manners, like those of Henry Higgins and Dora Delaney, act as a force for democratic change in the play; his aristocratic love interest Lydia begins to use the street slang she has learned from him. Byron also invites comparison to Higgins by being passionately articulate in his disparagement of English aristocratic "snobbery" and condescension.[63]

After one of Byron's fights, a sportswriter ascribes a clever strategy used by the boxer to "colonial smartness," a reference to the years Byron spent in Australia, but also presumably to Byron's Irish background.[64] This line makes explicit Byron's foreignness in England, which is further signaled in the original novel during the scene in which Byron fights a Cockney called Teddy. Having been knocked to the floor, Teddy exclaims, "Be a Englishman [*sic*]; and don't hit a man when he's down."[65] Both the novel and the play provide a number of clues that the English-born Byron is not exactly English; clearly, this foreignness is related not only to the time he spent living abroad, but also to his Irish heritage.

One particularly interesting Irish Diasporic character from Shaw's dramatic canon is "Boss" Mangan from *Heartbreak House* (1919). Mangan is an Englishman of Irish stock, whose shrewdness in business and politics is much greater than that of the "mere English" who surround him.[66] The contrast between Mangan and his associates recalls the one set up by Shaw between the Irishman Doyle and the English "duffer" Broadbent in *John Bull's Other Island*, and between the Irishman Hector Malone and various, impoverished, English aristocrats in *Man and Superman*.[67]

Mangan possesses two weaknesses that Shaw associated with Irishness. The first is that he "drank too much formerly."[68] When Shaw spoke of the Irish weakness for alcohol, it was usually in relation to his own family members.[69] He once famously stated that, "I am a teetotaler because my family has already paid the Shaw debt to the distilling industry so munificently as to leave me no further obligation."[70] Mangan's second such weakness is that he is excessively materialistic due to an irrationally heightened "dread...of being poor."[71] This obsessive materialism is a trait Shaw gave to other Irish characters, including Teresa Driscoll and Mrs O'Flaherty from *O'Flaherty, VC* and some of the townspeople of Rosscullen in *John Bull's Other Island*. As was demonstrated in chapter 1, Shaw usually suggested that Irish poverty sharpened the wits of those who endured it. However, he clearly views an excessive materialism as a possible, negative side effect of that early deprivation.

During the course of the play, Shaw signals Mangan's hybrid Irish-English identity through the character's speech. In Act II, Mangan employs the Hiberno-English adjective "cute" (meaning "acute, sharp-witted, clever, shrewd").[72] Then, a few lines later, he uses the English expression "off my chump."[73] Likewise, towards the end of the play, Mangan says "jolly well" in the manner of an English gentleman, and, shortly thereafter, uses the phrase "fine talk" in the same Hiberno-English fashion as it is employed by Private O'Flaherty in *O'Flaherty, VC*, and in works by Shaw's Irish contemporaries, J. M. Synge and Winifred M. Letts.[74]

There are additional English characters from *Heartbreak House* who bear a (possibly) Irish surname and who also betray signs of Shavian Irishness: the "thinking...and drinking" Dunns.[75] Dunn without an *E* at the end is usually an English surname.[76] However, the fact that Mazzini Dunn, the "soldier of freedom," is named for the Italian revolutionary Giuseppe Mazzini (with whom his parents were friendly) may indicate an Irish background.[77] Giuseppe Mazzini's "vision of Italian nationalism was influential" in both Ireland and among the Diasporic Irish, despite the Italian's famous scepticism regarding the existence of a separate, distinct, Irish national identity.[78] Indeed, the fact that Mazzini Dunn and "Boss" Mangan grew up together suggests that they may even have been raised in the same Irish enclave in England.

An Irish Diasporic character who mirrors "Boss" Mangan in combining positive and negative Shavian Irish traits is "Snobby" O'Brien Price from the 1905 play *Major Barbara*. Like the admirable Irish figures in Shaw's other plays, "Snobby" is a thinker who possesses an ultra-realistic view of society and its workings. In particular, he is much less naïve about *laissez-faire* capitalism and the Salvation Army than the rest of the play's characters (with the possible exception of Andrew Undershaft). That said, despite "Snobby"'s "sharp" intellect, he is held back by his Shavian Irish weaknesses: he "drink[s] something cruel" when he gets the chance, and the struggle to survive has resulted in his being "capable of anything in reason except honesty or altruistic considerations of any kind."[79] Like "Boss" Mangan, he has become selfish and deceitful in his pursuit of gain (or at least out of his Irish horror of poverty). A further link between "Snobby" and Shaw's other Irish characters relates to his family background. Since "Snobby"'s middle name is O'Brien, it is probable that his formidable, fearsome mother—who we never meet—is another Shavian Irish woman with a fiery temper.

Shaw occasionally endowed characters with names recalled from his Irish childhood. On some occasions, this naming was effectively a private joke for Shaw. Few people would have known the real people that Shaw was referring to, and therefore, he did not intend the name to be an indicator of the character's Irishness. Two examples of this are Eliza Doolittle from *Pygmalion* and Louis Dubedat from *The Doctor's Dilemma*. According to a deed associated with Bushy Park (the Shaw ancestral home in Terenure),

Lidia Wilkinson—who was related to the Shaws by marriage—left a legacy to a woman called Eliza Doolittle of Cork.[80] While Shaw may have enjoyed naming his plucky flower seller after someone associated with his Irish family, he does not suggest in the play that there is anything particularly Irish about Eliza. (Indeed, her Doolittle father is a true Londoner from Hounslow, whose only non-English cultural input seems to be his mother's Welshness.) As regards Louis Dubedat, Shaw once indicated that he was aware of the presence of the character's unusual, Huguenot surname in Ireland.[81] However, throughout *The Doctor's Dilemma*, Dubedat speaks in the manner of the English leisure classes, and none of the play's characters (including the Irishman Cullen) give any indication that the young bounder might be from an Irish background.

On other occasions, Shaw would give his characters names familiar from his Irish childhood that were originally borne by relatively well-known people. Shaw was aware that Irish audience members and readers would link these characters to their real-life namesakes, and would assume that the characters had Irish backgrounds. A clear example of this is one mentioned earlier: the Young Islander Cashel Hoey's influence on the naming and characterization of Cashel Byron. Another example is Fergus Crampton, the "irritable" patriarch from the underrated 1898 comedy, *You Never Can Tell*.[82] As Peter Gahan has noted, Crampton's surname is clearly an allusion to Sir John Crampton, an Irish Anglican diplomat whose young wife left him for a Spanish Duke while he was posted in Madrid.[83] This incident caused "great scandal" in Dublin during Shaw's childhood, and Shaw must have remembered it in later life when creating an ornery character whose younger wife leaves him and moves to the Portuguese island of Madeira.[84] As a child, Shaw's attention would also presumably have been drawn to the Crampton saga, since Sir John Crampton's family seat in Enniskerry, Co. Wicklow was called (like the Shaw family seat) Bushy Park.

Throughout *You Never Can Tell*, Fergus Crampton speaks in a standard English manner, and none of the characters indicate that he is Irish. However, audiences can assume he is of Irish descent, thanks to a couple of obvious clues. First, his first name references a famous figure from Irish mythology. Second, his favorite drink is Irish whiskey.[85] In keeping with stereotypes regarding the Irish (and in line with Shaw's Irish Diasporic figures Mangan and Price), some of the play's characters indicate that Fergus used to drink too much.[86]

Those familiar with Shaw's Irish and Irish Diasporic characters will see other indications that Fergus is from an Irish background. His final falling out with his wife was due to the fact that he believed that his children should be regularly disciplined (as he was while growing up) and not spoiled. His belief in the benefits of a strict upbringing link him to Shavian Irish parents such as Hector Malone and Mrs Farrell, who—as was noted earlier— believe that their children have had it too easy while growing up in the United States and England, respectively. Shaw was famously against corporal punishment, and Fergus is rightly condemned in the play for his threatened introduction of it into the Crampton home.[87] However, Fergus and his creator would almost certainly concur over the contention in the preface to *John Bull's Other Island* that "when power and riches are thrown haphazard into children's cradles as they are in England, you get a governing class without industry, character, courage, or real experience."[88]

Fergus's other main Shavian Irish quality is the fact that he is a cynical straight-talker prone to blunt statements and wise aphorisms that explode the fanciful notions and tactful lies of others.[89] A further indication that we should view Fergus as Irish is Valentine's comparison of him to "a Jew," since Shaw repeatedly linked the Irish to the Jews in his work.[90] For example, in *John Bull's Other Island*, Larry Doyle says, "We Irishmen were never made to be farmers; and we'll never do any good at it. We're like the Jews: the Almighty gave us brains, and bid us farm them and leave the clay and the worms alone."[91] Likewise, in *Man and Superman*, the Irishman Malone is a shareholder in the Jew Mendoza's firm of brigands, and, in *The Doctor's Dilemma*, the Irishman Sir Patrick

Cullen and the Jew Leo Schutzmacher are the only two doctors who are not taken in by Louis Dubedat's lies.[92]

Irish readers and audience members familiar with Sir John Crampton would have noted other parallels between Shaw's fictitious Irish Diasporic character and the real-life Irish diplomat. In the play, Fergus is disappointed to see that his children have received very little religious education.[93] One imagines that Sir John Crampton would have been similarly distressed over such a discovery, since his family boasted a number of prominent Anglican clergymen.[94] Another tie between Fergus and Sir John is the fact that both are from solidly middle-class families. We are told in the stage directions that Fergus comes "from an old family in the aristocracy of trade."[95] Similarly, over preceding generations, Sir John's family was made up mainly of medical practitioners and the aforementioned churchmen; his father, a surgeon called Sir Philip, only secured the baronetcy through his groundbreaking medical work when John was 34.[96]

In *You Never Can Tell*, Fergus's family always get the better of him when consulting lawyers over the family's unusual living arrangements. This is because Fergus is eager to avoid scandal— something that Sir John, his real-life namesake (and subject of much Dublin gossip), was simply unable to do.[97]

Shaw's disparate handling of figures who bear Irish names but who were evidently not Irish by birth indicates that he was clearly ambivalent about the notion of second- and third-generation Irishness. Shaw usually had thoroughly considered views on the subjects he tackled in his prefaces and plays; thus, his contradictory treatment of the Diasporic Irish is unusual for him, but perhaps not surprising. Many, or perhaps most, Irish people today seem to hold such contradictory views regarding the Diaspora, as the actor and cultural ambassador Gabriel Byrne recently discussed in a widely debated radio interview on Dublin's Today FM.[98] While contemporary Irish critics and cultural commentators readily recognize the Irishness of certain members of the Diaspora (such as Martin McDonagh, Shane McGowan, or J. P. Donleavy), they find the supposed Irish identities of others (such as the conservative Fox News presenters Bill O'Reilly and Sean Hannity, or the producers of Hollywood films like *Far and Away* and *Leap Year*) difficult if not impossible to imagine.

In the end, although Shaw failed to conceive of an overarching theory regarding the Diasporic Irish, his instinct to assess the Irishness of people in the Diaspora on a case-by-case basis is sound. His most substantial, and also most subtle, portrait of an Irish Diasporic person is Henry Higgins, an Englishman of Irish descent, whose Irish background Shaw sees as having helped to give him his "sane" ideas regarding language and social class; as Shaw puts it in the preface to *John Bull's Other Island*, "England cannot do without its Irish...today because it cannot do without at least a little sanity."[99] Henry Higgins is Shaw's tribute to the many Irish Diasporic people who have brought fresh perspectives and dynamic, revolutionary energy to the new countries which they (and their families) have gradually learned to call home.

3
Shaw and Irish Anglican Preoccupations

An immersion in the literature produced in Ireland in the two and a half centuries leading up to Bernard Shaw's birth in 1856 reveals that three different Irish cultures were producing work in significant quantities: Irish Gaelic Catholics, Irish Anglicans (traditionally—and dubiously—called the Anglo-Irish), and Ulster Scots Presbyterians.[1] Less famous but still intriguing works were being produced by smaller Irish subcultures: especially Irish Methodists, Irish Quakers, and Irish Jews.[2] In studies on the Irish Shaw, such as this one, it should always be emphasized that Shaw belonged specifically to the Irish Anglican cultural tradition.

Irish Anglicans are often associated solely with political ascendancy and the Big House; in reality, theirs is a much broader tradition. This cultural group includes any Irish person of (at least partial) English, Welsh, or lowland Scottish descent, who is raised within an Anglophone, Church of Ireland milieu, and whose economic, social, and cultural life is significantly linked to Great Britain and/or British interests in Ireland.[3] While Irish Anglicans have (on average) owned more land and had greater access to political power than other groups in Ireland, they are, from a social class perspective, actually quite diverse.[4] Some are scions of the Big House, such as Maria Edgeworth, Lady Gregory, or Elizabeth Bowen; some are from urban, middle-class households, such as Oscar Wilde, Denis Johnston, or Samuel Beckett; some are from Anglican clerical families, such as Oliver Goldsmith,

Douglas Hyde, or Standish O'Grady; some are from families tied to the English (later British) military, such as William Congreve, Laurence Sterne, or Maud Gonne; some are even from poor farming or working-class laboring backgrounds, such as Shan F. Bullock, James Stephens, or Seán O'Casey (effectively refuting the popular belief that all Irish Protestants are well-to-do).[5] And, of course, some Irish Anglicans are from backgrounds that mix a few of these strands, such as W. B. Yeats, J. M. Synge, or C. S. Lewis.

Because Ireland's Anglican population historically occupied the unique position of "middle nation" between England and Ireland, Irish Anglican writing has its own singular preoccupations.[6] Elizabeth Bowen has suggested that many of these preoccupations date back at least to Jonathan Swift. (She once wrote of her subculture, "With Swift comes the voice.")[7] When attempting to describe the "outlook" peculiar to what she calls (in deference to tradition) the "Anglo-Irish," Bowen insisted that writers from this subculture—even those from middle-class backgrounds, such as J. S. Le Fanu—are obsessed by "the autocracy of the great country house" and by "family myth, fatalism, [and] feudalism."[8] W. J. McCormack, R. F. Foster, and Terry Eagleton have built on her ideas to suggest that there is a distinct tradition of "Irish Protestant Gothic," indulged in by writers from both Ascendancy and middle-class backgrounds.[9] These critics contend that, for obvious reasons, authors from Irish Anglican backgrounds have been attracted to stories of disinheritance and the disclosure of past sins.[10] The Gothic works these writers produce usually feature characters in big, spooky, ramshackle houses like the ones that many Irish Anglicans occupied as they lived in fear of retribution from the Catholic Irish and grew morbid watching their lands and their old, privileged way of life disappear.

Ultimately, an interest in Gothic themes is only one hallmark of the Irish Anglican mind. As important critics have observed, writers from this background have demonstrated an interest in stories of allegiance and betrayal (political and sexual).[11] They also have a habit of engaging in "nostalgia as protest."[12] While these are certainly important tropes within Irish Anglican literature, there are other concerns and obsessions that are frequently dealt with by writers from this subculture, only some of which have been highlighted by previous critics.

First and foremost, as Elizabeth Bowen has noted, the Irish Anglican perspective (and, by extension, Irish Anglican writing) are frequently marked by "subtle...anti-Englishness" and a marked "ambivalence as to all things English"—despite the belief among many Irish Anglicans that they are British as well as Irish.[13] I am not simply referring to the often repeated suggestion that writers from this subculture who moved to London "swoop[ed] down on the English," passing satirical comment on them with the power given to them by "having such a weird, outside view of the English" (to quote Bowen again).[14] I am arguing instead that there is a more consistent, understated—and occasionally not-so-understated—hostility aimed at the English by Irish Anglicans that dates back at least as far as works by Swift such as *The Drapier's Letters* (1724–5), *Gulliver's Travels* (1726–7), and "An Excellent New Ballad; or, The True English Dean to Be Hanged for Rape" (1730).

The literature produced by this subculture suggests that, in addition to "anti-Englishness," other significant hallmarks of the Irish Anglican mind include being proudly (and occasionally bigotedly) Protestant while at the same time showing a greater understanding of Roman Catholicism than Protestants in Britain or the United States; possessing a finely tuned sense of differences in social class (arguably inherited from their British forebears); being obsessed with misalliance (mixing between higher and lower social groups)—an obsession which often leads Irish Anglicans to suppress evidence of their own Catholic blood; and harboring a distrust of art and artifice and possessing a concomitant fear of disappearing too far into a world of dreams and the imagination (seen most markedly in the work of Samuel Beckett, especially his stripped-back drama and the consistently undermined stories told by his narrators). Finally, as Terence Brown, Seán Kennedy, Feargal Whelan, and the present writer have argued, there is a tendency in Irish Protestant art and letters to praise the beauty of the Irish landscape while ignoring the people who populate it.[15] For Irish Anglicans (and, indeed, for those from the other Irish Protestant traditions), confrontation with that populace requires a painful wrestling with historical injustice—injustice in which one's ancestors may have played a part.

The Irish Anglican preoccupations I have highlighted are present in a number of works by Bernard Shaw, but his Irish Anglican perspective is arguably most clearly evident in three plays which contain no Irish characters at all: *Saint Joan*, *The Man of Destiny*, and *Tragedy of an Elderly Gentleman*.[16] In these works, Shaw uses Surrogate Irish figures to explore issues that he was taught were of vital importance during his formative years within a Church of Ireland cultural milieu. Saint Joan (in the play that bears her name), Napoleon (from *The Man of Destiny*), and the long-livers (from *Tragedy of an Elderly Gentleman*) all occupy an adversarial crypto-Irish role when confronted with the English characters (or characters of English descent) included in these works, and Shaw uses them to explore issues close to the heart of his Irish Anglican community.

Shaw's 1923 masterpiece, *Saint Joan*, retells the story of Joan of Arc, the fifteenth-century teenager from the Vosges who dressed as a male soldier, led French troops to resounding victories over invading English forces, and was burned as a heretic for defying the Roman Catholic hierarchy. In the play and its preface, Shaw argues that Joan was "one of the first Protestant martyrs," since she prized her own conscience (and the voices of the saints who spoke to her) over the teachings and stipulations of the official Church.[17] Shaw also contends that she was "one of the first apostles of Nationalism," since she regarded the English presence in France as unnatural (she believed that France was for the French-speaking peoples and that the English must be sent back to their own English-speaking land).[18] Joan's negative feelings about foreign conquest mirrors Shaw's own Irish distaste for English colonialism, and this has led critics such as Declan Kiberd, James

Moran, and Audrey McNamara to contend that Shaw's Saint Joan can be seen as his portrait of the Irish Republicans (including young women) who fought during the tumultuous years of 1916–23.[19] These critics rightly point out that Shaw wrote much of *Saint Joan* while visiting his native Ireland, and that this visit occurred in the immediate aftermath of the Irish Civil War, undoubtedly influencing the play's content.

As Moran has noted, the "Irish dimension" that Shaw embedded in *Saint Joan* has influenced important theatrical productions of the play.[20] With Shaw's permission, the Belfast-born actor Siobhán McKenna translated *Saint Joan* into Irish for a 1950 production at Galway's An Taibhdhearc. By producing the play in the official first language of Ireland (a language that the English had advocated wiping out since at least the time of Edmund Spenser), McKenna and her colleagues drew clear attention to the play's implicit comments on Anglo-Irish politics.[21] In a celebrated English-language production at the Gate Theatre three years later (which subsequently toured to London, New York, and continental Europe), McKenna stressed the Irish angle again by playing Joan with an Irish accent. The Irish Diasporic actor Anne-Marie Duff did the same in a high-profile British Royal National Theatre production in 2007.[22] Interestingly, one could argue that the very first production of the play (staged in New York in late 1923) also nodded to the play's Irishness. The actress who created the part of the young saint was an Irish-American called Winifred Linehan, and Shaw was pleased to hear that discerning critics believed that "the spiritual and national qualities of Joan of Arc are fully represented in Miss Linehan's performance."[23]

Building on the work of Kiberd, Moran, and McNamara, as well as theatre practitioners from Linehan to McKenna to Duff, I want to suggest in this chapter that Joan can be seen not only as a Surrogate Irish character in the play but also—more specifically—as a Surrogate Irish *Anglican* one. As will be seen, Shaw reveals much about his own Irish Anglican mindset through his creation and use of Joan.

Shaw imbues the young saint with Irish Anglican "anti-English-ness." This is seen most obviously in the fact that, despite her distaste for swearing and her deep sanctity, she refers to the English throughout the play as the "goddams." Joan's "anti-Englishness" leads her and her supporters to condemn the wanton cruelty of the English repeatedly throughout the play.[24] Likewise, her antipathy to the English convinces her that she must drive them back to England through physical force; she even echoes the common Irish Republican sentiment that "the English...understand nothing but hard knocks and slashes."[25]

Joan's statement on this occasion is one of many instances in which Shaw ensures that the play's audiences and readers link Joan to the Irish revolutionary tradition—a tradition that was disproportionately influenced by Irish Anglicans, from Lord Edward Fitzgerald and Robert Emmet to Charles Stewart Parnell and Erskine Childers. A second instance is when Joan wants her supporters to yell "Up, Joan!" (echoing the famous cry of "Up the republic!").[26] Another is when one of her accusers says:

> I know as a matter of plain commonsense that the woman is a rebel; and that is enough for me...And all these rebellions are only excuses for her great rebellion against England.[27]

Shaw links Joan most obviously to the Irish Anglican revolutionary tradition in the play's preface, when he compares Joan's trial to that of the 1916 rebel, Sir Roger Casement.[28] Indeed, James Moran persuasively argues in his important book *Staging the Easter Rising: 1916 as Theatre* that Shaw based the character of Joan at least partially on the homosexual, gender-bending Casement.[29]

Casement is not the only freedom fighter of Irish Anglican descent that Shaw links to Joan. As Stanley Weintraub and Michael Holroyd have demonstrated, Joan was also based partially on the Welsh-born son of an Irish Anglican father and a Scottish mother, T. E. Lawrence—a man who was very proud of his Irishness and who, as I noted in chapter 2, Shaw nominated for the Irish

Academy of Letters.[30] Lawrence, of course, fought on behalf of various Arabic peoples against the Ottoman Empire.

Shaw further stresses Joan's Surrogate Irish Anglican status during the play's preface by comparing her military prowess to that of the great Irish-born general, the Duke of Wellington.[31] While Wellington was not a rebel in the sense that Joan, Casement, or Lawrence were, he was (as Shaw always loved to point out) disrespectful of the "English" way of doing things on the battlefield.[32]

All of this emphasis on Joan's Irish Anglican "anti-Englishness" can be taken too far, however. It is true that, in the scenes not involving Joan, Shaw continually makes jokes at the expense of English pride, hypocrisy, and mental "blunt[ness]."[33] He even suggests that one of Joan's English accusers is an ancestor of Edmund Spenser (who not only advocated the extermination of the Irish language but also of the Irish themselves).[34] However, Shaw also takes care to stress the good qualities of the English in the play. Most notably, it is an *English* soldier who comforts Joan by handing her a wooden cross as she burns at the stake. (Interestingly, this scene was always going to be in the play, from the time he first contemplated writing it in 1913.)[35] And, Shaw, a proud Protestant and contrarian, does not consider it an insult when the French characters contend that all Englishmen are "Protestants" and "heretics" at heart.[36] Furthermore, Shaw (like his character Dunois) thinks it is admirable that the English take their work "seriously," echoing Larry Doyle's praise of the English in *John Bull's Other Island*.[37] There is also implied praise of English magnanimity in the allusion to the statue built in memory of Saint Joan at Winchester Cathedral (referenced in the play's Epilogue), and there is implied disparagement of the Irish in the fact that Warwick's probably-Irish attendant Brian has pruriently gone to witness Joan's burning. Ultimately, the positive reflections on the English in the piece, when taken together with its "anti-English-ness," speak to Shaw's Irish Anglican "ambivalence" regarding the residents of the imperial center.

When writing on religion and Irish affairs, Bernard Shaw was always quick to point out that he was "violently and arrogantly Protestant by family tradition."[38] He was proud of his Protestant background, because it fit with his self-image as a reformer and a contrarian. As he put it in the preface to *John Bull's Other Island*, "The Protestant is...an individualist, a freethinker, a self-helper, a Whig, a Liberal, a mistruster and vilifier of the State, a rebel."[39] Shaw's Protestant pride led him to celebrate the freethinking and rebellious Joan as one of the world's first Protestants. However, as he points out in the preface to *Saint Joan*, he did not make the same mistake as previous Protestant chroniclers of Joan's story (including Shakespeare, Andrew Lang, and Mark Twain).[40] That is, he did not depict the Catholic authorities who executed Joan as corrupt and evil. His extensive exposure to the Catholic mind while growing up in Ireland had taught him that a perfectly reasonable and fair Catholic would have had to conclude—based on Catholic theology and Joan's revolutionary ideas—that Joan was a heretic who required correction. One of the brilliant strengths of Shaw's play, therefore, is the fact that the Catholic authorities who condemn her are not two-dimensional villains out of Victorian melodrama—they are merely doctrinaire Catholics struggling to do the right thing, according to the teachings of their Church. And, as Shaw is keen to emphasize in the preface to *Saint Joan*, the punishment of Joan (and the Roman Catholic torture of heretics generally) "was not cruelty for cruelty's sake, but cruelty for the salvation of Joan's soul."[41] To make sure that he captured this Catholic mindset correctly, Shaw read the play to two Irish priests, Father Leonard (with whom he also corresponded by letter regarding the play) and Father Sheehy.

Shaw's nuanced understanding of the Roman Catholic perspective goes far beyond that of Protestant writers from countries with a majority Protestant population, such as England, Scotland, or the United States. This intimate knowledge of Catholicism was (and is) open to Irish Protestants, since they are surrounded by so many people from Roman Catholic backgrounds. Some

Irish Protestant writers, including Irish Anglicans such as Shaw, Oscar Wilde, Winifred Letts, and C. S. Lewis, have shown great sympathy for and appreciation of aspects of Roman Catholicism in their work as a result of this exposure (even as they remained, with the exception of Wilde, doctrinally Protestant). Other Irish Protestants, including many Ulster Orangemen—a common straw man in Shaw's rhetorical arguments on religion and Irish politics—have used this intimacy to develop a strongly bigoted, though frequently well-informed, understanding of the doctrinal differences that separate Catholics and Protestants.[42]

Despite the fact that Shaw was one of those Irish Protestant writers who showed appreciation for aspects of Catholicism, he is not completely complimentary regarding Catholicism in the play: in Shaw's view (as in ours), the Catholic authorities treat Joan appallingly, despite the mundanity of their evil. Also, although Shaw demonstrates a remarkable openness to mysticism in the play, his Protestant soul still gives a rational explanation for Joan's voices, miracles, and quirks of behavior. In the end, as Kiberd notes, Shaw is aiming for a fusion of Catholicism and Protestantism in the play—a fusion that captures the strengths of both traditions.[43] He was driven to achieve this by his dissatisfaction with the Irish Anglican faith within which he was raised. He felt that Irish Anglicanism was not Protestant enough, once writing that it was not "a religion but a side in a political faction; actuated less by theological principle than by class prejudice."[44]

Despite Shaw's relative openness to the more admirable aspects of Catholicism, as well as his negative feelings towards aspects of his Church of Ireland background and his belief that people from divergent class backgrounds should not be afraid to procreate (as noted in chapter 1), Shaw had a curious blind spot in his otherwise liberal views: he possessed the Irish Anglican reluctance to admit of Roman Catholicism in his family tree. Shaw insists in the preface to *John Bull's Other Island* that "My extraction is the extraction of most Englishmen: that is, I have no trace in me of the commercially imported North Spanish strain which passes for aboriginal Irish."[45] However, Shaw himself admitted in a letter that, through his father George Carr Shaw, he was descended from the Fennells of Cappoquin, Co. Waterford, who (he neglects to add) were probably of Gaelic Catholic origin. (Although the name can derive from English immigrants to Ireland, genealogists suggest that the Carlow and Waterford Fennells descend from an old Gaelic family called Ó Fionnghail.)[46] Similarly, the Carrs of Wexford—also from his father's side of the family tree—may have been of Scottish descent (since this surname is a variant of the lowland Scottish surname Kerr) or they may have been descended from an Irish Gaelic family (since Carr can be the anglicized form of ten different Gaelic surnames).[47]

Complicating matters further, Shaw was always unsure about his paternity, believing that his biological father may have actually been his mother's music teacher, George John Vandeleur Lee. As Peter Gahan and John O'Donovan have noted, "in [Shaw's] copious writings on Lee...[he] never mentions Lee's Catholicism...a significant, if rare, exception to the general reliability of Shaw's accounts" regarding his past.[48] Given that Shaw may have been the son of an Irish Catholic father and that his mother and nominal father's ancestors had been in Ireland for centuries by the time of his birth, intermarrying with families of various origins, he could not actually claim with any certainty that he had "no trace" of "aboriginal" Irish blood. His desire to do so is clearly a manifestation of his Irish Anglican mindset, inculcated in him during his youth.

In many works by Irish Anglican writers, including—for example—*Love and a Bottle* (1698) by George Farquhar, *The House in the Churchyard* (1863) by J. S. Le Fanu, *The Big House of Inver* by Somerville & Ross (1925), and *Purgatory* by W. B. Yeats (1938), deep anxiety over Irish Anglican intermarriage with Irish Gaelic Catholics is expressed.[49] Even in relatively light-hearted works, such as Somerville & Ross's *Irish RM* stories (1898–1915), "Flurry" McCarthy Knox's status as a half-sir is signaled by the fact that he is part McCarthy (an Irish Gaelic surname) and part

Knox (a Protestant surname of lowland Scottish origin), with his "low" McCarthy blood presumably explaining why he does not come across as a pure gentleman.[50] (We are told that he looks like "a stableboy among gentlemen, and a gentleman among stableboys.")[51]

This belief in and value on Irish Anglican racial purity, however, is patently absurd; most Irish Anglican families have been in Ireland since at least 1600, and some date back to the arrival of the Normans in 1169. Therefore, they certainly intermarried with Irish Gaelic Catholics. Indeed, Elizabeth Bowen and J. M. Synge both admitted to having "aboriginal" Irish blood on the maternal side of their families. (Tellingly, they only admitted as much to people outside of Ireland: Synge in a letter to his German translator, Max Meyerfeld, and Bowen in an interview in the *Chicago Tribune Book World*.)[52] W. B. Yeats's Butler ancestors had significant Catholic and Protestant branches in the family.[53] Oscar Wilde had Ó Finn ancestors in his direct line, and Somerville & Ross were descended from the Doyles of Carlow, originally a Gaelic Catholic family.[54] (It should be noted that, since "Flurry" McCarthy Knox was based on one of Edith Somerville's own brothers, the cousins may have been acknowledging their mixed origins through their creation of the character.)[55] Oliver Goldsmith boasted Roman Catholic clergy in his recent family tree.[56] And the families of Richard Brinsley Sheridan and Edmund Burke were of Gaelic Catholic origin (indeed, in Burke's case, it was his own father who first conformed to the established church, while his mother remained Catholic).[57]

One of the few prominent Irish Anglican writers to freely discuss and openly accept Irish Anglican mixing with Catholics was Maria Edgeworth, which is remarkable given the socio-political climate within which she was writing. She readily admitted her own family's descent from the Catholic Tuites, and, in her Irish novels, she repeatedly implies that there has been much intermarriage between the Ascendancy and their Gaelic Catholic tenantry. In *Castle Rackrent* (1800), we are told that the Rackrents were originally the Catholic O'Shaughlins, and in *Ennui* (1809), we learn that the Glenthorns were originally the Catholic O'Shaughnessys. In *The Absentee* (1812), Grace Nugent, who is from a Catholic background, marries the Irish Anglican Lord Colambre.[58] As regards *Ormond* (1817), history tells us that the lords of Annaly (the heroine's family) were originally O'Farrells.[59] And, as we already noted in reference to Yeats, the Ormond Butlers had important Catholic branches in the family. Edgeworth may have been emboldened to proclaim her lack of horror regarding Protestant-Catholic intermarriage from a statement made by her friend and neighbor, Charlotte Brooke, author of the *Reliques of Irish Poetry* (1789), a book that profoundly influenced Edgeworth's work.[60] In the preface to the *Reliques*, Brooke writes that "the portion of [British] blood which flows in our veins is rather ennobled than disgraced by the mingling tides that descended from our heroic [Irish] ancestors."[61] Edgeworth and Brooke were much more open-minded than most Irish Anglican people in taking this view, and, indeed, proved themselves freer than even the liberal Shaw on this matter. It is true that Shaw frequently professed openness to cross-cultural and cross-class procreation, even within an Irish context.[62] Likewise, his fictional representatives in *John Bull's Other Island*—Larry Doyle and Peter Keegan—are Catholics, albeit relatively heretical ones. (The shrewd political philosopher Doyle and poetic mystic Keegan represent two sides of Shaw's multifarious personality.) However, his Irish Anglican background seems to have left him with a blind spot regarding the Catholic-Protestant mixing in his own family tree. Indeed, even when insisting in a 1941 piece on Ireland that "cross-breeding" is "all too the good," he still claims that his Irishness is not based on his family's intermarriage with Irish Gaels but on "the Irish climate...work[ing] on my stock for some centuries."[63]

There may have been an element of unconscious class snobbery in this, with Shaw not wanting people to suspect that he was from a lower social class background than he actually was (most Irish Catholics being of lower social standing than the Shaws). Despite

Shaw's socialist desire to see all become equal and his routine criticisms of middle-class hypocrisy and hyper-conformity, he was actually prouder of his bourgeois origins than one might expect. Indeed, he seems to have wished that his background had been *more* bourgeois. I am not simply referring to his rueful reference to the Shaws as "downstarts," his anger over the fact that his family was shunned by the wealthier branches of the Shaw family, or his initial reluctance to admit that he had attended the socially low Marlborough Street Central Model Boys' School.[64] In a 1949 letter about the selling of the Shaw ancestral home, Bushy Park, Shaw confirms that, despite his socialism, he maintained a sentimental soft spot for the bourgeoisie (it also reveals that, despite his fear of possessing Catholic ancestry, he was still very far from sectarian in his views). Shaw writes:

I shall not be sorry to see the Catholic bourgeoisie elegantly housed in the park: for my mother, who was a famous amateur singer, found that Providence gave good voices and musical faculty quite indiscriminately to Catholics and Protestants. The priests invited her to sing when there were special musical services in their chapels. The concerts of the Amateur Musical Society were rehearsed in our house; and the tenors, baritones, basses, and soprano[s] were all Catholics...In this way I learnt early that the Catholic bourgeoisie, instead of being, as I had been taught, an inferior class on its way to hell, was in fact more cultivated and much kinder and better mannered than the Protestant.[65]

In this quote, Shaw may comment negatively on the bigotry and false sense of superiority rife in his own class and community, but he still shows a respect and affection for the bourgeois atmosphere within which he was raised. This respect and affection led him to emphasize in *Saint Joan*, and its preface, the historically true fact that Joan was not a peasant or a shepherdess, as she is often depicted, but "the young lady of the farm"—the daughter of a prosperous farmer "who was one of the headmen of his village, and transacted its feudal business for it with the neighboring squires and their lawyers."[66] While Joan can relate well to the lower-class characters in the play, her proto-middle-class social standing is repeatedly stressed.[67] In fact, she is even described in Shaw's stage directions as "respectably dressed."[68] Shaw's efforts in this regard led T. S. Eliot to accuse Shaw of turning Joan into a "middle-class reformer," which Eliot believed was an act of "sacrilege."[69] Shaw, however, had considerable respect for middle-class reformers. Indeed, he was one himself, and his desire to see poverty eradicated seems, at times, grounded in his desire to see rough, lower-class manners—engendered by lack of money and lack of access to education—eradicated.[70] Declan Kiberd correctly notes that, "As a Fabian, Shaw had a strong desire to make bourgeois lifestyles available to all."[71] Shaw's socialist dream therefore seems to involve *everyone* in society becoming middle-class—though without the hunger for respectability and the sheep-like conformity that, in his view, afflicted most middle-class people to their spiritual detriment.

Incidentally (and crucially), Shaw's middle-class pride is a sign of the cosmopolitanism and freedom of expression he gained by leaving Ireland.[72] As he notes through Larry Doyle in *John Bull's Other Island*, people in early twentieth-century Ireland did not "brag" about being "middle-class": "in Ireland youre either a gentleman or youre not. [*sic*]"[73] As R. F. Foster has shown, Irish Anglicans were very sensitive to gradations of status within the large category that the Irish in *John Bull's Other Island* call "gentlemen" and that Irish speakers called the *duine uasal* ("noble persons," but often used in Shaw's time for anyone from the middle and upper classes).[74] However, even when Irish Anglicans were in trade and the professions, they were reluctant to refer to themselves as middle-class, and preferred to perpetuate a subtle, unspoken social code, which involved them subtly shunning those of a slightly lower rank or those who violated hidden class taboos. (A good example of this is when Shaw himself was "dropped" by well-to-do Protestant boys after he briefly attended the Marlborough Street School.)[75] The socialist and cosmopolitan Shaw—with his globally minded class consciousness and the freedom given to him by escaping his small, Irish subculture—was willing to speak openly about class (both from an economic and a social point of view) and was even happy to put concrete names on Ireland's various social classes.[76]

Towards the end of *Saint Joan*, we are told that Joan danced around fairy trees and prayed at magic wells as a girl, recalling the Irish Literary Revival's interest in fairies and holy wells. This is merely one more example of Shaw's desire to link Joan to Ireland in the play. However, *Saint Joan* is not simply an Irish play and the character of Joan is not simply an Irish figure—no matter how much Shaw's creation and use of her may have been influenced by his Irish Anglican perspective. Just as Shaw tempers the play's anti-Englishness, he also complicates any reductive correlation between Joan and the Irish. It is true that Shaw seems to have based the character on freedom fighters of Irish extraction: Casement, Lawrence, and, as McNamara has shown, the brave women who were involved in Ireland's revolutionary struggle in the early twentieth century.[77] However, Shaw's main model for the character—and the only person he ever admitted to basing the character upon—was an English woman: Mary Hankinson, who hosted (and led the physical fitness training at) the Fabian Summer Schools he attended each year.[78] In fact, since Hankinson was from Cheshire, Shaw actually imbues Joan's dialogue with North of England inflections, in contrast to the more conventional Home Counties English spoken by the rest of the characters. This move enabled Shaw to maintain the play's internal consistency and to avoid over-stressing the Irish angle. Indeed, Shaw was so worried about over-selling the Irish angle that he preferred the part being played by an English actress and specified that the part could be played with any rural English dialect but "not Irish."[79]

Thus, while Shaw was certainly using the character of Joan to comment on Anglo-Irish relations, he also wanted the character to be a symbol to people of all nations, as he insisted in a letter to a Roman Catholic nun, his friend Sister Laurentia (née Margaret MacLachlan).[80] Arguably, this internationalist (some might say, deracinated) perspective also betrays his Irish Anglican background, since he demonstrates that he is not bound solely by considerations related to the island of Ireland.

Key aspects of *Saint Joan* were anticipated by a play that Shaw wrote at the start of his career: *The Man of Destiny* (1897), a play about the young Napoleon which is set in Italy. The two plays are linked in various ways. First, as Tracy J. R. Collins has noted, the female lead in *The Man of Destiny*, the Strange Lady, is a physically and psychologically strong woman who, like Joan, cross-dresses as a soldier.[81] Second, the two plays tell the story of successful French generals—generals who Shaw often compared to each other, including twice in the preface to *Saint Joan*.[82] Finally, and most importantly for our purposes, in each play Shaw uses a French historical figure as a Surrogate Irish character. In *The Man of Destiny*, Napoleon is linked subtly and repeatedly to the Irish. As with Joan, the nature of Napoleon's crypto-Irishness, and the ways in which the character is used, betray Shaw's enduringly Irish Anglican mindset.

In the play, Napoleon's Corsican background is strongly empha-sized, and the character himself notes that he is a "French citizen but not a Frenchman."[83] By highlighting this aspect of Napoleon's background, the Irishman Shaw is hinting that Napoleon, coming from an island off of the French mainland, is analogous to Irish people under the Union, who are from an island off of Great Britain and who are British citizens but who are patently not English.

To Shaw's mind, Corsica's status and treatment within the French polity is analogous to Ireland's under the English crown. Shaw was infuriated that the English regularly regarded the Irish as "back-ward, superstitious, and uncivilized" natives despite the fact that Ireland was technically equal to England under the Act of Union.[84] He therefore has the French Strange Lady use the word "Corsican" as an insult twice, and has her repeatedly pronounce Napoleon's surname in the Italian—and not the French—way, thereby sign-aling Corsica's marginalized, effectively foreign status.[85]

An implied connection between Ireland and Corsica is also made when Shaw has Napoleon reference the Corsican "love for stories"—a love traditionally associated with the Irish in British discourse.[86] And, at the end of the play, a further link is made when Shaw suggests that marginalized islander status is something that Napoleon shared with his great adversary, the Irish Duke of Wellington. Towards the end of the play, Napoleon's Italianate Corsican origins are linked to the "Iron Duke"'s Irish background when the young Napoleon muses: "An English army led by an Irish general: that might be a match for a French army led by an Italian general."[87]

We know definitively that Corsica and Ireland were linked in this way in Shaw's mind from a letter that he wrote in 1921 to an Irish-American admirer, Ignatius MacHugh. In the letter, Shaw—still smarting from the fact that he was not selected as a delegate to the 1917–18 Irish Convention—addresses the unpopularity of his cosmopolitan viewpoint among certain pockets of Nationalist opinion in Ireland, and links his native island to Napoleon's:

> I find myself without real influence in Ireland because I am without provincial illusions; and I cannot be persuaded that it would be better if I had a narrower outlook and greater popularity. I cannot help being a bad Irishman any more than Napoleon could help being a bad Corsican... [I]t is impossible to deal with modern political problems from the standpoint of a small island which is a century behind in social development, even though that century has been one of frightful degradation in England.[88]

Intriguingly (for our purposes), the status of marginalized islander does not just apply to Napoleon, Wellington, and Shaw; it also extends to Shaw's real-life model for the character of Napoleon: the actor-manager Richard Mansfield, with whom Shaw always had a strained relationship.[89] Mansfield was born in Berlin to an English father and a Russian mother (the famous singer Ermina Rudersdorhff) and actually spent a significant part of his childhood on the island of Heligoland—an island in the North Sea which belonged to Britain during Mansfield's childhood but is now ruled by Germany. Although Mansfield was partially educated at the Derby School in England and based in London for part of his twenties, he actually spent most of his adult life in the United States. Therefore, Mansfield was (like Napoleon, Wellington, and Shaw) a provincial outsider from a small island attempting to do great things on the world stage.

Of course, *The Man of Destiny*'s main link to Anglo-Irish politics is Napoleon's incendiary speech at the end of the play, in which he attempts to explain the reasons for English success but often in terms that are deeply insulting. During this speech, Shaw uses Napoleon to voice his own Irish—or, more precisely, Irish Anglican—"anti-Englishness." This speech rehearses many of Larry Doyle and Peter Keegan's ideas regarding the English, as expressed in *John Bull's Other Island*. Shaw's Napoleon believes, like those later Irish characters, that the English do everything on principle, even their most appalling deeds:

> When [an Englishman] wants a thing, he never tells himself that he wants it. He waits patiently until there comes into his mind, no one knows how, a burning conviction that it is his moral and religious duty to conquer those who have got the thing he wants. Then he becomes irresistible...There is nothing so bad or so good that you will not find Englishmen doing it; but you will never find an Englishman in the wrong. He does everything on principle. He fights you on patriotic principles; he robs you on business principles; he enslaves you on imperial principles; he bullies you on manly principles; he supports his king on loyal principles, and cuts off his king's head on republican principles. His watchword is always duty; and he never

forgets that the nation which lets its duty get on the opposite side to its interest is lost.[90]

The anti-Englishness underpinning this tirade and other remarks in the play (at one point, Napoleon and the Strange Lady agree that the English are "very stupid") made *The Man of Destiny* extremely popular in Ireland in the decades after its first production.[91] Indeed, of all of Shaw's early plays, *The Man of Destiny* was the one that Yeats requested permission to produce when he was planning the Irish National Theatre Society's 1903 offerings.[92] Similarly, the play, despite its relatively minor status in the Shaw canon, has been produced numerous times in Ireland, including seven times by the Abbey. (As Nelson O'Ceallaigh Ritschel has pointed out, *The Man of Destiny* was also popular in early twentieth-century Dublin because of Nationalist interest in Napoleon's ties to the Irish rebellions of 1798 and 1803.)[93]

Shaw's Irish Anglican mind is not only revealed through Napoleon's anti-Englishness. Shaw's subconscious partiality for people of his own class background is also clearly manifest in the play. In the stage directions, Napoleon's "shabby-gentility" is referenced; in Shaw's autobiographical writings he proudly speaks of "my own class: the Shabby Genteel."[94] Likewise, Napoleon voices some of Shaw's middle-class pride (and awareness of his class's weaknesses) when he explains to the Strange Lady that:

There are three sorts of people in the world, the low people, the middle people, and the high people. The low people and the high people are alike in one thing: they have no scruples, no morality. The low are beneath morality, the high above it. I am not afraid of either of them: for the low are unscrupulous without knowledge, so that they make an idol of me; whilst the high are unscrupulous without purpose, so that they go down before my will...It is the middle people who are dangerous: they have both knowledge and purpose. But they, too, have their weak point. They are full of scruples—chained hand and foot by their morality and respectability.[95]

Shaw's interest in gradations of class recurs a little later when Napoleon finds one of the Strange Lady's remarks to be surprisingly "vulgar"; he says, "I took you for a lady: an aristocrat. Was your grandfather a shopkeeper, pray?" When she answers that he was English, Napoleon believes that this explains everything, since "the English are a nation of shopkeepers."[96]

In this scene, Shaw's suggestion that a person's manners might have been corrupted by a grandparent mixing with a spouse from a lower social rank links to the Irish Anglican fear of misalliance. However, despite Shaw's heightened sensitivity to social mixing as promulgated in him by his Irish subculture, his views cannot be linked unequivocally to those Irish Anglicans who have suggested that English blood and Irish Protestant pedigree are nobler than an Irish Gaelic lineage. (A good example of someone who holds this snobbish view is Yeats; witness his reference to the Synges as "a very old Irish family"—are not Irish Gaelic genealogies and surnames some of the oldest in Europe?—and his belief that the new generation of Irish poets sprang from "base beds").[97] In *The Man of Destiny*, Shaw may suggest that the Strange Lady has been harmed by her "shopkeeperish" English blood, but he also suggests that Irish blood of any stripe is empowering: Napoleon concludes that the Strange Lady owes her clever, non-English brains to her Irish grandmother.[98] In this instance, Shaw is sticking to his principle that mixing with a person from a marginalized background might actually improve one's offspring ("cross-breeding [is]...all to the good"), even if he is contradicting his belief expressed elsewhere that "there is no Irish race any more than there is an English race or a Yankee race."[99]

One of the clearest indications that Shaw is using Napoleon as a Surrogate Irish character is the fact that he gives the general traits that he associates elsewhere with the Irish. Shaw describes Napoleon in the stage directions as "imaginative without illusions."[100] This links directly to Shaw's description of the Irish (defined in contrast to the English) in the preface to *John Bull's Other Island*:

> The Englishman is wholly at the mercy of his imagination, having no sense of reality to check it. The Irishman, with a far subtler and more fastidious imagination, has one eye always on things as they are... [The] Irish [have] a power of appreciating art and sentiment without being duped by them into mistaking romantic figments for realities.[101]

In a similar vein, Shaw describes Napoleon as "a merciless cannonader of political rubbish."[102] This links him to the Irish characters in Shaw's other plays, who (as we noted in chapters 1 and 2) often voice hard truths to those around them.

In the preface to *Saint Joan*, Shaw wrote approvingly that Joan was "as much a realist as Napoleon."[103] Elsewhere, Shaw contends that Napoleon had "no illusions," was not sentimental, and was wonderfully pragmatic as a ruler.[104] These remarks, along with Shaw's characterization of the general in *The Man of Destiny* and 1921's *Tragedy of an Elderly Gentleman* (in which Napoleon briefly appears as the Emperor of Turania), reveal Shaw's Irish Anglican value on realism and practicality and distrust of disappearing into dreams and the imagination.[105] In Shaw's own case, this distrust was linked not only to the values promoted within his Irish subculture but also to his regrets over what he considered his own wasted boyhood. Michael Holroyd explains:

> The beauty of [Shaw's childhood] Dalkey evoked a happiness that 'takes you out, far out, of this time and this world'; but such 'imaginative feasts' starved him of reality, he later claimed, and delayed his development. 'With a little more courage & a little more energy I could have done much more; and I lacked these because in my boyhood I lived on my imagination instead of my work.'[106]

Shaw channeled his anger over the dreaminess that the Irish landscape seemed to produce in him into some of Larry Doyle's speeches in *John Bull's Other Island*.[107] However, he was not alone among Irish Anglican writers in this fear of being made indolent by the ethereal Irish landscape. C. S. Lewis expresses the same fear in his poem "Irish Nocturne" (1919).[108] Likewise, fear of sloth combined with appreciation for the Irish landscape underpins many of Samuel Beckett's early stories, as various critics have pointed out. Writing about idleness in Beckett's work, Feargal Whelan has compellingly argued that "for a Protestant man, and in particular a bourgeois Protestant young man, sloth is the greatest of all sins" (betraying, as it does, what Max Weber famously termed the "Protestant work ethic").[109] Certainly, the prolific and workaholic Shaw fought hard against sloth in his own life and regularly advocated that others do the same. Perhaps Irish Anglican writers have been taunted by their dual inheritance of the Protestant work ethic and British efficiency into believing that they should be working as hard as they possibly can (and certainly much harder than their Catholic neighbors). Under such pressure, the seductive power of the beautiful Irish landscape becomes the enemy of the machine-like industry that they believe is required of them.

As has been noted, *The Man of Destiny* was not to be Napoleon's only appearance in a Shaw play. He appears in thinly veiled disguise as the Emperor of Turania in 1921's *Tragedy of an Elderly Gentleman*. This play is the fourth part of *Back to Methuselah*, a cycle of five plays that attempts to demonstrate that humankind, with the help of the Life Force, can once again learn to live for hundreds of years, as they did in early Biblical times. The last three parts of the cycle (*The Thing Happens, Tragedy of an Elderly Gentleman,* and *As Far As Thought Can Reach*) take place in the future, and try to picture a world in which people live for centuries. *Tragedy of an Elderly Gentleman* is set in the Burren and Galway city in 3000 AD, at a time when some of the world's population are "long-livers" but most are "shortlived people."[110] The "long-livers" live in Britain and Ireland, and the "shortlivers" in the rest of the world.[111]

The British Empire has become the British Commonwealth and its capital has moved to Baghdad, because "the Englishman" of 3000 AD has come to believe that Mesopotamia is "the true cradle of his race."[112] In the play, we are told that the long-livers who reside in Ireland are not really Irish, because the Irish nation died out after leaving Ireland and helping to lead "the struggle for national independence" in countries all around the world.[113] The English Elderly Gentleman, who is visiting Ireland with his family, explains that

> The Irish, who had lost all their political faculties by disuse except that of nationalist agitation, and who owed their position as the most interesting race on earth solely to their sufferings...[became known] in the very countries they had helped set free...as intolerable bores.[114]

Unwanted in the countries they had moved to, the Irish were convinced by an English archbishop to move back to Ireland. When they landed in the Burren, however, and saw that the fields contained "no earth, only stone," they left for England the next day and "no Irishman ever again confessed to being Irish, even to his own children."[115] Scared by the example of the Irish, "the dispersed Jews did the same lest they should be sent back to Palestine. Since then the world, bereft of its Jews and its Irish, has been a tame dull place."[116] (This is yet another instance of Shaw linking the Irish with the Jews.)

As Peter Gahan has noted, the long-livers who reside in Ireland, while not ethnically Irish, "have become more Irish than the Irish themselves and exemplify the positive qualities that Shaw found gave Irishmen a type of wisdom, an objectivity in dealing with subjects other than Ireland."[117] Shaw is once again stressing that the Irish climate produces the Irish perspective. However, he is also betraying his Irish Anglican mindset through these Surrogate Irish long-livers.

The long-livers are, in keeping with Shaw's Irish Anglican values and his depictions of the Irish in other works, hyper-realists and fact-facers, disdaining metaphorical language, sentimental rhetoric, and pomp and ceremony. This is stressed right from the play's opening moments. The play starts with the English Elderly Gentleman sentimentally announcing to a female long-liver that he is in Ireland because he is making "a pious pilgrimage" back to the "islands [that] were once the centre of the British Commonwealth during a period now known as the Exile."[118] The mercilessly practical long-liver replies: "I do not understand. You say you have come here on a pious pilgrimage. Is that some new means of transport?"[119]

The Surrogate Irish long-livers also repeatedly express Shaw's Irish Anglican "anti-Englishness": they are used by Shaw to insult "red-faced Englishmen," "English...fatheads," and London ("Was London a place of any importance?").[120] One of the long-livers even echoes Shaw's belief that "Irish air will change even an English man or woman so usefully that two years of it should be made part of their compulsory education, just to make their minds flexible."[121]

Issues around social class and misalliance are also raised once again by Shaw through these Surrogate Irish characters. The socialistic long-livers have developed a classless society. Thus, they are frankly bewildered by the English Elderly Gentleman's insistence on making distinctions between himself (as a "gentleman") and "the lower classes," including "agricultural laborers" and "paupers."[122] Similarly, whereas the Elderly Gentleman scorns American "social promiscuity," favors a society which is "organized in a series of highly exclusive circles," and looks down upon "the natives" of "savage" countries, the long-livers have no issues with racial mixing.[123] One of them remarks, "we are not particular about our pigmentation."[124] This is a clear indication of the long-livers' Surrogate Irish status, since, just as Shaw was always ready to link the Irish to the Jews, he was also quick to link them to people from Asia and Africa. For example, Shaw approvingly compared his own mother to a South Sea Islander when discussing her lack of concern for English conventions of behavior.[125] In *John Bull's Other Island* and its preface, Shaw repeatedly compares Ireland to non-white countries that have been exploited by the British Empire, including Egypt, India, and China.[126] In the same play, Peter Keegan is defrocked for being open to the spiritual views of "a black...Hindoo."[127] Most notably, the Black Girl in Shaw's novella *The Adventures of the Black Girl in Her Search of God* (1932) marries a red-haired Irishman at the end; Shaw explains that their children "were charmingly coffee-colored."[128]

As Shaw undoubtedly knew, the Irish actually have a very mixed record with regards to interracial relations. On the one hand, as sociologists and historians have proven, the Irish have readily mixed with other races in the Diaspora (Billie Holiday and Mohammed Ali—to name two famous examples—are the descendants of such unions).[129] On the other hand, the Irish have also been prominently involved in violent, racist protests such as the Draft Riots in New York City during the American Civil War, anti-Chinese rallies in California in the late nineteenth century, and the anti-busing protests in Boston in the mid-1970s. By setting *Tragedy of an Elderly Gentleman* in an Ireland devoid of the Irish, Shaw is able to maintain (and freely express) his idealistic views of the Irish with regards to mixing without having to address actual Irish racism or confront the unconscious class prejudice that sometimes arose in his analysis when dealing with Ireland in all of its complex reality.

Interestingly, Shaw's decision to set the play in an Ireland devoid of Irish people is yet another manifestation of his stubbornly Irish Anglican perspective. *Tragedy of an Elderly Gentleman* fits into a long tradition of works by Irish Protestants which celebrate the Irish landscape, but in a way that ignores or removes the Irish populace. In 1988, Terence Brown noted this phenomenon in the work of Protestant poets such as William Allingham, W. B. Yeats, Louis MacNeice, Michael Longley, Richard Murphy, and James Simmons.[130] In 2005, Seán Kennedy traced this trope in the memoirs published by Irish Anglicans in the decades after independence and linked it to the barren landscapes in the work of Samuel Beckett.[131] More recently, Feargal Whelan has linked these depopulated landscapes in Beckett to the famous landscapes painted by Irish Anglican artists such as Paul Henry and to studies by Irish Protestant naturalists—such as Robert Praeger and John Joly—who insisted on studying the physical landscape of Ireland in minute detail while ignoring the populace who reside in that landscape.[132] In an article in the *Irish Studies Review*, I have linked this trope to the following remark from Belfast writer C. S. Lewis:

> The country [around Ulster] is very beautiful and if only I could deport the Ulstermen and fill their land with a populace of my own choosing, I should ask for no better place to live.[133]

Since Lewis based the topography of Narnia in *The Chronicles of Narnia* (1950–6) on his native Ulster and the Narnian landscape on the area around Carlingford Lough in Co. Louth, it is clear that, in his most famous works, he did in fact replace the Irish with "a populace of [his] own choosing."[134] Given Lewis's conflicted feelings regarding the Irish populace, this is hardly surprising. Lewis claimed to feel "a natural repulsion to noisy, drum-beating, bullying Orangemen," who he compared to the Klu Klux Klan and McCarthyites.[135] Lewis also wrote, in the context of Ireland, that "conquest is an evil productive of almost every other evil both to those who commit and to those who suffer it," and noted in his autobiography that he "hated whatever [he] knew or imagined of the British Empire."[136] Thus, he clearly felt Irish Anglican guilt over his subculture's historic mistreatment of the Irish Gaelic population. In *The Chronicles*, Lewis's personal feelings regarding Irish Catholics and Protestants led him to replace these groups with animals and mythical creatures who spoke—like Lewis—a mix of Hiberno-English and London/Home Counties English.[137] In making this decision, Lewis was not completely ignoring the Irish socio-political situation; as Nicole du Plessis has noted, most of the novels in *The Chronicles of Narnia* involve a people being taken over—or nearly taken over—to their detriment by imperialistic invaders or supernatural beings.[138] (I would add that this is also the plot of all three of Lewis's science fiction novels.) Thus, Lewis is voicing his Irish anti-colonial views without confronting the difficult personal obstacles that writing about Ireland directly would have involved for someone from an Ulster Unionist household who regarded himself as both Irish and British.[139]

Shaw does something similar to Lewis in *Tragedy of an Elderly Gentleman*. As Gahan and Moran have shown, Shaw is subtly commenting on Anglo-Irish relations in this play.[140] He finds it easier, however, to comment on the situation from a remove; specifically—like other Irish Protestant writers, painters, and scientists—he frees himself from personal and socio-historical baggage by first removing the Irish populace from the Irish landscape. This strand in Irish Protestant art and letters is, of course, not without its potentially sinister side. When the descendants of colonizers repeatedly try to picture an Ireland devoid of the Irish, it cannot help but stir up thoughts of English commentators such as Spenser who called for the extermination of the Irish—or even memories of cruel Irish landlords such as Lady Gregory's future husband, W. H. Gregory, who, during the Famine, sponsored the Gregory Clause (an amendment to the Irish poor law "which exempted anyone who held more than a quarter of an acre from obtaining famine relief unless they gave up their land").[141] While such genocidal measures were clearly far from the minds of Shaw, Lewis, Beckett, and other Irish Protestant writers and painters when creating their depopulated Irish landscapes, they do speak to the discomfort felt by these artists in confronting the populace with whom their families had such conflicted histories.

In recent decades, critics have frequently and blithely asserted that Shaw only wrote one Irish play—*John Bull's Other Island*.[142] Even if we excuse these critics for their ignorance of the excellent (but relatively little-known) *O'Flaherty, VC*, the definitiveness of such an assertion suggests that these critics complacently assume that Shaw was relatively uninterested in writing about the land of his birth. Critics who make such an assumption fail to recognize that Shaw occasionally wanted to comment on Irish affairs from an angle, by writing plays featuring Surrogate Irish characters. An important example of such a play is *Tragedy of an Elderly Gentleman*. Given that this play is actually set in Ireland and that it features the Surrogate Irish long-livers, it certainly deserves to be regarded as Shaw's third Irish play. As we have seen, other plays in which Shaw explores Irish issues through the use of Surrogate Irish characters include *Saint Joan* and *The Man of Destiny*, both of which are set on the Continent and both of which tell the stories of celebrated French generals.

Clearly, the settings and subjects of Shaw's plays featuring Surrogate Irish characters complicate his popular reputation as a writer of English society plays. Indeed, each of these plays addresses matters of pan-European (and even global) concern, even as they simultaneously—and pointedly—address Irish politics and history. Critics who ignore Shaw's Irish intentions in these plays—including the degree to which these scripts are permeated by his Irish Anglican perspective—fail to appreciate crucial aspects of these remarkable and complex works.

4
Shaw and the Stage Englishman in Irish Literature

Part I: The Stage Englishman in Irish literature

Much has been written by critics about the phenomenon of the Stage Irishman in English drama. For centuries, the Irish were depicted on the English stage as ugly, drunken, sentimental, pugnacious, patriotic buffoons. But how have the English been portrayed in Irish fiction and drama? While Irish writers have resisted the temptation to create deeply offensive ciphers like the Stage Irishman, over the past two centuries a number of important dramatists and fiction writers have repeatedly placed English characters into their work in order to take satirical swipes at the English and their handling of Ireland. These characters may not be crude caricatures like the Stage Irishman, but they are far from completely objective portraits of English people. In fact, even in the cases where these writers intended their English characters to be good, or at least harmless, they still used these portraits to reveal what they saw as drawbacks or peculiarities in the English national character.[1] One of the most famous Stage Englishmen in Irish literary history is, of course, Tom Broadbent from *John Bull's Other Island*, but, as this chapter will demonstrate, Broadbent must be contextualized within a long, under-considered, virtually invisible, *tradition* of Irish writing, in which the commendable Irish Self is repeatedly contrasted with the less admirable English Other. Curiously, despite the prevalence of satirical representations of the

English in Irish literature, the Stage Englishman, as a phenomenon in its own right, has received relatively little critical attention.

Several critics have described individual characters in Irish literature as Stage Englishmen, but there has been no serious theorizing on the subject. By far the most comprehensive examination of the Stage Englishman is the chapter entitled "The Stage Englishman of the Irish Drama: Boucicault and the Politics of Empathy" in Elizabeth Butler Cullingford's groundbreaking and seminal study *Ireland's Others* (2001), but her essay focuses almost exclusively on the English characters in Dion Boucicault's Irish melodramas.[2] Cullingford does touch on the subject more broadly in three other chapters in the same book, but there are two crucial differences between my work and Cullingford's.[3] First, she seems to define a Stage Englishman as *any* English character appearing in an Irish work, whereas I believe that it is vitally important to consider just how the English figure is being used. As such, I have only regarded characters as Stage English if they are employed for subversive, anti-English satirical purposes. Secondly, Cullingford only examines male Stage English figures, in the belief that "Englishness remains almost completely identified with maleness" in Irish drama and film.[4] While I will not be covering film in this chapter, my engagement with Irish drama and fiction will reveal that the Irish literary canon actually contains a number of fascinating Stage English females. (With some hesitation, I include these characters in the generic category Stage Englishman, just as previous critics have included female characters in their studies of the Stage Irishman.)

Other than Cullingford—whose work I will regularly engage with during this chapter—critics have mainly used the term Stage Englishman in relation to Broadbent. While some of these commentators have examined specific ways in which Broadbent could be seen as a Stage Englishman (including Declan Kiberd, Nicholas Grene, David Krause, and Michael Holroyd), none have done so at any great length.[5] Elsewhere, Kiberd has briefly put forward the view that Oscar Wilde, while living in England, played the role of the Stage Englishman, and Violet Powell has, in passing, described some of Somerville & Ross's characters as Stage Englishmen.[6] More recently, John Nash has looked at Haines in Joyce's *Ulysses* as a Stage Englishman, but, again, not at great length.[7] Heinz Kosok concludes two different essays with brief analysis of the Stage Englishmen in works by writers such as Charles Macklin, Lady Morgan, Seán O'Casey, Louis D'Alton, Brendan Behan, Brian Friel, and, of course, Shaw.[8] And Anthony Roche, in like spirit, has called Teddy in Friel's *Faith Healer* (1979) a Stage Englishman and suggested a link between Broadbent and Lieutenant Yolland in Friel's *Translations* (1980).[9] My decision to examine satirical representations of the English has partially been inspired by the work of these important critics, whose provocative allusions to the Stage Englishman are, to my eyes, begging to be teased out.

Before embarking on my analysis, I should point out that, just as previous critics have used the terms Stage Irishman and Stage Englishman to refer to characters from both drama and fiction, I will be examining characters from plays, novels, and short stories in this chapter. There are two other reasons why I have decided to label these characters *Stage* English, even though some of them do not actually appear on a stage. First, the fact that these otherwise believable English characters exist even partially for satirical purposes recalls their similarity to the Stage Irishman. (In the works referenced in this chapter, an English character enters an Irish scene, revealing the author's feelings about the English, just as, historically, the Stage Irishman entered an English scene, revealing the author's view of the Irish.) Secondly, the English characters that Irish writers place in their work often project a very stagey, consciously heightened Englishness, and therefore it is no stretch to call such creations—even those from novels and short stories—*Stage* Englishmen.

Stage English characters in Irish literature are curious creatures, because they are, in many ways, very realistic characters, and yet are also meant to serve as satirical portraits of the English. Their realism lies in the fact that they possess the three requirements that Andrew Bennett and Nicholas Royale have suggested are key components of "life-like" characters in fiction:

> The first requirement is for such a character to have a plausible name and to say and do things that seem convincingly like the kinds of things that people do in so-called 'real-life'...The second requirement is a certain complexity...To be life-like, a fictional character should have a number of different traits— traits or qualities which may be conflicting or contradictory...[H]is or her words and actions should appear to originate in multiple impulses. Thirdly, however, these tensions, contradictions, multiplicities should cohere in a single identity...It is this tension, between complexity and unity, that makes a character...both interesting and credible.[10]

Wedded to this realism, in the case of Stage English characters, is what Deidre Shauna Lynch would call their "pragmatics of character"—that is, their employment as anti-English satirical tools.[11] While the definition of satire is hotly contested, a helpful recent definition comes from critic Jill E. Twark:

> Satirical humor is produced when humor is directed pointedly or aggressively against an object to illustrate its flaws or to censure it in some way. Satire may serve to teach or uplift morally.[12]

In the works covered in this chapter, Irish writers create English characters who are quite realistic but then point up their idiosyncrasies to demonstrate what they see as the negative sides of the English national character or to critique English attitudes to Ireland and the Irish. These characters are often the sole representative of England in the Irish scenes in which they appear. Since they are presented, and come across, as very realistic portraits of English people, when they turn out to be—for instance—cruel or condescending or excessively practical, their flaws seem like completely plausible faults of the English generally, not merely hysterical defamations trumped up by the literary representatives of a hurt and subjected people.[13]

While subversive intentions may have prevented Irish writers from creating English characters who are as strictly realistic as, say, Austen's Elizabeth Bennet or Dickens's Mr Pickwick, the desire among Irish writers to approach realism with their Stage English portraits, without actually reaching it, is intentional. Their satire gains extra bite when they imply that the heightened viciousness or absurdity demonstrated by the Stage Englishman is not far from the actual viciousness or absurdity of real English people in Ireland. As the Irish-American fiction writer and critic Flannery O'Connor has observed, the more a writer makes their characters "real" and "believable"—in terms of their physical appearance, as well as their "personalit[ies]" and "motivations"—the more likely it is that readers will accept it when, in the name of pushing a message, the writer breaks with the natural order of things (for example, by engaging in satirical "exaggeration" or introducing the supernatural).[14] As such, the authors highlighted in this chapter—be they dramatists or fiction writers—deliberately make their Stage English characters very true to life so that audiences will hear (and accept) their message when they pass negative satirical comment on the English.

In recognizing that these English characters are not completely realistic, we might be tempted to conclude that the Stage Englishman is just as much of a racist caricature as the Stage Irishman, with the only difference being that the Stage Englishman is drawn with a bit more subtlety. That would be a mistake, however, because the charges that Irish writers have brought against the English through their use of the Stage Englishman have not been exceedingly unjust. In works featuring Stage English characters, Irish writers have made perceptive observations about general English behavior and attitudes, especially as exemplified by the English abroad.

In particular, these writers have identified the stagey, extreme, self-conscious Englishness that English visitors to Ireland before, and even after, Irish independence projected. As various commentators have observed, when English people went to the colonies belonging to the British Empire, they felt the pressure to embody for "the natives" what a good English person should be—refined in manners, graceful under pressure, and ever rational and efficient.[15] According to V. S. Naipaul and Philip Woodruff, the "peculiar quality" of the English in colonies like India was ascribable to "this affectation of being very English, this sense of a nation at play, acting out a fantasy."[16] Within an Irish context, a famous example of this is Anthony Trollope, who, as R. F. Foster and Victoria Glendinning have pointed out, "actually acquired his typical 'English' mode of address and behavior in Ireland."[17] The Irish writers highlighted in this chapter incorporated this "affectation of being very English" into their Stage English portraits, and, in that way, made their characters more true to life. Few English writers, except those who had observed the English in the colonies—such as E. M. Forster or Somerset Maugham—picked up on this sense of Englishness as a self-conscious, performative identity.

Class politics was a significant factor behind this projection of extreme Englishness. "At the height of their power," the English colonials were not only intent on "playing at being English," they were intent on "playing at being English of a certain class."[18] In attempting to show the natives through their bodies and their manner of speaking just how (supposedly) civilized, rational, efficient, and honorable a person could become by following English ways, these mainly middle-class civil servants and army personnel were mimicking English upper-class manners.[19] Since they were not from the background that they were projecting, there was a greater amount of artifice than usual in their daily performance of Englishness. The Irish writers who have incorporated Stage Englishmen in their work suggest that when this performance of Englishness was brought to Ireland, it struck different segments of the Irish population differently. The Ascendancy, who regarded themselves as aristocratic and who had, in some cases, been educated in England, detected what they regarded as middle-class vulgarity just below the surface of these faux-posh English army officers, government bureaucrats, and their wives, and they were offended by it. The Catholic Irish, meanwhile, were struck by how "unnatural" the English were.[20] Little wonder, considering they may not have been seeing the real English person at all but an English mask.

Of course, as in all the colonies, the Irish had much greater exposure to the dominant English culture than the English ever did to the culture of the subordinate Irish.[21] This helps explain the Irish writer's ability to make subtler (perhaps truer) satirical portraits of the English than the English were able to do of the Irish. Educated within a British school system heavily biased in favor of English books and plays, Irish writers were quite familiar with English values and manners and were therefore able to detect that there was often something not quite genuine in the way the English in Ireland were acting. The Irish writers discussed in this chapter seem ever aware of this stagey performance of Englishness by the English characters they create.

The Stage English males created by Irish writers usually fall into two categories. They are often either "racist, officious hypocrites" or "sentimental, romantic duffers." The racist, officious hypocrites are often cold and cruel; they believe they can size up Ireland and the Irish in a short amount of time; and they routinely behave in a manner that violates their verbally professed principles. Famous examples of such characters include Lord Craiglethorpe from Edgeworth's *Ennui* (1809), Basil Leigh Kelway from the Somerville & Ross story "Lisheen Races, Second-Hand" (1899), the Magistrate from Lady Gregory's *Spreading the News* (1904), the Hangman and his assistant from Behan's *The Quare Fellow* (1954), Captain Lancey from Friel's *Translations* (1980), Tom Bailey from Christina Reid's *The Belle of the Belfast City* (1989), Richard Gore from Friel's *The Home Place* (2005), and the brutish English "tommies" featured in works by numerous playwrights.[22] Notable sentimental, romantic duffers include Harry Lorrequer from Charles Lever's *The Confessions of Harry Lorrequer* (1839), Maxwell Bruce from the Somerville & Ross story "The Last Day of Shraft" (1906), Angel from Behan's *The Big House* (1957), Teddy from Friel's *Faith Healer* (1979), and Lieutenant Yolland from Friel's *Translations* (1980).[23] Shaw's Broadbent is an ingenious combination of these two English male types, and, in the decades that followed the premiere of *John Bull's Other Island*, important Irish writers followed Shaw's example by creating Stage Englishmen who are a combination of racist, officious hypocrite and sentimental, romantic duffer (as shall be discussed in more detail below).

With regards to Stage English females, Irish writers often depict English women as either middle-class arrivistes who look down on both the Protestant Irish and the Catholic Irish for being dirty, poor, unpredictable, and potentially violent, or else as shallow innocents who regard the Irish as noble savages. These two types are simply female versions of the racist, officious hypocrite and the sentimental, romantic duffer. Examples of the female racist, officious hypocrite include Lady Dashfort from Edgeworth's *The Absentee*, Lady O'Shane (née Scraggs) and Mrs McCrule (née Black) from Edgeworth's *Ormond*, Alice Hervey from Somerville & Ross's *Irish RM* stories, Lilia (and arguably Lady Latterly) from Bowen's *A World of Love* (1955), Boadicea Baldcock from Behan's *The Big House*, and Lady Elizabeth Montgomery Bailey, QC from Reid's *The Belle of the Belfast City*.[24] Female sentimental, romantic duffers include Philippa from Somerville & Ross's *Irish RM* stories, Edith Paston from Mary Lavin's short story "Limbo" (1956), and—crucially for our purposes—Lady Madigan from Shaw's *O'Flaherty, VC*.[25]

Why did Irish writers settle on these two types for the English?[26] First, it must be stressed that they were not writing in a vacuum; as the title of Shaw's first Irish play suggests, he (like other Irish writers) was very conscious of prevailing stereotypes of the English, especially the figure of John Bull.[27] In creating the two Stage English types, Irish writers chose to either directly contradict the positive qualities and faint flaws associated with John Bull or to exaggerate those qualities and flaws until they became grievous English national failings. If John Bull is plain-speaking and matter-of-fact, then Irish writers suggest through their Stage English satirical portraits that the English are prosaic and unimaginative; if John Bull detests sentiment, then Irish writers suggest that the English are cold and unfeeling, or else they insist that the English are actually absurdly sentimental; Irish writers respond to John Bull's compulsive desire to come up with a practical solution to every problem by creating Stage Englishmen who naïvely believe that they can size up (and solve) Ireland's problems quickly and easily.[28] From the point of view of postcolonial theory, Irish writers who base their views of the English on what the English say about them-selves are in Frantz Fanon's second "national" phase—a phase in which fiery assertions of national pride and cultural dignity are "logically inscribed from the same point of view as that of colonialism."[29]

This second phase perspective also helps explain why so many Irish writers have employed these two Stage English types. These types relate directly to the impression that many Irish people had of the English when Ireland was a crown possession (note that writers from British-ruled Northern Ireland, such as Brian Friel and Christina Reid, continue to employ these two types). English people posted to Ireland who attempted to rule the country with ruthless efficiency and an iron fist naturally struck Irish people as racist, officious hypocrites, because, while claiming to uphold justice and fair-play, they actively perpetuated discrimination and inequality. Those English people who, out of naïveté or guilt or a combination of the two, engaged in "reverse mimicry" upon moving to Ireland—that is, who "went native"—were also deemed unworthy of respect.[30] Their overly idealistic view of Ireland, their excitement over Ireland's perceived exoticism, and their laziness or ineptitude (produced by rich idleness or holding nonsensical jobs in a corrupt colonial administration) led Irish people to regard these naïve souls as sentimental, romantic duffers.

The fact that Shaw and later writers mixed these two types to produce more complex English characters, betrays their desire to enter Fanon's third and final stage of national self-discovery (the "liberationist"), in which—as was noted in chapter 1—"binaries are exploded in a sort of Hegelian synthesis."[31] Of course, it would fall to mid-to-late twentieth-century writers who were more fully in Fanon's third phase—such as Frank O'Connor, Kate O'Brien, and John McGahern—to create Stage English characters who were free of the two, traditional, Stage English types. The Stage English characters created by these third phase writers (including—to name the most obvious examples—'Awkins and Belcher from O'Connor's "Guests of the Nation" (1931), Helen Archer from O'Brien's *The Land of Spices* (1942), and Mrs Sinclair from McGahern's "Oldfashioned" (1985)) are sympathetic, complex characters who merely possess one or more Stage English flaws: for example, hypocrisy, officiousness, sentimentality, coldness, legalism, and the like. (Their possession of pointedly and conventionally English national faults is what makes these characters mildly satirical portraits and not simply well-rounded, English characters.)[32]

There is one final point to make regarding my use of the term Stage Englishman before moving on to discuss Shaw's use of the figure. The term suggests—because of the precedent of the lowly Stage Irishman—that the Stage Englishman is someone to be laughed at or pitied. We may also guess, given the link to the Stage Irishman, that the Stage Englishman must be unsuccessful. Many of the Stage English characters in Irish literary history (including some of those discussed in this chapter) are quite successful in the works in which they appear. Those with an agenda in Ireland often achieve their (usually anti-Irish) aims. Despite these successes, Irish authors repeatedly imply that these Stage English characters are still to be laughed at or pitied, because, as English people, they are less artistic, spiritual, knowing, or humane than the Irish are. This betrays the Irish authors' subversive aims, and it is noteworthy that the authors often achieve these aims through use of the common Irish trope of the heroic failure, in which the defeated Irish are nobler than those who have beaten them. As we shall see, this idea relates directly to the ending of Shaw's *John Bull's Other Island*, the play which introduced Tom Broadbent—that important and highly influential Stage Englishman—to the world.

Part II: The Stage English figure in Shaw's Irish plays

Given Shaw's Irish Anglican "anti-Englishness" and his habit of regularly disparaging the English in his plays, one could argue that most of his English characters are, on some level, Stage English—especially since he often uses them to expose what he regards as English foibles.[33] In my theorizing of the Stage Englishman, however, I reserve the term for English characters placed into Irish scenes. It is therefore in Shaw's three plays set in Ireland—*John Bull's Other Island, O'Flaherty, VC*, and *Tragedy of an Elderly Gentleman*—that his English characters become completely and unequivocally Stage English. Although all three of these plays were discussed in previous chapters, in a study on the Irish Shaw, they are worthy of further and deeper analysis.

John Bull's Other Island, a drama which attempts to overturn old stereotypes of the English and the Irish, was originally written for the new Abbey Theatre in Dublin. However, Yeats's indifference to the play and the fact that it was "beyond the resources" of the fledgling national theatre meant that it premiered at the Royal Court in London instead.[34] Critics make much of the fact that the play was initially intended for an Irish audience, but Shaw knew that the play would eventually be seen by both Irish and English audiences; that is why he claimed that his mission in writing the play was "to teach Irish people the value of an Englishman... [and] to shew the Englishman his own absurdities."[35]

As part of this mission, Shaw endowed the character of Tom Broadbent, an English gentleman, with comically heightened Stage English "absurdities."[36] Indeed, Broadbent unknowingly contradicts everything that he (and presumably English audiences) believe about the English, because his character is identical to that which the English have ascribed to the Irish for centuries—he is, to use Doyle's words, "a romantic duffer."[37] But Shaw does not just endow Broadbent with the stereotypically Irish traits of sentimentality, romanticism, and laziness. He also shows the Englishman to be hypocritical, racist, lacking in tact, and full of a ruthless and heartless money-making instinct that regularly offends Irish sensibilities. Thus, while Irish writers often depict English males as either sentimental, romantic duffers or racist, officious hypocrites, Shaw creates, in Broadbent, an Englishman who is both.

Broadbent's sentimentality regarding England, Ireland, and love is profound. His naïve belief in the nobility of England and the English manifests itself in statements that demonstrate a disconnection from reality, because they admit of no sin or even self-interest in the English heart. Broadbent says things like "I'm a lover of liberty, like every true Englishman," ignoring the economic slavery produced by the British Empire around the world and, potentially, by his own firm in Ireland.[38] Despite calling himself a liberal, he says that "we English must place our capacity for government without stint at the service of nations who are less fortunately endowed in that respect; so as to allow them to develop in perfect freedom to the English level of self-government."[39] He extols the English gift for "common sense" and says "whatever you say, Larry, [the Irish] like an Englishman. They feel they can trust him, I suppose."[40] He seems to sincerely believe the stereotype of the no-nonsense Englishman, who can be trusted never to lie in self-interest but to always speak, as he says himself, "in earnest: in English earnest."[41] This, despite the fact that he must be aware on some level of grievances that colonized peoples have against the English for broken treaties and suspended human rights.

After hearing about Matt Haffigan's past troubles with his land-lord and the laws emanating from Westminster, Broadbent says "this gentleman's sufferings should make every Englishman think. It is want of thought rather than want of heart that allows such iniquities to disgrace society."[42] This remark acquits the English of culpability for the oppression of the Irish poor by suggesting that the English are not fully aware that such exploitation takes place. This anticipates the Englishman Haines's remark in *Ulysses* that "it seems history is to blame"—and not England—for the troubles resulting from England's colonization of Ireland.[43] Broadbent's belief in England is so great that towards the end of the play he tells Keegan, the defrocked Irish priest and mystical prophet: "I see no evils in the world—except, of course, natural evils—that cannot be remedied by freedom, self-government, and English institutions. I think so, not because I am an Englishman, but as a matter of common sense."[44]

His sentimentality also extends to his notions of Ireland. Rather than observe Ireland upon arrival, to see it as it really is, he has come with a full set of ideas about Ireland, prepared to find only them. He speaks of "the melancholy of the Keltic race" and repeatedly of the cleverness and "wit" of the Irish.[45] He speaks of Keegan's "delightful Irish humor" and calls this earnest mystic "a whimsical Irishman."[46] When he meets Nora for the first time at the Round Tower, he is bowled over by "the magic of this Irish scene, and...the charm of your Irish voice," adding later "all the harps of Ireland are in your voice."[47] He says of the Irish: "their faults are on the surface: at heart they are one of the finest races on earth."[48] At a certain point, having found less humor than he expected, Broadbent does not change his stereo-typical ideas about the Irish. He merely decides that the struggle for Home Rule has resulted in a situation where "their sense of humor is in abeyance: I noticed it the moment we landed. Think of that in a country where every man is a born humorist!"[49] After running over a pig in his motorcar, Broadbent says, "I am glad it happened, because it has brought out the kindness and

sympathy of the Irish character to an extent I had no concep-
tion of."[50] He little suspects the fact that the villagers have been
repeating the story of the pig's demise *ad nauseum*, laughing at
Broadbent behind his back.

Broadbent's sentimentality regarding romantic love and family
also arise repeatedly in the play. His is the traditional English
middle-class sentiment regarding marriage, underwritten by a
sincere belief in the notion that "a single man in possession of
a good fortune, must be in want of a wife" and that the woman
of lesser means that he courts must be grateful for his attentions
and proposal(s).[51] Thus, Broadbent ascribes Nora's resistance to
his charms to her "Irish delicacy," ignoring the possibility that
she might not be attracted to him or might expect a courtship
that lasts longer than a couple of days.[52] In keeping with his
ideas of the ideal, dignified English proposal, he ceremoniously
announces to Nora that "you have inspired in me a very strong
attachment," leading her to exclaim: "Why do you talk to me in
that unfeeling nonsensical way?"[53] After she refuses his proposal,
Broadbent looks like he is going to cry. Nora, "almost awestruck,"
says: "Youre not going to cry, are you? I never thought a man
could cry. Dont."[54] The fact that Nora has never seen a man cry
pre-empts Broadbent's protest that "I'm not crying. I- I- I leave that
sort of thing to your damned sentimental Irishmen. You think I
have no feeling because I am a plain unemotional Englishman,
with no powers of expression."[55] Nora, helping Shaw to overturn
old stereotypes, wisely responds, "Whatever may be the matter
with you, it's not want of feeling."[56]

When Nora does eventually accept his proposal, he does not
lessen his dependence on sentiment nor give any indication that
the house will admit ideas from outside the English middle-class
tradition. He announces: "We're not going to have any rows: we're
going to have a solid four-square home: man and wife: comfort
and common sense. And plenty of affection, eh (*he puts his arm
round her with confident proprietorship*)?" According to Shaw's stage
directions, Nora responds "coldly" to this.[57]

This sentimental, romantic Englishman is also a duffer. As was noted in chapter 1, he is prone to cant and the ready-made ideas handed to him by his schooling and the newspapers. This is why Shaw regards him as "intellectually lazy."[58] What's more, his work ethic pales in comparison to that of the Irish characters in the play. Indeed, one of the traditional stereotypes that is exploded in the play is that of the lazy Irishman versus the hard-working Englishman. As was suggested in chapter 1, it is Doyle who is the workaholic in the engineering firm, not Broadbent, and Doyle is perhaps even the "evil genius" behind the Syndicate's schemes in Rosscullen.[59] Also, Haffigan's manic but economically unsound work ethic has caused him trouble his whole life, resulting—among other things—in his losing a farm because he improved it until he could no longer afford to rent it.[60] This is a world away from the stereotype of the lazy Irishman that Broadbent somehow still believes in (he says that "industrious[ness]" is "remarkable...in an Irishman"), despite the evidence in front of him every day of his working life.[61]

The sentimental, romantic duffer side of Broadbent's personality is the one that wins the sympathy of the audience. Shaw makes clear, however, that Broadbent also has a dark side: he is a racist, officious hypocrite. It is this dark side which brings Broadbent his worldly success, including his purchase of the town and his grabbing of the parliamentary nomination. This synthesis of the two English types can be seen as Shaw's attempt to reach for Fanon's third phase, in which old stereotypes are complicated or exploded, but, as a writer still caught in the grip of the second phase, Shaw cannot help but make the Englishman Broadbent much less sympathetic than the Irishman Doyle. The most obvious difference between Broadbent and Doyle is that the cynical Irish fact-facer is far less sentimental and romantic than the Englishman. However, Shaw also makes clear that Doyle does not share Broadbent's racism, his ruthless officiousness (when it comes to making money), or his hypocrisy.

Broadbent (despite claiming to be a liberal) is a full-blown racist, repeatedly making anti-Semitic and anti-Irish remarks.[62] By contrast, Doyle is proud of his Irishness and, as I noted in chapter 3, happily compares the Irish to the Jews, to the advantage of both.[63] Broadbent's comical lack of tact is never more pronounced than when he makes anti-Irish remarks in the mistaken assumption that the Irish share his belief in the superiority of the English. For example, he tells Larry without the intention of being insulting that "there are great possibilities for Ireland. Home Rule will work wonders under English guidance."[64] A little later, he tells Larry that issues like "Home Rule, South Africa, Free Trade, and putting the Church schools on the education rate...are not serious to you as they are to an Englishman." When Doyle responds, "What! not even Home Rule!," Broadbent replies, "Not even Home Rule. We owe Home Rule not to the Irish but to our English Gladstone."[65] Of course, to Doyle's ears, this is wildly insulting, and a shocking dismissal of the efforts of members of the Irish party in the British parliament throughout the late nineteenth century, especially those of Charles Stewart Parnell.

Broadbent's racism is also manifest in his unconscious belief that Ireland is more like the colonies than it is like an equal member of the United Kingdom. This is never clearer than when Broadbent, like Haines in *Ulysses* (another English liberal Unionist), "pack[s] a gun before coming over to Ireland to mix with, i.e. exploit, the natives."[66] However, in order to suggest that there is a perverse truth in Broadbent's view of Ireland as a subdued but potentially dangerous colony, Shaw, throughout the play and its preface, repeatedly links Ireland's plight to that of other countries that have been exploited by the British Empire (as I noted in chapter 3).[67] In contrast to Broadbent's muddled, contradictory views regarding the Empire, Shaw unequivocally regards British colonialism as "pushing forward 'civilization' in the shape of rifles & pistols in the hands of Hooligans, aristocratic *mauvais sujets* and stupid drifters."[68]

The other big contrast between Doyle and Broadbent is Doyle's inability to be as ruthless in matters of business as Broadbent is. Whereas Doyle is prepared to employ Haffigan and the rest of the men of Rosscullen after they have been kicked off of their farms, Broadbent will not hear of it. He heartlessly and ruthlessly says, "It really doesnt pay now to take on men over forty even for unskilled labor, which I suppose is all Haffigan would be good for. No: Haffigan had better go to America, or into the Union, poor old chap! Hes worked out, you know: you can see it." Doyle, attempting to overcome his scruples regarding the inevitable hardship that Haffigan will face, consoles himself by saying, "Haffigan doesnt matter much. He'll die presently." Broadbent, ever the sentimentalist, is "shocked," saying, "Oh come, Larry! Dont be unfeeling. It's hard on Haffigan. It's always hard on the inefficient."[69] But Larry is not being unfeeling. He is facing the facts regarding Haffigan's future. He knows how bad things will get for Haffigan if Broadbent refuses to employ him and sincerely believes that death will come as a relief to the hopeless old man. Broadbent's ability to avoid confronting that much gruesome reality by disingenuously expressing sympathy for Haffigan is, Shaw implies, much more "unfeeling."

The fact that Doyle has a more sensitive conscience than Broadbent is part of a pattern in Shaw's plays. Shaw's reverse snobbery and socialist beliefs (discussed in chapter 1) led him to regularly portray Irish characters and working-class characters as more morally scrupulous than English gentlemen. An important example is one already cited: Sir Patrick Cullen's long memory and Sir Colenso Ridgeon's short one regarding the patients they have failed in *The Doctor's Dilemma*. Shaw's belief in the shameless lack of scruples among English gentlemen is best articulated by Sir Orpheus Midlander in the play *Geneva* (1938), when he innocently marvels that "people have such extraordinary consciences when they have not been educated at an English public school."[70]

Compounding Broadbent's racism and officiousness is the fact that—as was noted briefly in chapter 1—he speaks and behaves hypocritically throughout the play. Having seized Nora in his arms within moments of first meeting her, Broadbent defends himself against her accusation that he is not behaving like a gentleman with the assertion: "I think you will accept the fact that I'm an Englishman as a guarantee that I am not a man to act hastily or romantically."[71] He then immediately proposes marriage to her, thus (in his eyes) proving that his intentions are honorable. He attempts to use the English reputation for coldness to act rashly and quickly with Nora, both in this scene and in all of their meetings until her acceptance of his proposal.

We see more of his hypocrisy in his business dealings. When he hears of all that Haffigan has overcome in his life, Broadbent tells those assembled that "only a great race is capable of producing such men," even though he already knows that his plans for the village will result in Haffigan having to end his days in the United States or more likely the work house.[72] He states at one point that "there are only two qualities in the world: efficiency and inefficiency, and only two sorts of people: the efficient and the inefficient. It dont matter whether theyre English or Irish. I shall collar this place, not because I'm an Englishman and Haffigan and Co. are Irishmen, but because theyre duffers and I know my way about."[73] He says this even though he has already learned how hard-working Haffigan and the others are on their inefficient farms and that his own Irish business partner (and perhaps the secret behind his success) calls him a "duffer" to his face.[74] His championing of a suspect English efficiency justifies England's and his own presence in Ireland.

Broadbent's hypocrisy also extends to his campaign for parliament. His emotional speech that the member for Rosscullen should make contributions to Father Dempsey's valuable work in the village is actually a savvy bribe intended to reduce clerical opposition to his own candidacy. Also, Broadbent's ostentatious displays of English liberal self-hatred lead him to call the Union Jack "a detestable symbol of a decadent Imperialism" and to celebrate when "an English expedition [is] bet in a battle in Inja somewhere,"[75] but we know that he actually believes in the benevolent influence of the Empire on the global scene. Hence, this self-hatred comes across as a tactic intended to reassure the Irish voters that he is anti-English and thus fools them into supporting him.

Finally, we also see Broadbent's hypocrisy in his dealings with the mystic Keegan, who has an inordinate influence in the town. Although Broadbent says that he "would [not] flatter any man," when he sees Keegan late in the play, he decides he will approach him because he "controls nearly as many votes as Father Dempsey," adding "what really flatters a man is that you think him worth flattering."[76] Then during his conversation with Keegan, he applauds the work of Ruskin, Shelley, and Carlyle, but shows through his concomitant discussions of his business plans that he has no intention of taking their ideas seriously. As Keegan assesses the matter after their talk, "Mr Broadbent spends his life inefficiently admiring the thoughts of great men, and efficiently serving the cupidity of base money hunters."[77] For his part, Broadbent defends this disjunction in his thinking by saying that great thinkers like Ruskin, Shelley, and Carlyle (and Keegan) are important because "they keep up the moral tone of the community" and because "they improved my mind: they raised my tone enormously."[78] The fact that he has no intention of changing his plans based on their ideas or on Keegan's withering assessment of the Syndicate demonstrates Shaw's belief in the "intellectual laziness" of the English.[79] In Shaw's view, the English love great ideas but will not do the intellectual or political work required upon hearing new, powerful truths.

Throughout the play and its preface, Shaw indicates that hypocrisy is not just a quirk in Broadbent's personality but in fact an English trait generally. Yet, critics have debated whether Shaw believes that Broadbent and the English are aware of their hypocrisy. A close reading of the play and Shaw's other writings suggests that Shaw feels that the English are in some way not fully aware of their hypocrisy. Their hypocrisy is, according to Shaw, a mental tic that they use instinctively whenever they set out to succeed at something. In the play, Doyle describes the *almost* innocent English use of hypocrisy thus:

A caterpillar when it gets into a tree, instinctively makes itself look exactly like a leaf; so that both its enemies and its prey may mistake it for one and think it not worth bothering about...The world is as full of fools as a tree is full of leaves. Well, the Englishman does what the caterpillar does. He instinctively makes himself look like a fool, and eats up all the real fools at his ease while his enemies let him alone and laugh at him for being a fool like the rest.[80]

Shaw, in a letter to an American friend from 1904, suggests some culpability on the part of the English in regards to this hypocrisy because of the fact that it is based on a "stupidity" that is "voluntary"; but there is still the suggestion on Shaw's part that this "brainlessness," though "knavish," is more a sin of omission than commission because of the Englishman's lack of understanding how it works.[81] It is as much an instinct as the caterpillar's ability to hide. The English elect to charge at life and "grab" things unthinkingly because doing so seems to help them succeed, and, therefore, in keeping with the spirit of this "voluntary stupidity," they refuse to analyze this habit of mind lest it lead them to repent and reduce their effectiveness in the world.[82] As Shaw says in the same letter:

Cromwell said that no man goes further than the man who doesn't know where he is going; and in that you have the whole secret of English success. What is the use of being bright, subtle, witty, genial, if these qualities lead to the subjugation and poverty of India and Ireland[?][83]

During one conversation, Doyle tells Broadbent, "I never stop wondering at that blessed old head of yours with all its ideas in watertight compartments, and all the compartments warranted impervious to anything that it doesnt suit you to understand."[84] Doyle's contemplations on this aspect of Broadbent's English mind leads him to formulate his caterpillar theory of English success based on a semi-conscious hypocrisy. Likewise, after listening to Broadbent discuss politics and business, Keegan is eventually driven to tell Broadbent that in his youth he would have called him a hypocrite. This is because Broadbent has stated that his candidacy for the Rosscullen seat would be won because "an Englishman with no humbug about him, who will talk straight common sense and take his stand on the solid ground of prin- ciple and public duty, must win his way with men of all classes," while at the same time agreeing with Keegan that he "will get into parliament because [he] want[s] to get into it badly enough to be prepared to take the necessary steps to induce the people to vote for [him]."[85] He does not seem to recognize the deep contradic- tion between standing on principle to win and being prepared to do anything to win. Keegan then goes on to echo the Shaw/Doyle caterpillar theory when he voices his own theory that "the secret of the Englishman's strange power" is due to his ability to "let not the right side of [his] brain know what the left side doeth."[86]

Commentators like Kiberd seem to suggest that Broadbent's use of the "voluntary stupidity" that allows the Englishman to succeed is part of a deliberate, pre-meditated plan on Broadbent's part, formulated in London, to take over Rosscullen for his own, selfish, purely financial ends. Kiberd writes: "Broadbent is merely playing the stage Englishman in Ireland, the better to get the villagers off guard and into his pocket." [87] Such a reading implies that Broadbent knows he is going over to Rosscullen to be made fun of by the locals and believes that this will be the key to his success. But Broadbent seems completely unaware of how foolish he appears to the Irish. He really *is* swept up in emotion when he rashly proposes to Nora. He *is* truly moved by what he takes to be the villagers' kindness in the wake of the auto accident which killed the pig, little suspecting that they are laughing at him and, in fact, repeating the story to each other for laughs. And he seems to earnestly believe in the good that the English can do for Rosscullen and Ireland, with a naïve, sincere belief. It is only in carrying out this good (only one part of which is his own financial gain) that the question of hypocrisy arises, because, in the game of life, in Shaw's view, an Englishman will attempt to succeed *by any means necessary*, even if it means contradicting a principle that on another occasion he has defended or promoted. (This links to Napoleon's speech regarding English success in *The Man of Destiny*, quoted at length in chapter 3.) Though Broadbent does this repeatedly, he cannot understand the accusations of hypocrisy leveled at him by Doyle and Keegan. According to Shaw (again as articulated in the Napoleon speech), this is because an Englishman will fearlessly do whatever it takes to achieve his aim, but will always make sure he can justify his actions with a pre-formulated motivation or principle that is accepted in wider, English society. As long as he can explain that his actions are, for instance, helping to bring about greater efficiency, satisfying his own or someone else's sense of honor (an important motivation for the English characters in Shaw plays like *Man and Superman*), keeping up the moral tone of the community, or preserving a woman's delicacy, then he feels justified in doing exactly what he wants to do. This is why keeping ideas in separate compartments is so helpful in allowing an Englishman to achieve his own ends. Broadbent, for instance, never lets his belief in efficiency be tempered by his compassionate liberal politics (political beliefs that are so sincere that he has fallen out with his father over them).

At the end of the play, Broadbent appears on the surface to have triumphed over Larry and the town of Rosscullen (winning Nora and the parliamentary nomination, as well as—together with Larry—buying up the town). Some critics, such as Elizabeth Butler Cullingford, Declan Kiberd, Michael Holroyd, and Alfred Turco Jr., have therefore concluded that *John Bull's Other Island* reinforces the old Arnoldian stereotypes of the efficient Saxon and the ineffectual Celt, only with more subtlety.[88] Cullingford writes:

> [D]espite Shaw's claim to be dismantling fictions about the English, in many respects Broadbent replicates the 'standard'

stage English type...[H]is xenophobia, earnestness, lack of humour, energy, efficiency and ultimate victory confirm Arnold's analysis.[89]

Such a reading, however, drastically undervalues Shaw's strenuous efforts to reverse certain, old stereotypes of the English and the Irish in the play. As I noted above, Shaw (most notably through the characterizations of Doyle and Broadbent) portrays the Irish as more hard-working than the English, and suggests that it is the English who are sentimental, not the Irish. Also, Broadbent's tears and the fact that he is constantly at Nora's mercy prior to their engagement, are clearly part of Shaw's attempt to contradict the Arnoldian idea that the Irish are a feminine race and the English masculine.[90]

Cullingford feels that this attempt to contradict Arnold is undermined by the fact that Broadbent and Doyle agree that England "made a man" of the Irishman and because "Broadbent's tears...do not feminize him for long...[W]hen he has finally won [Nora] he reverts to masculine chivalry and *'confident proprietorship.'*"[91] The "manhood" that Doyle gained by going to England, however, is not gender-related. The men are referring to his gaining of professional and personal maturity. Doyle was improved by entering (in his words) "the big world," obtaining a maturity that could have been gained by moving from the small world of Rosscullen to *any* cosmopolitan place where people "take a question seriously and give a serious answer to it."[92] And Doyle's maturity and seriousness are not solely down to his experience of *English* life—he has also spent time working in the United States. As for Broadbent's tears being an aberration, we as an audience know that not only are his tears genuine, but also that his act of "masculine chivalry and *'confident proprietorship'*" is a mask worn in deference to the gender politics of his time and, perhaps (in Shaw's eyes), another manifestation of his English hypocrisy. He is pretending to a strength that he does not in fact possess.

In the play, Shaw also disputes Arnold's description of the Celts as more spiritual and less materialistic than the English. This stereotype was happily accepted by Revival writers such as AE (George Russell) and the early Yeats, but Shaw sends it up through the financial greed of the small landowners of Rosscullen.[93] He contradicts this stereotype again in *O'Flaherty, VC* (as we will see later in this chapter) through the mercenary way in which O'Flaherty's mother and sweetheart view life. Shaw argues in these plays that the Irish have had to focus very much on money, because their finances have always been under threat. It is prosperous Englishman like Broadbent who can afford to applaud the sentiments of Ruskin, Shelley, and Carlyle, and enjoy the "charm" of the Land of Saints and Scholars.[94] Though Keegan is spiritual and non-materialistic and believes Ireland to be a holy place, the play implies that, despite the clarity of his apocalyptic vision, Irishmen like Keegan are on the way out, retreating to the Round Towers. The new breed of Irishman appears in the play in several forms: the anti-dreaming Doyle, Doyle's humorless father (as Shaw noted, "It is a point of honor with the modern Irishman to have no sense of humor"), and the "arriviste rural Catholic Middle Class" villagers.[95] The ascension of such people may not signify a good prognosis for Ireland's immediate future but is perhaps inevitable in a postcolonial society which has been forced into "full reaction against both servility and the Stage Irishman" in an attempt to escape the English colonizer's view of the Irish people and establish a truer picture of the nation's soul.[96]

It is noteworthy that Shaw described Andrew Undershaft, the unredeemed Superman and carrier of the Life Force in his next play, *Major Barbara* (1905), as "Broadbent and Keegan rolled into one."[97] As Holroyd has written, "Undershaft embodies Shaw's concept of the Life Force, a mindless, aimless power for good-or-evil depending (like all technology) on what human beings themselves decide to do with it."[98] In *Major Barbara*, Undershaft's work will be refined in the next generation by his more enlightened daughter and son-in-law. In the same way, perhaps Shaw was saying that the world's future (and by extension, Ireland's) lies with the ability to assimilate the vision of Keegan with the worldly power of someone like Broadbent, his partner Doyle, or members of the new Irish Catholic middle class. At the turn of the twentieth century, however, Shaw seemed to be saying that the Irish first had to learn to resist the urge to disappear into dreams and derision and to push themselves into the world of action, even if it meant making mistakes, until it could reincorporate the Keegan side of the nation's character. Shaw seemed to be saying that, if the Irish did not leave behind dreaming and derision, they would be much more likely to be swallowed up by the financial titans of Britain and the United States.

Critics who believe that *John Bull* reinforces Arnoldian stereotypes stress that Doyle, the ineffectual Celt, loses Nora and the parliamentary nomination to Broadbent, the efficient Englishman, at the end of the play. As I have hinted throughout this chapter, however, this is a wildly simplified reading of the ending. As Nicholas Grene correctly contends, Doyle (as the "evil genius" behind the Syndicate's scheme) is much more victorious at the play's end than such critics give him credit for.[99] That said, Shaw clearly implies that there are ways in which Doyle's Irishness has held him back. We may, as an audience, believe his lengthy explanations of why he did not want the local parliamentary seat, but it is hard to be convinced by his indifference to the loss of Nora. Indications are that he did in fact want her, but was too reluctant or afraid to act (once again betraying a national weakness compared to the English ability to just *do*). He betrays his true feelings for Nora (and perhaps for the parliamentary nomination) when his father asks, "Why would you be such a fool as to let him take the seat in parliament from you?" Larry, glancing at Nora, answers: "He will take more than that from me before hes done here."[100] He betrays his feelings again later, when he says: "Nora, dear, dont you understand that I'm an Irishman, and hes an Englishman. He wants you; and he grabs you. I want you; and I quarrel with you and have to go on wanting you."[101] And finally, Larry's viciously anti-Irish anger at the end and his relish at how the Syndicate will transform (deface?) Rosscullen follow directly on from his learning that Broadbent has become engaged to Nora, and may be directed at himself for having lost her by being too Irish.[102] Some measure of failure on Larry's part (and on that of Keegan and the other Irish characters) must be acknowledged to justify Shaw's remark in the preface that, "Writing the play for an Irish audience, I thought it would be good for them to be shewn very clearly that the loudest laugh they could raise at the expense of the absurdest Englishman was not really a laugh on their side; that he would succeed where they would fail."[103] Indeed, as mentioned in chapter 1, one could argue that, at the end, Keegan and Doyle fall prey to the two Irish flaws that Shaw warns about throughout the play and its preface: Keegan's retreat to the Round Tower and his defeated confession that he may actually vote for Broadbent seem like the actions of an Irishman disappearing into dreams, and Doyle's angry approval of the Syndicate's drastic plans for Rosscullen and his insulting of Keegan smack of Irish derision.

Despite Broadbent's successes at Doyle's expense, I would contend that the Irish characters (and presumably Irish audiences) are consoled at the end of the play by the fact that, when all is said and done, the Irishmen Doyle and Keegan still see life much more clearly than "God's Englishman."[104] Broadbent, of course, is too blinded by pride (and Stage English "intellectual laziness") to see this. Doyle's and Keegan's clear intellectual superiority provide a different kind of victory for the Irish characters at the end—a subversive, almost hidden victory, firmly within the tradition of heroic Irish failure, ever beloved of Irish writers and historians.[105] That said, this subtle victory could be seen as an example of the Irish taking consolation once again in derision and dreams, since they are scornfully looking down on the English and since their intellectual superiority does not bring about tangible, earthly rewards.

When *John Bull's Other Island* premiered in London, it became Shaw's first major success. Something that is rarely pointed out about Shaw's career is *John Bull's* role in winning him mainstream acceptance on the English stage. As Michael Holroyd has written, "In the summer of 1903, Shaw published *Man and Superman*: it was his twelfth play, he was in his forty-eighth year and still almost wholly unknown to British audiences."[106] In response to the success of *John Bull's Other Island* at the Royal Court in late 1904, however, six other Shaw plays went into production in London in 1905.

The Conservative Prime Minister, Arthur Balfour, was so enamoured with *John Bull's Other Island* that he attended it five times during its initial run, and King Edward VII laughed so hard at the play that he broke the chair he was sitting on.[107] In light of all this English enjoyment, one has to ask what exactly English audiences were laughing at. Shaw himself was shocked by their appreciation and feared that he had failed to convey his message(s) properly. Shaw had set out, among other things, to point out the faults in the English character, and, in the 1907 preface to play, he admits to being surprised that the English did not seem to mind him pointing out these faults. He writes that English audiences "were perfectly willing to allow me to represent Tom Broadbent as infatuated in politics, hypnotized by his newspaper-leader-writers and parliamentary orators into an utter paralysis of his common sense, without moral delicacy or social tact, provided I made him cheerful, robust, goodnatured, free from envy, and above all, a successful muddler-through in business and love."[108] "The English," he realized, "are avowed muddlers—rather proud of it, in fact."[109]

In that same preface, he goes on to abuse the English—his Irish reverse snobbery in full flight.[110] He contrasts the "clearheaded, sane" Irish with the "hysterical, nonsense-crammed, fact-proof, truth-terrified, unballasted sport of all the bogey panics and all the silly enthusiasms that now calls itself 'God's Englishman.'"[111] Shaw was attempting to drive home the criticisms of the English that he made in the play but which London audiences had failed to recognize. The fact that the English were not insulted by *John*

Bull's Other Island but rather enjoyed it curiously endorses Shaw's belief (expressed by Doyle in the play) that the English do not recognize when the Irish are laughing at them.[112]

As Holroyd has wisely pointed out, the fact that Shaw wrote an ostensibly tongue-in-cheek (though surprisingly serious) programme note for a later English production, which included "a 'personal appeal' to the audience not to demoralize the actors with shouts of laughter and noisy applause," indicates that he remained deeply uncomfortable with the English laughing so heartily at the play and feared that their laughter meant that the play was a "failure."[113] With his next Irish play, *O'Flaherty, VC*, Shaw would not give the audience the opportunity to misinterpret his aims, and the anti-war, pro-Irish, anti-English ideas expressed in the play would result in it failing to get an English production until five years after its composition, with many of its most offensive arguments made irrelevant due to the end of the Great War.

O'Flaherty, VC (written in 1915 and first published and performed in 1917) is, like Shaw's first Irish play, deeply concerned with Anglo-Irish relations. Specifically, Shaw believed that Irish recruiting for the Great War was being "badly bungled" by the British government.[114] As he writes in the play's brilliant preface, "incomprehensible as it seems to an Englishman, Irish patriotism does not take the form of devotion to England and England's king."[115] Therefore, he reasoned, recruiting drives based on appeals to British patriotism, highlighting war aims that were only of great concern to the English public, were bound to end in failure. Likewise, Shaw regarded the decision by Dublin Castle to plaster the walls of Irish cities and towns with posters asking potential recruits to "Remember plucky, little, Catholic Belgium" as particularly ill-conceived, despite the fact that Ireland was itself a small, predominantly Catholic country:

> The folly of asking an Irishman to remember anything when you want him to fight for England was apparent to everyone outside the Castle: FORGET AND FORGIVE would have been

more to the point. Remembering Belgium and its broken treaty led Irishmen to remember Limerick and its broken treaty; and the recruiting ended in a rebellion...[116]

Shaw's solution to the problem was to write a play that encouraged the Irish to join the British Army in response to real concerns that they might have: frustration with the tediousness of life in unexciting Ireland and/or a desire to escape unhappy domestic situations.

Accordingly, in the play, Shaw appeals to the Irishman's love of "change and adventure" by showing that O'Flaherty, in going to serve in France, has escaped the "discontent" that plagues many men who stay in Ireland—a discontent born of the "thwarted curiosity" and "deadly boredom" that maddens the ambitious Irishman and causes him to fall into an "ignorance and insularity [that] is a danger to himself and his neighbors."[117] Similarly, Shaw's belief that "the happy home of the idealist...is not common at present" led him to demonstrate in the play that, by joining the army, young Irishmen like the fictional O'Flaherty would be able to "escape from [the] tyrants and taskmasters, termagants and shrews" that call themselves "our fathers, our mothers, our wives and our children."[118] In the preface, Shaw points out that it was for this reason that he "did not endow O'Flaherty with an ideal Irish colleen for his sweetheart, and gave him for his mother a Volumnia of the potato patch rather than an affectionate parent from whom he could not easily have torn himself."[119]

The play is set in front of the Irish country house of Sir Pearce Madigan, an Irish Anglican gentleman and landlord to the O'Flaherty family. Madigan, a British Army General, has been leading a recruiting drive in Ireland and has brought O'Flaherty back from France to tell the Irish of the heroic exploits which have won him the Victoria Cross. Since Madigan and O'Flaherty are currently recruiting near the Madigan estate, Sir Pearce has taken the opportunity to invite O'Flaherty and his mother to tea at the Big House. O'Flaherty's girlfriend, Teresa Driscoll, is a maid at the Big House, so a reunion with her is also to take place.

The play reiterates many of Shaw's feelings on the Irish national character first expressed in *John Bull's Other Island*. As was noted earlier in this book, the idea that the Irish are cynical fact-facers is present in O'Flaherty's enunciation of clear-headed insights regarding the Great War, newspaper propaganda, class politics, and Anglo-Irish relations—insights which he expresses freely and fearlessly to all, emboldened by his exposure to "the wide world."[120] Likewise, O'Flaherty's mother may be—as was also previously noted—too blinded by hatred for the English, but she is also a very practical woman whose poverty has taught her important lessons about the nature of the world.

Mrs O'Flaherty is additionally used by Shaw to reiterate his theory, first advanced in *John Bull* through the depiction of the Rosscullen villagers, that the Irish are fond of petty one-upmanship. O'Flaherty points out that his mother, as she walks to the Big House, will "stop...at every house on the way to show herself off and tell them where she's going, and fill the whole parish with spite and envy."[121]

O'Flaherty's mother, and, to an even greater extent, his girlfriend, also recall the villagers of Rosscullen in that financial hardship has taught them to be very concerned about money. They are far from being the spiritual, non-materialistic, other-worldly Celts celebrated by many Irish Revivalists. His girlfriend, in particular, seems much less concerned with O'Flaherty's health and well-being than with the money to be made through soldiering, and she seems to hope that he gets injured so that he can get a wound pension on top of his normal pension and the VC pension.[122] Teresa, like Nora from *John Bull* and Mrs Farrell from *Press Cuttings*, also reiterates Shaw's belief in the unshakeable pride and lack of sentimentality that Irish women possess. When O'Flaherty goes to kiss his sweetheart, Shaw writes that "Teresa, without losing her Irish dignity, takes the kiss as appreciatively as a connoisseur might take a glass of wine," before sitting down, full of self-possession, next to O'Flaherty.[123]

While much of the play re-explores ideas already examined in *John Bulls Other Island*, new ground is broken through the play's Stage English character: Sir Pearce's wife, Lady Madigan. Unusually for the characters discussed in this chapter, she is a Stage English figure who never actually appears on stage. She is away on holidays in London, but what O'Flaherty and Sir Pearce say about her gives a vivid indication of her character. As will be seen, Lady Madigan strongly resembles Philippa from the *Irish RM* stories of Somerville & Ross, in that she is an English woman who regards the Irish as noble savages.

In the Somerville & Ross story "Philippa's Fox-Hunt" (1899), Major Yeates, the Irish RM, finally marries Philippa, his fiancée of five years. Philippa regards her introduction to Ireland with glee, as "a gigantic picnic in a foreign land."[124] According to the Major, she is "adorably callous" to his house's shortcomings, including "rat-holes in the hall floor [that] were nailed up with pieces of tin biscuit boxes" and a front hall in which "the casual visitor could, instead of leaving a card, have easily written his name in the damp on the walls."[125] He adds:

[Philippa] held long conversations daily with Mrs Cadogan, in order, as she informed me, to acquire the language...[S]he engaged kitchen-maids because of the beauty of their eyes, and housemaids because they had such delightfully picturesque old mothers.[126]

While Philippa is quite lovely and open-hearted, her naïve affection for all things Irish (including Irish poverty and, in a later story, the Irish language) does strike one as the condescending regard of a colonial charmed by the natives. Sir Pearce's English wife in *O'Flaherty, VC* possesses a similarly naïve and unwittingly condescending attitude. As O'Flaherty says to Sir Pearce:

[Your wife] was always a kind friend to the poor. Little her lady-ship knew, God help her, the depth of divilment that was in us: we were like a play to her. You see, sir, she was English: that was how it was. We was to her what the Pathans and Senegalese was to me when I first seen them: I couldnt think, somehow, that they were liars, and thieves, and backbiters, and drunkards, just like ourselves or any other Christians. Oh, her lady-ship never knew all that was going on behind her back: how would she?[127]

Unlike Philippa and Lady Madigan, the Major and Sir Pearce, as Irishmen, know much of the "divilment" that is in the Irish people (though as a Resident Magistrate, Major Yeates knows significantly more).[128] For Yeates and Sir Pearce, the Irish people do not hold the same exotic magic as they do for their English wives. A good example of this is Sir Pearce's view of Irish Catholics, which contrasts sharply with the view of his overly sentimental English wife. Madigan believes that Irish Catholics can become like "wild beasts" when in a rage and is worried about getting "too familiar" with them, whereas his English wife thinks they are colorful and harmless and gives the Irish Catholic children pennies in an attempt to make a personal connection with them.[129]

O'Flaherty regards Lady Madigan's ignorance regarding "all that was going on behind her back" as innocent, excusing it on the grounds that "she was English" and would therefore be unable to suspect or detect Irish "divilment."[130] He compares it to his own feeling that the Asians and Africans that he has met as a soldier also initially seemed more noble and less sinful than the people he grew up around. O'Flaherty's connecting of his own perspective with Lady Madigan's is another case of Shaw reaching for Fanon's third phase of "synthesis." However, there are still plenty of jibes made by Shaw against the English in the play, all designed to make the Irish look like the superior nation. Each of these jibes betrays the fact that Shaw was still actually in Fanon's second "national" phase. One prominent example of Shaw praising the Irish at the expense of the English is the stage direction in which he writes:

> [Mrs O'Flaherty] turns threateningly to her son with one of those sudden Irish changes of manner which amaze and scandalize less flexible nations.[131]

This reminds us of Shaw's praise of Ireland's "flexibility of mind" over England's excessive literal-mindedness in *Tragedy of an Elderly Gentleman* and his journalism.[132]

Three other notable examples of Shaw remaining in Fanon's second "national" phase come from the preface. It opens with Shaw comically suggesting the superiority of Irish soldiers over English ones:

> The British officer seldom likes Irish soldiers; but he always tries to have a certain proportion of them in his battalion, because, partly from a want of common sense which leads them to value their lives less than Englishmen do (lives are really less worth living in a poor country), and partly because even the most cowardly Irishman feels obliged to outdo an Englishman in bravery if possible, and at least to set a perilous pace for him, Irish soldiers give impetus to those military operations which require for their spirited execution more devilment than prudence.[133]

Later in the preface, after describing various mistakes made by the English in their handling of various Great War-related matters, including their irresponsible use of bigoted, jingoistic propaganda, Shaw writes that "the British blockade won the war; but the wonder is that the British blockhead did not lose it."[134] According to Shaw, one of the wartime blunders made by the English was their brutal suppression of the 1916 Rising, in which British forces "quite unnecessarily" reduced the Dublin city center to ruins and executed the "leading prisoners of war."[135] Shaw, playing the

Shavian role of cool Irish rationalist analyzing the ways of the (supposedly) irrational English, concludes that

> Really it was only the usual childish petulance in which John Bull does things in a week that disgrace him for a century, though he soon recovers his good humor, and cannot understand why the survivors of his wrath do not feel as jolly with him as he does with them.[136]

As these examples demonstrate, Shaw, in *O'Flaherty, VC*, is once again depicting the Irish as canny, brave, incisive thinkers, superior to the brutish, sentimental, unimaginative English.

Since *O'Flaherty, VC* was, according to Shaw, "a recruiting poster in disguise," he wrote it with the Abbey Theatre's Irish audience in mind.[137] Upon completing the play in September 1915, he sent it to Lady Gregory, who gladly accepted it. While the play was in rehearsal, however, St John Ervine (who was managing the theatre singlehandedly while Yeats was in London and Lady Gregory was in the United States) was forced to pull the production; Augustine Birrell, Secretary for Ireland, and W. F. Bailey, an Abbey trustee, advised Ervine that, no matter how honorable Shaw's intentions in the play, its aggressively candid views regarding Ireland were liable to be misinterpreted by the Irish public. Birrell and Bailey argued that the play could cause riots, which would not only hurt Irish recruiting but might also lead Dublin Castle to revoke the theater's license.[138] Shaw did not have to be convinced that riots were a very real possibility. As he confessed in a letter to Lady Gregory while composing the play, its "picture of the Irish character will make... [Synge's] Playboy seem like a patriotic rhapsody by comparison," and he boasted, with typical Shavian bravado, that the play might prove to be "a barricade for the theatre to die gloriously on."[139] Ervine's decision to pull the play meant that the Abbey, for the second time, chose not to stage an excellent Shaw play set in his home country of Ireland.

Unproduced in Ireland, a disappointed Shaw had to find other ways to get the play's message into public discourse about the war. Shaw encountered complete resistance from London producers, however, because he was widely perceived by the British public to be pro-German.[140] Although Shaw made it abundantly clear in his journalism that the United Kingdom had to stand up to German aggression, his exceedingly candid views regarding certain unsavory aspects of the war and his highlighting of the lies and distortions included in much British war propaganda were perceived as wantonly unpatriotic. Without a forthcoming English production, Shaw finally got the play produced by RFC Officers at the Western Front in Treizennes, France, on February 3, 1917. Robert Loraine directed the piece, and the cast included three Irishmen (Captain Denis Mulholland played O'Flaherty; Lieutenant Desmond de Burgh played Mrs O'Flaherty; and Lady Gregory's son, Robert, played Teresa).[141] Shaw attended the dress rehearsal and laughed riotously throughout. In August of that year, Shaw managed to have the play published in *Hearst's Magazine* in New York, and, three months later, he read it to 250 wounded soldiers at a hospital near his home in Ayot St Lawrence, Hertfordshire. He wrote to Lady Gregory that the soldiers "gave me three cheers, and laughed a good deal; but the best bits were when they sat very tight and said nothing."[142] Although Shaw may not have suspected as much, their silence may have been in response to the inappropriate levity with which he treated the horrors of life at the Front in the play.

Shaw published the play in book form after the war was over in 1919, and finally got the play produced professionally in 1920 (there were independent productions in both New York and London that year). By that time, however, with the war over, much of the play's subject matter was politically irrelevant and many of its controversial views harmless, and Shaw was disappointed that it was only being produced and published in book form "now that it can no longer do any good."[143] Although the 1920 London production was put on by the Abbey touring company, they did not bring the play back to Dublin, where Irish men and women were waging the War of Independence. As Christopher Innes has written, "*O'Flaherty, VC* was still felt to be too much of a challenge to Nationalist sensitivities, even more than a year after the end of the Great War."[144] The fact that so many Irish families lost loved ones in the Great War might also have dampened Irish enthusiasm for the play at the time. Indeed, as one of the Abbey directors, Lady Gregory would have been involved in the decision not to bring the play back to Dublin, and her son Robert (who, as noted above, created the role of Teresa Driscoll) died fighting in Italy on January 23, 1918.[145]

While it might be assumed that a play on such a timely issue would have little role in Shaw's later career, the reading by Shaw to the wounded soldiers at Ayot set a precedent. He found that it was the one play from his repertoire that was particularly popular at public readings. "It never fails when I read it,"[146] he boasted to the BBC, and, as such, it was the play he chose to read for his first BBC radio broadcast in 1924. English audiences enjoyed hearing Shaw, an Irish author, read a play that required him to use a variety of Irish accents. He also surprised the BBC staff and the listeners at home by bursting into a few bars of "It's a Long Way to Tipperary," which features prominently in the play. Cecil Lewis of the BBC, who had approached Shaw to do the broadcast, informed the author that

> Everyone I have met so far is unanimous in the opinion that it was the best thing that has ever been broadcast... People seem to think that it is uncanny that a playwright should be actually able to sing *Tipperary* and assume three or four different voices as well. I think they are right. In any case the ease and intimacy which you achieved without any practice or rehearsal leaves us, the regular broadcasters, gasping.[147]

Even an English reviewer who did not enjoy the broadcast, believing that the BBC should have hired actors for the different parts, admired Shaw's "brave attempt" at "changing his voice to suit the different characters."[148]

Given the damning criticisms of England in *O'Flaherty, VC*, it is perhaps surprising that the English found the play so amusing. (A typical early review from an English newspaper describes the play as a "delightful frolic.")[149] The worrying conclusion is that Shaw may have been getting laughs from English audiences for simply representing the Irish characters in the play in a comic light, and even—in the case of the BBC broadcast—for reading parts like those of O'Flaherty, his mother, and his girlfriend in a broad Irish accent (and singing a quasi-Irish song). Once again, as with *John Bull's Other Island*, Shaw's serious intentions seem to have been obscured by the English desire and propensity to laugh at the Irish.

Perhaps to avoid a repeat of this phenomenon, for his third and final play set in Ireland, *Tragedy of an Elderly Gentleman* (1921), Shaw featured no Irish characters in the cast and made the Stage English figure more central to the action and more absurd than in either of his previous Irish efforts. In chapter 3, I suggested that Shaw's removal of the Irish from the Irish landscape in *Tragedy of an Elderly Gentleman* placed the play into a tradition of works by Irish Protestants which celebrate the physical landscape of Ireland while ignoring the country's inhabitants. For Shaw, this motivation for removing the Irish would have been a subconscious one; he had other, more conscious and deliberate reasons for including the extinction of the Irish in the work. First, he wanted to warn the Irish that they had to learn how to use more than just their revolutionary political muscles. Second, he wanted to indulge in some pro-Irish reverse snobbery. Even though Shaw implies that the Elderly Gentleman's retelling of Irish history is too full of sentiment, you still sense Shaw's joy at proclaiming, through this character, that the Irish are "the most interesting race on earth" and that the world would be "a tame dull place" without them.[150] In keeping with his use of reverse snobbery in other plays, he gets to reiterate that the Irish owe their superiority "solely to their sufferings."[151] Finally, Shaw seems to have removed the Irish from the equation in this play, because he could use the long-livers to play the role of practical, intellectually superior inhabitants of Ireland without having to imbue them with "Oirish" traits and speech patterns that audiences (particularly English ones) might be tempted to laugh at, thus undermining the play's criticisms of the English. As was mentioned in chapter 3, the fact that the long-livers have an Irish cast of mind also helps promote his theory, first proposed in the preface to *John Bull's Other Island*, that what we think of as the Irish perspective owes much to the power of the unique climate in Ireland.

Tragedy of an Elderly Gentleman includes four English characters. Of these, the Elderly Gentleman and the British Envoy (a deeply corrupt politician) recall Tom Broadbent by being both racist, officious hypocrites and sentimental, romantic duffers; the Envoy's wife and daughter (both shallow tourists) recall Lady Madigan in being easily impressed with what they regard as the exotic souvenirs and performances on offer at the temple in Galway. Since the Elderly Gentleman is the most fully developed of these characters and since it is mainly through him that Shaw explores different Stage English faults than the ones that preoccupied him in his earlier Irish plays, he is the main focus of my analysis.

The loquacious Elderly Gentleman is not merely racist, but also extremely sexist and classist, and Shaw implies that these attitudes are typical of well-to-do English conservatives like the Elderly Gentleman. The character's racism—as I noted in chapter 3—manifests itself in his habit of categorizing all countries as either "civilized" or "savage"; he even refers to people from less developed countries as "the natives."[152] His sexism is evident from his distaste for females who behave "improper[ly]" and his belief that men should only speak to "a married lady" about sexual matters, since unmarried women's sexual innocence must be preserved.[153] Shaw mocks the Elderly Gentleman's sexism most expertly when he has the Stage Englishman refer to a "lady doctor." Confusion ensues, because the long-liver he is speaking to thinks that the Elderly Gentleman is referring to a butterfly.

The long-liver explains, "You spoke of a lady doctor. The word is known here only as the name of a butterfly."[154] The Elderly Gentleman's classist aggression—also noted in Chapter 3—manifests itself in his firm belief in both "private property" and the British "caste system," as well as his denigration of "agricultural laborer[s]," "paupers," and the "lower classes," and his insistence that he not be confused with them, since he is "well-bred" and "a gentleman."[155]

Since English puritanical social morality is one of Shaw's main targets in this play (much more so than in the earlier Irish plays), Shaw completes his portrait of an English enemy of progress by imbuing the Elderly Gentleman with a dogged determination to conform to a set of prudish, obsolete manners and to maintain a meaningless propriety. Shaw generates most of the play's comedy from the Elderly Gentleman's efforts to adhere to these manners and proprieties and from the inability of the ultra-practical, Surrogate Irish long-livers to comprehend why he is so bound up by them. His sexual prudishness, his fear about engaging in activities that are "scandalous" or in "questionable taste," and his desire to hang on to his "dignity" in all circumstances are met with bewilderment and incomprehension by the long-livers.[156] A great example is when the Elderly Gentleman and his party are about to enter the temple in Galway, to meet The Oracle. He nervously asks Zoo, a long-liver, how they should behave when inside, explaining, "We desire to behave in a becoming manner." Zoo, with Irish naturalness, says, "Behave just how you feel. It doesn't matter how you behave."[157] As in *Fanny's First Play* and *Pygmalion*, Shaw is attempting to show that English decorum is based on a set of arbitrary, learned manners, and, just as he enjoyed having Dora Delaney and Henry Higgins aggressively contravene those proprieties in the earlier plays, he enjoys having the long-livers expose the absurdity of them here.

In *Tragedy of an Elderly Gentleman*, Shaw does not merely reiterate his previous criticisms of the English fixation on decorum— he moves his argument on. He argues that when the members of a society agree to pose as more dignified than they actually are, it creates a situation in which people are sensitive about having that dignity outraged. In this play, the Elderly Gentleman often construes the words or actions of the long-livers to be calculated affronts to his dignity. Of course, they are not—the long-livers are oblivious to the effect they are having on the Elderly Gentleman's pride, and they cannot even relate to the feelings of shame and abasement that he is experiencing. They literally do not understand what he means when he accuses them of "gross impertinence," of "sneering" at his activities, or of "taking a great liberty" at his expense.[158] This is the Irishman Shaw using a Stage English figure to expose the irrationality endemic in English social discourse.

In keeping with his plan of criticizing English Phariseeism, Shaw has the Elderly Gentleman's Stage English hypocrisy mainly reside, not in matters of commerce and politics (as with *John Bull's* Broadbent), but in his tendency to pretend to a propriety that he cannot maintain. The Elderly Gentleman occasionally swears, has fits of temper, or says sexually suggestive things that he must immediately apologize for in order to maintain his pose as a moral paragon. After an angry outburst at Zoo, he says, "I withdraw what I said."[159] Being relentless realists, the long-livers cannot understand metaphorical figures of speech, especially those that are cover-ups for wrongdoing (like "our hearts are in the right place" and "I throw myself upon your indulgence"), so Zoo asks him plainly and reasonably, "How can you withdraw what you said?"[160] At another point, when the Elderly Gentleman swears in front of Zoo and she does not hold it against him, he is very pleased. He says "I feels almost as if I were at the club," a place where he can be looser morally than he is at home.[161] This is Shaw once again exposing the hypocrisy endemic in English codes of behavior. He is suggesting that it would be much more honest if the English maintained the same moral standards wherever they were and whoever they were with, as the Surrogate Irish long-livers do.

The Elderly Gentleman is not merely a hypocritical, prudish, chauvinistic political conservative; as I mentioned above, he is also, at times, a sentimental, romantic duffer. His sentimentality is manifest not only in the fact that he has made this "pious pilgrimage" to Britain and Ireland, but also in his tendency to wax lyrical about the heroes of English history. At one point he says, with as much sentimentality as any Stage Irishman, "When I think of... [those] strong silent men, ruling an empire on which the sun never set, my eyes fill with tears: my heart bursts with emotion."[162]

A large part of the Elderly Gentleman's romanticism is his Stage English love of spectacle (another trait that Shaw gave to the Elderly Gentleman but not to Broadbent). The long-livers are aware of this English predilection, so, when people from the British government come to see The Oracle, they put on a Wizard of Oz-like show for them. Even though the shortlived visitors know that the show is a sham, we are told that they are always "deeply impressed" (and, in some cases, awestruck) by it.[163] This is Shaw's comment on what the English historian John Allen Giles has called "that love of pomp and ceremony, which, to a certain extent, has always belonged to the English character."[164] (For examples of this love, consider English coronations and other ornate state ceremonies.) The long-livers, playing the role of Shavian Irish realists, regard the pomp as ridiculous, and offend the English party with their "levity" before and during the solemn meeting with The Oracle.[165] Being good Shavian Irish pragmatists, however, the long-livers recognize that they *have* to put on the show. As Zoo says to the Envoy, "If you wont believe in anyone who is not dressed-up, why, we must dress-up for you."[166] Shaw is mocking the English need to have their authority figures, such as judges, professors, and royalty, dress in costumes that supposedly denote authority and power.

In chapter 3, the anti-English insults enunciated by the Surrogate Irish long-livers were highlighted. Shaw also mocks the English in the play by having the Elderly Gentleman allude to

Britons with preposterously "Englishy" names. He mentions his admiration for "modern spiritual leaders [like] Blitherinjam, Tosh and Spiffkins," as well as the "father of history, Thucyderodotus Macollybuckle."[167] The two main British political parties are "the Potterbills" and "the Rotterjacks," and even the Elderly Gentleman himself is given a childishly Stage English name—"Joseph Popham Bolge Bluebin Barlow, O. M."—of which he is inordinately proud.[168]

The relentlessness of Shaw's disparagement of the English and praise of the Irish throughout the play are further confirmation that he is in Fanon's second "national" phase, fixated on emphasizing to his audience the idea that "green is beautiful." Once again, however, Shaw is reaching for the third phase of "synthesis" through his depiction of the Elderly Gentleman's death.

The Elderly Gentleman was warned at the beginning of the play by a long-liver that it was dangerous for "shortlived people to come to this country," because, after prolonged exposure to the much wiser ways of the long-livers, they become afflicted by "a deadly disease called discouragement."[169] Accordingly, the Elderly Gentleman comes to see how foolish the English he lives among are, compared to these wise long-livers. Like Swift's Gulliver desiring to remain among the Houyhnhnm, the Elderly Gentleman proclaims at the end of the play that he wishes to remain in Ireland among the long-livers.[170] He explains to The Oracle that he simply cannot go back to Baghdad, because "I cannot live among people to whom nothing is real. I have become incapable of it through my stay here." The Oracle warns him that staying will result in an expedited death by "discouragement," to which the Elderly Gentleman responds, "If I go back I shall die of disgust and despair. I take the nobler risk. I beg you, do not cast me out."[171] The Oracle has compassion for him and lets him remain in Ireland, but, as The Oracle offers the Elderly Gentleman her hands, she stares steadily into his eyes and the Elderly Gentleman "stiffens" and dies.[172] The Oracle expresses sadness over the fact that she could not have done more for him.

The English Elderly Gentleman's realization at the end of the play that he is not wise, as well as his noble desire to remain among those who have a firmer grasp on reality, signify that, as in Shaw's two previous Irish plays, he is once again reaching for Fanon's third phase in which simplistic dualities are broken down. He has made the Stage Englishman in this play not merely absurd, but also the *hero* of this tragedy. While acknowledging that this ending is an attempt by Shaw to escape from the simple formula of noble Irish versus ignoble English, his relentless criticisms of the English and constant praising of the Irish results in a play which remains firmly in Fanon's second phase.

In any honest study of *Tragedy of an Elderly Gentleman*, it must be admitted that it is not a great play. While Michael Holroyd is overly harsh when he contends that it is the "weakest play of the [*Back to Methuselah*] cycle," the play certainly has its faults.[173] Many viewers and readers of it have undoubtedly sympathized with famous Dublin theatre-goer Joseph Holloway, who left the play's Irish debut at the Gate Theatre in 1930 after the first act because he was "somewhat bored" by all the long speeches made by the Elderly Gentleman—a character Holloway describes as "volubility itself."[174] (Of course, this is just the reaction we should expect from a man with such populist taste.) In spite of the play's weaknesses, it is still of vital importance to any study on the Irish Shaw or on Shaw and the English. Not only does it give us more insight into Shaw's Irish reverse snobbery and his perspective on the English national character, it also reveals his desire to take a new tack in his third and final Irish play. Distressed by the ways his incisive, critical portraits of the English in Ireland were undermined in his earlier plays by the English propensity to laugh at all things Irish, he made his Stage English character even more absurd and completely removed representations of Irishness from the work. This partially results in a less entertaining play, but also demonstrates Shaw's relentless desire to develop as a playwright, ever ready to adjust his methods to better communicate his ideas to an audience.

Without a doubt, the most disturbing aspect of the play for contemporary audiences is the fact that, in it, Shaw (like many on the far left and far right between the World Wars) seems open to the idea of exterminating "undesirables."[175] It is true that in Shaw's case, the "undesirables" are those whose stubborn conservatism and "dead thought" are preventing the spread of a truly equal society, free from gender, race, and class discrimination.[176] However, the willingness among the long-livers to contemplate the mass murder of all shortlivers (on the assumption that their childishly conservative moral and socio-political outlooks are beyond redemption) and even to slaughter any of their own children whom they discover to be "evil" (or simply shortlived throwbacks) smacks too much of Nazi extermination of "undesirables" for contemporary minds.[177] It also seems to justify the criticisms made by C. S. Lewis, who was, in many other respects, "an admirer of Bernard Shaw's work."[178] Lewis claimed that the "alien, cold…intelligence" and "ruthless…will" of the Shavian Superman made him "superhuman in power [but] subhuman in cruelty," his "monstrosity of form" the result of his ultra-rational "elimination of pity."[179] Of course, Shavians could rightly argue that the long-livers are only contemplating their world-wide extermination plan, and that The Oracle's mercy towards the converted Elderly Gentleman at the end of the play is a sign that (1) the long-livers are not, in fact, lacking in pity, and that (2) the Elderly Gentleman's conversion at the end will convince sceptical long-livers that shortlivers are capable of acknowledging and surrendering to superior wisdom.[180]

Regardless of the play's problems, it is certainly full of fascinating ideas and compelling stage pictures. As such, it is certainly unwise for critics to overlook or lightly dismiss it.

Part III: After Broadbent

In the decades following Shaw's groundbreaking creation of Tom Broadbent, a number of important Irish playwrights and fiction writers copied Shaw in creating Stage English characters who were a combination of racist, officious hypocrite and sentimental, romantic duffer. The most notable examples of such characters are Haines from James Joyce's *Ulysses* (1922), Gerald Lesworth from Elizabeth Bowen's *The Last September* (1929), Basil Stoke and Cyril Poges from Seán O'Casey's *Purple Dust* (1940), and Leslie Williams and Monsewer from Brendan Behan's *The Hostage* (1958).

Although James Joyce famously criticized Shaw for being one of the Irish writers who chose to play "court jester to the English," critics such as Martha Fodaski Black and Peter Gahan have demonstrated that Shaw actually left a significant imprint on Joyce's work.[181] In this book, I have already drawn important parallels between Tom Broadbent and the Englishman Haines from *Ulysses*; however, their biggest connection is that both characters combine the two, traditional, Stage English types.

During Haines's relatively brief appearances in *Ulysses*, he is revealed to be a racist, officious hypocrite through his anti-Semitic remarks, his violent dreams inspired by time in the colonies, and his bringing of a gun to Ireland (despite his supposed love for the country). His sentimental, romantic duffer nature is most clearly displayed through his naïve but sincere interest in the Irish Revival. The Englishman's interest in the Irish language and his hurrying from the National Library to buy Douglas Hyde's *Love Songs of Connaught* are treated with a mix of pity and derision in the novel.

Like Broadbent and the Elderly Gentleman, Haines is used by his creator to slyly demonstrate English inferiority to the Irish; there are several indications throughout *Ulysses* that Haines is less clever than "Buck" Mulligan and Stephen Dedalus, the two Irishmen with whom he resides in the Martello Tower. Haines even hopes to make a collection of Stephen's ingenious sayings. That said, Joyce, through the unreliable narrator, subtly demonstrates (with third phase generosity) that the sinister traits ascribed to a Stage English figure may simply be projections born in the mind of an Irish character. For example, as readers, we are well aware that Stephen may be unjust in assuming that Haines's smile is aimed at the "wild Irish" who surround him. Likewise, we know that Stephen's subconscious linking of Haines's smile to the deceitful "smile of a Saxon" from the old Irish proverb may be more a sign of Stephen's anti-English prejudice than a true indication that Haines is duplicitous. In fact, in Stephen's more generous moments, he even concedes that Haines is "not all unkind" and that his interest in Ireland makes him less a "usurper" than a "penitent thief."[182]

Elizabeth Bowen is another writer who followed Shaw in creating a Stage English character who combined the two, traditional, Stage English types. Bowen was well-acquainted with Shaw's work. Maud Ellman has demonstrated that *Pygmalion* was an important influence on Bowen's late novel, *Eva Trout* (1968), and Bowen herself refers to Shaw and his work a number of times in her literary journalism.[183] For example, when discussing the "cosmic devouring laughter" which is "most heard" in Ireland and which—she implies—is inflected with derision, she cites the laughter of the townspeople of Rosscullen after Broadbent's running over of the pig.[184]

In Bowen's most famous Irish work, *The Last September* (1929), the main Stage Englishman (and a central character in the novel) is Gerald Lesworth—a British soldier who has been stationed near Danielstown, a Big House modeled on Bowen's Court, during the Irish War of Independence.[185] He has formed an attachment to the Irish Lois Farquhar, an orphaned young woman who lives at Danielstown with her uncle and aunt, Lord and Lady Naylor. Gerald and his English soldier friends are entertained regularly at Danielstown, and it is during these scenes that Bowen most pointedly demonstrates what she regards as the negative aspects of the English national character. Most notably, she indicates that Gerald is both a racist, officious hypocrite and a sentimental, romantic duffer.

Gerald's racism is linked to his sincere and almost childlike belief in the British Empire, which greatly surprises the Irish characters Lois and Laurence.[186] At one point, Gerald is shocked to learn that the Naylors, despite being part of the Ascendancy, are actually friendly with some of the rebels. It is as though Gerald, in his dreams of helping to spread and maintain the British Empire, has never regarded the general populace of the colonies as people that one might get to know personally; they are merely there for the English (and their colonial representatives) to subdue, civilize, and exploit for labor.

Gerald's officiousness is present in his desire for "correctness" and his devotion to duty. Lois is intimidated by the idea of marrying Gerald, because she says that in English country-house life, even one's dog must be "correct."[187] And we know that Lois is wise to suspect that Gerald will want everything to be impeccably correct in their future home: as the narrator has already revealed, he fantasizes about one day possessing a neat family home in "confident English country[side]" and longs for the day when the British Empire will be "accurately, finally fenced about and all raked over."[188]

Gerald's "bright and abstract" sense of "his duty" is his guiding light through life.[189] (Bowen writes that life for Gerald is "a succession of practical adjustments, into which the factor of personality did not enter at all.")[190] Later in the novel, she hints that this abstract sense of duty for its own sake is not just peculiar to Gerald but might be an English trait generally. When Lady Naylor suggests in a letter to Gerald's mother after his death that "it must always be some consolation to think how happy his life had been," the English mother writes back to say that "*her* first consolation [is] to think he died in so noble a cause."[191] Their different philosophies of life are writ large here. Bowen suggests that the Irish are primarily concerned with the *quality* of a person's life, whereas the English, with their more abstract view of life, hope to be able to say on their deathbed, like Lord Nelson, "Thank God, I have done my duty."[192]

Gerald's sentimental, romantic side is seen most clearly in his impulsive actions during his courtship of Lois (unexpectedly visiting her after being out all night on duty and kissing her without warning). With his iron-clad sense of duty and discipline, these lapses are a betrayal of his own values, and are therefore examples of Stage English hypocrisy.

In the novel, Bowen suggests that Gerald's main Stage English foible is that he is an intellectual duffer—a fault that the formidable Lady Naylor believes he shares with English people generally. Lady Naylor avers that all Irish people (Protestant and Catholic alike) are "thinkers," fond of intellectual contemplation, and she cites Mrs Pat Gregan on her estate as an example. By contrast, she finds the English to be a "people with so little brain."[193] In the case of Gerald, the other Irish characters agree with her negative assessment of his intellect. Lois, Marda, and Lady Naylor criticize him for having a "matter of fact," "cutting book," "unoriginal" mind and for talking in a way that is "square and facty, compact with assumptions."[194]

Seán O'Casey was a tremendous admirer of Shaw's work (and a personal friend of Shaw and his wife, Charlotte), and he followed Shaw in repeatedly using Stage Englishmen in his drama. In two of O'Casey's early plays, 1923's *The Shadow of a Gunman* (set during the War of Independence) and 1926's *The Plough and the Stars* (set during the 1916 Rising), vicious English soldiers come on to the stage, speaking in low Cockney accents and abusing the residents of Dublin tenements, even those loyal to the crown. These soldiers seem to relish being cruel to the Irish in the name of their "dooty" and display shocking ignorance of the Irish sociopolitical situation.[195]

In contrast to the brief appearances by these characters, the Stage Englishmen in O'Casey's *Purple Dust* (first published in 1940 and first produced in 1945) are more central to the play's action and are much more fully developed as characters, though they still remain somewhat cartoonish (thereby making lengthy, nuanced analysis of them rather difficult).[196] In the play, the two Englishmen, Basil Stoke and Cyril Poges, attempt to refurbish an Irish castle and are maddened by the ways of their Irish mistresses and the Irish workmen whom they hire to do the restoration.

Perhaps unsurprisingly, given O'Casey's admiration for Shaw, his portraits of Stoke and Poges are heavily indebted to Shaw's depiction of Broadbent; like Shaw's first Stage Englishman, these characters are combinations of the two, traditional, Stage English types. Indeed, *Purple Dust* essentially makes the same case against the English as *John Bull's Other Island*, the only significant difference being that O'Casey does not make even the slightest attempt to suggest "the value of an Englishman," as Shaw does.[197]

Stoke and Poges (their surnames are derived from the quintessentially English-sounding place name of Stoke Poges in Buckinghamshire), are racist against the Irish and the other "primitive peoples" in the colonies of the British Empire; are hypocritical (constantly accusing the Irish of vices that they themselves possess); are sentimental regarding the English, the Irish, the benefits of country life, and love (foolishly settling money on their gold-digging Irish partners); have been rendered useless in practical matters by their prosperity; are less hardworking than the Irish characters; do not realize when the Irish despise them or are laughing at them; have a violent belief in "efficiency"; and often affect poses of "stateliness," "dignity," and confident, "smiling" heartiness as a protection against circumstances that are overwhelming them. They, like Broadbent (and Haines from *Ulysses*), have also brought a gun to Ireland, out of fear of the Irish and their supposedly wild land, which they compare at various points to "jungle," "desert," and "wilderness."[198]

O'Casey's inability to break new ground with these Stage English characters speaks to the overwhelming influence that *John Bull's Other Island* had upon him. Brendan Behan, who also loved Shaw's first Irish play (he liked to boast that he had the preface to the play "almost by heart"), managed to create Stage English characters in *The Hostage* (1958) who both drew upon Shaw but who were also, in key respects, innovative characters in the history of Irish drama.[199]

One innovative aspect of Behan's *The Hostage* is that the main Stage English character, a British soldier called Leslie Williams, is working-class. As Elizabeth Butler Cullingford has rightly argued, Behan's decision to move the "working-class stage Englishman" from his usual "minor role" into a more important one was new for Irish drama and was suggested to him by Frank O'Connor's short story, "Guests of the Nation."[200] The effect of this story on Behan's work, particularly *The Hostage*, has been historically overstated by critics (important Behan critics agree that *The Hostage* only bears superficial resemblance to O'Connor's story).[201] However, its use of working-class Englishmen as main characters certainly would have appealed to the socialist Behan, who enjoyed depicting the accents and manners of the urban, working-class English boys he knew during his time in borstal.

Also innovative was Behan's decision to make a Stage Englishman the sympathetic hero of the piece. Although Behan imbues Leslie with significant Stage English flaws, he makes the soldier's hero status clear when he first appears onstage in *An Giall* (1958), the original Irish-language version of *The Hostage*. As Leslie enters the brothel where the IRA will be holding him hostage, a hornpipe called "The Blackbird" is playing on the radio (to which Kate and Teresa are dancing wildly), and, as Richard Wall has pointed out, "the Irish word for '*londubh*' (blackbird) is also a metaphor for hero."[202] Of previous Stage Englishmen in Irish drama, only Shaw's Elderly Gentleman can be described as a play's hero, and he is a much less "attractive" character than Leslie.[203]

Leslie is a "decent chap" most of the time; in fact, he is a sentimental romantic in his dealings with Teresa and in his desire to see the best in his Irish captors.[204] However, when provoked, he comes out with racist remarks against the Irish, blacks, and Asians. At one point, when singing of his beloved London, he sings that he "wish[es] the Irish, the niggers and the wogs...were kicked out and sent back home."[205] The main manifestations of his anti-Irish racism are his disrespectful reference to Irish Gaelic as "Garlic," his twice-repeated view that there are too many Irish in London, and the fact that he subscribes to traditional anti-Irish stereotypes.[206] He believes the Irish are all heavy drinkers ("we just let them drink their way through [London]"), "great" storytellers, and a bit "barmy."[207] Also, his Ireland is a fetishized Ireland of songs like "When Irish Eyes Are Smiling," a song he sings in Act III but which, tellingly, the Irish characters do not know.[208]

Leslie's officiousness and hypocrisy are present in his reflexive devotion to his duty and to the crown, when put under pressure. In both *An Giall* and *The Hostage*, when Leslie learns that the IRA might kill him if the Republican in custody in Belfast is hanged, his British patriotism comes out aggressively; he proudly sings and hums British patriotic songs and becomes much more critical of the Irish. This makes a sharp contrast with his earlier friendliness towards the Irish characters and his previous anti-royalist remarks.[209] Behan is suggesting that the English pretend to be open to the ways and the people from other countries, but, in an instant, if challenged, will revert to jingoistic patriotism. This is in line with Shaw's theory that the English pretend to be fools but are willing and able to turn and devour the real fools if a situation demands it.

Perhaps Leslie's main Stage English flaw is the fact that his political ignorance marks him out as an intellectual duffer, especially when compared to most of the play's Irish characters. Despite being a British soldier assigned to Northern Ireland, Leslie is deeply ignorant about Ireland, British imperialism, and the world. Behan is suggesting, like Shaw often did, that one of the biggest tragedies of the English attempt to rule Ireland was the fact that the English never took the trouble to get to know the country.[210] The Irish characters have to repeatedly point out to Leslie the bad things that England has done in Ireland, Cyprus, Africa, and Asia, as well as to Jews at home in England.[211] Leslie's ignorance of these English atrocities (and his belief that they have nothing to do with him, despite the fact that he is serving outside England as a soldier in the British Army) is made clear when he answers Meg's question, "What are you doing poking your nose into our [Irish] affairs?" with: "[W]hat affairs? What do I know about Ireland or Cyprus, or Kenya or Jordan or any of those places?"[212] Likewise, when Teresa mentions that Monsewer "fought for Ireland," Leslie asks, "Why, was somebody doing something to Ireland?" Teresa, scandalized, says, "Wasn't England, for hundreds of years?" Leslie's response echoes that of Stage English characters such as Broadbent and Haines, who are happy to forget history and mystified by the long Irish memory: "That was donkey's years ago. Everybody was doing something to someone in those days."[213] This statement is particularly appalling, given that Leslie is currently serving in Northern Ireland, where, as far as the Nationalist community is concerned, Englishmen like Leslie are *still* doing something to them.

While Behan criticizes British imperialism in the play (partially through his characterization of the unwitting stooge Leslie), he is also hard on militant Republicanism. Indeed, Behan pushes an essentially pacifist message. Like his character Pat in *The Hostage*, "the H Bomb...got [Behan] scared of the little bombs," and it is abundantly clear that he regards Leslie's death at the end of the play as a useless tragedy.[214] The pacifist Behan ingeniously incarnates the madness of both militant nationalism and militant imperialism in the figure of Monsewer—the confused, English-born Irish Republican and owner of the brothel. Monsewer, as Cullingford has suggested, is a Stage Irishman and a Stage Englishman all at the same time.[215]

Throughout the play, Behan, with a reverse snobbery that would do Shaw proud, mocks the Eton and Oxford educated Monsewer, suggesting that he is a sentimental romantic whose political delusions are the product of an upper-class Englishness that he will never escape, no matter how hard he tries. Like the proverbial out-of-touch, upper-class English officers in the Crimea or miles behind the line in World War I, Monsewer is hopelessly cut off from the realities of the situation he finds himself in. He has, like these officers, lost himself in a fantasy world of heroes and high ideals. Monsewer actually believes that "everybody in [the] house are gaels, patriots or Republicans on the run" and not the "pimps, prostitutes, [and] decayed gentlemen" that they so obviously are.[216] Indeed, he perfectly fits Shaw's description (from the preface to *John Bull's Other Island*) of an Englishman who is living "wholly at the mercy of his imagination, having no sense of reality to check it," and who is "drunk with glory."[217]

Monsewer's ostentatious (and patently absurd) performance of Irishness—begun after "discover[ing]" "one day" that he was "Anglo-Irish"—involves him wearing a kilt everywhere, speaking Irish, and playing the bagpipes.[218] His duffer laziness is demonstrated by the fact that he is terrible on the bagpipes and that his Irish language skills are deeply suspect. As Declan Kiberd has observed, "when he spoke Irish to bus-conductors, we are gravely informed, he had to bring an interpreter with him, so that the man would let him off. (Presumably, his British dialect of Irish was incomprehensible.)"[219] And, when the Soviet sailor speaks to him in Russian, he mistakes it for Irish and answers with some basic, beginner's Irish.[220] Intellectual laziness is also indicated by his use of bagpipes (as opposed to *uilleann* pipes) and his wearing of a kilt—not to mention his use of the term "laddie."[221] These are all evidence that he is "confusing Scottish with Irish customs."[222] (John Brannigan interestingly links this strand in Monsewer's character to the Scottish/Irish confusion associated with Tim Haffigan in *John Bull's Other Island*.)[223]

Throughout the play, Behan indicates that Monsewer's performance of Irishness is only a surface affectation. Deep down, he is still the English public schoolboy raised on Empire rhetoric, as he unwittingly reveals in unguarded moments. For example, when he first gets talking to Leslie, they bond over cricket, and this self-proclaimed Irish patriot, whose "rabid Anglophobia" means that he "would rather be called 'Monsewer' than" be addressed *as Bearla*, ends up proudly praising English as "the language of Shakespeare and Milton."[224] Behan's implication is that, unlike previously Unionist Irish Protestants who have genuinely come around to the Nationalist cause, the English Monsewer has not had a true, deep, principled conversion. He has merely traded imperialist violence for nationalist violence. This becomes abundantly clear when Monsewer (who, throughout the play, has uttered the work's most spine-chillingly fanatical Republican sentiments) becomes disoriented by his chat with Leslie. Losing himself in Etonian reminiscence, he begins to sing a song that celebrates Englishness and reveals him to be yet another Stage English racist, officious hypocrite.[225]

In the song, the famous "The Captains and the Kings," Monsewer's racism is revealed when he sings of his belief in "the white man's burden" and sings "praise God that we are white.../ And better still we're English."[226] His moralistic officiousness, which is alluded to earlier in the play when Pat explains to Meg that "Monsewer is terrible strict and honest [because]...he's an Englishman," is also made clear in the song.[227] First, Monsewer echoes the old adage "the playing-fields of Eton" and "Harrow" taught Englishmen like himself discipline and "Christian ethics," and gave them physical strength.[228] Second, Behan has Monsewer praise English "old ladies" for having "stern faces," which reveal their moral seriousness and personal discipline.[229] And Monsewer is clearly a hypocrite: when he sings that "far away in dear old Cyprus,/Or in Kenya's dusty land,/[We]...bear the white man's burden" and adds that, when stationed "in West Belfast," "we sigh for dear old England," he not only proves his Englishness once and for all, but also proves that he is not on the side of oppressed peoples, like the other Nationalists in the play.[230] He is, and always has been, an imperialist. In coming to Ireland, he found it easy to become a Republican, because he was prepared to fight to take the North from England, just as his English imperialist predecessors fought to wrestle other lands away from those that ruled them.

As the important Stage English characters in the work of Joyce, Bowen, O'Casey, and Behan indicate, Shaw was a pivotal figure in the history of the Irish use of the Stage Englishman. After his creation of Broadbent, writers saw that they could make their satirical portraits of the English more complex by combining the two, traditional, Stage English types. No longer would characters have to be two-dimensional figures such as thuggish soldiers, condescending English snobs, or sycophantic lovers of all things

Irish. Of course, later third phase writers who were less driven by political circumstances to emphasize the equality—or even the superiority—of the Irish were more prepared to create fully developed English characters who just happened to possess one or more Stage English faults.

Shaw would presumably have loved to be that fair to the English. In his journalism, he regularly castigated Irish Nationalists in Ireland and the United States for believing that "the Irish are the salt of the earth and that all other races are comparatively barbarous, degraded, sordid, irreligious, ungenerous, tyrannical, and treacherous, and that this inferiority is essentially and disgustingly marked in the case of 'the English race.'"[231] Nevertheless, Shaw (as we have seen from many passages quoted in this chapter and throughout this book) was not exempt from championing the Irish and maligning the English in just such a way. It seems he was never quite able to let go of his "inextinguishable pride in being an Irishman" and the "quite irrational" "inborn sense of superiority to all who have had the misfortune to be born in other countries."[232] This is yet more proof of his enduringly Irish outlook.

Conclusion

In Daniel Corkery's notorious 1931 study, *Synge and Anglo-Irish Literature*, he claims that Shaw is one of the Irish Protestant writers "for whom Ireland was never a *patria* in any sense."[1] This book has demonstrated just how preposterous such a statement is; Shaw maintained a strongly Irish outlook throughout his life, and it inspired or significantly informed most of his best work. Critics and commentators after Corkery have continued to exclude Shaw from the truly Irish canon (one thinks of Brian Friel's contention that Shaw "no more belong[s] to Irish drama than John Field belongs to Irish music or Francis Bacon to Irish painting").[2] However, the vast majority of critics have included Shaw but kept him quarantined among the London-based Irish writers from Church of Ireland backgrounds who set most of their work in England and who wrote primarily for English audiences. As chapter 3 affirms, Shaw certainly belongs to the Irish Anglican literary tradition. However, given the time period in which he wrote, his pro-Irish reverse snobbery, the subject matter handled in his plays, his literary influences, and his personal and professional connections, he should also be considered part of the Irish Literary Revival. The arguments in the body of this book demand that Shaw's position with respect to more mainstream Irish writing be reassessed, and the idea of Shaw as a Revival writer is by no means far-fetched.[3]

Studies of the Irish Literary Revival inform us that, in the late nineteenth and early twentieth centuries, a group of Irish writers emerged who sought to rehabilitate Ireland's national image through the creation of artistically ambitious literature; these writers drew inspiration from Irish mythology, history, and politics, as well as continental European culture. The authors of these studies, however, usually fail to recognize that this traditional definition of a Revival writer could just as easily apply to Bernard Shaw. As I will demonstrate here, Shaw shared important artistic and philosophical aims with the acknowledged members of the Revival, and was, in fact, socially and professionally connected to some of them. Most critics have excluded him from the movement, however, because of the erroneous assumption—already disproved in this book—that he was not very interested in writing about his native country. Narrow-gauge Nationalist critics have also excluded him because they never appreciated views of his which they regard as too British. I am referring to (1) Shaw's belief that Ireland benefits greatly from being English-speaking (and his related—often comedic—disparagement of attempts to revive the Irish language); (2) his willingness to use the term "Britons" for the residents of all four countries in the Atlantic Archipelago (traditionally called the British Isles); and (3) the fact that, although he was in favor of Home Rule, he believed that Ireland should maintain some sort of political tie to the countries of Great Britain for the purposes of commerce and defense.[4] Further to this last point, he believed that the complete severance of ties with Britain was the dream of "Impossibilists" who did not realize that an independent Irish state would never assimilate the Ulster Protestants if it required them to completely deny their Britishness; Shaw also believed that these "Impossibilists" underestimated the degree to which Ireland's and Britian's fates were linked in the event of international war.[5] (Shaw rightly believed that the only reason that neutral Ireland's ports were not seized by Britain or the United States during World War II was because the Allies had access to the ports in Northern Ireland—that is, Irish neutrality was only made possible by partition.)[6] In this book, I have shown that Shaw was fiercely proud of his Irishness (in spite of his socialist/internationalist desire to see bigoted and violent patriotism become less of a force in the world). We must therefore consider the nature of Shaw's conscious—or even unconscious—Britishness (as well as the nature of Britishness generally), and ask if possessing a degree of Britishness necessarily excludes a writer from consideration as an Irish Revivalist.

When analyzing the views and work of Irish Anglicans (including Shaw), we should expect some Britishness of language and perspective. People from an Irish Gaelic Catholic background may only be British to the extent that all people from the British colonies entered a state of cultural "hybridity" through exposure to ideas and personnel from the imperial center (or due to unique biographical circumstances, such as where they were educated).[7] For those from Irish Anglican and Ulster Scots Presbyterian backgrounds, however, this hybridity is much more pronounced. Writers from these parallel Irish traditions are quite ready to admit to being influenced by the language(s) and culture(s) of Great Britain, and this influence is often apparent in the settings and narrative/dramatic voices featured in their work. While commentators such as Corkery and Friel might be ready to exclude Irish Anglicans and Ulster Scots writers from the Irish canon for displaying such openness to Britain, the Good Friday Agreement affirms that Britishness and Irishness are not necessarily mutually exclusive terms. Indeed, with the exception of those diehard Orange Protestants who insist on their Britishness while denying their Irishness or even Northern Irishness, most people from Irish Protestant backgrounds are very proud of their Irishness, even as they continue to acknowledge their cultural and/or political Britishness.[8] It has been justly and ruefully noted that English critics have frequently seized upon the Britishness of Irish Protestant writers, while ignoring their Irishness, in an effort to claim them for England. In deciding whether or not to claim these writers back, however, Irish critics have frequently made the mistake of either dismissing any writers whose work smacks of "literary Unionism" or remaining wilfully blind to the cultural, political, and familial ties that such writers inevitably have to Britain.[9] While not denying the very real and very painful injustices perpetrated over centuries by Irish Unionists in the name of the British state (including the suppression of Irish Catholic civil rights in Northern Ireland in my own lifetime), the discerning critic must be open to acknowledging both the Irishness *and* the Britishness of Ireland's culturally hybrid Protestant writers. In the spirit of the Good Friday Agreement, critics should employ the word Irish in a way that accommodates writers from all traditions on the island. This is particularly crucial, since so many of Ireland's most important writers over the past three centuries were extremely proud of their Irishness and yet were also, on some level, British.

While these views are certainly contentious, part of the anger that they rouse may stem from the fact that, among Irish and British commentators, the term British is often mistakenly conflated with the term English. When Irish Protestants claim to be British, they are analogous to people from Scotland and Wales making such a claim; people from these countries invoke the idea of Britishness to signal their participation in a political and cultural partnership with *all* of the countries in the Atlantic Archipelago/British Isles. Indeed, as Michael Gardiner has demonstrated, the concept of Britishness was actually developed and promoted by the Scots in the eighteenth century, as a means of creating a supranational identity that accommodated the Scottish, Welsh, English, and—depending on the commentator—Irish peoples. As Gardiner has also shown, however, the Scottish, Welsh, and Irish elements that were meant to be included in the British identity were quickly overwhelmed by the contribution of the more powerful (and numerous) English. Thus, between the 1740 composition by a Scot of "Rule, Britannia!" and the propagation of English imperial propaganda during the mid-Victorian era, "the British stress had moved from Scottish demands to be *included within* Britain, to

English assumptions of *standing for* Britain."[10] England's hijacking of the concept of Britishness (and the confusion and resentment that have resulted) has meant that "a fully unified British culture [has] never appeared."[11] Anger at English hegemony (political and cultural) within the British scheme has led to much anti-English feeling, not only in Ireland but also in Scotland, Wales, and even Cornwall; this has contributed to the move towards British devolution in recent decades.[12]

It is certainly true that, when Irish Protestants have performed Britishness in their daily lives, it has occasionally collapsed into an "ersatz... Englishness," due mainly to the confusion over the terms British and English.[13] By and large, however, British within an Irish Anglican or Ulster Scots context has never meant simply English. This is particularly true because of the antipathy that many Irish Protestants have traditionally felt towards the English (I am referring, of course, to the "subtle... anti-Englishness" and "ambivalence as to all things English" discussed earlier in this book).[14] Such "anti-Englishness" is especially marked in the work of the Revival writers who were from Protestant backgrounds (which is, of course, most of the major writers associated with the movement)— witness their passionate longing for "de-anglicization."[15] Indeed, the ironic thing about critics excluding Shaw from the Revival for his perceived Britishness is the degree to which the entire Revival was underwritten by (and, some would argue, undermined by) the cultural Britishness of most of its key participants. Samuel Beckett was alluding to this aspect of the Revival when he famously scorned the Revivalists for being "Victorian Gael[s]," as was Patrick Kavanagh when he called the Revival "a thoroughgoing English-bred lie."[16] Thankfully, in recent decades, critics such as Vivien Mercier, Declan Kiberd, and Elaine Sisson have increasingly begun to stress the prim, Victorian, British public school flavor that seems to characterize much Revival writing and rhetoric.[17] There are few better examples of this Britishness than Sisson's observation that even the fiercely Nationalist, Christian Brothers-educated Pádraig Pearse chose to make St Enda's essentially an Irish Gaelic version of a British public school.[18] (Perhaps Pearse's English father left more of an imprint on his son than is usually credited.)

That such deference to the British way of doing things should prevail among people raised in a crown possession during the height of the British Empire should hardly be surprising, especially given where most of the Revivalists (including others who have been wrongly excluded from the movement—such as Oscar Wilde, Somerville & Ross, and James Joyce) were educated.[19] While the curriculum in all schools in Ireland prior to independence was British in orientation—as was noted in Chapter 4—most of the Revivalists (including Shaw) attended private schools and/or elite universities that were much more explicitly tied into the British imperial system and that were much more consciously fixated on instilling British Victorian values in their pupils. George Moore attended Oscott College; AE attended the Rathmines School; J. M. Synge and Douglas Hyde were alumni of Trinity College Dublin; George Birmingham went to Haileybury College and Trinity; Edith Somerville, Violet Martin Ross, and Winifred Letts were educated at Alexandra College; Oscar Wilde went to Portora Royal School and Trinity (before heading to Oxford); Shaw attended Wesley College; Edward Martyn went to Belvedere College; and James Joyce was educated at Clongowes Wood and Belvedere.[20] While Martyn's and Joyce's schools may have been Catholic, their ethos was still indebted to British notions of civility and gentlemanly behavior/pursuits. For example, Joyce's alma maters made the pointed decision to focus on (supposedly) genteel sports such as rugby and cricket instead of more democratic games like soccer or—after the founding of the GAA—Irish sports like hurling and Gaelic football. Among the major Revival writers, the only exceptions to this British private school/elite university background—other than Pearse (discussed earlier)—were Yeats, Gregory, James Stephens, and O'Casey. Each of them, however, had what could be seen as upbringings heavily influenced by Britishness.

Despite Yeats's concealment of the fact in his autobiographical writings, much of his education was conducted in London and was therefore extremely British. Lady Gregory was educated at home by "English...governesses" and was even tutored in the Irish language by an Englishwoman, Norma Bothwick.[21] Stephens attended the Meath Protestant Industrial School, founded by Lord Meath, which David H. Hume has shown was very Empire-oriented in its culture and curriculum.[22] Finally, O'Casey, while poorly educated, was from a Church of Ireland background, raised by a mother of Irish Anglican stock. Thus, even his upbringing was more British than that of most children brought up in Ireland. Indeed, O'Casey's evangelical Anglican background was shared by several of the Revival writers, and, as Vivian Mercier, W. J. McCormack, and Feargal Whelan have shown, Irish Anglican evangelicalism in the late nineteenth and early twentieth centuries had much in common with Anglican evangelicalism across the Irish Sea.[23] This evangelical background explains why O'Casey's views regarding Catholic Ireland were "tinged with Orangism," as Alan Simpson and others have observed.[24]

Having established that Britishness need not be a cause for exclusion from the Revival—indeed, it is (to a great extent) a reason for *inclusion*—we can now examine the ways in which Shaw fulfils even the traditional definitions of a Revival writer.

In 1991, Declan Kiberd wondered if critics had erred in failing to recognize the degree to which Wilde and Shaw were "dynamic contributors to the national revival," because

> If Wilde and Shaw had not toppled the stage Irishman from his plinth and cleared the necessary intellectual space, it is doubtful whether Yeats and Synge could ever have set up a successful theatre in Dublin, and certain that much Irish writing would have taken a very different course.[25]

However, the "toppling of the stage Irishman" and providing the Revivalists with an inspiring example of an Irish intellectual were not Shaw's only contributions to the Irish Literary Revival. Critics too often overlook the fact that Shaw was actually an *active* part of the Revival, through his long association with the Abbey Theatre. Many studies of the Revival discuss the Abbey's fight to stage Shaw's *The Shewing-up of Blanco Posnet* in 1909, in defiance of Dublin Castle.[26] Some also point out that *John Bull's Other Island* was originally intended for the Abbey. Most, however, ignore the numerous other ties between Shaw and the Revivalist project at the Abbey.[27]

The first such tie is the degree to which Shaw was personally close to Yeats and Lady Gregory. Not only did Shaw see Yeats regularly in London, he also stayed with Lady Gregory at Coole or her summer house, Mount Vernon, on a number of occasions. The closeness of the tie between Shaw and Gregory is proven by the settings of two of his three Irish plays. According to a letter that Shaw sent to Lady Gregory, the play *O'Flaherty, VC*, which takes place in front of an Irish Big House, is set on the "front porch" at Coole.[28] And the first act of Shaw's third Irish play—*Tragedy of an Elderly Gentleman*—is set in Burrin, Co. Clare.[29] Burrin is a village in northwest Clare that phonetically shares a name with the region in which it is located, the Burren, and it is also the village where Lady Gregory's summer house, Mount Vernon, was located—a house where Shaw and his wife occasionally stayed with the Abbey co-founder.[30] On these trips to Coole and Mount Vernon, Yeats, Gregory, and Shaw discussed the possibility of the Abbey premiering both *John Bull's Other Island* and *O'Flaherty, VC*.

The closeness of the tie between Shaw and Gregory is also proven by the fact that he incorporated helpful recommendations from her when writing *The Shewing-up of Blanco Posnet* and *Saint Joan*. Gregory, whose work Shaw greatly respected (he once compared her to Molière), famously convinced him to incorporate the "Kiltartan sneeze" into *Saint Joan*.[31] During the crucial scene in which the wind changes direction, enabling the French to attack the English, Shaw's script originally called for a pennon to start waving in a different direction. Gregory wisely suggested that he have a soldier sneeze instead, since her tenants in Kiltartan (a townland outside of Gort, which was part of the Coole estate) told her that they often sneeze when the wind shifts.[32]

While the Abbey chose not to premiere *John Bull's Other Island* in 1904, they did produce it in 1916 and revived it (along with several other Shaw plays) throughout the late teens and 1920s. In fact, the Abbey has been credited by critics with helping to firmly establish Shaw's reputation in Ireland.[33] Likewise, though *O'Flaherty, VC* was not produced by the Abbey as planned in 1915, an Abbey touring company did mount a well-received production of it in London in 1920. Thus, these two Irish plays have stronger ties to the Abbey than most critics imply. Also, Shaw's negotiations with Yeats and Gregory over them, the association in the Irish public mind between Shaw's plays and the Abbey, the numerous fund-raising lectures that Shaw gave on behalf of the Abbey between 1904 and 1921, and the fact that he turned down an offer to be the third director of the theater after Synge's passing demonstrate that he was much more deeply involved in the Abbey's Revivalist project throughout this period than is usually credited. And, although critics like to focus on Yeats's repeatedly rude remarks about Shaw, they often ignore the fact that he was happy to have people associate Shaw with his theater; a sign of this is the fact that *The Shewing-up of Blanco Posnet* was included in various, early Abbey tours, including the first tour to the United States in 1911, despite the fact that (as James Joyce asserted) it is a relatively "flimsy" piece.[34]

Some might protest that, no matter how intimate a relationship may have existed between Shaw, Yeats, and Gregory, there is little to connect the work of Shaw and Synge, other than Kiberd's suggestion that the plays of both men are—like Oscar Wilde's—"verbal opera."[35] However, Nelson O'Ceallaigh Ritschel has recently shown that Shaw and Synge responded quite sensitively to each other's work. Ritschel has persuasively argued that key aspects of Synge's *In the Shadow of the Glen* (1903) influenced Shaw's *John Bull*, which in turn influenced Synge's treatment of the new rural middle classes in *The Playboy of the Western World*

(1907). (Synge read *John Bull's Other Island* as he traveled by train to Belmullet, Co. Mayo, where the seeds for his masterpiece were first sown.) *The Playboy* was subsequently an important intertextual presence in both *The Shewing-up of Blanco Posnet* (written as Synge was dying) and *O'Flaherty, VC*.[36]

I would suggest that there are other important connections between these two great dramatists. Synge once said that great art is reached when "the dreamer is leaning out to reality or [when] the man of real life is lifted out of" reality into dreams.[37] This quote perfectly sums up the main theme of *John Bull's Other Island*—a play in which Shaw wants to see Irish dreamers become more realistic and wants cynical, Irish fact-facers to become more mystical. Finally, the "brutal[ity]" that Synge wanted to see returned to verse and drama is not dissimilar to the brutality that Shaw directed at middle-class complacency and Victorian sentiment in his socially conscious drama.[38]

Shaw's ties to the Abbey and its playwrights are not his only connection to the Irish Literary Revival; his work recalls that of many Revivalists in being inspired by both continental European culture and Irish socio-political concerns. Shaw openly declared his debts to the European artists Henrik Ibsen and Richard Wagner, writing studies on both of them, *The Quintessence of Ibsenism* (1891, rev. 1913 and 1922) and *The Perfect Wagnerite* (1898, rev. 1902, 1907, and 1922).[39] Likewise, Shaw's three greatest plays draw on continental European sources. *Saint Joan*, as we know, tells the story of the celebrated French saint; *Pygmalion* is based on the Classical myth of Galatea and Pygmalion; and *Man and Superman* was inspired by the various legends surrounding Don Juan, including Mozart's retelling of the libertine's adventures in the opera, *Don Giovanni* (1787).[40] *Saint Joan* is, naturally, set in France, and Acts III and IV of *Man and Superman* are set in Spain; however, these are only two of many Shaw plays set (in whole or in part) on the Continent which cover topics of Europe-wide relevance. The others include *Widowers' Houses* (1892), *Arms and the Man* (1894), *The Man of Destiny* (1897), *Androcles and the Lion*

(1912), *Great Catherine* (1914), *Annajanska, the Bolshevik Empress* (1918), *The Glimpse of Reality* (1926), *The Six of Calais* (1934), and *Geneva* (1938).

As regards Irish concerns, Shaw was similar to Yeats and O'Casey in using drama to comment on important events from Irish history and contemporary Anglo-Irish relations. Just as Yeats drew on Irish myth and key moments in Nationalist history in *Cathleen ni Houlihan* (1902) (co-written with Gregory) and *The Dreaming of the Bones* (1919), and just as O'Casey commented on the major events which occurred in Dublin between 1914 and 1923 in his first four plays, Shaw addressed important Irish watersheds in his drama. As I contended earlier in this book (supported by the work of Kiberd, Moran, McNamara, and Gahan), *Tragedy of an Elderly Gentleman* and *Saint Joan* are Shaw's somewhat veiled comments on Anglo-Irish relations during the tumultuous period of 1916–23, and Shaw deals explicitly with the Land Purchase Acts of 1885 and 1903 in *John Bull's Other Island*, and Irish involvement in the Great War in *O'Flaherty, VC*. As I also noted earlier, Shaw alludes to Irish mythology in the 1898 comedy *You Never Can Tell* by naming an Irish Diasporic character after Fergus mac Róich from the Ulster Cycle. Similarly, as Peter Gahan contends, *Tragedy of an Elderly Gentleman*'s account of a man deteriorating and dying rapidly upon exposure to Ireland and its inhabitants recalls the near-instant aging and death of Oisín upon his return to Ireland from Tír na nÓg in the Fenian Cycle.[41]

Ultimately, the biggest connection between Shaw's work and that of the acknowledged Revivalists is his second phase tendency to insist that the Irish are not only equal to, but in many ways superior to, their English colonial masters. As this book has demonstrated, Shaw was as aware and proud of his Irish national identity as any member of the Revival; he also knew that his Irish background left an indelible imprint on his work. From the outset of his career to the end of his long life, he always emphasized that "being an Irishman, I do not always see things exactly as an

Englishman would."[42] Between his enduringly Irish outlook and the true greatness of his best work, Shaw deserves to be regarded as a vitally important figure—a giant—at the very heart of the Irish literary canon.

Notes

Introduction

1. Michael Holroyd. *Bernard Shaw Volume 1 (1856–1898): The Search for Love.* London: Penguin, 1988. 27.
2. Bernard Shaw. "Shaw Speaks to His Native City (1946)." In *The Matter with Ireland.* Ed. Dan H. Laurence and David H. Greene. 2nd ed. Gainesville: University Press of Florida, 2001. 334–8. 334. During the course of this book, I cite several pieces from this selection of Shaw's Irish writings. However, this is the only time that I will cite *The Matter with Ireland*'s full bibliographical details in the endnotes. Henceforth, the first time that I cite essays, articles, or letters from this volume in each chapter, I will indicate that they are from *The Matter with Ireland* and provide their complete page numbers; the rest of the bibliographical information for these pieces can—of course—be found in the Bibliography.
3. Shaw, "Shaw Speaks to His Native City," 334.
4. Bernard Shaw. "Ireland Eternal and External (1948)." In *The Matter with Ireland.* 339–41. 339.
5. In this study, the dates used for each play refer to either the first publication or the first production, whichever came first. (Shaw sometimes published his plays in book form or in periodicals before he was able to get them produced, especially early in his career.)
6. R. F. Dietrich. "Foreward." In *Shaw, Synge, Connolly, and Socialist Provocation.* By Nelson O'Ceallaigh Ritschel. Gainesville: University Press of Florida, 2011. xi–xiii. xi. Emphasis in original.
7. Of course, while the action in *Man and Superman* starts in England, the later acts are set in Spain and Hell.
8. Critics and commentators during Shaw's own lifetime and in the decades since have often referred to his habit of compulsively contradicting popular notions and overturning conventional stereotypes as "mere"or "typical" "Shavian perversity." See, for example, Frank Wadleigh Chandler. *Aspects of Modern Drama.* London: Macmillan, 1914. 310; William Irvine. *The Universe of G.B.S.* New York: Russell, 1968. 283; Allardyce Nicoll. *English Drama, 1900–1930: The Beginnings of the Modern Period.* Cambridge: Cambridge University Press, 1973. 355; Nicholas Grene. *Bernard Shaw: A Critical View.* London: Macmillan, 1987. 30, 111; Nicholas Grene. "Introduction." In *Pygmalion.* By Bernard Shaw. London: Penguin, 2003. xvii.
9. Bernard Shaw. "The Irish Players (1911)." In *The Matter with Ireland.* 71–77. 77.
10. Bernard Shaw. *John Bull's Other Island.* London: Penguin, 1984. 78.

11. Shaw, "Ireland Eternal and External," 340. I am not using the more general term Irish Protestant for this very specific subculture, because it is too vague—that is, it is not forensic enough. It is true that, in Ireland, the word Protestant was originally used exclusively for members of the established (Anglican) Church of Ireland, but, over the past two centuries, it has come to refer to people from any reformed Christian sect. Anyone who has read the rude remarks made by Jonathan Swift, Lady Morgan (née Sydney Owenson), and Shaw regarding Ulster Scots Presbyterians will be aware that there are deep cultural distinctions between the various Protestant subcultures in Ireland. That said, in this book, I do occasionally use the term Irish Protestant when making observations that apply to people from all of the reformed denominations.

   In the name of precision, I must further qualify my use of the word Anglican. The Church of Ireland has traditionally emphasized that, while it is part of the Anglican Communion, it is an Irish church with origins that are distinct from those of the Church of England. Although the Church of Ireland's break with Rome was intimately tied to the English king Henry VIII's, the Church of Ireland drafted and adopted its own 104 Articles 19 years before adopting the Church of England's 39 Articles, and the English church's 39 Articles did not take precedence until 1660. Likewise, the Church of Ireland and the Church of England did not technically unite until the Act of Union in 1800; even then, they remained (and remain) independent churches.

   While these facts might have dissuaded me from using the term Anglican in times past, I am quite happy using the term now, since, in recent years, the Church of Ireland has increasingly stressed its affiliation with the Anglican Communion. For example, its official website is www.ireland.anglican.org, and some of its churches—including the iconic Peppercanister Church (St Stephen's) in Dublin—have even removed the words Church of Ireland from their signs, replacing them with "(Anglican)" or "Anglican Church." This change in emphasis may be ascribable to the fact that the Anglican Communion has a reputation for being more liberal regarding gender equality, homosexuality, and divorce than most Christian churches; the Church of Ireland might be hoping to attract those whose beliefs or life circumstances have alienated them from the other Irish churches.

   I should also make clear here that, in this book, I use the terms Protestant, Catholic, Anglican, Presbyterian, and so on to signal cultural affiliations, not to imply doctrinaire religious belief among all members of these communities.

12. Bernard Shaw. "Eamon De Valera and the Second World War (1940–1944)." In *The Matter with Ireland*. 319–26. 324.

13. Audrey McNamara. "Bernard Shaw's *Saint Joan*: An Irish Female Patriot." ACIS Conference. University College Dublin. June 11, 2014. Conference Paper.

14. See Leonard W. Conolly. "Introduction." In *Pygmalion*. By Bernard Shaw. London: Methuen/New Mermaids, 2008. xxv, xlix–l; A. M. Gibbs. *Bernard Shaw: A Life*. Gainesville: University Press of Florida, 2005. 331, 333; Arnold Silver. *Bernard Shaw: The Darker Side*. Stanford, CA: Stanford University Press, 1982. 180; Diderik Roll-Hansen. "Shaw's *Pygmalion*: The Two Versions of 1916 and 1941." *Review of English Studies* 8.3 (July 1967): 81–90; St John Irvine. *Bernard Shaw: His Life, Work and Friends*. London: Constable, 1956. 460.

As regards *Mrs Warren's Profession* and *Misalliance*, Nicholas Grene has previously discussed some of the dramaturgical issues in these works. (Grene, *Bernard Shaw: A Critical View*, 20–25, 101.) I would add some additional points to his astute observations. At the end of Act II in *Mrs Warren's Profession*, Shaw intends that we feel uneasy about the reconciliation reached between Vivie Warren and her mother; we are meant to sense that this is a peace predicated on misunderstanding. Specifically, he wants us to spot that Mrs Warren only discusses the brothel she used to run with her sister in Brussels, and we are therefore meant to assume that the previously shrewd Vivie has naïvely concluded that her mother is no longer a brothel keeper (despite the fact that Mrs Warren still works on the continent and will not tell Vivie exactly what she does). Needless to add, given Vivie's intelligence, such an assumption is not automatic for audience members.

Shaw's other subtle indication that all is not well at the end of Act II is the final line of the stage directions, in which he writes that Mrs Warren "embraces her daughter protectingly, instinctively looking upward for divine sanction." (Bernard Shaw. *Mrs Warren's Profession*. In *Plays Unpleasant*. London: Penguin, 2000. 179–286. 252.) In every performance I have seen of this play—including high-profile productions at the Abbey's Peacock Theatre in 2000 and the Gate Theatre in 2013—this non-verbal unease has proven impossible to communicate. As a result, audience members who believe that Vivie reconciled with her mother while in full possession of the facts—and who have failed to spot Mrs Warren's mimed supplication—find it confusing when it is later revealed that Vivie assumed that her mother was no longer involved in the so-called White Slave Trade; for such audience members, it feels like a fresh complication plucked out of the air. Shaw should have indicated more clearly in the dialogue towards the end of Act II that Mrs Warren was withholding information and that Vivie (despite her smarts and independence of mind) is credulous enough to reach such an erroneous conclusion.

In *Misalliance*, the acrobat Lina Szczepanowska's shocking entrance and her extraordinary claim that, every day for the past 150 years, a member of her family has deliberately risked their lives as a point of honor stun audiences who thought they were witnessing a relatively straightforward, naturalistic comedy of ideas. While this scene (and others like it) inspired an admiring Bertolt Brecht to call Shaw a theatrical "terrorist," productions of *Misalliance* are usually bent out of shape by this sudden intrusion of expressionism and, in my experience, seldom recover. (Bertolt Brecht. "Ovation for Shaw." In *G.B. Shaw: A Collection of Critical Essays*. Ed. R. J. Kaufmann. Englewood Cliffs, NJ: Prentice Hall, 1965. 15–18. 15. This essay was originally written in 1926.)

15. Three strong Shaw plays that are not analyzed in this study (because of their lack of obvious Irish content) are *Widowers' Houses* (1892), *Arms and the Man* (1894), and *Village Wooing* (1933). However, Nelson O'Ceallaigh Ritschel, Declan Kiberd, and Michael Holroyd have found evidence of the Irish Shaw even in these. For *Widowers' Houses*, see Nelson O'Ceallaigh Ritschel. *Shaw, Synge, Connolly, and Socialist Provocation*. Gainesville: University Press of Florida, 2011. 9–17. For *Arms and the Man*, see Declan Kiberd. *Irish Classics*. London: Granta, 2000. 340–59. For *Village Wooing*, see the comparison of the Irishman Shaw with the character of A in Michael Holroyd. *Bernard Shaw Volume 3 (1919–1950): The Lure of Fantasy*. New York: Vintage, 1991. 331–3.

It should be admitted that some of the plays analyzed and promoted in this study arguably have—like the interesting but flawed plays slighted above—dramaturgical issues: I am thinking specifically of *Major Barbara*, *The Doctor's Dilemma*, and *Heartbreak House*. These plays are, however, still fascinating, and, like most Shaw plays, are more compelling in performance than one would ever guess from just reading the scripts. (For sensitive discussions of the dramaturgical issues in these plays, see Grene, *Bernard Shaw: A Critical View*, 52, 78, 84–100, 114–31.)

1   Shaw and the Rise of Reverse Snobbery

1. Denis Johnston. "Giants in Those Days." In *Orders and Desecrations*. Ed. Rory Johnston. Dublin: Lilliput, 1992. 175–201. 177.
2. Michael Roper. *Masculinity and the British Organisation Man since 1945*. Oxford: Oxford University Press, 1994. 56.
3. Antony Miall and David Milsted. *The Xenophobe's Guide to the English*. London: Oval, 1999. 19–20.
4. John Belcham. *Irish, Catholic and Scouse: The History of the Liverpool Irish, 1800–1939*. Liverpool: Liverpool University Press, 2007. 323.
5. Daniel Nelson and Laura Neack. *Global Society in Transition: An International Politics Reader*. New York: Kluwer, 2002. 176.
6. Harold M. Hodges. *Social Stratification: Class in America*. New York: Schenkman, 1964. 122.
7. Ihab Hassan. "POSTmodernISM." *New Literary History* 3.1 (Fall 1971): 5–30. 25; Terry Eagleton. *The Illusions of Postmodernism*. Oxford: Wiley-Blackwell, 1996. 113–18.
8. John R. Reed. *Old School Ties: The Public School in British Literature*. Syracuse, NY: Syracuse University Press, 1964. 116. See also Lynda Mugglestone.

Talking Proper: The Rise of Accent as Social Symbol. Oxford: Oxford University Press, 2007; Ulrike Altendorf. *Estuary English: Levelling at the Interface of RP and South-Eastern Britain*. Tubingen: Gunter Narr Verlag, 2003.

9. James L. White and James H. Cones. *Black Man Emerging: Facing the Past and Seizing a Future in America*. New York: Routledge, 1999. 108.
10. R. F. Foster. *The Oxford Illustrated History of Ireland*. Oxford: Oxford University Press, 2001. 316.
11. Colin Graham. *Deconstructing Ireland: Identity, Theory, Culture*. Edinburgh: Edinburgh University Press, 2001. 165.
12. Bernard Shaw. *Man and Superman*. London: Penguin, 2004. 181; 184; 185.
13. Bernard Shaw. *John Bull's Other Island*. London: Penguin, 1984. 14.
14. Shaw, *John Bull's Other Island*, 83.
15. Shaw, *John Bull's Other Island*, 139.
16. Shaw, *John Bull's Other Island*, 9.
17. Shaw, *John Bull's Other Island*, 10; 83; 86; 158.
18. As quoted in Michael Holroyd. *Bernard Shaw Volume 2 (1898–1918): The Pursuit of Power*. New York: Vintage, 1991. 81. This quote comes from the "Author's Instructions to the Producer." It should be noted that Shaw spelled certain words in his own idiosyncratic way: for example, he always spelled show as "shew," as is evident from this quote and from the title of his 1909 play, *The Shewing-up of Blanco Posnet*.
19. Bernard Shaw. *Getting Married/Press Cuttings*. London: Penguin, 1986. 265.
20. Shaw, *Press Cuttings*, 266.
21. Shaw, *Press Cuttings*, 269.
22. Shaw, *Press Cuttings*, 261.
23. Shaw, *Press Cuttings*, 238.
24. Shaw, *Press Cuttings*, 240, 258.
25. Bernard Shaw. *The Shewing-up of Blanco Posnet/Fanny's First Play*. London: Penguin, 1987. 131.
26. Bernard Shaw. *Back to Methuselah*. London: Penguin, 1990. 206.
27. Bernard Shaw. *O'Flaherty, V.C.* In *Selected Short Plays*. New York: Penguin, 1987. 253–77. 270.
28. Shaw, *O'Flaherty, VC*, 270.
29. It should be noted that there are arguably other Shaw plays with Irish characters. Nurse Guinness from *Heartbreak House* (1919) is sometimes played as Irish, including in a recent (2014) production at the Abbey Theatre. This is presumably because her surname invokes the name of the famous Irish stout. However, the surname Guinness can actually be of either Irish or Scottish origin, and Shaw gives various indications in the text that we should view this character as Scottish—most notably, her syntax and her use of Stage Scottishisms such as "ducky." (Bernard Shaw. *Heartbreak House*. London: Penguin, 1976. 51, 52, 53, 54, 57, 98, 100.) (Although ducky is also used in the north of England, it is originally Scottish and

derives from the Scots word *tokie*, "a fondling term for a child.") (See John Jamieson, John Johnstone, and John Longmuir. *Jamieson's Dictionary of the Scottish Language*. Edinburgh: Nimmo, 1867. 568; A. S. Palmer. *Folk-Etymology*. New York: Haskell, 1969. 105.) If Nurse Guinness were to be played as Irish, her Bible-infused speech (for example, "he has no place to lay his head this night") and her Scottishisms suggest that she should ideally be played as Ulster Scots. (Shaw, *Heartbreak House*, 157.)

Shamrock from the Fifth Fable of *Farfetched Fables* (1950) is effectively an Irish character—just as Rose is English and Thistle is Scottish. However, Shamrock's part is not large enough to inspire fruitful, detailed analysis.

30. For more on the history of anti-Irish racism in the English media, see Liz Curtis. *Nothing But the Same Old Story: The Roots of Anti-Irish Racism*. Belfast: Sásta, 1996.

31. Bernard Shaw. *Widowers' Houses*. In *Plays Unpleasant*. London: Penguin, 2000. 29–96. 86.

32. Shaw, *Man and Superman*, 88.

33. Shaw, *Man and Superman*, 218.

34. W. J. McCormack and Kim Walker. "Introduction." In *The Absentee*. By Maria Edgeworth. Oxford: Oxford University Press, 1988. xx.

35. Helen Gilbert and Joanne Tompkins. *Post-colonial Drama: Theory, Practice, Politics*. London: Routledge, 1996. 2.

36. Brian Friel. *Translations*. In *Plays 1: Philadelphia, Here I Come!/The Freedom of the City/Living Quarters/Aristocrats/Faith Healer/Translations*. London: Faber, 1996. 377–451. 417; 399.

37. Declan Kiberd. "From Nationalism to Liberation." In *The Irish Writer and the World*. Cambridge: Cambridge University Press, 2005. 146–57. See also Frantz Fanon. *The Wretched of the Earth*. Harmondsworth: Penguin, 1970. 166–99. Despite the fact that my engagement with postcolonial theory in this book is built mainly around the three (now rather shopworn) postcolonial phases, readers will note that my use of Fanon and Kiberd is augmented by ideas from critics involved in Subaltern Studies, such as Homi Bhabha and Gayatri Spivak, and those who have sought to complicate the application of postcolonial theory to Ireland, such as Colin Graham and David Lloyd. This is because Ireland is in an "anomalous" position vis-à-vis colonialism; while the country was historically treated as a colony by the English, it was also, through the Act of Union, at the very center of the British Empire, conspiring (through military service and jobs in the colonies) in the subjugation of other colonies. My embracing of this tension will be especially evident in the Conclusion, in which I discuss the conscious and unconscious Britishness of Shaw and other Revival-era Irish writers. (David Lloyd. *Anomalous States: Irish Writing and the Post-Colonial Moment*. Durham, NC: Duke University Press, 1993.)

38. Kiberd, "From Nationalism to Liberation," 151.

39. Declan Kiberd. *Inventing Ireland: The Literature of the Modern Nation*. London: Vintage, 1995. 61; Kiberd, "From Nationalism to Liberation," 151.

40. As Fintan O'Toole points out in his biography of Sheridan, the playwright and politician usually referred to himself as Irish, not English. However, when under suspicion of treasonous sympathies in the wake of the 1798 Rebellion, he referred to himself as "an Englishman" in a parliamentary speech to allay the fears of his colleagues and the public. (Fintan O'Toole. *A Traitor's Kiss: A Life of Richard Brinsley Sheridan.* New York: Farrar, Strauss and Giroux, 1998. 331.) With regards to Edgeworth, a childhood split between England and Ireland meant that she was able to sometimes present herself as an Irishwoman and sometimes, to convince English readers of her impartiality in championing Ireland, to depict herself as one "neither born nor bred in Ireland," despite having spent 6 of her first 18 years there. However, it should also be noted that, in her private letters, Edgeworth refers to "the English" as though she herself is not English. (Maria Edgeworth. *An Essay on Irish Bulls.* Dublin: University College Dublin Press, 2006. 122; Maria Edgeworth. *Chosen Letters.* Ed. F. V. Barry. London: Cape, 1931. 48, 109, 277, 339, 344, 448.)

    By contrast with Sheridan and Edgeworth, Shaw once wrote: "I never think of an Englishman as my countryman. I should as soon apply that term to a German." (Shaw, *John Bull's Other Island*, 11.)

41. Robert Tracy. *The Unappeasable Host: Studies in Irish Identities.* Dublin: UCD Press, 1998. 31. See also Robert Tracy. "Maria Edgeworth and Lady Morgan: Legality versus Legitimacy." *Nineteenth-Century Fiction* 40 (June 1985): 1–22. Glorvina is the Irish heroine in Morgan's novel *The Wild Irish Girl* (1806). She marries the Englishman Horatio, the son of an earl, at the end of the book. It should be noted here that Tracy also applies the term "the Glorvina solution" to situations in which the gentleman who marries the colleen is "Anglo-Irish" (that is to say, a native Irish member of the Protestant Ascendancy).

42. W. B. Yeats compared Shaw's "Irish mind" to that of an Irish "country rapscallion" in W. B. Yeats. *The Letters of W.B. Yeats.* Ed. Allan Wade. London: Hart-Davis, 1954. 35.

43. What was groundbreaking was Shaw's application of such an inclusive theory to Ireland, where warring religious and political allegiances made the definition of an Irish person contentious. As Joep Leersson has pointed out, since the late eighteenth century commentators from other countries—including William Temple, the abbé Du Bos, Cheyne, and Montesqieu—were happy to propose or endorse such a "climatological" theory of nationality, but among Irish commentators, only Goldsmith had hinted at such a view. For more on the early history of the climatological theory, see Joep Leerssen. *Mere Irish and Fíor-Gael: Studies in the Idea of Irish Nationality, Its Development and Literary Expression prior to the Nineteenth Century.* Cork: Cork University Press, 1996. 26–29.

44. Shaw, *John Bull's Other Island*, 11.

45. Like Shaw, sociologist Elizabeth Throop believes that "begrudgery" is rife in Irish society; she defines "begrudgery" as the society-wide tendency to

"feel envy at another's good fortune" and to "flatten social differences" through the use of (often humorous) mockery and insult, thus "ensuring everyone's equality." (Elizabeth A. Throop. *Net Curtains and Closed Doors: Intimacy, Family, and Public Life in Dublin.* Westport, CT: Greenwood, 1999. 53.)

46. Shaw, *O'Flaherty, VC,* 256.
47. A. M. Gibbs. *The Art and Mind of Shaw: Essays in Criticism.* London: Macmillan, 1983. 39.
48. It should be noted here that Peter Gahan has shown that Shaw chose the first name of Fanny for the title character of *Fanny's First Play*, because of the similarity between Fanny O'Dowda's life and Fanny Burney's. (Both women attempted to hide their early literary efforts from their fathers.) (See Peter Gahan. *Shaw Shadows: Rereading the Texts of Bernard Shaw.* Gainesville: University Press of Florida, 2004. 167–8.)

2   Shaw and the Irish Diaspora

1. The name is also clearly a private tribute to Shaw's longtime gardener at his home in Ayot St Lawrence, Hertfordshire—an Englishman called Henry Higgs.
2. Edward MacLysaght. *The Surnames of Ireland.* Dublin: Irish Academic Press, 1985. 157. According to the National Genealogical Office, in 1996, Higgins was the 79th most common surname in Ireland. (See "Surname History: Higgins." *Irish Times.com.* n.d. Web. 26 December 2012.) Although Higgins is a very common surname in both Ireland and the Irish Diaspora (including among those who settled in Britain), it should be noted that, in England, it is occasionally—though much more rarely—a diminutive of the names Higg or Hick. (See P.H. Reaney and E.M. Wilson, *A Dictionary of English Surnames.* London: Routledge, 1991. 1606.)
3. Bernard Shaw. "The Irish Players (1911)." In *The Matter with Ireland.* 71–77. 72.
4. Daniel J. Leary's observation about the character names in Shaw's *Heartbreak House* (1919) could easily be applied to most Shaw plays: "the unusual names surely evoke symbolic undertones." (Daniel J. Leary. "Entry for *Heartbreak House*." In *The Reader's Encyclopedia of World Drama.* Ed. John Gassner and Edward Quinn. New York: Dover, 2002. 414.)
5. On Shaw's reputation as someone who was dismissive of the Diasporic Irish, see Micheál Ó hAodha. "Some Irish American Theatre Links." In *America and Ireland, 1776–1976: The American Identity and the Irish Connection.* Ed. Con Howard, David Noel Doyle, and Owen Dudley Edwards. Westport, CT: Greenwood, 1980. 295–306. 300; Matthew Pratt Guteri. *The Color of Race in America: 1900–1940.* Cambridge, MA: Harvard UP, 2002. 79; John H. Houchin. *Censorship of the American Theatre in the Twentieth Century.* Cambridge: Cambridge UP, 2003. 59–60; James Moran. "Meditations in Time of Civil War: *Back to Methuselah* and *Saint Joan* in

Production, 1919–1924." *SHAW: The Annual of Bernard Shaw Studies* 30 (2010): 147–60. 150–1.

6. Bernard Shaw. *John Bull's Other Island*. London: Penguin, 1984. 113; 14.
7. Bernard Shaw. *Man and Superman*. London: Penguin, 2004. 180.
8. Maria Edgeworth. *Castle Rackrent/Ennui*. London: Penguin, 1992. 224.
9. Violet Powell. *The Irish Cousins: The Books and Background of Somerville and Ross*. London: Heinemann, 1970. 148; E.Œ. Somerville & Martin Ross. *The Irish R.M.* London: Abacus, 2005. 431.

   I should point out that, although Major Yeates is sometimes described as an Englishman by critics and was depicted as one in the celebrated UTV/RTÉ One/Channel Four television series based on the stories, he is, in fact, an Irish Anglican. Indeed, he repeatedly expresses pride in his Irish blood and nationality. (Somerville & Ross, *The Irish RM*, 8, 21, 91, 273, 336, 585.)

10. James Joyce. *A Portrait of the Artist as a Young Man*. Ware: Wordsworth, 1992. 145.
11. Shaw, *John Bull's Other Island*, 9. Shaw reiterated the view that the Irish speak the English language better than the English do on a number of occasions. See Bernard Shaw. "The Gaelic League (1910)." In *The Matter with Ireland*. 63–65. 64; Bernard Shaw. "A Note on Aggressive Nationalism (1913)." In *The Matter with Ireland*. 91–94. 93; Bernard Shaw. "Why Devolution Will Not Do (1919–20)." In *The Matter with Ireland*. 213–26. 219; Bernard Shaw. "On Throwing Out Dirty Water (1923)." In *The Matter with Ireland*. 285–9. 287; Bernard Shaw. "The Greatest Living Irishman? (1941)." In *The Matter with Ireland*. 327–8. 328; Bernard Shaw. "A Film Industry for Ireland (1945–47)." In *The Matter with Ireland*. 331–3. 332.
12. Bernard Shaw. *Pygmalion*. New York: Dover, 1994. xii. The Dover edition reprints the original 1916 text of the play. As noted in the Introduction to this book, many important Shaw critics, including Leonard Conolly, A.M. Gibbs, Arnold Silver, Diderik Roll-Hansen, and St John Irvine, have argued that this original version is superior to the later 1939 Constable and 1941 Penguin versions, which were altered to their aesthetic detriment by Shaw himself. I should point out, however, that the portions of the play I am examining in this chapter are not from the radically altered sections of the text.
13. Leonard Conolly. "Introduction." In *Pygmalion*. By Bernard Shaw. London: Methuen/New Mermaids, 2008. xx.
14. Shaw was fond of pointing out that, according to geneticists, the people of Ireland, Scotland, Wales, Cornwall, and the Isle of Man are not racially Celtic. (See, for example, Bernard Shaw. "The New Nation (1917)." In *The Matter with Ireland*. 174–5.) Actually, this is not completely true: according to recent studies, there is some indication of Celtic migration into Iron Age Britain and Ireland. However, Shaw was right to question the racial construction of a common Celtic identity across Ireland and Britain, given that the relatively small number of Celts who arrived made little

impact on Irish and British gene pools. That said, the Celts did make a significant cultural impact: Irish and Scottish Gaelic, Welsh, Cornish, and Manx are all Celtic languages derived from Common Celtic. Therefore, when I occasionally refer to Celts in this book, I am alluding to a common ethnic tie based on linguistics and culture, not perpetuating Arnoldian myths from Irish and British discourse regarding the Celtic race.

15. Conrad Brunström. *Thomas Sheridan's Career and Influence: An Actor in Earnest*. Lewisburg, PA: Bucknell University Press, 2011. 86, 94.
16. The remark was made by the English parliamentarian, Nathaniel Wraxall. As quoted in Fintan O'Toole. *A Traitor's Kiss: A Life of Richard Brinsley Sheridan*. New York: Farrar, Strauss and Giroux, 1998. 206.
17. Tina O'Toole. *The Irish New Woman*. Houndmills: Palgrave Macmillan, 2013. 27.
18. See, for example, "George Bernard Shaw's First Visit to America" (1928 Fox Movietone newsreel). *YouTube.com*. December 25, 2008. Web. December 11, 2012; "George Bernard Shaw Says to Abolish the Constitution" (1931 Fox Movietone newsreel). *YouTube.com*. January 7, 2010. Web. December 11, 2012.
19. See, for example, "George Bernard Shaw Giving a Speech at a Dinner in Honor of Albert Einstein." *YouTube.com*. December 10, 2010. Web. December 11, 2012.
20. It is also possible that Henry's Irish ancestry may be exclusively on his father's side, and his brother may be a Protestant clergyman because of family roots other than those provided by the Higgins branch of the family.
21. Recently, Fintan O'Toole provocatively suggested that "the confirmed bachelor" Higgins is probably a closeted homosexual, given his interest in "dressing Eliza" and his private collection of Japanese kimonos. (Fintan O'Toole. "Shaw Was an Anarchist: Where is all the Chaos?" *Irish Times* May 14, 2011. B9.)
22. See, for example, Diarmaid Ferriter. *Occasions of Sin: Sex and Society in Modern Ireland*. London: Profile, 2009. 103; C.S. Lewis, as quoted in Peter Milward. "What Lewis Has Meant for Me." In *C.S. Lewis Remembered: Collected Reflections of Students, Friends and Colleagues*. Ed. Harry Lee Poe and Rebecca Whitten Poe. Grand Rapids, MI: Zondervan, 2006. E-book/n. pag.
23. As it concerns Higgins's possible Irishness, it should be noted that, while Irish males in England married significantly later than their English counterparts in 1851, reflecting "a general postponement of marriage by migrants during the famine years," over the ensuing decades, the "demographic behaviour" of the Irish in England "slowly became like that of the host population." (Lynn Hillen Lees. *Exiles of Erin: Irish Migrants in Victorian London*. Manchester: Manchester University Press, 1979. 153; 138, 138.)
24. Shaw, *Pygmalion*, 6, 79; 49.

25. Shaw, *Pygmalion*, 49.
26. In both plays, the pejorative adjective "low" is used to describe rough or vulgar people, manners, and actions. (Shaw, *Pygmalion*, 16, 70; Bernard Shaw. *The Shewing-up of Blanco Posnet/Fanny's First Play*. London: Penguin, 1987. 127, 155.)
27. Shaw, *Pygmalion*, 66.
28. For an important article on the notion of "passing" in *Pygmalion*, see Kimberly Bohman-Kalaja. "Undoing Identities in Two Irish Shaw Plays: *John Bull's Other Island* and *Pygmalion*." *SHAW: The Annual of Bernard Shaw Studies* 30 (2010): 108–32. Bohman-Kalaja argues that *Pygmalion* is an Irish play, but she regards Eliza and not Higgins as the character who is "Irish-by-association." (Bohman-Kalaja, "Undoing Identities in Two Irish Shaw Plays," 120.) Eliza's possible Irishness will be discussed later in this chapter.
29. Shaw, *Pygmalion*, 39.
30. Maria Edgeworth. *Ormond*. Dublin: Gill and Macmillan, 1990. 5.
31. Shaw, *Pygmalion*, 35.
32. Elizabeth Bowen. *The Last September*. Harmondsworth: Penguin, 1987. 134.
33. In contrast to Mrs Higgins, the mothers of Shaw, Wilde, and Yeats remained stubbornly Irish after moving to London. Of course, Lucinda Shaw and Lady Jane Wilde had much bigger personalities than Susan Yeats did.
34. For Afro-Caribbean and Asian youths in Britain rejecting "artificial" English manners and "proper" speech in favor of cultural distinctiveness (as the children of Jewish and Irish families did in earlier decades), see Errol Lawrence. "In the Abundance of Water the Fool is Thirsty: Sociology and Black 'Pathology.'" In *The Empire Strikes Back: Race and Racism in 70s Britain*. Ed. The Centre for Cultural Studies at the University of Birmingham. Oxford: Taylor & Francis, 2005. 93–139. (See especially p. 108–9, 120–9.) It should be noted that Lawrence sums up the research regarding this phenomenon without always agreeing with it.
35. For the Irish use of alliteration when insulting others, especially in the work of Swift and Synge, see Declan Kiberd. *Inventing Ireland: The Literature of the Modern Nation*. London: Vintage, 1995. 187.
36. For more on the relative informality of Irish manners (compared to the manners of other European countries), see Éilis Ní Dhuibhne. "The Irish." In *Europeans: Essays on Cultural Identity*. Ed. Åke Daun and Sören Jansson. Lund: Nordic Academic Press, 1999. 47–65.
37. Virginia Woolf. *The Diary of Virginia Woolf, Volume 4*. Ed. Anne Olivier Bell, with Andrew McNellie. New York: Harcourt, 1982. 210.
38. Shaw, *Pygmalion*, 8.
39. Shaw, *Pygmalion*, 70.
40. Shaw, *Pygmalion*, 39.
41. Shaw, *Pygmalion*, 24, 25, 28.
42. Shaw, *Pygmalion*, 8.

43. See, for example, Brendan Behan. *The Big House*. In *The Complete Plays*. New York: Grove, 1978. 359–384. 361; Brian Friel. *The Home Place*. London: Faber, 2005. 16.

44. Conolly, Introduction, *Pygmalion*, xxi.

45. Shaw, *Pygmalion*, 20.

46. Shaw, *John Bull's Other Island*, 83, 86, 158.

47. Bernard Shaw. *Collected Letters, 1911–1925*. Ed. Dan H. Laurence. New York: Viking, 1985. 111.

48. For Shaw's dismissive remarks regarding "American Gaels," see Shaw, "The Irish Players," 71, 74–7; Bernard Shaw. "Ireland and the First World War (1914)." In *The Matter with Ireland*. 101–4. 103; Bernard Shaw. "Irish Nonsense about Ireland (1916)." In *The Matter with Ireland*. 112–19. 112–13. For his negative opinions of "Clan na Gael Irishmen" from Britain, see Shaw, "The Irish Players," 72, 73–74, 76; Bernard Shaw. "The Eve of Civil War (1922)." In *The Matter with Ireland*. 273–5. 275. See also Shaw's letter quoted in Tim Pat Coogan. *Wherever Green Is Worn: The Story of the Irish Diaspora*. New York: Palgrave Macmillan, 2001. 122.

49. Shaw, "The Irish Players," 71, 74; 77.

50. Shaw, "The Irish Players," 72. The narrowly Nationalist Devoy first attracted Shaw's ire, because he was involved in organizing protests against the Abbey Theatre players during their 1911–12 American tour. He and his followers were particularly angered by the representation of the Irish in Synge's *The Playboy of the Western World* (1907)—despite the fact that many of them admitted to never having read or seen the play. Shaw, who greatly admired *The Playboy*, argued that the flaws in Synge's Irish characters were the flaws of all mankind. (Shaw, "A Note on Aggressive Nationalism," 94.) He believed that the inability of the protesters to recognize this, and their naïve belief in the heightened purity of the Irish, proved how little they knew of Irish reality. These protesters, and other Irish Diasporic people who seemed to believe in the singular nobility of the Irish, inspired many of Shaw's angriest anti-Diaspora remarks.

51. Shaw, *John Bull's Other Island*, 78.

52. Shaw, "Why Devolution Will Not Do," 219; Bernard Shaw. "Socialism and Ireland (1919)." In *The Matter with Ireland*. 233–49. 248; Bernard Shaw. "An Appeal to the IRA (1940)." In *The Matter with Ireland*. 310–18. 314; Bernard Shaw. "Eamon De Valera and the Second World War (1940–44)." In *The Matter with Ireland*. 319–26. 324; Bernard Shaw. "Ireland Eternal and External (1948)." In *The Matter with Ireland*. 339–41. 340. See also Bernard Shaw. *Dramatic Opinions and Essays with an Apology, Volume 2*. New York: Brentano's, 1906. 324.

53. See Jay R. Tunney. *The Prizefighter and the Playwright: Gene Tunney and Bernard Shaw*. Tonawanda, NJ: Firefly, 2010.

54. Bernard Shaw. *Back to Methuselah*. London: Penguin, 1990. 194.

55. Bernard Shaw. *Captain Brassbound's Conversion*. In *Three Plays for Puritans*. London: Penguin, 1970. 255–347. 319. It is possible that Kearney is

Shaw's nod to the Wexford-born John Barry (1745–1803), who is widely considered the Father of the American Navy. Special thanks to Nelson O'Ceallaigh Ritschel for suggesting this to me.

56. Shaw, *Captain Brassbound's Conversion*, 329.
57. Maria Edgeworth. *The Absentee*. Oxford: Oxford University Press, 1988. 5.
58. Shaw, *Captain Brassbound's Conversion*, 328. Kearney's American upbringing would also help to explain this preference for bluntness, as Americans were generally thought to be very straightforward.
59. The novel was written in 1882 and rejected by numerous publishers. It was then published serially in a socialist magazine, *To-Day*, between April 1885 and December 1886, and was finally published in book form together with *The Admirable Bashville* in 1901, after Shaw had established himself as a playwright.
60. Peter Gahan. "Introduction: Bernard Shaw and the Irish Literary Tradition." *SHAW: The Annual of Bernard Shaw Studies* 30 (2010): 1–26. 4.
61. In the play, we are given surnames from both sides of Byron's family tree. Other than de Courcy, which is a celebrated Irish surname of Norman origin, the surnames are all deeply English. One possible exception is FitzAlgernon, which, as Barney Rosset has half-hinted, could conceivably be Irish, given its *Fitz* prefix. (See Barney Rosset. *Shaw of Dublin: The Formative Years*. Harrisburg: Pennsylvania State University Press, 1964. 147.)
62. Bernard Shaw. *The Admirable Bashville*. In *Selected Short Plays*. Harmondsworth: Penguin, 1987. 1–41. 11; 12, 37. Just as the character of Private O'Flaherty prefers the dangers of life at the Front to living with his mother, Byron prefers prizefighting and even prison to reuniting with his mother.
63. Shaw, *The Admirable Bashville*, 23.
64. Shaw, *The Admirable Bashville*, 18.
65. Bernard Shaw. *Cashel Byron's Profession*. New York: Brentano's, 1904. 165.
66. In English discourse regarding Ireland, it was common for the Catholic tenantry to be referred to as the "mere Irish"—to differentiate them from Protestants who were loyal to the English crown and who were considered culturally hybrid. Here, I am using the word mere to similarly indicate a non-hyphenated identity. (For more on the term "mere Irish," see Joep Leerssen. *Mere Irish and Fíor-Gael: Studies in the Idea of Irish Nationality, its Development and Literary Expression prior to the Nineteenth Century*. Cork: Cork University Press, 1996.)
67. Shaw, *John Bull's Other Island*, 78. Peter Gahan has suggested that Alfred "Boss" Mangan might be based on the Dublin-born newspaper mogul, Alfred Harnsworth, later Lord Northcliffe, since they share a first name and since Harnsworth had "the same influence on the government" that Mangan claims to possess in *Heartbreak House*. (Peter Gahan. "Shaw's Irish Outlook FIRST DRAFT." Message to the author. September 24, 2014. E-mail.)
68. Bernard Shaw. *Heartbreak House*. London: Penguin, 1976. 99.

69. See Michael Holroyd. *Bernard Shaw: The One-Volume Definitive Edition.*
    London: Vintage, 1998. 2–3, 53; Daniel Dervin. *Bernard Shaw: A*
    Psychological Study. Lewisburg: Bucknell UP, 1975. 112.
70. As quoted in Hesketh Pearson. *G.B.S.: A Full Length Portrait.* New York and
    London: Harper, 1942. 49.
71. Shaw, *Heartbreak House*, 102.
72. Shaw, *Heartbreak House*, 97; Eric Patridge, Tom Dalzell, and Terry Victor.
    The Concise New Partridge Dictionary of Slang and Unconventional English.
    London: Routledge, 2008. 181. Although this use of the word cute is
    known throughout Britain and Ireland, it is most popular by far in Ireland.
    In *An Essay on Irish Bulls* (1803), Maria Edgeworth even suggests that the
    expression is of Irish origin, and, as various scholars have pointed out, it
    has remained current in Ireland in expressions like "country cute" (used
    conspicuously in James Joyce's "The Dead" (1914)) and "cute hoor" (often
    applied today to corrupt politicians). (See Maria Edgeworth. *An Essay*
    on Irish Bulls. Dublin: University College Dublin Press, 2006. 68; James
    Joyce. *Dubliners.* London: Penguin, 1956. 213; Bernard Share. *Slanguage:*
    A Dictionary of Irish Slang. Dublin: Gill & Macmillan, 1997. 139; Patridge
    et. al., *The Concise New Partridge of Dictionary of Slang and Unconventional*
    English, 181; Terence Patrick Dolan. *A Dictionary of Hiberno-English: The*
    Irish Use of English. 3rd ed. Dublin: Gill & Macmillan, 2012. 76.)
73. Shaw, *Heartbreak House*, 97.
74. Shaw, *Heartbreak House*, 144; 145. For the use of "fine talk" in Shaw's
    O'Flaherty, VC, as well as in the work of Synge and Letts, see Bernard Shaw.
    O'Flaherty, V.C. In *Selected Short Plays.* New York: Penguin Books, 1987.
    253–77. 273; J.M. Synge. *Collected Works II: Prose.* Ed. Alan Price. Oxford:
    Oxford University Press, 1966. 107; W.M. Letts. "For Sixpence." In *Songs*
    from Leinster. London: Smith, Elder & Co., 1914. 40–41. 41. Although
    Letts was born in Manchester, she was educated at Alexandra College in
    Dublin and spent most of her adult life in Ireland. Her poems frequently
    employ Hiberno-English dialect.
75. Shaw, *Heartbreak House*, 120.
76. Reaney and Wilson, *A Dictionary of English Surnames*, 996; John Grenham.
    Clans and Families of Ireland: The Heritage and Heraldry of Irish Clans and
    Families. Dublin: Gill and Macmillan, 1993. 106.
77. Shaw, *Heartbreak House*, 60, 62, 150, 152.
78. Colin Barr. Abstract for "Giuseppe Mazzini and Irish Nationalism, 1845–
    70." In *Giuseppe Mazzini and the Globalization of Democratic Nationalism,*
    1830–1920. Ed. C. A. Bayly and E. F. Biagini. Oxford: Oxford University
    Press, 2008. 402.
79. Bernard Shaw. *Major Barbara.* New York: Penguin, 1978. 75; 76; 75.
80. See a copy deed of release (AR/add/52/22) among the Shaw Family Papers in
    the Dublin City Archives, housed at the Pearse Street Library in Dublin 2.
81. Shaw, "The Irish Players," 72. The surname Dubedat is actually mentioned
    four times in James Joyce's *Ulysses*. (See Joyce, *Ulysses*, 223, 608, 686.) It is

noteworthy that Joyce's protagonist, Leopold Bloom, mentions that there are Dubedats in Killiney, since that is the next village down the coast from Shaw's childhood Dalkey.

82. Bernard Shaw. *You Never Can Tell.* In *Plays Pleasant.* Harmondsworth: Penguin, 1949. 229–348. 324.
83. Peter Gahan. "Shaw Book Series for Palgrave Macmillan." Message to the author. 18 April 2014. E-mail.
84. Gahan, "Shaw Book Series for Palgrave Macmillan."
85. Shaw, *You Never Can Tell*, 277, 329.
86. Shaw, *You Never Can Tell*, 277, 316, 329.
87. For Shaw's condemnations of corporal punishment, see, for example, the "Under the Whip" section of the preface to *Misalliance.* (Bernard Shaw. *Misalliance/The Fascinating Foundling.* Harmondsworth: Penguin, 1984. 59–61.) See also Bernard Shaw. "Child-Beating: A Bishop's Letter from Mr Bernard Shaw." *The Irish Times* February 25, 1928. 9.
88. Shaw, *John Bull's Other Island*, 23.
89. Shaw, *You Never Can Tell*, 254, 256, 277–8, 279, 285.
90. Shaw, *You Never Can Tell*, 238.
91. Shaw, *You Never Can Tell*, 120.
92. Shaw also memorably links the Irish and the Jews in his brilliant 1896 review of Dion Boucicault's *The Colleen Bawn.* (See Bernard Shaw. "Dear Harp of my Country!" In *The Portable Shaw.* Ed. Stanley Weintraub. New York: Penguin, 1986. 111–16. 114.)
93. Shaw, *You Never Can Tell*, 276, 280.
94. Edward Walford. *The County Families of the United Kingdom; or, Royal Manual of the Titled and Untitled Aristocracy of Great Britain and Ireland.* London: Hardwicke, 1869. 247; Charles Croslegh. *Descent and Alliances of Croslegh: or Crossle, or Crossley, of Scaitcliffe; and Coddington, of Oldbridge; and Evans, of Eyton Hall.* London: Moring/De La More, 1904. 11–12, 42.
95. Shaw, *You Never Can Tell*, 251.
96. Gahan notes the interesting fact that a statue erected in honor of Sir Philip Crampton at the junction of College Street with D'Olier Street and present-day Pearse Street is actually mentioned twice in James Joyce's *Ulysses.* (Gahan, "Shaw Book Series for Palgrave Macmillan"; James Joyce. *Ulysses.* London: Penguin, 2000. 114, 217.)
97. In addition to the characters highlighted in this chapter, it should be noted that it is possible to see other characters from Shaw's oeuvre as depictions of people from the Irish Diaspora who possess Shavian Irish qualities. Although I treated Dora Delaney and Count O'Dowda from *Fanny's First Play* as Irish-born above, it is conceivable that they are actually representations of Irish Diasporic people, since it is ultimately impossible to determine for certain if their knowledge of Ireland is first- or second-hand. Dora may have simply heard the name Carrickmines from an Irish parent. (Shaw, *Fanny's First Play*, 131.) And Count O'Dowda's description of his own Irish identity is somewhat distanced:

when the noble aesthete proudly protests that he is not English to a theatre critic who has come to see his daughter's play, he explains that his *"family* is Irish" and that he has lived "all... [his] life" in Italy. (Shaw, *Fanny's First Play*, 112. Emphasis mine.) These comments suggest that the Count may never have lived in Ireland at all.

Similarly, in *The Doctor's Dilemma*, we are told that Sir Patrick Cullen's name, physiognomy, manners, and cast of mind, as well as "occasional turn[s] of speech," betray his Irishness, but we are also told that he has spent "all his life" in England. Shaw is presumably indicating that Cullen left Ireland at a relatively young age, as Shaw did himself. (This would explain why we are told that Cullen has gotten "acclimatized" to England.) (Bernard Shaw. *The Doctor's Dilemma*. London: Penguin, 1987. 95.) However, it is also possible that Cullen is Shaw's depiction of a Diasporic Irish person whose character and speech remain remarkably Irish.

Finally, although I indicated above that Nurse Guinness from *Heartbreak House* is a Scottish and not an Irish Guinness, it is also possible that this servant (criticized by Lady Utterwood for the "casual impudence" of her manner) is a Scottish—or even northern English—person of Irish descent. (Shaw, *Heartbreak House*, 55.)

98. For a transcript of this November 5, 2012 interview about The Gathering 2013, as well as discussions of the public debate that ensued in its aftermath, see "Come Gather 'Round People Wherever You Roam" (Transcript of Today FM interview with Gabriel Byrne). *Broadsheet.ie*. November 5, 2012. Web. December 11, 2012. Byrne harshly criticized the shallow sentimentality and cynical materialism driving the project, saying that the organizers of the campaign "have to understand that the bridge between the Diaspora and the people of Ireland is broken...And unless you understand what it is that the Diaspora feel about Ireland and the fact that, once your people have emigrated, you don't really care where they're gone to, unless they're your kids, then emigration takes on a very, very different emotional sense for you."

99. Shaw, *John Bull's Other Island*, 9–10.

3   Shaw and Irish Anglican Preoccupations

1. For an excellent sense of these three traditions coexisting, see Andrew Carpenter, ed. *Verse in English from Eighteenth-Century Ireland*. Dublin: Four Courts, 1998.

2. Notable writers from these backgrounds include the Methodist poet Mary Tighe (1772–1810), the Methodist novelist Selina Bunbury (1802–82), the Quaker poet John Perrot (d. 1665), the Quaker fiction writer Mary Leadbeater (1758–1826), and the various Jewish poets highlighted in Louis Hyman. *The Jews of Ireland: From Earliest Times to the Year 1910*. London: Jewish Historical Society of England/Jerusalem: Israel Universities Press,

1972. Early accounts of Irish Travellers were invariably written by preju-
diced non-Travellers. (See Jane Helleiner. *Irish Travellers: Racism and the
Politics of Culture.* Toronto: University of Toronto Press, 2003.)

3. It should be noted that important Irish Anglican writers also possessed
some French Huguenot ancestry (for example, Charles Maturin, J. S. Le
Fanu, Dion Boucicault, and Samuel Beckett). As many historians have
noted, the influx of Huguenots into Ireland between the late seventeenth
and early eighteenth centuries reinvigorated the Irish Anglican community socially and (given the Huguenot work ethic, knowledge of specialist
crafts, and interest in banking) financially.

4. This is repeatedly emphasized in Colin Murphy and Lynne Adair, ed.
Untold Stories: Protestants in the Republic of Ireland, 1922–2002. Dublin:
Liffey, 2002.

5. Although James Stephens's parents were married in a Presbyterian Church,
he was raised mainly within the Church of Ireland after the early death of
his father and his entrance into the Meath Protestant Industrial School.

6. Joep Leerssen. *Mere Irish and Fíor-Gael: Studies in the Idea of Irish Nationality,
Its Development and Literary Expression prior to the Nineteenth Century.* Cork:
Cork University Press, 1996. 11.

7. Elizabeth Bowen. "Review of *The Anglo-Irish*, by Brian Fitzgerald." In *The
Mulberry Tree: Writings of Elizabeth Bowen.* Ed. Hermione Lee. London:
Virago, 1986. 174–6. 176.

8. Elizabeth Bowen. "Preface to *Uncle Silas*, by Sheridan Le Fanu." In *The
Mulberry Tree: Writings of Elizabeth Bowen.* Ed. Hermione Lee. London:
Virago, 1986. 100–13. 101.

9. See W. J. McCormack. "Irish Gothic and After." In *The Field Day Anthology
of Irish Writing, Volume II.* Ed. Seamus Deane et. al. Derry: Field Day, 1991.
832–54; R. F. Foster. "Protestant Magic: W.B. Yeats and the Spell of Irish
History." In *Paddy & Mr Punch.* London: Allen Lane, 1993. 212–32; Terry
Eagleton. *Heathcliff and the Great Hunger.* London: Verso, 1995. 187–99.

10. Although these critics use the generalized term Irish Protestant, all of the
major Protestant Gothic writers have been from Church of Ireland backgrounds: Charles Maturin, J. S. Le Fanu, Bram Stoker, Somerville & Ross,
W. B. Yeats, Lady Gregory, Elizabeth Bowen, and Samuel Beckett. Shaw
could also be added to this list, since, early in his career, he wrote a Gothic
short story set in Ireland called "The Miraculous Revenge" (1885).

11. See, for example, W. J. McCormack. *From Burke to Beckett: Ascendancy,
Tradition and Betrayal in Literary History.* Cork: Cork University Press,
1994; Clair Wills. *That Neutral Island: A Cultural History of Ireland During
the Second World War.* London: Faber, 2008. 174.

12. Declan Kiberd. *Irish Classics.* London: Granta, 2000. 107–23.

13. Elizabeth Bowen. "The Idea of France." In *People, Places, Things: Essays
by Elizabeth Bowen.* Ed. Allan Hepburn. Edinburgh: Edinburgh University
Press, 2008. 61–65. 62–63; Elizabeth Bowen. "Coming to London."
In *The Mulberry Tree: Writings of Elizabeth Bowen.* Ed. Hermione Lee.

London: Virago, 1986. 85–89. 86. Of course, in these essays (as in all her work), she refers to this subculture as the Anglo-Irish. She is one of the few Irish Anglican writers to happily use this controversial moniker. That said, as Neil Corcoran has pointed out, Bowen "specifically, and repeatedly, chose" the unhyphenated title of "'Irish' writer" (as opposed to "'Anglo-Irish' writer") for herself. (Neil Corcoran. *Elizabeth Bowen: The Enforced Return*. Oxford: Oxford University Press, 2004. 14.)

14. Elizabeth Bowen. "Portrait of a Woman Reading." In *Listening In: Broadcasts, Speeches and Interviews*. Ed. Allan Hepburn. Edinburgh: Edinburgh University Press, 2010. 235–9. 239; 238. In this passage, she is referring specifically to Richard Brinsley Sheridan.

15. Terence Brown. *Ireland's Literature*. Mullingar: Lilliput, 1988. 189; Seán Kennedy. "'The Beckett Country' Revisited: Beckett, Belonging and Longing." In *Ireland: Space, Text, Time*. Ed. Liam Harte, Yvonne Whelan and Patrick Crotty. Dublin: Liffey, 2005. 135–44; Feargal Whelan. "Samuel Beckett and the Irish Protestant Imagination." Diss. University College Dublin, 2014. Chapter 2; David Clare. "C.S. Lewis: An Irish Writer." *Irish Studies Review* 18.1 (February 2010): 17–38. 24.

16. Although these plays contain no Irish-born characters, it should be admitted that towards the end of *The Man of Destiny*, the French Strange Lady discloses that she has an Irish grandmother. Therefore, despite the fact that her reference to this Irish ancestor is almost an afterthought, she is technically an Irish Diasporic person. (Indeed, her Irish blood will be discussed in more detail later in this chapter.) Also, in the futuristic *Tragedy of an Elderly Gentleman*, although we are told that the Irish are extinct, one of the characters claims that the O'Mulligans, the "wild…ancestors of the aboriginal inhabitants" of Ireland, still roam the island's west coast. (Bernard Shaw. *Back to Methuselah*. London: Penguin, 1990. 198.)

17. Bernard Shaw. *Saint Joan*. London: Penguin, 1957. 7.

18. Shaw, *Saint Joan*, 7.

19. Declan Kiberd. *Inventing Ireland: The Literature of the Modern Nation*. London: Vintage, 1995. 418–39; James Moran. "Meditations in Time of Civil War: *Back to Methuselah* and *Saint Joan* in Production, 1919–1924." *SHAW: The Annual of Bernard Shaw Studies* 30 (2010): 154–8; James Moran. *Staging the Easter Rising: 1916 as Theatre*. Cork: Cork University Press, 2005. 94–102; Audrey McNamara. "Bernard Shaw's *Saint Joan*: An Irish Female Patriot." ACIS Conference. University College Dublin. June 11, 2014. Conference Paper.

20. Moran, "Meditations in Time of Civil War," 158.

21. For this production, McKenna had the French characters speak in Connaught Irish and the English characters in Munster Irish. For more information on this production, see the Siobhán McKenna and An Taibhdhearc archives housed at the Hardiman Library at the National University of Ireland, Galway.

22. Moran, "Meditations in Time of Civil War," 158.
23. Bernard Shaw. *Collected Letters, 1911–1925* Ed. Dan H. Laurence. New York: Viking, 1985. 896.
24. Shaw, *Saint Joan*, 60, 125, 133, 139.
25. Shaw, *Saint Joan*, 84.
26. Shaw, *Saint Joan*, 85.
27. Shaw, *Saint Joan*, 100.
28. Shaw, *Saint Joan*, 26–27.
29. Moran, *Staging the Easter Rising: 1916 as Theatre*, 94–99. Shaw famously wrote a defiant defense for Casement to read at his trial; although the Irish Anglican revolutionary loved the speech, he was advised not to use it by his lawyers. (This defense is reprinted in full in Bernard Shaw. "Roger Casement (1916–37), Part II." In *The Matter with Ireland*. 129–35.) As Moran notes, there are many parallels between the arguments in this defense and those employed by Joan in the play.
30. See Stanley Weintraub. "'Lawrence of Arabia': Bernard Shaw's Other Saint Joan." *South Atlantic Quarterly* 64 (Spring 1965): 194–205; Michael Holroyd, *Bernard Shaw Volume 3: The Lure of Fantasy*. New York: Vintage, 1991. 82–88.
31. Shaw, *Saint Joan*, 20–21. Shaw makes another connection between Joan and an Irish person when he links her execution to the eighteenth-century burning of a Dublin woman accused of coining. (See Shaw, *Saint Joan*, 30.)
32. Bernard Shaw. *John Bull's Other Island*. London: Penguin, 1984. 12–13.
33. Shaw, *Saint Joan*, 92; see also Shaw, *Saint Joan*, 89, 92, 93, 118.
34. Shaw, *Saint Joan*, 89.
35. Shaw, *Collected Letters, 1911–1925*, 201–2. This letter to Mrs Patrick Campbell also indicates that he always saw writing the play as an Irish mission: "English literature must be saved (by an Irishman, as usual) from having nothing to show concerning Joan except the piffling libel in [Shakespeare's] *Henry VI*."
36. Shaw, *Saint Joan*, 99; 96.
37. Shaw, *Saint Joan*, 104. See also Shaw, *John Bull's Other Island*, 82.
38. Shaw, *John Bull's Other Island*, 9. See also Bernard Shaw. "The Protestants of Ireland (1912)." In *The Matter with Ireland*. 78–83; Bernard Shaw. "Brogue-Shock (1917)." In *The Matter with Ireland*. 147–52. 147; Bernard Shaw. "How to Settle the Irish Question (1917)." In *The Matter with Ireland*. 153–73. 161; Bernard Shaw. "On St Patrick's Cathedral (1935)." In *The Matter with Ireland*. 305; Bernard Shaw. "Eamon De Valera and the Second World War (1940–44)." In *The Matter with Ireland*. 319–26. 321; Shaw, *Collected Letters, 1911–1925*, 882; Bernard Shaw. *Collected Letters, 1926–1950*. Ed. Dan H. Laurence. New York: Viking Penguin, 1988. 728.
39. Shaw, *John Bull's Other Island*, 18.
40. It should be noted that some scholars believe that Shakespeare was Roman Catholic. In the preface to *Saint Joan*, Shaw hedges his bets by stating that

"Although [Shakespeare] was a Catholic by family tradition, his figures are all intensely Protestant, individualist, sceptical, self-centred in everything but their love affairs, and personal and selfish even in them." (Shaw, *Saint Joan*, 42.)

41. Shaw, *Saint Joan*, 31.

42. For Shaw's negative feelings towards Orangemen, see, for example, Shaw, *Saint Joan*, 31; Shaw, *John Bull's Other Island*, 57–58; Shaw, *Back to Methuselah*, 56; Shaw, *Collected Letters, 1911–1925*, 799; Shaw, "The Protestants of Ireland," 79; Bernard Shaw. "The Third Home Rule Bill and Ulster (1913)." In *The Matter with Ireland*. 84–90. 88–89; Bernard Shaw. "A Note on Aggressive Nationalism (1913)." In *The Matter with Ireland*. 91–94. 92–93; Bernard Shaw. "Wake Up, Ulster! (1914)." In *The Matter with Ireland*. 98–100; Shaw, "How to Settle the Irish Question," 161–5; Bernard Shaw. "Socialism and Ireland (1919)." In *The Matter with Ireland*. 233–49. 244; Bernard Shaw. "The Irish Censorship (1928)." In *The Matter with Ireland*. 293–8. 294. Bernard Shaw. "An Appeal to the IRA (1940)." In *The Matter with Ireland*. 310–18. 312–14.

43. Kiberd, *Inventing Ireland*, 419–25.

44. Bernard Shaw. *An Autobiography 1856–1898*. Ed. Stanley Weintraub. New York: Reinhardt, 1970. 14.

45. Shaw, *John Bull's Other Island*, 9. This claim might seem to contradict his boast in the same preface that one of his ancestors was an abbess, but the nun in question was actually a convert. Indeed, Shaw advertises this by noting that her brother was an Orangeman. (Shaw, *John Bull's Other Island*, 9.)

46. Michael O'Laughlin. *The Book of Irish Families, Great & Small*. Kansas City, MO: Irish Roots, 2002. 109. For Shaw's discussion of his Fennell antecedents, see Shaw, *Collected Letters, 1926–1950*, 430.

47. Patrick Woulfe. *Irish Names and Surnames*. Dublin: Gill, 1922. 54, 64, 72, 88, 89. For Shaw's discussion of his Carr antecedents, see Shaw, *Collected Letters, 1926–1950*, 652.

48. Peter Gahan. *Shaw Shadows: Rereading the Texts of Bernard Shaw*. Gainesville: University Press of Florida, 2004. 65. See also John O'Donovan. *Shaw and the Charlatan Genius: A Memoir*. Dublin: Dolmen, 1965. 36–38.

49. In Farquhar's *Love and a Bottle*, which is set in England, the Irish Anglican rake, Roebuck, is repulsed by the idea of marrying Mrs Trudge, the Irish Catholic woman who he impregnated back in Ireland and who has followed him across the Irish Sea. Mrs Trudge's Catholicism is signaled by a humorous Irish song she sings about flirtation after Mass. (The song, although performed during the first run, was not included in the first edition of the play. It was, however, published as a separate broadsheet. Because of its unusual publication history, it is not always included in editions of the play. For more on this, see Shirley Strum Kenny, ed. "Notes." In *The Works of George Farquhar, Volume I*. By George Farquhar. Oxford: Oxford University Press, 1988. 11–12, 16–17.)

Le Fanu's *The House in the Churchyard* features a doomed love affair between the Protestant Richard Devereux and the Catholic Nan Glynn. Although *The Big House of Inver* was written after Violet Martin Ross's death, the plot was suggested to Somerville by a letter that Ross sent her, in which she discussed the history of a Big House family she knew in Co. Galway who were "awful [and] half peasant" due to intermarriage with local "country women" and the "men in the yard." (E.Œ. Somerville & Martin Ross. *The Selected Letters of Somerville & Ross*. Ed. Gifford Lewis. London: Faber, 1989. 294.) These sentiments suggest that, despite Martin's reputation for tolerance towards Roman Catholicism, she cannot be completely exonerated from the views expressed in the novel. (For Martin's openness regarding Catholicism, see Gifford Lewis. "Editor's Note." In *The Selected Letters of Somerville & Ross*. By E.Œ. Somerville & Martin Ross. London: Faber, 1989. 97.)

In Yeats's *Purgatory*, the Old Man is convinced that his blood is polluted, because his mother, a lady of the Big House, stooped to sleep with his father, a groom from the training stables. The Old Man stabs and kills both his father and his son: his low-born father for having burned down the august Big House while drunk and his son in order to stop genetic "pollution" from being passed on to a subsequent generation. (W. B. Yeats. *Purgatory*. In *Eleven Plays of William Butler Yeats*. Ed. A. Norman Jeffares. New York: Macmillan, 1964. 197–206. 205.) In an interview with the *Irish Independent*, Yeats said that he wrote the play because of his "interest in certain problems of eugenics" and in order to express his approval for Nazi legislation that "enable[s] old families to go on living where their fathers lived." (As quoted in McCormack, *From Burke to Beckett*, 362.) Despite such chilling remarks, critics like W. J. McCormack, Robert Tracy, and Derek Hand have noted ambiguities in the play (such as the fact that the Old Man is clearly mad) which demonstrate that Yeats was aware of "the spurious nature of fascist aristocracy, Hitlerian authority," and harsh government policies based on racial discrimination. McCormack also rightly suggests that Yeats's "class-hatred," "sectarianism," and even his belief in "selective breeding" actually have their roots, not in European Fascism, but in "his inheritance of Protestant Ascendancy." (McCormack, *From Burke to Beckett*, 365; 363; 363; 363; 364; see also Robert Tracy. *The Unappeasable Host: Studies in Irish Identities*. Dublin: University College Dublin Press, 1998. 126–9; Derek Hand. "The *Purgatory* of W.B. Yeats." Purgatory: International Conference on Irish Literature and Culture. St Patrick's College, Drumcondra. November 27, 2010. Plenary Address.)

50. For more on the significance of "Flurry" McCarthy Knox's name, see Julie Ann Stevens. *The Irish Scene in Somerville & Ross*. Dublin: Irish Academic Press, 2007. 172–80.

51. E.Œ. Somerville & Martin Ross. *The Irish R.M.* London: Abacus, 2005. 10.

156   *Notes*

52. J. M. Synge. *The Collected Letters of J.M. Synge, Volume One (1871–1907)*. Ed. Ann Saddlemyer. Oxford: Clarendon, 1983. 129; Bowen, "Portrait of a Woman Reading," 235.
53. Claire Connolly. "Introduction." In *Ormond*. By Maria Edgeworth. London: Penguin, 2000. xiv.
54. Davis Coakley. *Oscar Wilde: The Importance of Being Irish*. Dublin: Town House, 1994. 12; Gifford Lewis. *Edith Somerville: A Biography*. Dublin: Four Courts, 2005. 14. Wilde's ancestors anglicized the name to Fynn.
55. For Aylmer Somerville as the model for "Flurry" McCarthy Knox, see Gifford Lewis, *Edith Somerville: A Biography*, 156, 325, 345.
56. McCormack, *From Burke to Beckett*, 326–8; Michael Griffin. *Enlightenment in Ruins: The Geographies of Oliver Goldsmith*. Lewisburg, PA: Bucknell University Press, 2013. 19–22.
57. Further to this point, it is possible that Oliver Goldsmith's Catholic antecedents did not just include those who married into the Goldsmith line. There is evidence to suggest that the Goldsmith surname itself was an anglicized version of the Gaelic name Mac Gabhann or McGowan, and that the name change was made when the family converted to Protestantism. (See Griffin, *Enlightenment in Ruins*, 19–20.)
58. For Grace's Catholic origins, see W. J. McCormack. *Ascendancy and Tradition in Anglo-Irish Literary History From 1789 to 1939*. Oxford: Clarendon, 1985. 139–47.
59. W. J. McCormack. "Introduction." In *Ormond*. By Maria Edgeworth. Dublin: Gill & Macmillan, 1990. xi. In the novel, Edgeworth spells it Annally with two Ls but the real midlands family spelled it as Annaly with one *L*.
60. When discussing Charlotte Brooke's influence on Edgeworth, most critics focus on Edgeworth's interest in "Gracey Nugent" (the Turlough O'Carolan song she probably first learned from the *Reliques*) and the ways in which the song may have helped her to formulate the character of Grace Nugent from her 1812 novel *The Absentee*. It is also common for critics to focus on the ways in which Edgeworth faithfully carried on Brooke's mission of explaining the Irish people to an English audience in works such as *Castle Rackrent* (1800) and *An Essay on Irish Bulls* (1803).
61. Charlotte Brooke. *Reliques of Irish Poetry*. Ed. Lesa Ní Mhunghaile. Dublin: Irish Manuscripts Commission, 2009. viii.
62. Shaw's support for such mixing is, of course, central to his 1910 play *Misalliance*. For his openness to "cross-breeding" within an Irish context, see, for example, Shaw, "Eamon De Valera and the Second World War," 324.
63. Shaw, "Eamon De Valera and the Second World War," 324. It is noteworthy that in *John Bull's Other Island*, neither Shaw nor his characters comment on the Catholic Nora's betrothal to the Protestant Broadbent. Perhaps this marriage is less troubling to Irish people on either side of the religious divide, because Broadbent is an *English* and not an Irish Protestant.

Also, some might read Shaw's famous claim that there was never "any such species as [the] Anglo-Irish" as an example of his conceding that Irish Catholics and Irish Anglicans share many common ancestors (given the racial overtones of the word "species"). However, after making that statement, Shaw goes on to repeat his theory that everyone who is raised in the Irish climate—regardless of their genetic ancestry—takes on Irish characteristics and is therefore Irish. (Bernard Shaw. "Ireland Eternal and External (1948)." In *The Matter with Ireland*. 339–41. 340.)

64. See Bernard Shaw. "Preface: Fragments of Autobiography." In *The Matter with Ireland*. 1–13. 1–6; W. R. Rodgers, ed. "George Bernard Shaw." In *Irish Literary Portraits: W. B. Yeats, James Joyce, George Moore, J. M. Synge, George Bernard Shaw, Oliver St John Gogarty, F. R. Higgins, AE (George Russell)*. London: BBC, 1972. 116–41. 119.

65. Shaw, *Collected Letters, 1926–1950*, 857.

66. Shaw, *Saint Joan*, 12.

67. Shaw, *Saint Joan*, 55, 78, 108, 128.

68. Shaw, *Saint Joan*, 52.

69. As quoted in Holroyd, *Bernard Shaw Volume 3*, 84.

70. This is made especially clear in some of Henry Higgins's speeches in *Pygmalion* (1912). See especially Bernard Shaw. *Pygmalion*. New York: Dover, 1994. 70.

71. Kiberd, *Irish Classics*, 352.

72. In his study *Shaw, Synge, Connolly and Socialist Provocation*, Nelson O'Ceallaigh Ritschel repeatedly stresses the internationalism of Shaw's perspective, compared to the more narrowly national perspective of the writers traditionally associated with the Irish Literary Revival. (See Nelson O'Ceallaigh Ritschel. *Shaw, Synge, Connolly and Socialist Provocation*. Gainesville: University Press of Florida, 2011.)

73. Shaw, *John Bull's Other Island*, 88. It must be pointed out here that, in Shaw's work, he refused to add apostrophes to most conjunctions. He only added them when omitting them would cause confusion—for example, can't versus cant.

74. R. F. Foster. *Paddy &Mr Punch*. London: Allen Lane, 1993. 198–9.

75. Bernard Shaw. *Sixteen Self Sketches*. New York: Dodd, 1949. 43.

76. See, for example, Shaw, "Preface: Fragments of Autobiography," 1.

77. McNamara, "Bernard Shaw's *Saint Joan*: An Irish Female Patriot."

78. See Brian Tyson. *The Story of Shaw's Saint Joan*. Montreal: McGill-Queen's, 1982. 17–18. See also Shaw, *Collected Letters, 1911–1925*, 554–5.

79. Shaw, *Collected Letters, 1926–1950*, 526. See also Shaw, *Collected Letters, 1911–1925*, 842; Shaw, *Collected Letters, 1926–1950*, 508, 666.

80. Shaw, *Collected Letters, 1911–1925*, 897.

81. Tracy J. R. Collins. "Shaw's Athletic-Minded Women." In *Shaw and Feminisms: On Stage and Off*. Ed. D. A. Hadfield and Jean Reynolds. Gainesville: University Press of Florida, 2013. 19–36. 32. As Collins notes,

the title character in the 1918 short play *Annajanska, the Bolshevik Empress* is another cross-dressing female soldier.

82. Shaw, *Saint Joan*, 8, 21.
83. Bernard Shaw. *The Man of Destiny*. In *Plays Pleasant*. Harmondsworth: Penguin, 1949. 178–228. 200.
84. R. F. Foster, *The Oxford Illustrated History of Ireland*. Oxford: Oxford University Press, 2001. 316.
85. Shaw, *The Man of Destiny*, 203, 210; 195, 198.
86. Shaw, *The Man of Destiny*, 206.
87. Shaw, *The Man of Destiny*, 227.
88. Shaw, *Collected Letters, 1911–1925*, 729.
89. For Mansfield as Shaw's model for Napoleon, see Bernard Shaw. *Collected Letters, 1898–1910*. Ed. Dan H. Laurence. New York: Dodd, 1972. 34; Michael Holroyd. *Bernard Shaw Volume 1 (1856–1898): The Search for Love*. London: Penguin, 1988. 349.
90. Shaw, *The Man of Destiny*, 225–6.
91. Shaw, *The Man of Destiny*, 226.
92. W. B. Yeats. *The Collected Letters of W.B. Yeats, Volume III, 1901–1904*. Ed. John Kelly and Ronald Schuchard. Oxford: Clarendon, 1994. 302.
93. Ritschel, *Shaw, Synge, Connolly and Socialist Provocation*, 226.
94. Shaw, *The Man of Destiny*, 179; Shaw, "Preface: Fragments of Autobiography," 1.
95. Shaw, *The Man of Destiny*, 224–5.
96. Shaw, *The Man of Destiny*, 224.
97. W. B. Yeats. *The Collected Works of W.B. Yeats, Volume III: Autobiographies*. Ed. William H. O'Donnell and Douglas N. Archibald. New York: Scribner, 1999. 415; W. B. Yeats. "Under Ben Bulben." In *The Collected Works of W.B. Yeats, Volume I: The Poems*. Ed. Richard J. Finneran. New York: Scribner, 1997. 333–6. 335. As noted earlier, Yeats's snobbery was (in the words of W. J. McCormack) a product of "his inheritance of Protestant Ascendancy." (McCormack, *From Burke to Beckett*, 364.) However, to Yeats's credit, he was also aware that his disdain for the products of "base beds" may have been (at least, in part) a subliminal, psychological reaction to the fact that his Irish Anglican Muse, Maud Gonne, rejected his numerous proposals and married the lower-middle-class Catholic, John MacBride. (See journal entry number 17 in W. B. Yeats. *Memoirs*. Ed. Denis Donoghue. London: Papermac/Macmillan, 1988. 145.)
98. Shaw, *The Man of Destiny*, 226–7.
99. Shaw, "Eamon De Valera and the Second World War," 324; Shaw, *John Bull's Other Island*, 11.
100. Shaw, *The Man of Destiny*, 178.
101. Shaw, *John Bull's Other Island*, 11–13.
102. Shaw, *The Man of Destiny*, 179.
103. Shaw, *Saint Joan*, 21.

104. Shaw, *Saint Joan*, 8; Shaw, "Preface: Fragments of Autobiography," 9; Shaw, *Collected Letters, 1926–1950*, 68–69. See also, Shaw, *Collected Letters, 1911–1925*, 615.
105. During Napoleon's cameo in *Tragedy of an Elderly Gentleman*, his realism and freedom from illusion are continually stressed. See especially Shaw, *Back to Methuselah*, 224, 227.
106. Holroyd, *Bernard Shaw Volume 1*, 28.
107. See, for example, the famous speech regarding "heart-scalding... dreaming." (Shaw, *John Bull's Other Island*, 81–2.)
108. C. S. Lewis. "Irish Nocturne." In *Spirits in Bondage: A Cycle of Lyrics*. San Diego: Harcourt, 1984. 9–10.
109. Feargal Whelan. "*A Dirty Low-Down Low-Church Protestant High-Brow*: The Shape of Protestantism in Samuel Beckett's Work." *Emerging Perspectives* 1.1 (Autumn 2010): 4–15. 5. See also Max Weber. *The Protestant Ethic and the Spirit of Capitalism*. Trans. Peter Baehr and Gordon C. Wells. London: Penguin, 2002.
110. Shaw, *Back to Methuselah*, 221; 191.
111. Shaw, *Back to Methuselah*, 207. Curiously, in the play, Shaw spells long-livers with a hyphen and shortlivers without one.
112. Shaw, *Back to Methuselah*, 204.
113. Shaw, *Back to Methuselah*, 205.
114. Shaw, *Back to Methuselah*, 206.
115. Shaw, *Back to Methuselah*, 206.
116. Shaw, *Back to Methuselah*, 206.
117. Peter Gahan. "John Bull's Other War: Bernard Shaw and the Anglo-Irish War, 1918–1921." *SHAW: The Annual of Bernard Shaw Studies* 28 (2008): 209–38. 219.
118. Shaw, *Back to Methuselah*, 191.
119. Shaw, *Back to Methuselah*, 191.
120. Shaw, *Back to Methuselah*, 238; 205; 223.
121. Bernard Shaw. "Shaw Speaks to His Native City (1946)." In *The Matter with Ireland*. 334–8. 337. See Shaw, *Back to Methuselah*, 194.
122. Shaw, *Back to Methuselah*, 193.
123. Shaw, *Back to Methuselah*, 238; 238; 217; 207.
124. Shaw, *Back to Methuselah*, 238.
125. Shaw, *An Autobiography*, 184.
126. Shaw, *John Bull's Other Island*, 10, 24–25, 35, 38–52, 94, 140, 158.
127. Shaw, *John Bull's Other Island*, 140.
128. Bernard Shaw. *The Black Girl in Search of God and Some Lesser Tales*. Harmondsworth: Penguin, 1966. 83. Given Shaw's openness to interracial mixing, his repeated linking of the Irish to Jews, Asians, and Africans, and his belief in the political and sexual liberation of women, it should be abundantly clear by this point that the eugenic implications of some of his remarks regarding "cross-breeding" are in no way equitable to the

racist and misogynistic views of most nineteenth- and twentieth-century eugenicists.

129. For more on the Irish mixing with other races in the United States (especially African-Americans and Chinese people), see Noel Ignatiev. *How the Irish Became White*. New York: Routledge, 1995.

130. Brown, *Ireland's Literature*, 189–202. Simmons was from a Presbyterian background, but the rest of these poets were raised Anglican.

131. Kennedy, "'The Beckett Country' Revisited," 135–44.

132. Whelan, "Samuel Beckett and the Irish Protestant Imagination," Chapter 2. The Belfast-born Praeger was from a Unitarian background, and Joly was the son of a Church of Ireland minister.

133. C. S. Lewis. *All My Road Before Me: The Diary of C.S. Lewis, 1922–1927*. Ed. Walter Hooper. London: HarperCollins, 1993. 105. I make this link in Clare, "C.S. Lewis: An Irish Writer," 24.

134. For more on Narnia's Irish source landscapes, see Clare, "C.S. Lewis: An Irish Writer," 26.

135. C. S. Lewis. *Collected Letters, Volume 1: Family Letters, 1905–1931*. Ed. Walter Hooper. London: HarperCollins, 2000. 330; C. S. Lewis. *An Experiment in Criticism*. Cambridge: Cambridge University Press, 1961. 127.

136. C. S. Lewis. "Edmund Spenser, 1552–99." In *Studies in Medieval and Renaissance Literature*. Cambridge: Cambridge University Press, 1998. 121–45. 123; C. S. Lewis. *Surprised by Joy: The Shape of My Early Life*. New York: Harcourt, 1984. 173.

137. Clare, "C.S. Lewis: An Irish Writer," 20–21.

138. Nicole M. DuPlessis. "ecoLewis: Conservationism and Anticolonialism in *The Chronicles of Narnia*." In *Wild Things: Children's Culture and Ecocriticism*. Ed. Sidney I. Dobrin and Kenneth B. Kidd. Detroit: Wayne State University Press, 2004. 115–27.

139. Clare, "C.S. Lewis: An Irish Writer," 19–24.

140. Gahan, "John Bull's Other War," 209–38; Moran, "Meditations in Time of Civil War," 148–54.

141. Seán Kennedy. "Edmund Spenser, Famine Memory and the Discontents of Humanism in *Endgame*." *Samuel Beckett Today/Aujourd'hui* 24 (2012): 105–20. 111.

142. See, for example, David Krause. "John Bull's Other Island." In *Modern Irish Drama*. Ed. John P. Harrington. New York: Norton, 1991. 488–92. 489; Sanford V. Sternlicht. *A Reader's Guide to Modern Irish Drama*. Syracuse: Syracuse University Press, 1998. 19; Adam Feldman. "Shaw Business: David Staller's Project Shaw Offers GBS from A to Z." *Time Out New York*. July 13, 2006. Web. July 1, 2014; Colin Murphy. "A Major Hit 100 Years Ago, It's Been a Long Wait to See Shaw's 'Barbara' at the Abbey." *The Irish Independent* August 3, 2013. Web. July 1, 2014; John Davenport. "G.K. Chesterton: Nationalist Ireland's English Apologist." *Studies: An Irish Quarterly Review* 103.410 (Summer 2014): 178–92. 189–90.

4   Shaw and the Stage Englishman in Irish Literature

1. For an important account of the rise and persistence of notions of an English and an Irish national character, see Seamus Deane. "Irish National Character, 1790–1900." In *The Writer as Witness: Literature as Historical Evidence*. Ed. Tom Dunne. Cork: Cork University Press, 1987. 90–113. I should note, however, that Deane often conflates notions of English and British national character, even when it is clear that a non-English commentator like Edmund Burke is attempting to describe a version of the British national character that accommodates the traits of all four countries in the so-called British Isles.

   Joep Leerssen has also effectively demonstrated that Irish literature has, since the eighteenth century, been fixated on the Enlightenment notion that each country possesses a national character. (See Joep Leerssen. *Mere Irish and Fíor-Gael: Studies in the Idea of Irish Nationality, Its Development and Literary Expression prior to the Nineteenth Century*. Cork: Cork University Press, 1996.)

   As my analysis in chapter 3 makes clear, I believe that Ireland has been a multicultural society for centuries. And, like Michael Gardiner, I would like to see Englishness become less associated with racial ancestry. (See the chapter "England without the Cricket Test" in Michael Gardiner. *The Cultural Roots of British Devolution*. Edinburgh: Edinburgh University Press, 2004. 102–30). I therefore view most attempts by writers to describe or depict the Irish and English national characters with wariness and suspicion—especially since most commentators seem to formulate simplistic, essentialist constructions of Irishness and Englishness that do not take into account qualities associated with minority cultures within each polity. That said, the topics covered in this book—but especially in this chapter—require me to repeatedly compare and contrast the Irish and the English (or to analyze Shaw's comparing and contrasting of the two nations), and I am keenly aware that in the process I, at times, run the risk of making the kind of essentialist generalizations that I have criticized in the work of others.

2. Elizabeth Butler Cullingford. *Ireland's Others: Ethnicity and Gender in Irish Literature and Popular Culture*. Cork: Cork University Press, 2001. 13–36.

3. The three chapters alluded to are entitled "Decent Chaps: Gender, Sexuality and Englishness in Twentieth-Century Irish Drama and Film," "There's Many a Good Heart Beats under a Khaki Tunic," and "Brits Behaving Badly." See Cullingford, *Ireland's Others*, 37–95.

4. Cullingford, *Ireland's Others*, 37.

5. Declan Kiberd. *Inventing Ireland: The Literature of the Modern Nation*. London: Vintage, 1995. 57; Nicholas Grene. *Bernard Shaw: A Critical View*. London: Macmillan, 1987. 76; David Krause. "John Bull's Other Island." In *Modern Irish Drama*. Ed. John P. Harrington. New York: Norton, 1991. 488–92. 490; Michael Holroyd. *Bernard Shaw: The One-Volume Definitive Edition*. London: Vintage, 1998. 303.

6. Kiberd, *Inventing Ireland*, 36; Violet Powell. *The Irish Cousins: The Books and Background of Somerville and Ross*. London: Heinemann, 1970. 74, 148.

7. John Nash. *James Joyce and the Act of Reception: Reading, Ireland, Modernism*. Cambridge: Cambridge University Press, 2006. 44.

8. Heinz Kosok. "John Bull's Other Ego: Reactions to the Stage Irishman in Anglo-Irish Drama." In *Medieval and Modern Ireland*. Ed. Richard Wall. London: Rowan & Littlefield, 1988. 19–33; Heinz Kosok. "John Bull's Other Eden." *SHAW: The Annual of Bernard Shaw Studies* 30 (2010): 175–90.

9. Anthony Roche. *Contemporary Irish Drama: From Beckett to McGuinness*. New York: St Martin's, 1995. 119, 249.

10. Andrew Bennet and Nicholas Royale. *An Introduction to Literature, Criticism and Theory*. 4th ed. Harlow: Pearson, 2009. 65.

11. Deidre Shauna Lynch. *The Economy of Character: Novels, Market Culture, and the Business of Inner Meaning*. Chicago: University of Chicago Press, 1998. 4. Lynch defines "pragmatics of character" as how writers "use" their characters to understand, comment on, and "instruct" readers about the society in which they live. This helps an author's contemporary readership to understand how to feel about, and how to "imagine themselves as participants in," their ever-shifting social, political, and economic landscape. (Lynch, *The Economy of Character*, 4; 4; 11; 11).

12. Jill E. Twark. *Humor, Satire, and Identity: Eastern German Literature in the 1990s*. Berlin: de Gruyter, 2007. 14.

13. The fact that Stage English figures often seem to represent the English generally would indicate that they fit into Alex Woloch's "synecdoche" category of characters—secondary figures who represent an abstract idea or a larger group of people. That said, Woloch regards these "synecdoche" characters as invariably "flat," whereas most Stage English figures are quite "round," as we shall see during the course of this chapter. (Alex Woloch. *The One vs. the Many: Minor Characters and the Space of the Protagonist in the Novel*. Princeton: Princeton University Press, 2003. 69.) Also, some Stage English characters (including Shaw's Broadbent and Elderly Gentleman) are central to the works in which they appear—that is to say, they are not secondary figures.

14. Flannery O'Connor. *Mystery and Manners: Occasional Prose*. London: Faber, 1984. 105; 153; 105–6; 153; 162. It should be pointed out that O'Connor also believes that the setting must be extremely "believable." (O'Connor, *Mystery and Manners*, 27, 70.)

15. For example, see Kiberd, *Inventing Ireland*, 420; R. F. Foster, *Paddy & Mr Punch*. London: Allen Lane, 1993. 282, 292–6; V. S. Naipaul. *An Area of Darkness*. London: Vintage, 2002. 199–215; Philip Woodruff. *The Men Who Ruled India, Volume 2: The Guardians*. London: Cape, 1954. 94. Philip Woodruff was a pen name of Philip Mason, the famous Raj novelist. Naipaul, in this chapter of *An Area of Darkness*, acknowledges and quotes from Woodruff's work.

16. Naipaul, *An Area of Darkness*, 213. See also, Woodruff *The Men Who Ruled India, Volume 2*, 94.
17. Foster, *Paddy & Mr Punch*, 293. This transformation is examined in greater detail in Victoria Glendinning. *Trollope*. London: Pimlico, 1991.
18. Naipaul, *An Area of Darkness*, 212.
19. Naipaul, *An Area of Darkness*, 212; Kiberd, *Inventing Ireland*, 420.
20. For the initial, Irish distaste for "unnatural" and "artificial" English manners during the sixteenth and seventeenth centuries, see the chapter "Forging the Nation: the Irish Problem" in Thomas Scanlon. *Colonial Writing and the New World, 1583–1671: Allegories of Desire*. Cambridge: Cambridge University Press, 1999. 68–92; see also the chapter "A Civil Offer: The Failure to Adopt English Customs" in John Patrick Montaño. *The Roots of English Colonialism in Ireland*. Cambridge: Cambridge University Press, 2011. 282–334. For the continued Irish Catholic "antimony" to "English manners" through "the latter part of the nineteenth century," see Tom Inglis. *Global Ireland: Same Difference*. New York: Routledge, 2008. 128; see also Kiberd, *Inventing Ireland*, 151.
21. For the Englishness imposed on the Irish through education, see John Coolahan. "The Irish and Others in Irish Nineteenth Century Textbooks." In *The Imperial Curriculum: Racial Images and Education in the British Colonial Experience*. Ed. J. A. Mangan. London: Routledge, 1993. 54–63.
22. The most famous examples are the thuggish English soldiers in O'Casey's *The Shadow of a Gunman* (1923) and *The Plough and the Stars* (1926) and in Friel's *The Freedom of the City* (1973).
23. It should be admitted that, while most sentimental, romantic duffers are lazy or poor at their jobs, Maxwell Bruce from Somerville & Ross's "The Last Day of Shraft" is applying himself assiduously to the study of the Irish language. That said, the fact that he does not notice that the Irish people he meets are humoring and patronizing him throughout the story speaks to his duffer lack of wit.
24. Actually, although Boadicea Baldcock begins Behan's *The Big House* with a mixture of fear and racist condescension towards the Irish, she becomes much more of a female sentimental, romantic duffer after she moves back to England. She starts to miss Ireland and insists that she and her husband move back. Her new, sentimental resolve to love Ireland and the Irish is destroyed in an instant, however, when she and her husband discover that "Chuckles" Genokey, their Irish "man of affairs" (as she describes him with comically Stage English hyperbole), has badly swindled them. (Brendan Behan. *The Big House*. In *The Complete Plays*. New York: Grove, 1978. 359–384. 383.)
    Behan's pessimistic treatment of Boadicea's (temporary) conversion could be his reaction to the numerous English characters from nineteenth-century Irish fiction who go from initially hating Ireland to later loving it. Horatio from Lady Morgan's *The Wild Irish Girl* (1806) is

arguably the first—and most famous—character of this type. (For others, see Kosok, "John Bull's Other Eden," 186–8.) While one could argue that these characters convert from racist, officious hypocrite to sentimental, romantic duffer, I do not consider them Stage English, because they are not biting satirical portraits. In fact, the authors use these characters to deliberately flatter their English readers; they suggest that, with more exposure to Ireland and the Irish, the English will coolly and rationally change their negative attitudes. (It should be noted that three of the characters included in Kosok's analysis are not Stage English for the simple reason that they are in fact English-educated *Irish* people: I am referring to Ormsby Bethel from Maturin's *The Wild Irish Boy* (1808), Lord Colambre from Edgeworth's *The Absentee* (1812), and Major Yeates from Somerville & Ross's *Irish RM* stories (1898–1915). For such characters, embracing Ireland involves accepting their own Irishness and abandoning—or, at least, attempting to suppress—the prejudices and values inculcated in them during their years in England.)

25. It should be noted that Lavin's Edith Paston is subconsciously classist regarding the lower-class Irish and that her naïve regard for Ireland is not based on its exoticism but on her blinkered determination to see only its similarities to England.

26. It must be emphasized that these are loose categories that most Stage English figures fall into and are not relatively stable, essentialized stereotypes that Irish writers unreflectively employ whenever they want to create a Stage English character. Since a stereotype is "an idea or character etc. that is standardized in a conventional form without individuality" (OED), it is clearly the painfully predictable Stage Irishman, and not the widely variable Stage English figure, which is an example of a stereotype. As my analysis in this chapter suggests, I regard the "racist, officious hypocrite" and the "sentimental, romantic duffer" as wide-ranging character types but not as narrow stereotypes.

27. While the Scottish writer John Arbuthnot's creation of John Bull may have been influenced by subversive, (mildly) anti-English sentiments, subsequent English writers and caricaturists softened the figure until it became harmless as a critique of the English. For a concise but nuanced discussion of John Bull, see Miles Taylor. "John Bull." *Oxford Dictionary of National Biography*. May 2006. Web. August 1, 2013.

28. It should be noted that Shaw deliberately endowed Broadbent with other traits occasionally associated with John Bull over the past three centuries: Broadbent is, like some caricatures of John Bull, uneven in temper, the dupe of politicians, and overly patriotic.

29. Frantz Fanon, *The Wretched of the Earth*. Harmondsworth: Penguin, 1970. 170.

30. For more on "reverse mimicry," see Kristin Swenson Musselman. "The Other I: Questions of Identity in *Un Vie de Boy*." In *Francophone Post-colonial*

Cultures: Critical Essays. Ed. Kamal Sahli. Lanham, MD: Lexington Books, 2003. 126–37. 133–6.

31. Declan Kiberd. "From Nationalism to Liberation." In *The Irish Writer and the World*. Cambridge: Cambridge University Press, 2005. 146–57. 151.

32. Frank O'Connor also features English characters with one or more Stage English flaws in the short stories "The English Soldier" (1934), "The Babes in the Wood" (1947), "The Custom of the Country" (1947), "The Weeping Children" (1951), "Adventure" (1953), and "Eternal Triangle" (1954).

33. To take an example from Shaw's very first play, *Widowers' Houses*, when he introduces one of the main characters—an Englishman called Cokane—he takes the opportunity to express his pity or disdain for what he sees as the man's English foibles. Cokane has "affected manners" and is "fidgety, touchy, and constitutionally ridiculous in uncompassionate eyes." (Bernard Shaw. *Widowers' Houses*. In *Plays Unpleasant*. London: Penguin, 2000. 29–96. 31.) Shaw's are, presumably, such eyes—more evidence of his Irish outlook. (Of course, Cokane's surname provides another clue as to why he is "fidgety.")

Other obvious satirical portraits of the English from Shaw plays set outside of Ireland include Britannus from *Caesar and Cleopatra* (1901) and John de Stogumber from *Saint Joan*.

34. Bernard Shaw. *John Bull's Other Island*. London: Penguin, 1984. 7. For more on the Abbey's decision to turn this play down, see Norma Jenckes. "The Rejection of Shaw's Irish Play: *John Bull's Other Island*." *Éire-Ireland* 10 (Spring 1975): 38–53.

35. As quoted in Michael Holroyd. *Bernard Shaw Volume 2 (1898–1918): The Pursuit of Power*. New York: Vintage, 1991. 81. Shaw's use of the word absurdities is telling here. When Oliver Goldsmith, writing as the Chinese "Citizen of the World," attempted to sum up the nations of Europe for his Chinese readers, he spoke of:

the delicacy of Italy, the formality of Spain, the cruelty of Portugal, the fears of Austria, the confidence of Prussia, the levity of France, the avarice of Holland, the pride of England, [and] the absurdity of Ireland[.] (Oliver Goldsmith. *The Citizen of the World, or, Letters from a Chinese Philosopher, Residing in London, to His Friends in the East, Volume 1*. Bungay: Child, 1820. 26.)

While the Longford-born Goldsmith writes of "the pride of England," the Irishman Doyle in *John Bull's Other Island* warns Broadbent that "you don't know what Irish pride is," with the strong hint that it is much more potent than its English equivalent. (Shaw, *John Bull's Other Island*, 88.) Between this and Shaw's stated intention to show *English* and not Irish absurdity, we see that Shaw was writing not only against the English tradition but also, to some degree, the Irish Anglican one.

36. Interestingly, the play's working-class English character—the valet Hodson—is depicted in a relatively sympathetic and non-satirical manner.

37. Shaw, *John Bull's Other Island*, 78.
38. Shaw, *John Bull's Other Island*, 72.
39. Shaw, *John Bull's Other Island*, 82.
40. Shaw, *John Bull's Other Island*, 83; 126.
41. Shaw, *John Bull's Other Island*, 104.
42. Shaw, *John Bull's Other Island*, 127.
43. James Joyce. *Ulysses*. London: Penguin, 2000. 24.
44. Shaw, *John Bull's Other Island*, 141.
45. Shaw, *John Bull's Other Island*, 80; 75, 77, 86.
46. Shaw, *John Bull's Other Island*, 139.
47. Shaw, *John Bull's Other Island*, 103; 104.
48. Shaw, *John Bull's Other Island*, 108.
49. Shaw, *John Bull's Other Island*, 130. That said, Shaw does not actually want to suggest that the Irish are less humorous than everyone thinks. He still believes they are funnier than the English, who are pitied by the Irish characters for their inability to tell good jokes. (Shaw, *John Bull's Other Island*, 133.)
50. Shaw, *John Bull's Other Island*, 135.
51. Jane Austen. *Pride and Prejudice*. New York: Barnes & Noble, 1993. 1.
52. Shaw, *John Bull's Other Island*, 149.
53. Shaw, *John Bull's Other Island*, 148.
54. Shaw, *John Bull's Other Island*, 149.
55. Shaw, *John Bull's Other Island*, 149.
56. Shaw, *John Bull's Other Island*, 149.
57. Shaw, *John Bull's Other Island*, 150.
58. Shaw, *John Bull's Other Island*, 14.
59. Kiberd, *Inventing Ireland*, 58.
60. While some would argue that the story of Haffigan is a reaffirmation of the stereotype of the foolish Irishman, Shaw, firmly in the grip of Fanon's second phase, is actually suggesting that the noble Irish cannot conceive of a people who would administer laws allowing good tenants to be coldly forsaken in this way.
61. Shaw, *John Bull's Other Island*, 111.
62. Shaw, *John Bull's Other Island*, 72, 75, 77, 80, 86, 88, 127.
63. Shaw, *John Bull's Other Island*, 120.
64. Shaw, *John Bull's Other Island*, 82.
65. Shaw, *John Bull's Other Island*, 85.
66. Declan Kiberd. *Ulysses and Us: The Art of Everyday Living*. London: Faber, 2009. 51.
67. Shaw, *John Bull's Other Island*, 10, 24–25, 35, 38–52, 94, 140, 158.
68. Bernard Shaw, *Collected Letters, 1898–1910*. Ed. Dan H. Laurence. New York: Dodd, 1972. 98.
69. Shaw, *John Bull's Other Island*, 157.
70. Bernard Shaw. *Geneva*. In *Plays Political*. London: Penguin, 1986. 305–461. 385.

71. Shaw, *John Bull's Other Island*, 105.
72. Shaw, *John Bull's Other Island*, 111.
73. Shaw, *John Bull's Other Island*, 157.
74. Shaw, *John Bull's Other Island*, 78.
75. Shaw, *John Bull's Other Island*, 124; 125.
76. Shaw, *John Bull's Other Island*, 153.
77. Shaw, *John Bull's Other Island*, 160–1.
78. Shaw, *John Bull's Other Island*, 162; 163.
79. Shaw, *John Bull's Other Island*, 14.
80. Shaw, *John Bull's Other Island*, 86.
81. Shaw, *Collected Letters, 1898–1910*, 394; 394; 395; 395.
82. Shaw, *Collected Letters, 1898–1910*, 394; 394.
83. Shaw, *Collected Letters, 1898–1910*, 394.
84. Shaw, *John Bull's Other Island*, 83.
85. Shaw, *John Bull's Other Island*, 138–9; 138.
86. Shaw, *John Bull's Other Island*, 139.
87. Kiberd, *Inventing Ireland*, 57.
88. Cullingford, *Ireland's Others*, 39; Elizabeth Butler Cullingford. "Gender, Sexuality, and Englishness." In *Gender and Sexuality in Modern Ireland*. Ed. Anthony Bradley and Maryann Gialanella Valiulis. Amherst: University of Massachusetts Press, 1997. 159–86. 162–3; Kiberd, *Inventing Ireland*, 61; Holroyd, *Bernard Shaw Volume 2*, 87; Alfred Turco. *Shaw's Moral Vision: The Self and Salvation*. Ithaca: Cornell University Press, 1976. 178 ff.
89. Cullingford, *Ireland's Others*, 39.
90. Brad Kent persuasively argues that Nora has more agency and personal strength than is usually credited by critics in Brad Kent. "The Politics of Shaw's Irish Women in *John Bull's Other Island*." In *Shaw and Feminisms: On Stage and Off*. Ed. D. A. Hadfield and Jean Reynolds. Gainesville: University Press of Florida, 2013. 73–91.
91. Shaw, *John Bull's Other Island*, 83; Cullingford, *Ireland's Others*, 39. Cullingford is quoting from p. 150 of *John Bull's Other Island*. The italics are due to the fact that this phrase appears in Shaw's stage directions.
92. Shaw, *John Bull's Other Island*, 83, 120; 82.
93. R. F. Foster writes compellingly of "Thomas Davis's use of anti-materialism as a strategy of distinguishing Irish against English values, and asserting [Irish] moral superiority thereby," and notes that this "line was later adopted by Yeats as well as by de Valera." (Foster, *Paddy & Mr Punch*, 29.)
94. Shaw, *John Bull's Other Island*, 103.
95. Bernard Shaw. "Touring in Ireland, Part II (1916)." In *The Matter with Ireland*. Ed. David H. Greene and Dan H. Laurence. 1st ed. London: Hart-Davis, 1962. 97–99. 99; Kiberd, *Inventing Ireland*, 51. Part II of the essay "Touring in Ireland" is missing from the second edition of *The Matter with Ireland*.
96. Shaw, "Touring in Ireland," 99.

97. Shaw, *Collected Letters, 1898–1910*, 542.
98. Holroyd, *Bernard Shaw Volume 2*, 109.
99. Nicholas Grene. *The Politics of Irish Drama: Plays in Context from Boucicault to Friel.* Cambridge: Cambridge University Press, 1999. 33–34.
100. Shaw, *John Bull's Other Island*, 142.
101. Shaw, *John Bull's Other Island*, 153.
102. It could be argued that Broadbent's infatuation with Nora is just one of many examples from colonial literature of a "civilized" man falling in love with "some mysterious woman of the native tribe," with "the woman, like the colony," being regarded by the suitor as "a mystery to be penetrated." (Kiberd, *Inventing Ireland*, 620.) Indeed, this plot strand recalls Gayatri Spivak's famous description of "colonialism" as "white men...saving brown women from brown men," because Broadbent "saves" Nora from marriage to Larry or some other Irishman. (Gayatri Spivak. *A Critique of Postcolonial Reason: Toward a History of the Vanishing Present*. Cambridge, MA: Harvard University Press, 1999. 287.)
103. Shaw, *John Bull's Other Island*, 7–8.
104. Shaw, *John Bull's Other Island*, 10.
105. This strand in Irish thinking crosses political lines: note how Ulster Unionists celebrate the heroic loss of life on the Somme on July 1, 1916.
106. Holroyd, *Bernard Shaw Volume 2*, 48.
107. Holroyd, *Bernard Shaw Volume 2*, 99. It should be noted that Balfour's enjoyment of the play was not simply ascribable to an English instinct to laugh at the Irish. He would presumably have viewed Broadbent as an amusing satirical portrait of his political enemies in the Liberal Party, and, having served as the Secretary for Ireland in 1887, he undoubtedly enjoyed comparing Shaw's observations regarding Anglo-Irish relations to his own experiences and conclusions.
108. Shaw, *John Bull's Other Island*, 8.
109. Shaw, *John Bull's Other Island*, 32.
110. See, particularly, Shaw, *John Bull's Other Island*, 8–14.
111. Shaw, *John Bull's Other Island*, 9; 10.
112. Shaw, *John Bull's Other Island*, 137.
113. Holroyd, *Bernard Shaw Volume 2*, 100. He is quoting from the programme note that Shaw wrote for the 1913 production of *John Bull's Other Island* at the Kingsway Theatre in London.
114. Bernard Shaw. *O'Flaherty, VC*. In *Selected Short Plays*. New York: Penguin, 1987. 253–77. 255.
115. Shaw, *O'Flaherty, VC*, 256.
116. Shaw, *O'Flaherty, VC*, 255.
117. Shaw, *O'Flaherty, VC*, 256.
118. Shaw, *O'Flaherty, VC*, 256.
119. Shaw, *O'Flaherty, VC*, 256.
120. Shaw, *O'Flaherty, VC*, 263.

121. Shaw, *O'Flaherty, VC*, 264.
122. Seán O'Casey, who was a great admirer of Shaw, would borrow this aspect of the plot for his Great War play, *The Silver Tassie* (1929). For a detailed comparison of *O'Flaherty, VC* and *The Silver Tassie*, see Anthony Roche. *The Irish Dramatic Revival, 1899–1939*. London: Bloomsbury Methuen, 2015. 95–96.
123. Shaw, *O'Flaherty, VC*, 271.
124. E. Œ. Somerville & Martin Ross. *The Irish RM*. London: Abacus, 2005. 111.
125. Somerville & Ross, *The Irish RM*, 111.
126. Somerville & Ross, *The Irish RM*, 111.
127. Shaw, *O'Flaherty, VC*, 264.
128. Sir Pearce is aware of some of his tenants' mischief—such as their poaching of his salmon, rabbits, and cow's milk—and their habit of stretching the truth for dramatic effect, but is very shocked to learn of their lack of loyalty to England, their financial double-dealing, and their prayers for his conversion. Writers from the Ascendancy, such as Edgeworth, Somerville & Ross, and Bowen, repeatedly suggest in their work that even the most staunchly Unionist landlords are very familiar with the ways and views of the Irish tenantry (including the ways in which they are being swindled by them), but have deliberately decided to "not notice" such things, empowered by that great Irish Anglican sense of detachment. Shaw's inability to capture this unique "'ascendency' outlook" in his portrait of Sir Pearce arguably betrays the fact that he is a middle-class Dublin Protestant and not a country gentleman. It is rather surprising that Shaw was unable to better capture this Ascendency perspective since his wife was from the Ascendency and often made him stay at the Big Houses of her relations and friends on their return trips to Ireland. However, it could also be argued that Shaw was aware that he was exaggerating Madigan's ignorance of the Catholic Irish, and was doing so simply for comic effect. (Elizabeth Bowen. *The Last September*. Harmondsworth: Penguin, 1987. 82; Elizabeth Bowen. "Preface to *Uncle Silas*, by Sheridan Le Fanu." In *The Mulberry Tree: Writings of Elizabeth Bowen*. Ed. Hermione Lee. London: Virago, 1986. 100–13. 101.)
129. Shaw, *O'Flaherty, VC*, 275; 276.
130. Shaw, *O'Flaherty, VC*, 264.
131. Shaw, *O'Flaherty, VC*, 268.
132. Bernard Shaw. *Back to Methuselah*. London: Penguin, 1990. 194; Bernard Shaw. "Shaw Speaks to His Native City (1946)." In *The Matter with Ireland*. 2001. 334–8. 337.
133. Shaw, *O'Flaherty, VC*, 255.
134. Shaw, *O'Flaherty, VC*, 256.
135. Shaw, *O'Flaherty, VC*, 255.
136. Shaw, *O'Flaherty, VC*, 255.
137. Shaw, *O'Flaherty, VC*, 255.

138. Bernard Shaw. *Collected Letters, 1911–1925*. Ed. Dan H. Laurence. New York: Viking, 1985. 308.
139. Shaw, *Collected Letters, 1911–1925*, 309.
140. At this time, the Dramatist Club asked Shaw not to attend their meetings due to his (perceived) war position. With regards specifically to *O'Flaherty, VC*, Shaw had high hopes that the London producer Arthur Bourchier would stage the play in early 1916. However, Bourchier told him that the play was "unbearable" in the current political climate. (As quoted in Stanley Weintraub. *Bernard Shaw 1914–1918: Journey to Heartbreak*. London: Routledge, 1973. 144.)
141. For more on this production, see David Gunby. "The First Night of *O'Flaherty, VC*." *SHAW: The Annual of Bernard Shaw Studies* 19 (1999): 85–97.
142. Shaw, *Collected Letters, 1911–1925*, 517.
143. Shaw, *O'Flaherty, VC*, 257.
144. Christopher Innes. "Defining Irishness: Bernard Shaw and the Irish Connection on the English Stage." In *A Companion to Irish Literature, Volume One*. Ed. Julia M. Wright. Chichester: Wiley, 2010. 35–49. 44.
145. W. B. Yeats wrote two brilliant poems in tribute to Robert: "An Irish Airman Forsees His Death" and "In Memory of Major Robert Gregory," both of which were included in the collection *The Wild Swans at Coole* (1919).
146. Shaw, *Collected Letters, 1911–1925*, 882.
147. As quoted in Leonard W. Conolly. *Bernard Shaw and the BBC*. Toronto: University of Toronto Press, 2009. 12.
148. Conolly, *Bernard Shaw and the BBC*, 13.
149. A review by "Wayfarer" in the London newspaper *Nation* (later *The Nation* and eventually *The New Statesman*), as quoted in Weintraub, *Journey to Heartbreak*, 126.
150. Shaw, *Back to Methuselah*, 206.
151. Shaw, *Back to Methuselah*, 206.
152. Shaw, *Back to Methuselah*, 197; 207; 217.
153. Shaw, *Back to Methuselah*, 196–7; 202.
154. Shaw, *Back to Methuselah*, 192.
155. Shaw, *Back to Methuselah*, 194; 238; 193; 193; 193; 194; 208.
156. Shaw, *Back to Methuselah*, 198; 202; 243.
157. Shaw, *Back to Methuselah*, 242.
158. Shaw, *Back to Methuselah*, 195; 196; 216.
159. Shaw, *Back to Methuselah*, 217.
160. Shaw, *Back to Methuselah*, 215; 243; 217.
161. Shaw, *Back to Methuselah*, 201.
162. Shaw, *Back to Methuselah*, 204.
163. Shaw, *Back to Methuselah*, 242.
164. John Allen Giles. *The Life and Letters of Thomas à Becket, Volume 1*. London: Whittaker, 1846. 76.

165. Shaw, *Back to Methuselah*, 235, 242.
166. Shaw, *Back to Methuselah*, 233.
167. Shaw, *Back to Methuselah*, 214; 239.
168. Shaw, *Back to Methuselah*, 246; 198.
169. Shaw, *Back to Methuselah*, 191.
170. Several critics have compared the end of this play to the end of *Gulliver's Travels*. See, for example, F. D. Crawford. "Shaw among the Houyhnhnms." *The Shaw Review* 19 (September 1976): 102–19; Weintraub, *Journey to Heartbreak*, 307; Louis Crompton. *Shaw the Dramatist*. Lincoln: University of Nebraska Press, 1969. 175; Michael Holroyd. *Bernard Shaw Volume 3 (1919–1950): The Lure of Fantasy*. New York: Vintage, 1991. 50; Peter Gahan. *Shaw Shadows: Rereading the Texts of Bernard Shaw*. Gainesville: University Press of Florida, 2004. 241.
171. Shaw, *Back to Methuselah*, 249.
172. Shaw, *Back to Methuselah*, 249.
173. Holroyd, *Bernard Shaw Volume 3*, 50.
174. Joseph Holloway. *Joseph Holloway's Irish Theatre: Volume One, 1926–1930*. Ed. Robert Hogan and Michael O'Neill. Dixon, CA: Proscenium, 1968. 68.
175. The Nazis infamously classified portions of the German population (including Jews, Gypsies, homosexuals, and the handicapped) as "undesirables" and sought to exterminate them. (Michael Haas. *International Human Rights: A Comprehensive Introduction*. 2nd ed. Oxford and New York: Routledge, 2014. 86.)
176. Shaw, *Back to Methuselah*, 200.
177. Shaw, *Back to Methuselah*, 217.
178. C. S. Lewis. *Collected Letters, Volume 3: Narnia, Cambridge and Joy, 1950–1963*. Ed. Walter Hooper. San Francisco: HarperCollins, 2007. 65. Although Lewis frequently criticized Shaw in his literary criticism, fiction, and Christian apologetics, his work shows a deep engagement with Shaw's oeuvre (as various critics have pointed out). It is noteworthy that in private letters he was much more open about his "enthusiasm for Shaw." (C. S. Lewis. *Collected Letters, Volume 2: Books, Broadcasts, and the War, 1931–1949*. Ed. Walter Hooper. San Francisco: HarperCollins, 2004. 28.)
179. C. S. Lewis. *Out of the Silent Planet/Perelandra*. London: Voyager/HarperCollins, 2000. 87; 58; 87; 58; Lewis. *Collected Letters, Volume 3*. 1535.
180. We can also guess that Shaw is not on the side of the long-livers who advocate mass extermination from the compassionate nature of his politics generally and from remarks such as those made by the Shavian hero Higgins in *Pygmalion*: Higgins asserts that those who "are always shrieking to have troublesome people killed" are "cowards," because life was intended by its creator to be full of "trouble." (Bernard Shaw. *Pygmalion*. New York: Dover, 1994. 68.)

Towards the end of Shaw's life, he did advocate the execution of those who were proven to be criminally insane, but also stipulated that "criminals who can be reformed raise no problem and should be left out of the discussion. If they are reformable, reform them: that is all." (Bernard Shaw. "Capital Punishment (December 5, 1947)". In *The Letters of Bernard Shaw to* The Times. Ed. Ronald Ford. Dublin: Irish Academic Press, 2007. 268–269. 269.)

181. James Joyce. "Oscar Wilde: The Poet of *Salomé*." In *Occasional, Critical, and Political Writing*. Ed. Kevin Barry. Oxford: Oxford University Press, 2000. 148–51. 149. For Black and Gahan's work linking Shaw and Joyce, see Martha Fodaski Black. *Shaw and Joyce: "The Last Word in Stolentelling."* Gainesville: University Press of Florida, 1995; Gahan, *Shaw Shadows*, 85–86, 260, 273; Peter Gahan. "Introduction: Bernard Shaw and the Irish Literary Tradition." *SHAW: The Annual of Bernard Shaw Studies* 30 (2010): 1–26. 2–3.

182. Joyce, *Ulysses*, 27; 27; 24; 28; 238.

183. For Ellmann's linking of *Pygmalion* and *Eva Trout*, see Maud Ellmann. *Elizabeth Bowen: The Shadow Across the Page*. Edinburgh: Edinburgh University Press, 2004. 216–17. For Bowen's reflections on Shaw, see Elizabeth Bowen. "Pictures and Conversations." In *The Mulberry Tree: Writings of Elizabeth Bowen*. Ed. Hermione Lee. London: Virago, 1986. 265–98. 276; Elizabeth Bowen. "James Joyce." In *People, Places, Things: Essays by Elizabeth Bowen*. Ed. Allan Hepburn. Edinburgh: Edinburgh University Press, 2008. 239–47. 243; Elizabeth Bowen. "Review of *James Joyce's Dublin*, by Patricia Hutchins." In *Elizabeth Bowen's Selected Irish Writings*. Ed. Eibhear Walshe. Cork: Cork University Press, 2011. 186–8. 187; Elizabeth Bowen. "Bowen's Court, 1958." In *Elizabeth Bowen's Selected Irish Writings*. Ed. Eibhear Walshe. Cork: Cork University Press, 2011. 188–97. 194.

184. Bowen, "James Joyce," 243.

185. Like Shaw, Bowen suffers from critics assuming that she wrote only one Irish work. However, twelve of her short stories and four of her novels have Irish settings. Nine of these short stories were published together as *Elizabeth Bowen's Irish Stories* in 1978, five years after her death. A tenth—"The Back Drawing-Room"—originally appeared in *Ann Lee's and Other Stories* from 1926 and was later included in her *Collected Stories* of 1980. Two more—"The Good Earl" and "Candles in the Window"—were published in a volume of previously uncollected stories called *The Bazaar and Other Stories* in 2008. With regards to her novels, two of them—*The Last September* (1929) and *A World of Love* (1955)—are set entirely in Ireland. In *The House in Paris* (1935), the characters move between France, England, and Ireland, and in *The Heat of the Day* (1948), the action is split between England and Ireland. Bowen was working on a fifth Irish novel (entitled *The Move-In*) at the time of her death.

186. Bowen, *Last September*, 92–93.
187. Bowen, *Last September*, 175.
188. Bowen, *Last September*, 87.
189. Bowen, *Last September*, 92.
190. Bowen, *Last September*, 41.
191. Bowen, *Last September*, 205. Emphasis in original.
192. As quoted in James Stanier Clarke and John McArthur. *The Life and Services of Horatio Viscount Nelson.* Cambridge: Cambridge University Press, 2010. 242.
193. Bowen, *Last September*, 26–27.
194. Bowen, *Last September*, 66; 95; 185; 84.
195. Seán O'Casey. *The Plough and the Stars.* In *Three Dublin Plays: The Shadow of a Gunman/Juno and the Paycock/The Plough and the Stars.* London: Faber, 1998. 149–247. 236.
196. Indeed, Kosok argues that Stoke and Poges "are caricatured to such an extent that there is no way of mistaking them for realistic characters." Kosok rightly notes that, while the last Stage Englishman to appear in O'Casey's dramatic canon—Lord Leslieson from *The Moon Shines on Kylenamoe* (1961)—is still deeply absurd, he is treated with much more sympathy by his creator; during the course of the play, Leslieson's initial "pride and stiffness finally turn into an almost touching helplessness." (Kosok, "John Bull's Other Ego," 31; 32.)
197. As quoted in Holroyd, *Bernard Shaw Volume 2*, 81. O'Casey describes the powerful effect that reading *John Bull's Other Island* had on him in the third volume of his autobiography, *Drums under the Window*. (Seán O'Casey. *Drums under the Window*. London: Macmillan, 1946. 200–7.) Several critics have noted the play's strong influence on his work, particularly on *Purple Dust*. (See Saros Cowasjee. *Seán O'Casey: The Man behind the Plays*. Edinburgh and London: Oliver and Boyd, 1963. 156–66; Ronald Rollins. *Seán O'Casey's Drama*. Tuscaloosa: University of Alabama Press, 1979. 65–77; Heinz Kosok. *O'Casey the Dramatist*. Gerrards Cross: Colin Smythe, 1985. 166–8; Christopher Murray. *Seán O'Casey: Writer at Work*. Dublin: Gill & Macmillan, 2004. 265; Kosok, "John Bull's Other Eden," 181–3.)
198. Seán O'Casey. *Purple Dust*. In *Three More Plays by Seán O'Casey: The Silver Tassie/Purple Dust/Red Roses for Me*. London: Papermac/Macmillan, 1965. 115–220. 136; 173; 150; 203; 161; 58; 166; 186.
199. Brendan Behan. *Borstal Boy*. London: Arrow, 1990. 251; Brendan Behan. *Confessions of an Irish Rebel*. London: Arrow, 1991. 121.
200. Cullingford, *Ireland's Others*, 57.
201. See, for example, Ted E. Boyle. *Brendan Behan*. New York: Twayne, 1969. 88–89; John Brannigan. *Brendan Behan: Cultural Nationalism and the Revisionist Writer*. Dublin: Four Courts, 2002. 42; Richard Wall. "Introduction." In *An Giall/The Hostage*. By Brendan Behan. Washington, DC: Catholic University of America Press, 1987. 2. There is a much

stronger case to be made for the story's influence on the early Behan short story, "The Execution," as John Brannigan has demonstrated. (Brannigan, *Brendan Behan*, 52–57.)

202. Richard Wall. "Notes." In *An Giall/The Hostage*. By Brendan Behan. Washington, DC: Catholic University of America Press, 1987. 48.
203. Grene, *The Politics of Irish Drama*, 162.
204. Cullingford, *Ireland's Others*, 37.
205. Brendan Behan. *The Hostage*. In *The Complete Plays*. New York: Grove, 1978. 127–237. 206.
206. Behan, *The Hostage*, 190; 186, 206.
207. Behan, *The Hostage*, 186; 195; 217.
208. Behan, *The Hostage*, 221.
209. For Leslie's anti-royalist remarks, see Behan, *The Hostage*, 181, 185. After Leslie realizes that the IRA might execute him, he confesses, in song, that "I love my royal-ty [*sic*]." (Behan, *The Hostage*, 206.)
210. As if accusing his original London audiences of such ignorance, Behan repeatedly has the characters in *The Hostage* explain basic aspects of Irish history, Irish culture, or the Irish perspective, either straight to the audience, or by engineering scenes in which the Irish characters are forced to explain such things. (Behan, *The Hostage*, 145–6, 160, 180, 196, 197.) When his characters break the fourth wall in some of these scenes, Behan is virtually taunting his English audiences with their ignorance of Ireland.
211. Behan, *The Hostage*, 163, 179, 192, 202, 206, 215, 223.
212. Behan, *The Hostage*, 223.
213. Behan, *The Hostage*, 185–6.
214. Behan, *The Hostage*, 133.
215. Cullingford, *Ireland's Others*, 46.
216. Behan, *The Hostage*, 139; 129.
217. Shaw, *John Bull's Other Island*, 11; 12.
218. Behan, *The Hostage*, 143.
219. Kiberd, *Inventing Ireland*, 524.
220. Behan, *The Hostage*, 137.
221. Behan, *The Hostage*, 135, 159, 187, 188, 193, 233.
222. Branningan, *Brendan Behan*, 119.
223. Branningan, *Brendan Behan*, 119.
224. Kiberd, *Inventing Ireland*, 524; 524; Behan, *The Hostage*, 190.
225. Given the incendiary, anti-English use to which Behan puts this song (and the jingoistic, racist song sung by Leslie), I cannot agree with Nicholas Grene's assessment that the songs in *The Hostage* are simply "showstopping set-pieces which have had all the political harm taken out of them." (Grene, *The Politics of Irish Drama*, 164.)
226. Behan, *The Hostage*, 192; 193.
227. Behan, *The Hostage*, 142.
228. Behan, *The Hostage*, 192; 193; 192.
229. Behan, *The Hostage*, 193.

230. Behan, *The Hostage*, 192. Prior to his chat with Leslie and his singing of "The Captains and the Kings," the only verbal hints that Monsewer gives of his own Englishness are confined to his spontaneous use of phrases like "by Jove" and his references to people as "chap" and "sonny." (Behan, *The Hostage*, 179, 190, 191; 234; 194.) Of course, the other characters, and Behan in the stage directions, repeatedly reference Monsewer's Englishness. Examples include Leslie's observation that Monsewer has the "same face, same voice" as his Colonel and Behan's description of Monsewer as "looking like Baden Powell." (Behan, *The Hostage*, 189; 133.)

231. Bernard Shaw. "Irish Nonsense about Ireland (1916)." In *The Matter with Ireland*. 112–9. 113. See also Bernard Shaw. "The Irish Players (1911)." In *The Matter with Ireland*. 71–77. 73; Bernard Shaw. "A Note on Aggressive Nationalism (1913)." In *The Matter with Ireland*. 91–94. 91–92; Bernard Shaw. "Ireland and the First World War (1914)." In *The Matter with Ireland*. 101–4. 103; Bernard Shaw. "How to Settle the Irish Question (1917)." In *The Matter with Ireland*. 153–73. 157; Bernard Shaw. "The Dominion League (1919)." In *The Matter with Ireland*. 205–8. 206; Bernard Shaw. "On Throwing Out Dirty Water (1923)." In *The Matter with Ireland*. 285–9. 287, 289.

232. Bernard Shaw, "Roger Casement (1916–37)." In *The Matter with Ireland*. 127–46. 135; Shaw, "How to Settle the Irish Question," 157; 157. See also Bernard Shaw. "Why Devolution Will Not Do (1919–20)." In *The Matter with Ireland*. 213–26. 222; Bernard Shaw. "Ireland Eternal and External (1948)." In *The Matter with Ireland*. 339–41. 340.

Conclusion

1. Daniel Corkery. *Synge and Anglo-Irish Literature*. Cork: Cork University Press, 1931. 3.

2. Brian Friel. *Essays, Diaries, Interviews: 1964–1999*. Ed. Christopher Murray. London: Faber, 1999. 51. This quote is from the essay "Plays Peasant and Unpeasant," which originally appeared in the *Times Literary Supplement* on March 17, 1972. The title of this essay, of course, derives from the title of Shaw's first play collection, *Plays Pleasant and Unpleasant* (1898). Friel asserts that Shaw and other Irish Protestant playwrights should be excluded from the Irish canon because they "wrote within the English tradition, for the English stage and for the English people." (Friel, *Essays, Diaries, Interviews: 1964–1999*, 51.)

3. For a wider consideration of Shaw's relationship to the Irish canon, see Peter Gahan. "Introduction: Bernard Shaw and the Irish Literary Tradition." *SHAW: The Annual of Bernard Shaw Studies* 30 (2010): 1–26.

4. For Shaw's championing of the Irish use of English and his disparagement of efforts to revive Irish, see, for example, Bernard Shaw. "The Gaelic League (1910)." In *The Matter with Ireland*. 63–65; Bernard Shaw. "A Note

on Aggressive Nationalism (1913)." In *The Matter with Ireland*. 91–94. 93; Bernard Shaw. "Irish Nonsense about Ireland (1916)." In *The Matter with Ireland*. 112–9. 114; Bernard Shaw. "Literature in Ireland (1918)." In *The Matter with Ireland*. 176–9. 177; Bernard Shaw. "On Throwing Out Dirty Water (1923)." In *The Matter with Ireland*. 285–9. 287; Bernard Shaw. "The Greatest Living Irishman? (1941)." In *The Matter with Ireland*. 327–8. 328; Bernard Shaw. "Shaw Speaks to His Native City (1946)." In *The Matter with Ireland*. 334–8. 335.

For examples of Shaw referring to all of the residents of the Atlantic Archipelago as "Britons," see Bernard Shaw. *Back to Methuselah*. London: Penguin, 1990. 191, 204; Bernard Shaw. *The Millionairess*. In *Plays Extravagant*. London: Penguin, 1991. 213–320. 226. (Since the publication of J. G. A. Pocock's influential essay "British History: A Plea for a New Subject" in 1975, scholars have increasingly used the term Atlantic Archipelago in an effort "to avoid the political and ethnic connotations of 'the British Isles.'" (Krishan Kumar. *The Making of English National Identity*. Cambridge: Cambridge University Press, 2003. 6. See also J. G. A. Pocock. "British History: A Plea for a New Subject." *The Journal of Modern History* 47.4 (December 1975): 601–21. 606–7.))

Shaw's conviction that Ireland needed to maintain some ties with Britain requires lengthier explanation. Shaw believed Ireland should rule itself, but remain a voluntary member of the British Empire. He also believed that Scotland and Wales should rule themselves, and that no country needed Home Rule—that is, a local focus on local affairs—as badly as England did.

Shaw also recommended that the British Empire be converted into the British Commonwealth, with each country having its own National Parliament and sending representatives to what Shaw called the Imperial Conference. Due to their strong, mutual economic and military interests, he believed that England, Ireland, Scotland, and Wales should also send representation to a Federal Parliament of the British Isles.

In Shaw's opinion, Ireland needed to stay tied (on some level) to England, because small countries are always dependent on their more powerful neighbors, economically and militarily, whether they like to admit it or not. (For more on this, see Shaw, "Irish Nonsense about Ireland," 116; Bernard Shaw. "The Easter Week Executions (1916)." In *The Matter with Ireland*. 124–6. 124; Bernard Shaw. "How to Settle the Irish Question (1917)." In *The Matter with Ireland*. 153–73. 154–5, 167–9; Bernard Shaw. "Sir Edward Carson's Other Island (1918)." In *The Matter with Ireland*. 202–4; Bernard Shaw. "The Dominion League (1919)." In *The Matter with Ireland*. 205–8; Bernard Shaw. "Why Devolution Will Not Do (1919–20)." In *The Matter with Ireland*. 213–26. 217–22; Bernard Shaw. "Socialism and Ireland." In *The Matter with Ireland*. 233–49. 245–6; Bernard Shaw. "Ireland Eternal and External (1948)." In *The Matter with Ireland*. 339–41. 341.)

5. See Shaw, "How to Settle the Irish Question," 153–73; Shaw, "The Dominion League," 208; Bernard Shaw. "The British Offer (1921)." In *The Matter with Ireland*. 262–7; Bernard Shaw. "Eire – Ulster – Britain (1938)." In *The Matter*

with Ireland. 306–7. 307; Bernard Shaw. "An Appeal to the IRA (1940)." In *The Matter with Ireland.* 310–8. 311–13.

6. Bernard Shaw. "Eamon De Valera and the Second World War (1940–44)." In *The Matter with Ireland.* 319–26. 326; Shaw, "Ireland Eternal and External," 341.

7. As Homi Bhabha explains in his landmark study, *The Location of Culture* (1994), the cultural mixing and interplay that inevitably occurs between the colonizers and the residents of a colony results in the creation of a "liminal space, in-between the designations of identity." In this space, we find "cultural hybridity" which "erases any essentialist claims for the inherent authenticity or purity of cultures" (Homi K. Bhabha. *The Location of Culture.* London: Routledge, 1994. 5; 5; 83).

8. To the bewilderment of many outside observers in the United Kingdom and Ireland, many diehard Orange Protestants in Northern Ireland affirm their allegiance to a union of nations but not to any of the nations within that union. For examples of this mindset, see Paddy Logue, ed. *Being Irish.* Dublin: Oak Tree, 2000. 27–29, 288–90.

   In the 2011 UK census, 68.3 percent of Northern Irish Protestants described themselves as "British only," while 29.4 percent acknowledged being, at least on some level, "Irish" and/or "Northern Irish." In discussions of this phenomenon, it should be noted that many Northern Irish Protestants say that they have been made to feel that an Irish identity is not open to them, due to their British allegiance. (For the Northern Ireland portion of the 2011 UK census, see "Census 2011 Results for Northern Ireland." *Northern Ireland Statistics and Research Agency.* June 12, 2014. Web. October 16, 2014.)

9. Seamus Deane. *Heroic Styles: The Tradition of an Idea* [Field Day Pamphlet, No. 4]. Derry: Field Day, 1984. 10.

10. Michael Gardiner. *The Cultural Roots of British Devolution.* Edinburgh: Edinburgh University Press, 2004. 15. Emphasis in original.

11. Gardiner, *The Cultural Roots of British Devolution*, 14.

12. There is no greater indication of Scottish alienation within the British scheme than the 2014 referendum in which 45 percent of Scots voted for independence from the United Kingdom.

13. Edna Longley. *The Living Stream: Literature and Revisionism in Ireland.* Newcastle: Bloodaxe, 1994. 194.

14. Elizabeth Bowen. "The Idea of France." In *People, Places, Things: Essays by Elizabeth Bowen.* Ed. Allan Hepburn. Edinburgh: Edinburgh University Press, 2008. 61–65. 62–63; Elizabeth Bowen. "Coming to London," In *The Mulberry Tree: Writings of Elizabeth Bowen.* Ed. Hermione Lee. London: Virago, 1986. 85–89. 86.

15. For the most concise articulation of this, see Douglas Hyde. "The Necessity for De-Anglicizing Ireland." In *Irish Writing in the Twentieth Century: A Reader.* Ed. David Pierce. Cork: Cork University Press, 2000. 2–13.

16. Samuel Beckett. "Recent Irish Poetry." In *Disjecta: Miscellaneous Writings and a Dramatic Fragment.* Ed. Ruby Cohn. London: Calder, 1983. 70–76.

178   *Notes*

70; Patrick Kavanagh, as quoted in Darcy O'Brien. *Patrick Kavanagh*.
Lewisburg, PA: Bucknell University Press, 1975. 23.

17. Vivian Mercier. "Victorian Evangelicalism and the Anglo-Irish Literary
Revival." In *Literature and the Changing Ireland*. Ed. Peter Connolly.
Gerrards Cross: Colin Smythe, 1980. 59–101; Declan Kiberd. *Inventing Ireland: The
Literature of the Modern Nation*. London: Vintage, 1995. 31, 44, 182, 275,
296, 299, 537, 552; Elaine Sisson. *Pearse's Patriots: St Enda's and the Cult of
Boyhood*. Cork: Cork University Press, 2004. 16, 52, 69, 104, 116, 134–6.

18. Sisson, *Pearse's Patriots*, 104.

19. For more on viewing Oscar Wilde and Somerville & Ross as Revival writers,
see David Clare. "Wilde, Shaw, and Somerville and Ross: Irish Britons,
Irish Revivalists, or Both?" *Irish Studies Review* 22.1 (February 2014):
91–103. For more on viewing Joyce as a Revival writer, see P. J. Mathews.
*Revival: The Abbey Theatre, Sinn Fein, The Gaelic League and the Co-operative
Movement*. Cork: Cork University Press, 2003. 110–15; John Wilson Foster.
"The Irish Renaissance, 1890–1940: Prose in English." In *The Cambridge
History of Irish Literature, Volume II*. Ed. Margaret Kelleher and Philip
O'Leary. Cambridge: Cambridge University Press, 2006. 113–80. 154–6;
Declan Kiberd. *Ulysses and Us: The Art of Everyday Living*. London: Faber,
2009. 33–36.

20. C. S. Lewis's first volume of poetry, *Spirits in Bondage* (1919), could certainly
be deemed a Revival work (given its focus on Irish mythology and the
Irish landscape). Lewis attended Campbell College in Belfast, an exclusive
public school where Samuel Beckett, an Old Portoran, later taught; Lewis
also attended Wynyard School and Malvern College in England, followed
by Oxford.

21. Elizabeth Coxhead. *Lady Gregory: A Literary Portrait*. New York: Harcourt,
1961. 10.

22. David H. Hume. "Empire Day in Ireland." In *'An Irish Empire'?: Aspects of
Ireland and the British Empire*. Ed. Keith Jeffery. Manchester: Manchester
University Press, 1996. 149–68. 152.

23. Mercier, "Victorian Evangelicalism and the Anglo-Irish Literary Revival,"
75–76, 83, 92; W. J. McCormack. *Fool of the Family: A Life of J.M. Synge*.
New York: New York University Press, 2000. 176–7, 431–6; Feargal Whelan.
"Samuel Beckett and the Irish Protestant Imagination." Diss. University
College Dublin, 2014. Chapter 1.

24. Alan Simpson. *Beckett and Behan and a Theatre in Dublin*. London:
Routledge, 1962. 172. For quotes from others accusing O'Casey of sectari-
anism, see Christopher Murray. *Seán O'Casey: Writer at Work*. Dublin: Gill
& Macmillan, 2004. 288–9, 331.

25. Declan Kiberd. "The London Exiles: Wilde and Shaw." In *The Field Day
Anthology of Irish Writing, Volume 2*. Ed. Seamus Deane et al. Derry: Field
Day, 1991. 372–6. 373.

26. For a comprehensive account of this controversy, see the chapter "The
Shewing-up of Dublin Castle: Lady Gregory, Shaw, and *Blanco Posnet*,

August 1909" in Lucy McDiarmid. *The Irish Art of Controversy*. Dublin: Lilliput, 2005. 87–122.

27. One book that is devoted to Shaw's relationship with the Abbey is Dan H. Laurence and Nicholas Grene, eds. *Shaw, Lady Gregory, and the Abbey: A Correspondence and a Record*. Gerrards Cross: Colin Smythe, 1993. The Shaw-Abbey relationship is also explored in detail in Chapter 4 of Anthony Roche. *The Irish Dramatic Revival, 1899–1939*. London: Bloomsbury Methuen, 2015.

28. Bernard Shaw. *Collected Letters, 1911–1925*. Ed. Dan H. Laurence. New York: Viking, 1985. 309.

29. In the play, Shaw mistakenly places the village in Co. Galway. (Shaw, *Back to Methuselah*, 195.) While it is near the border between the two counties, it is in fact in Co. Clare. It should be noted that today the village is more popularly known as New Quay. That said, it is still referred to as Burrin or even Burren on some maps, and the old post office building bearing the name Burrin can still be spotted.)

30. This house still stands and currently operates as an upscale bed and breakfast.

31. For Shaw's comparison of Gregory to Molière, see Bernard Shaw. "The Irish Players (1911)." In *The Matter with Ireland*. 71–77. 74.

32. For more on this, see James Moran. "Meditations in Time of Civil War: *Back to Methuselah* and *Saint Joan* in Production, 1919–1924." *SHAW: The Annual of Bernard Shaw Studies* 30 (2010): 147–60. 156–7. Kiltartan is, of course, also the name that Lady Gregory gave to the Hiberno-English dialect she used in her plays.

33. Michael Holroyd. *Bernard Shaw Volume 2 (1898–1918): The Pursuit of Power*. New York: Vintage, 1991. 381; Christopher Fitz-Simon. *The Abbey Theatre: Ireland's National Theatre, The First 100 Years*. New York: Thames & Hudson, 2003. 43.

34. James Joyce. "Review of *The Shewing-up of Blanco Posnet*." In *Shaw: The Critical Heritage*. Ed. T. F. Evans. London: Routledge, 1976. 197–9. 199. This review was originally published in the Trieste newspaper *Il Piccolo della Sera* in September 1909.

35. Declan Kiberd. "The Language of Synge." The Abbey Theatre, Dublin. April 12, 2011. Public Lecture. The first person to describe Wilde's plays as "verbal opera" was W. H. Auden in W. H. Auden. "An Improbable Life: Review of *The Letters of Oscar Wilde*." *New Yorker* (March 9, 1963): 47.

36. See Nelson O'Ceallaigh Ritschel. *Shaw, Synge, Connolly, and Socialist Provocation*. Gainesville: University Press of Florida, 2011. Ritschel also suggests that Synge's last play, *Deirdre of the Sorrows*, may have been influenced by *John Bull's Other Island*. (Ritschel, *Shaw, Synge, Connolly, and Socialist Provocation*, 87–88.)

37. J. M. Synge. *Collected Works II: Prose*. Ed. Alan Price. Oxford: Oxford University Press, 1966. 347.

38. J. M. Synge. "Preface to *Poems and Translations*." In *Collected Works 1: Poems*. Ed. Robin Skelton. Oxford: Oxford University Press, 1968. xxxvi.

39. Shaw also repeatedly publicized his debts to the writers Leo Tolstoy, August Strindberg, and Anton Chekhov.
40. Bernard Shaw. *Man and Superman*. London: Penguin, 2004. 7–38.
41. Peter Gahan. "Things Irish: Review of *The Matter with Ireland* (Second Edition)." *SHAW: The Annual of Bernard Shaw Studies* 22 (2002): 200–8. 202.
42. Bernard Shaw. "The Playwright on His First Play." In *The Portable Bernard Shaw*. Ed. Stanley Weintraub. New York: Penguin, 1986. 48–56. 52.

Bibliography

Print, Web, and Audiovisual Sources

Altendorf, Ulrike. *Estuary English: Levelling at the Interface of RP and South-Eastern Britain*. Tubingen: Gunter Narr Verlag, 2003. Print.

Auden, W. H. "An Improbable Life: Review of *The Letters of Oscar Wilde*." *New Yorker* (March 9, 1963): 47. Print.

Austen, Jane. *Pride and Prejudice*. New York: Barnes & Noble, 1993. Print.

Barr, Colin. Abstract for "Giuseppe Mazzini and Irish Nationalism, 1845–70." In *Giuseppe Mazzini and the Globalization of Democratic Nationalism, 1830–1920*. Ed. C. A. Bayly and E. F. Biagini. Oxford: Oxford University Press, 2008. 402. Print.

Beckett, Samuel. "Recent Irish Poetry." In *Disjecta: Miscellaneous Writings and a Dramatic Fragment*. Ed. Ruby Cohn. London: Calder, 1983. 70–76. Print.

Behan, Brendan. *Borstal Boy*. London: Arrow, 1990. Print.

———. *The Complete Plays*. New York: Grove, 1978. Print.

———. *Confessions of an Irish Rebel*. London: Arrow, 1991. Print.

Belcham, John. *Irish, Catholic and Scouse: The History of the Liverpool Irish, 1800–1939*. Liverpool: Liverpool University Press, 2007. Print.

Bennet, Andrew and Nicholas Royale. *An Introduction to Literature, Criticism and Theory*. 4th ed. Harlow: Pearson Education, 2009. Print.

Bhabha, Homi K. *The Location of Culture*. London: Routledge, 1994. Print.

Black, Martha Fodaski. *Shaw and Joyce: "The Last Word in Stolentelling."* Gainesville: University Press of Florida, 1995. Print.

Bohman-Kalaja, Kimberly. "Undoing Identities in Two Irish Shaw Plays: *John Bull's Other Island* and *Pygmalion*." *SHAW: The Annual of Bernard Shaw Studies* 30 (2010): 108–32. Print.

Bowen, Elizabeth. "Bowen's Court, 1958." In *Elizabeth Bowen's Selected Irish Writings*. Ed. Eibhear Walshe. Cork: Cork University Press, 2011. 188–97. Print.

———. "Coming to London." In *The Mulberry Tree: Writings of Elizabeth Bowen*. Ed. Hermione Lee. London: Virago, 1986. 85–89. Print.

———. "The Idea of France." In *People, Places, Things: Essays by Elizabeth Bowen*. Ed. Allan Hepburn. Edinburgh: Edinburgh University Press, 2008. 61–65. Print.

———. "James Joyce." In *People, Places, Things: Essays by Elizabeth Bowen*. Ed. Allan Hepburn. Edinburgh: Edinburgh University Press, 2008. 239–47. Print.

———. *The Last September*. Harmondsworth: Penguin, 1987. Print.

———. "Pictures and Conversations." In *The Mulberry Tree: Writings of Elizabeth Bowen*. Ed. Hermione Lee. London: Virago, 1986. 265–98. Print.

———. "Portrait of a Woman Reading." In *Listening In: Broadcasts, Speeches and Interviews*. Ed. Allan Hepburn. Edinburgh: Edinburgh University Press, 2010. 235–9. Print.

———. "Preface to *Uncle Silas*, by Sheridan Le Fanu." In *The Mulberry Tree: Writings of Elizabeth Bowen*. Ed. Hermione Lee. London: Virago, 1986. 100–13. Print.

———. "Review of *James Joyce's Dublin*, by Patricia Hutchins." In *Elizabeth Bowen's Selected Irish Writings*. Ed. Eibhear Walshe. Cork: Cork University Press, 2011. 186–8. Print.

———. "Review of *The Anglo-Irish*, by Brian Fitzgerald." In *The Mulberry Tree: Writings of Elizabeth Bowen*. Ed. Hermione Lee. London: Virago, 1986. 174–6. Print.

Boyle, Ted E. *Brendan Behan*. New York: Twayne, 1969. Print.

Brannigan, John. *Brendan Behan: Cultural Nationalism and the Revisionist Writer*. Dublin: Four Courts, 2002. Print.

Brecht, Bertolt. "Ovation for Shaw." In *G.B. Shaw: A Collection of Critical Essays*. Ed. R. J. Kaufmann. Englewood Cliffs, NJ: Prentice Hall, 1965. 15–18. Print.

Brooke, Charlotte. *Reliques of Irish Poetry*. Ed. Lesa Ní Mhunghaile. Dublin: Irish Manuscripts Commission, 2009. Print.

Brown, Terence. *Ireland's Literature*. Mullingar: Lilliput, 1988. Print.

Brunström, Conrad. *Thomas Sheridan's Career and Influence: An Actor in Earnest*. Lewisburg, PA: Bucknell University Press, 2011. Print.

Carpenter, Andrew, ed. *Verse in English from Eighteenth-Century Ireland*. Dublin: Four Courts, 1998. Print.

"Census 2011 Results for Northern Ireland." *Northern Ireland Statistics and Research Agency*. June 12, 2014. Web. October 16, 2014.

Clare, David. "C.S. Lewis: An Irish Writer." *Irish Studies Review* 18.1 (February 2010): 17–38. Print.

———. "Wilde, Shaw, and Somerville and Ross: Irish Britons, Irish Revivalists, or Both?" *Irish Studies Review* 22.1 (February 2014): 91–103. Print.

Clarke, James Stanier and John McArthur. *The Life and Services of Horatio Viscount Nelson*. Cambridge: Cambridge University Press, 2010. Print.

Coakley, Davis. *Oscar Wilde: The Importance of Being Irish*. Dublin: Town House, 1994.

Collins, Tracy J. R. "Shaw's Athletic-Minded Women." In *Shaw and Feminisms: On Stage and Off*. Ed. D. A. Hadfield and Jean Reynolds. Gainesville: University Press of Florida, 2013. 19–36. Print.

"Come Gather Round People Wherever You Roam" (Transcript of Today FM interview with Gabriel Byrne). *Broadsheet.ie*. November 5, 2012. Web. December 11, 2012.

Connolly, Claire. "Introduction." In *Ormond*. By Maria Edgeworth. London: Penguin, 2000. Print.

Conolly, Leonard W. *Bernard Shaw and the BBC*. Toronto: University of Toronto Press, 2009. Print.

———. "Introduction." In *Pygmalion*. By Bernard Shaw. London: Methuen/ New Mermaids, 2008. Print.

Coogan, Tim Pat. *Wherever Green Is Worn: The Story of the Irish Diaspora*. New York: Palgrave Macmillan, 2001. Print.

Coolahan, John. "The Irish and Others in Irish Nineteenth Century Textbooks." In *The Imperial Curriculum: Racial Images and Education in the British Colonial Experience*. Ed. J. A. Mangan. London: Routledge, 1993. 54–63. Print.

Corcoran, Neil. *Elizabeth Bowen: The Enforced Return*. Oxford: Oxford University Press, 2004. Print.

Corkery, Daniel. *Synge and Anglo-Irish Literature*. Cork: Cork University Press, 1931. Print.

Cowasjee, Saros. *Seán O'Casey: The Man behind the Plays*. Edinburgh and London: Oliver and Boyd, 1963. Print.

Coxhead, Elizabeth. *Lady Gregory: A Literary Portrait*. New York: Harcourt, 1961. Print.

Crawford, F. D. "Shaw among the Houyhnhnms." *The Shaw Review* 19 (September 1976): 102–19. Print.

Crompton, Louis. *Shaw the Dramatist*. Lincoln: University of Nebraska Press, 1969. Print.

Croslegh, Charles. *Descent and Alliances of Croslegh: or Crossle, or Crossley, of Scaitcliffe; and Coddington, of Oldbridge; and Evans, of Eyton Hall*. London: Moring/De La More, 1904. *Google Books*. Web. July 27, 2014.

Cullingford, Elizabeth Butler. "Gender, Sexuality, and Englishness." In *Gender and Sexuality in Modern Ireland*. Ed. Anthony Bradley and Maryann Gialanella Valiulis. Amherst: University of Massachusetts Press, 1997. 159–86. Print.

———. *Ireland's Others: Ethnicity and Gender in Irish Literature and Popular Culture*. Cork: Cork University Press, 2001. Print.

Curtis, Liz. *Nothing But the Same Old Story: The Roots of Anti-Irish Racism*. Belfast: Sásta, 1996. Print.

Davenport, John. "G.K. Chesterton: Nationalist Ireland's English Apologist." *Studies: An Irish Quarterly Review* 103.410 (Summer 2014): 178–92. Print.

Deane, Seamus. *Heroic Styles: The Tradition of an Idea* [Field Day Pamphlet, No. 4]. Derry: Field Day, 1984. Print.

———. "Irish National Character, 1790–1900." In *The Writer as Witness: Literature as Historical Evidence*. Ed. Tom Dunne. Cork: Cork University Press, 1987. 90–113. Print.

Dervin, Daniel. *Bernard Shaw: A Psychological Study*. Lewisburg: Bucknell University Press, 1975. Print.

Dietrich, R. F. "Foreward." In *Shaw, Synge, Connolly, and Socialist Provocation*. By Nelson O'Ceallaigh Ritschel. Gainesville: University Press of Florida, 2011. xi–xiii. Print.

Dolan, Terence Patrick. *A Dictionary of Hiberno-English: The Irish Use of English.* 3rd ed. Dublin: Gill & Macmillan, 2012. Print.

DuPlessis, Nicole M. "ecoLewis: Conservationism and Anticolonialism in *The Chronicles of Narnia.*" In *Wild Things: Children's Culture and Ecocriticism.* Ed. Sidney I. Dobrin and Kenneth B. Kidd. Detroit: Wayne State University Press, 2004. 115–27. Print.

Eagleton, Terry. *Heathcliff and the Great Hunger.* London: Verso, 1995. Print.

———. *The Illusions of Postmodernism.* Oxford: Wiley-Blackwell, 1996. Print.

Edgeworth, Maria. *The Absentee.* Oxford: Oxford University Press, 1988. Print.

———. *Castle Rackrent/Ennui.* London: Penguin, 1992. Print.

———. *Chosen Letters.* Ed. F. V. Barry. London: Cape, 1931. Print.

———. *An Essay on Irish Bulls.* Dublin: University College Dublin Press, 2006. Print

———. *Ormond.* Dublin: Gill and Macmillan, 1990. Print.

Ellmann, Maud. *Elizabeth Bowen: The Shadow Across the Page.* Edinburgh: Edinburgh University Press, 2004. Print.

Fanon, Frantz. *The Wretched of the Earth.* Harmondsworth: Penguin, 1970. Print.

Feldman, Adam. "Shaw Business: David Staller's Project Shaw Offers GBS from A to Z." *Time Out New York.* July 13, 2006. Web. July 1, 2014.

Ferriter, Diarmaid. *Occasions of Sin: Sex and Society in Modern Ireland.* London: Profile, 2009. Print.

Fitz-Simon, Christopher. *The Abbey Theatre: Ireland's National Theatre, The First 100 Years.* New York: Thames & Hudson, 2003. Print.

Foster, John Wilson. "The Irish Renaissance, 1890–1940: Prose in English." In *The Cambridge History of Irish Literature, Volume II.* Ed. Margaret Kelleher and Philip O'Leary. Cambridge: Cambridge University Press, 2006. 113–80. Print.

Foster, R. F. *The Oxford Illustrated History of Ireland.* Oxford: Oxford University Press, 2001. Print.

———. *Paddy & Mr Punch.* London: Allen Lane, 1993. Print.

Friel, Brian. *Essays, Diaries, Interviews: 1964–1999.* Ed. Christopher Murray. London: Faber, 1999. Print.

———. *The Home Place.* London: Faber, 2005. Print.

———. *Plays 1: Philadelphia, Here I Come!/The Freedom of the City/Living Quarters/Aristocrats/Faith Healer/Translations.* London: Faber, 1996. Print.

Gahan, Peter. "Introduction: Bernard Shaw and the Irish Literary Tradition." *SHAW: The Annual of Bernard Shaw Studies* 30 (2010): 1–26. Print.

———. "John Bull's Other War: Bernard Shaw and the Anglo-Irish War, 1918–1921." *SHAW: The Annual of Bernard Shaw Studies* 28 (2008): 209–38. Print.

———. "Shaw Book Series for Palgrave Macmillan." Message to the author. April 18, 2014. E-mail.

———. *Shaw Shadows: Rereading the Texts of Bernard Shaw.* Gainesville: University Press of Florida, 2004. Print.

———. "Shaw's Irish Outlook FIRST DRAFT." Message to the author. September 24, 2014. E-mail.

———. "Things Irish: Review of *The Matter with Ireland* (Second Edition)." *SHAW: The Annual of Bernard Shaw Studies* 22 (2002): 200–208.

Gardiner, Michael. *The Cultural Roots of British Devolution*. Edinburgh: Edinburgh University Press, 2004.

"George Bernard Shaw Giving a Speech at a Dinner in Honor of Albert Einstein." *YouTube.com*. December 10, 2010. Web. December 11, 2012.

"George Bernard Shaw Says to Abolish the Constitution" (1931 Fox Movietone newsreel). *YouTube.com*. January 7, 2010. Web. December 11, 2012.

"George Bernard Shaw's First Visit to America" (1928 Fox Movietone newsreel). *YouTube.com*. December 25, 2008. Web. December 11, 2012.

Gibbs, A. M. *The Art and Mind of Shaw: Essays in Criticism*. London: Macmillan, 1983. Print.

———. *Bernard Shaw: A Life*. Gainesville: University Press of Florida, 2005. Print.

Gilbert, Helen and Joanne Tompkins. *Post-Colonial Drama: Theory, Practice, Politics*. London: Routledge, 1996. Print.

Giles, John Allen. *The Life and Letters of Thomas à Becket, Volume 1*. London: Whittaker, 1846. *Google Books*. Web. October 23, 2010.

Glendinning, Victoria. *Trollope*. London: Pimlico, 1991. Print.

Goldsmith, Oliver. *The Citizen of the World, or, Letters from a Chinese philosopher, Residing in London, to His Friends in the East, Volume 1*. Bungay: Child, 1820. *Google Books*. Web. September 3, 2010.

Graham, Colin. *Deconstructing Ireland: Identity, Theory, Culture*. Edinburgh: Edinburgh University Press, 2001. Print.

Grene, Nicholas. *Bernard Shaw: A Critical View*. London: Macmillan, 1987. Print.

———. "Introduction." In *Pygmalion*. By Bernard Shaw. London: Penguin Classics, 2003. Print.

———. *The Politics of Irish Drama: Plays in Context from Boucicault to Friel*. Cambridge: Cambridge University Press, 1999. Print.

Grenham, John. *Clans and Families of Ireland: The Heritage and Heraldry of Irish Clans and Families*. Dublin: Gill and Macmillan, 1993. Print.

Griffin, Michael. *Enlightenment in Ruins: The Geographies of Oliver Goldsmith*. Lewisburg, PA: Bucknell University Press, 2013. Print.

Gunby, David. "The First Night of *O'Flaherty, VC*." *SHAW: The Annual of Bernard Shaw Studies* 19 (1999): 85–97. Print.

Guteri, Matthew Pratt. *The Color of Race in America: 1900–1940*. Cambridge, MA: Harvard University Press, 2002. Print.

Haas, Michael. *International Human Rights: A Comprehensive Introduction*. 2nd ed. Oxford and New York: Routledge, 2014. Print.

Hand, Derek. "The *Purgatory* of W.B. Yeats." Purgatory: International Conference on Irish Literature and Culture. St Patrick's College, Drumcondra. November 27, 2010. Plenary Address.

Hassan, Ihab. "POSTmodernISM." *New Literary History* 3.1 (Fall 1971): 5–30. Print.

Helleiner, Jane. *Irish Travellers: Racism and the Politics of Culture*. Toronto: University of Toronto Press, 2003. Print.

Hodges, Harold M. *Social Stratification: Class in America*. New York: Schenkman, 1964. Print.

Holloway, Joseph. *Joseph Holloway's Irish Theatre: Volume One, 1926–1930*. Ed. Robert Hogan and Michael O'Neill. Dixon, CA: Proscenium, 1968. Print.

Holroyd, Michael. *Bernard Shaw: The One-Volume Definitive Edition*. London: Vintage, 1998. Print.

———. *Bernard Shaw Volume 1 (1856–1898): The Search for Love*. London: Penguin, 1988. Print.

———. *Bernard Shaw Volume 2 (1898–1918): The Pursuit of Power*. New York: Vintage, 1991. Print.

———. *Bernard Shaw Volume 3 (1919–1950): The Lure of Fantasy*. New York: Vintage, 1991. Print.

Houchin, John H. *Censorship of the American Theatre in the Twentieth Century*. Cambridge: Cambridge University Press, 2003. Print.

Hume, David H. "Empire Day in Ireland." In *'An Irish Empire'?: Aspects of Ireland and the British Empire*. Ed. Keith Jeffery. Manchester: Manchester University Press, 1996. 149–68. Print.

Hyde, Douglas. "The Necessity for De-Anglicizing Ireland." In *Irish Writing in the Twentieth Century: A Reader*. Ed. David Pierce. Cork: Cork University Press, 2000. 2–13. Print.

Hyman, Louis. *The Jews of Ireland: From Earliest Times to the Year 1910*. London: Jewish Historical Society of England/Jerusalem: Israel Universities Press, 1972. Print.

Ignatiev, Noel. *How the Irish Became White*. New York: Routledge, 1995. Print.

Inglis, Tom. *Global Ireland: Same Difference*. New York: Routledge, 2008. Print.

Innes, Christopher. "Defining Irishness: Bernard Shaw and the Irish Connection on the English Stage." In *A Companion to Irish Literature, Volume One*. Ed. Julia M. Wright. Chichester: Wiley, 2010. 35–49. Print.

Irvine, St John. *Bernard Shaw: His Life, Work and Friends*. London: Constable, 1956. Print.

Irvine, William. *The Universe of G.B.S.* New York: Russell & Russell, 1968. Print.

Jamieson, John, John Johnstone, and John Longmuir. *Jamieson's Dictionary of the Scottish Language*. Edinburgh: Nimmo, 1867. *Google Books*. Web. October 10, 2014.

Jenckes, Norma. "The Rejection of Shaw's Irish Play: *John Bull's Other Island*." *Éire-Ireland* 10 (Spring 1975): 38–53. Print.

Johnston, Denis. "Giants in Those Days." In *Orders and Desecrations*. Ed. Rory Johnston. Dublin: Lilliput, 1992. 175–201. Print.

Joyce, James. *Dubliners*. London: Penguin, 1956. Print.

———. "Oscar Wilde: The Poet of *Salomé*." In *Occasional, Critical, and Political Writing*. Ed. Kevin Barry. Oxford: Oxford University Press, 2000. 148–51. Print.

———. *A Portrait of the Artist as a Young Man*. Ware: Wordsworth, 1992. Print.

———. "Review of *The Shewing-up of Blanco Posnet*." In *Shaw: The Critical Heritage*. Ed. T.F. Evans. London: Routledge, 1976. 197–9. Print.

———. *Ulysses*. London: Penguin, 2000. Print.

Kennedy, Seán. "'The Beckett Country' Revisited: Beckett, Belonging and Longing." In *Ireland: Space, Text, Time*. Ed. Liam Harte, Yvonne Whelan, and Patrick Crotty. Dublin: Liffey, 2005. 135–44. Print.

———. "Edmund Spenser, Famine Memory and the Discontents of Humanism in *Endgame*." *Samuel Beckett Today/Aujourd'hui* 24 (2012): 105–20. Print.

Kenny, Shirley Strum, ed. "Notes." In *The Works of George Farquhar, Volume I*. By George Farquhar. Oxford: Oxford University Press, 1988. Print.

Kent, Brad. "The Politics of Shaw's Irish Women in *John Bull's Other Island*." In *Shaw and Feminisms: On Stage and Off*. Ed. D. A. Hadfield and Jean Reynolds. Gainesville: University Press of Florida, 2013. 73–91. Print.

Kiberd, Declan. *Inventing Ireland: The Literature of the Modern Nation*. London: Vintage, 1995. Print.

———. *Irish Classics*. London: Granta, 2000. Print.

———. *The Irish Writer and the World*. Cambridge: Cambridge University Press, 2005.

———. "The Language of Synge." The Abbey Theatre, Dublin. April 12, 2011. Public Lecture.

———. "The London Exiles: Wilde and Shaw." In *The Field Day Anthology of Irish Writing, Volume 2*. Ed. Seamus Deane et al. Derry: Field Day, 1991. 372–6. Print.

———. *Ulysses and Us: The Art of Everyday Living*. London: Faber, 2009. Print.

Kosok, Heinz. "John Bull's Other Eden." *SHAW: The Annual of Bernard Shaw Studies* 30 (2010): 175–190. Print.

———. "John Bull's Other Ego: Reactions to the Stage Irishman in Anglo-Irish Drama." In *Medieval and Modern Ireland*. Ed. Richard Wall. London: Rowan & Littlefield, 1988. 19–33. Print.

———. *O'Casey the Dramatist*. Gerrards Cross: Colin Smythe, 1985. Print.

Krause, David. "John Bull's Other Island." In *Modern Irish Drama*. Ed. John P. Harrington. New York: Norton, 1991. 488–92. Print.

Kumar, Krishan. *The Making of English National Identity*. Cambridge: Cambridge University Press, 2003. Print.

Laurence, Dan H. and Nicholas Grene, eds. *Shaw, Lady Gregory, and the Abbey: A Correspondence and a Record*. Gerrards Cross: Colin Smythe, 1993. Print.

Lawrence, Errol. "In the Abundance of Water the Fool Is Thirsty: Sociology and Black 'Pathology.'" In *The Empire Strikes Back: Race and Racism in 70s Britain*. Ed. The Centre for Cultural Studies at the University of Birmingham. Oxford: Taylor & Francis, 2005. 93–139. Print.

Leary, Daniel J. "Entry for *Heartbreak House.*" In *The Reader's Encyclopedia of World Drama.* Ed. John Gassner and Edward Quinn. New York: Dover, 2002. 414. Print.

Leerssen, Joep. *Mere Irish and Fíor-Gael: Studies in the Idea of Irish Nationality, its Development and Literary Expression prior to the Nineteenth Century.* Cork: Cork University Press, 1996. Print.

Lees, Lynn Hillen. *Exiles of Erin: Irish Migrants in Victorian London.* Manchester: Manchester University Press, 1979. Print.

Letts, W. M. *Songs from Leinster.* London: Smith, Elder & Co., 1914. 40–41. Print.

Lewis, C. S. *All My Road Before Me: The Diary of C.S. Lewis, 1922–1927.* Ed. Walter Hooper. London: HarperCollins, 1993. Print.

———. *An Experiment in Criticism.* Cambridge: Cambridge University Press, 1961. Print.

———. *Collected Letters, Volume 1: Family Letters, 1905–1931.* Ed. Walter Hooper. London: HarperCollins, 2000. Print.

———. *Collected Letters, Volume 2: Books, Broadcasts, and the War, 1931–1949.* Ed. Walter Hooper. San Francisco: HarperCollins, 2004. Print.

———. *Collected Letters, Volume 3: Narnia, Cambridge and Joy, 1950–1963.* Ed. Walter Hooper. San Francisco: HarperCollins, 2007. Print.

———. "Edmund Spenser, 1552–99." In *Studies in Medieval and Renaissance Literature.* Cambridge: Cambridge University Press, 1998. 121–45. Print.

———. *Out of the Silent Planet/Perelandra.* London: Voyager/HarperCollins, 2000. Print.

———. *Spirits in Bondage: A Cycle of Lyrics.* San Diego: Harcourt, 1984. Print.

———. *Surprised by Joy: The Shape of My Early Life.* New York: Harcourt, 1984. Print.

Lewis, Gifford. *Edith Somerville: A Biography.* Dublin: Four Courts, 2005. Print.

———. "Notes." In *The Selected Letters of Somerville & Ross.* By E.Œ. Somerville & Martin Ross. London: Faber, 1989. Print.

Logue, Paddy, ed. *Being Irish.* Dublin: Oak Tree, 2000. Print.

Longley, Edna. *The Living Stream: Literature and Revisionism in Ireland.* Newcastle: Bloodaxe, 1994. Print.

Lynch, Deidre Shauna. *The Economy of Character: Novels, Market Culture, and the Business of Inner Meaning.* Chicago: University of Chicago Press, 1998. Print.

MacLysaght, Edward. *The Surnames of Ireland.* Dublin: Irish Academic Press, 1985. Print.

Mathews, P. J. *Revival: The Abbey Theatre, Sinn Fein, The Gaelic League and the Co-operative Movement.* Cork: Cork University Press, 2003. Print.

McCormack, W. J. *Ascendancy and Tradition in Anglo-Irish Literary History from 1789 to 1939.* Oxford: Clarendon, 1985. Print.

———. *Fool of the Family: A Life of J.M. Synge.* New York: New York University Press, 2000. Print.

———. *From Burke to Beckett: Ascendancy, Tradition and Betrayal in Literary History*. Cork: Cork University Press, 1994. Print.

———. "Introduction." In *Ormond*. By Maria Edgeworth. Dublin: Gill & Macmillan, 1990. Print.

———. "Irish Gothic and After." In *The Field Day Anthology of Irish Writing, Volume II*. Ed. Seamus Deane et. al. Derry: Field Day, 1991. 832–54. Print.

McCormack, W. J. and Kim Walker. Introduction. *The Absentee*. By Maria Edgeworth. Oxford: Oxford University Press, 1988. Print.

McDiarmid, Lucy. *The Irish Art of Controversy*. Dublin: Lilliput, 2005. Print.

McNamara, Audrey. "Bernard Shaw's *Saint Joan*: An Irish Female Patriot." ACIS Conference. University College Dublin. June 11, 2014. Conference Paper.

Mercier, Vivian. "Victorian Evangelicalism and the Anglo-Irish Literary Revival." In *Literature and the Changing Ireland*. Ed. Peter Connolly. Gerrards Cross: Colin Smythe, 1980. 59–101. Print.

Miall, Anthony and David Milsted. *The Xenophobe's Guide to the English*. London: Oval, 1999. Print.

Milward, Peter. "What Lewis Has Meant for Me." In *C.S. Lewis Remembered: Collected Reflections of Students, Friends and Colleagues*. Ed. Harry Lee Poe and Rebecca Whitten Poe. Grand Rapids, MI: Zondervan, 2006. E-book.

Montaño, John Patrick. *The Roots of English Colonialism in Ireland*. Cambridge: Cambridge University Press, 2011. Print.

Moran, James. "Meditations in Time of Civil War: *Back to Methuselah* and *Saint Joan* in Production, 1919–1924." *SHAW: The Annual of Bernard Shaw Studies* 30 (2010): 147–60. Print.

———. *Staging the Easter Rising: 1916 as Theatre*. Cork: Cork University Press, 2005. Print.

Mugglestone, Lynda. *Talking Proper: The Rise of Accent as Social Symbol*. Oxford: Oxford University Press, 2007. Print.

Murphy, Colin. "A Major Hit 100 Years Ago, It's Been a Long Wait to See Shaw's 'Barbara' at the Abbey." *Irish Independent* August 3, 2013. Web. July 1, 2014.

Murphy, Colin and Lynne Adair, eds. *Untold Stories: Protestants in the Republic of Ireland, 1922–2002*. Dublin: Liffey, 2002. Print.

Murray, Christopher. *Seán O'Casey: Writer at Work*. Dublin: Gill & Macmillan, 2004. Print.

Musselman, Kristin Swenson. "The Other I: Questions of Identity in *Un Vie de Boy*." In *Francophone Post-colonial Cultures: Critical Essays*. Ed. Kamal Sahli. Lanham, MD: Lexington, 2003. 126–37. Print.

Naipaul, V. S. *An Area of Darkness*. London: Vintage, 2002. Print.

Nelson, Daniel and Laura Neack. *Global Society in Transition: An International Politics Reader*. New York: Kluwer, 2002. Print.

Ní Dhuibhne, Éilis. "The Irish." In *Europeans: Essays on Cultural Identity*. Ed. Åke Daun and Sören Jansson. Lund: Nordic Academic Press, 1999. 47–65. Print.

Nicoll, Allardyce. *English Drama, 1900–1930: The Beginnings of the Modern Period*. Cambridge: Cambridge University Press, 1973. Print.

Ó hAodha, Micheál. "Some Irish American Theatre Links." In *America and Ireland, 1776–1976: The American Identity and the Irish Connection*. Ed. Con Howard, David Noel Doyle, and Owen Dudley Edwards. Westport, CT: Greenwood, 1980. 295–306. Print.

O'Brien, Darcy. *Patrick Kavanagh*. Lewisburg, PA: Bucknell University Press, 1975. Print.

O'Casey, Seán. *Drums under the Window*. London: Macmillan, 1946. Print.

———. *Three Dublin Plays: The Shadow of a Gunman/Juno and the Paycock/The Plough and the Stars*. London: Faber, 1998.

———. *Three More Plays by Seán O'Casey: The Silver Tassie/Purple Dust/Red Roses for Me*. London: Papermac/Macmillan, 1965. Print.

O'Connor, Flannery. *Mystery and Manners: Occasional Prose*. London: Faber, 1984. Print.

O'Donovan, John. *Shaw and the Charlatan Genius: A Memoir*. Dublin: Dolmen, 1965. Print.

O'Laughlin, Michael. *The Book of Irish Families, Great & Small*. Kansas City, MO: Irish Roots, 2002. Print.

O'Toole, Fintan. "Shaw Was an Anarchist: Where is all the Chaos?" *Irish Times* May 14, 2011. B9. Print.

———. *A Traitor's Kiss: A Life of Richard Brinsley Sheridan*. New York: Farrar, Strauss and Giroux, 1998. Print.

O'Toole, Tina. *The Irish New Woman*. Houndmills: Palgrave Macmillan, 2013. Print.

Palmer, A. S. *Folk-Etymology*. New York: Haskell, 1969. Print.

Patridge, Eric, Tom Dalzell, and Terry Victor. *The Concise New Partridge Dictionary of Slang and Unconventional English*. London: Routledge, 2008. Print.

Pearson, Hesketh. *G.B.S.: A Full Length Portrait*. New York and London: Harper, 1942. Print.

Pocock, J. G. A. "British History: A Plea for a New Subject." *The Journal of Modern History* 47.4 (December 1975): 601–21. Print.

Powell, Violet. *The Irish Cousins: The Books and Background of Somerville and Ross*. London: Heinemann, 1970. Print.

Reaney. P. H. and E. M. Wilson, *A Dictionary of English Surnames*. London: Routledge, 1991. Print.

Reed, John R. *Old School Ties: The Public School in British Literature*. Syracuse, NY: Syracuse University Press, 1964. Print.

Ritschel, Nelson O'Ceallaigh. *Shaw, Synge, Connolly, and Socialist Provocation*. Gainesville: University Press of Florida, 2011. Print.

Roche, Anthony. *Contemporary Irish Drama: From Beckett to McGuinness*. New York: St Martin's, 1995. Print.

———. *The Irish Dramatic Revival, 1899–1939*. London: Bloomsbury Methuen, 2015. Print.

Rodgers, W. R., ed. "George Bernard Shaw." In *Irish Literary Portraits: W. B. Yeats, James Joyce, George Moore, J. M. Synge, George Bernard Shaw, Oliver St John Gogarty, F. R. Higgins, AE (George Russell)*. London: BBC, 1972. 116–41. Print.

Roll-Hansen, Diderick. "Shaw's *Pygmalion*: The Two Versions of 1916 and 1941." *Review of English Studies* 8.3 (July 1967): 81–90. Print.

Rollins, Ronald. *Seán O'Casey's Drama*. Tuscaloosa: University of Alabama Press, 1979. Print.

Roper, Michael. *Masculinity and the British Organisation Man since 1945*. Oxford: Oxford University Press, 1994. Print.

Rosset, Barney. *Shaw of Dublin: The Formative Years*. Harrisburg: Pennsylvania State University Press, 1964. Print.

Scanlon, Thomas. *Colonial Writing and the New World, 1583–1671: Allegories of Desire*. Cambridge: Cambridge University Press, 1999. Print.

Share, Bernard. *Slanguage: A Dictionary of Irish Slang*. Dublin: Gill & Macmillan, 1997. Print.

Shaw, Bernard. *The Admirable Bashville*. In *Selected Short Plays*. Harmondsworth: Penguin, 1987. 1–41. Print.

———. "An Appeal to the IRA (1940)." In *The Matter with Ireland*. Ed. Dan H. Laurence and David H. Greene. 2nd ed. Gainesville: University Press of Florida, 2001. 310–8. Print.

———. *An Autobiography 1856–1898*. Ed. Stanley Weintraub. New York: Reinhardt, 1970. Print.

———. *Back to Methuselah*. London: Penguin, 1990. Print.

———. *The Black Girl in Search of God and Some Lesser Tales*. Harmondsworth: Penguin, 1966. Print.

———. "The British Offer (1921)." In *The Matter with Ireland*. Ed. Dan H. Laurence and David H. Greene. 2nd ed. Gainesville: University Press of Florida, 2001. 262–7. Print.

———. "Brogue-Shock (1917)." In *The Matter with Ireland*. Ed. Dan H. Laurence and David H. Greene. 2nd ed. Gainesville: University Press of Florida, 2001. 147–52. Print.

———. "Capital Punishment (December 5, 1947)." In *The Letters of Bernard Shaw to* The Times. Ed. Ronald Ford. Dublin: Irish Academic Press, 2007. 268–269. Print.

———. *Captain Brassbound's Conversion*. In *Three Plays for Puritans*. London: Penguin, 1970. 255–347. Print.

———. *Cashel Byron's Profession*. New York: Brentano's, 1904. Print.

———. "Child-Beating: A Bishop's Letter from Mr Bernard Shaw." *The Irish Times* February 25, 1928. 9.

———. *Collected Letters, 1898–1910*. Ed. Dan H. Laurence. New York: Dodd, 1972. Print.

———. *Collected Letters, 1911–1925*. Ed. Dan H. Laurence. New York: Viking, 1985. Print.

———. *Collected Letters, 1926–1950*. Ed. Dan H. Laurence. New York: Viking Penguin, 1988. Print.

———. "Dear Harp of my Country!" In *The Portable Shaw*. Ed. Stanley Weintraub. New York: Penguin, 1986. 111–16. Print.

———. *The Doctor's Dilemma*. London: Penguin, 1987. Print.

———. "The Dominion League (1919)." In *The Matter with Ireland*. Ed. Dan H. Laurence and David H. Greene. 2nd ed. Gainesville: University Press of Florida, 2001. 205–8. Print.

———. *Dramatic Opinions and Essays with an Apology, Volume 2*. New York: Brentano's, 1906. Print.

———. "Eamon De Valera and the Second World War (1940–44)." In *The Matter with Ireland*. Ed. Dan H. Laurence and David H. Greene. 2nd ed. Gainesville: University Press of Florida, 2001. 319–26. Print.

———. "The Easter Week Executions (1916)." In *The Matter with Ireland*. Ed. Dan H. Laurence and David H. Greene. 2nd ed. Gainesville: University Press of Florida, 2001. 124–6. Print.

———. "The Eve of Civil War (1922)." In *The Matter with Ireland*. Ed. Dan H. Laurence and David H. Greene. 2nd ed. Gainesville: University Press of Florida, 2001. 273–5. Print.

———. "A Film Industry for Ireland (1945–47)." In *The Matter with Ireland*. Ed. Dan H. Laurence and David H. Greene. 2nd ed. Gainesville: University Press of Florida, 2001. 331–3. Print.

———. "The Gaelic League (1910)." In *The Matter with Ireland*. Ed. Dan H. Laurence and David H. Greene. 2nd ed. Gainesville: University Press of Florida, 2001. 63–5. Print.

———. *Geneva*. In *Plays Political*. London: Penguin, 1986. 305–461. Print.

———. *Getting Married/Press Cuttings*. London: Penguin, 1986. Print.

———. "The Greatest Living Irishman? (1941)." In *The Matter with Ireland*. Ed. Dan H. Laurence and David H. Greene. 2nd ed. Gainesville: University Press of Florida, 2001. 327–8. Print.

———. *Heartbreak House*. London: Penguin, 1976. Print.

———. "How to Settle the Irish Question (1917)." In *The Matter with Ireland*. Ed. Dan H. Laurence and David H. Greene. 2nd ed. Gainesville: University Press of Florida, 2001. 153–73. Print.

———. "Ireland and the First World War (1914)." In *The Matter with Ireland*. Ed. Dan H. Laurence and David H. Greene. 2nd ed. Gainesville: University Press of Florida, 2001. 101–4. Print.

———. "Ireland Eternal and External (1948)." In *The Matter with Ireland*. Ed. Dan H. Laurence and David H. Greene. 2nd ed. Gainesville: University Press of Florida, 2001. 339–41. Print.

———. "The Irish Censorship (1928)." In *The Matter with Ireland*. Ed. Dan H. Laurence and David H. Greene. 2nd ed. Gainesville: University Press of Florida, 2001. 293–8. Print.

———. "Irish Nonsense about Ireland (1916)." In *The Matter with Ireland*. Ed. Dan H. Laurence and David H. Greene. 2nd ed. Gainesville: University Press of Florida, 2001. 112–9. Print.

———. "The Irish Players (1911)." In *The Matter with Ireland*. Ed. Dan H. Laurence and David H. Greene. 2nd ed. Gainesville: University Press of Florida, 2001. 71–77. Print.

———. *John Bull's Other Island*. London: Penguin, 1984. Print.

———. "Literature in Ireland (1918)." In *The Matter with Ireland*. Ed. Dan H. Laurence and David H. Greene. 2nd ed. Gainesville: University Press of Florida, 2001. 176–9. Print.

———. "Mad Dogs in Uniform (1913)." In *The Matter with Ireland*. Ed. Dan H. Laurence and David H. Greene. 2nd ed. Gainesville: University Press of Florida, 2001. 95–97. Print.

———. *Major Barbara*. New York: Penguin, 1978. Print.

———. *Man and Superman*. London: Penguin, 2004. Print.

———. *The Man of Destiny*. In *Plays Pleasant*. Harmondsworth: Penguin, 1949. 178–228. Print.

———. *The Matter with Ireland*. Ed. Dan H. Laurence and David H. Greene. 2nd ed. Gainesville: University Press of Florida, 2001. Print.

———. *The Millionairess*. In *Plays Extravagant*. London: Penguin, 1991. 213–320. Print.

———. *Misalliance/The Fascinating Foundling*. Harmondsworth: Penguin, 1984. Print.

———. *Mrs Warren's Profession*. In *Plays Unpleasant*. London: Penguin, 2000. 179–286. Print.

———. "The New Nation (1917)." In *The Matter with Ireland*. Ed. Dan H. Laurence and David H. Greene. 2nd ed. Gainesville: University Press of Florida, 2001. 174–5. Print.

———. "A Note on Aggressive Nationalism (1913)." In *The Matter with Ireland*. Ed. Dan H. Laurence and David H. Greene. 2nd ed. Gainesville: University Press of Florida, 2001. 91–94. Print.

———. *O'Flaherty, V.C.* In *Selected Short Plays*. New York: Penguin, 1987. 253–77. Print.

———. "On St Patrick's Cathedral (1935)." In *The Matter with Ireland*. Ed. Dan H. Laurence and David H. Greene. 2nd ed. Gainesville: University Press of Florida, 2001. 305. Print.

———. "On Throwing Out Dirty Water (1923)." In *The Matter with Ireland*. Ed. Dan H. Laurence and David H. Greene. 2nd ed. Gainesville: University Press of Florida, 2001. 285–9. Print.

———. "Preface: Fragments of Autobiography." In *The Matter with Ireland*. Ed. Dan H. Laurence and David H. Greene. 2nd ed. Gainesville: University Press of Florida, 2001. 1–13. Print.

———. "The Playwright on His First Play." In *The Portable Bernard Shaw*. Ed. Stanley Weintraub. New York: Penguin, 1986. 48–56. Print.

———. "The Protestants of Ireland (1912)." In *The Matter with Ireland*. Ed. Dan H. Laurence and David H. Greene. 2nd ed. Gainesville: University Press of Florida, 2001. 78–83. Print.

———. *Pygmalion*. New York: Dover, 1994. Print.

———. "Roger Casement (1916–37)." In *The Matter with Ireland*. Ed. Dan H. Laurence and David H. Greene. 2nd ed. Gainesville: University Press of Florida, 2001. 127–46. Print.

———. *Saint Joan*. London: Penguin, 1957. Print.

———. "Shaw Speaks to His Native City (1946)." In *The Matter with Ireland*. Ed. Dan H. Laurence and David H. Greene. 2nd ed. Gainesville: University Press of Florida, 2001. 334–8. Print.

———. *The Shewing-up of Blanco Posnet/Fanny's First Play*. London: Penguin, 1987. Print.

———. "Sir Edward Carson's Other Island (1918)." In *The Matter with Ireland*. Ed. Dan H. Laurence and David H. Greene. 2nd ed. Gainesville: University Press of Florida, 2001. 202–4. Print.

———. *Sixteen Self Sketches*. New York: Dodd, 1949. Print.

———. "Socialism and Ireland (1919)." In *The Matter with Ireland*. Ed. Dan H. Laurence and David H. Greene. 2nd ed. Gainesville: University Press of Florida, 2001. 233–49. Print.

———. "The Third Home Rule Bill and Ulster (1913)." In *The Matter with Ireland*. Ed. Dan H. Laurence and David H. Greene. 2nd ed. Gainesville: University Press of Florida, 2001. 84–90. Print.

———. "Touring in Ireland (1916)." In *The Matter with Ireland*. Ed. David H. Greene and Dan H. Laurence. 1st ed. London: Hart-Davis, 1962. 92–9. Print. (*NOTE*: Part II of this essay is missing from the second edition of *The Matter with Ireland*.)

———. "Wake Up, Ulster! (1914)." In *The Matter with Ireland*. Ed. Dan H. Laurence and David H. Greene. 2nd ed. Gainesville: University Press of Florida, 2001. 98–100. Print.

———. "Why Devolution Will Not Do (1919–20)." In *The Matter with Ireland*. Ed. Dan H. Laurence and David H. Greene. 2nd ed. Gainesville: University Press of Florida, 2001. 213–26. Print.

———. *Widowers' Houses*. In *Plays Unpleasant*. London: Penguin, 2000. 29–96. Print.

———. *You Never Can Tell*. In *Plays Pleasant*. Harmondsworth: Penguin, 1949. 229–348. Print.

Silver, Arnold. *Bernard Shaw: The Darker Side*. Stanford, CA: Stanford University Press, 1982. Print.

Simpson, Alan. *Beckett and Behan and a Theatre in Dublin*. London: Routledge, 1962. Print.

Sisson, Elaine. *Pearse's Patriots: St Enda's and the Cult of Boyhood*. Cork: Cork University Press, 2004. Print.

Somerville, E. Œ. & Martin Ross. *The Irish R.M.* London: Abacus, 2005. Print.

———. *The Selected Letters of Somerville & Ross*. Ed. Gifford Lewis. London: Faber, 1989. Print.

Spivak, Gayatri. *A Critique of Postcolonial Reason: Toward a History of the Vanishing Present*. Cambridge, MA: Harvard University Press, 1999. Print.

Sternlicht, Sanford V. *A Reader's Guide to Modern Irish Drama*. Syracuse: Syracuse University Press, 1998. Print.

Stevens, Julie Ann. *The Irish Scene in Somerville & Ross*. Dublin: Irish Academic Press, 2007. Print.

"Surname History: Higgins." *Irish Times.com*. n.d. Web. December 26, 2012.

Synge, J. M. *The Collected Letters of J.M. Synge, Volume One (1871–1907)*. Ed. Ann Saddlemyer. Oxford: Clarendon, 1983. Print.

———. *Collected Works I: Poems*. Ed. Robin Skelton. Oxford: Oxford University Press, 1968. Print.

———. *Collected Works II: Prose*. Ed. Alan Price. Oxford: Oxford University Press, 1966. Print.

Taylor, Miles. "John Bull." *Oxford Dictionary of National Biography*. May 2006. Web. August 1, 2013.

Throop, Elizabeth A. *Net Curtains and Closed Doors: Intimacy, Family, and Public Life in Dublin*. Westport, CT: Greenwood, 1999. Print.

Tracy, Robert. "Maria Edgeworth and Lady Morgan: Legality versus Legitimacy." *Nineteenth-Century Fiction* 40 (June 1985): 1–22. Print.

———. *The Unappeasable Host: Studies in Irish Identities*. Dublin: University College Dublin Press, 1998. Print.

Tunney, Jay R. *The Prizefighter and the Playwright: Gene Tunney and Bernard Shaw*. Tonawanda, NJ: Firefly, 2010. Print.

Turco, Alfred. *Shaw's Moral Vision: The Self and Salvation*. Ithaca: Cornell University Press, 1976. Print.

Twark, Jill E. *Humor, Satire, and Identity: Eastern German Literature in the 1990s*. Berlin: de Gruyter, 2007. Print.

Tyson, Brian. *The Story of Shaw's Saint Joan*. Montreal: McGill-Queen's, 1982. Print.

Wadleigh Chandler, Frank. *Aspects of Modern Drama*. London: Macmillan, 1914. Print.

Walford, Edward. *The County Families of the United Kingdom; or, Royal Manual of the Titled and Untitled Aristocracy of Great Britain and Ireland*. London: Hardwicke, 1869. *Google Books*. Web. July 27, 2014.

Wall, Richard. "Introduction and Notes." In *An Giall/The Hostage*. By Brendan Behan. Washington, DC: Catholic University of America Press, 1987. Print.

Weber, Max. *The Protestant Ethic and the Spirit of Capitalism*. Trans. Peter Baehr and Gordon C. Wells. London: Penguin, 2002. Print.

Weintraub, Stanley. *Bernard Shaw 1914–1918: Journey to Heartbreak*. London: Routledge, 1973. Print.

———. "'Lawrence of Arabia': Bernard Shaw's Other Saint Joan." *South Atlantic Quarterly* 64 (Spring 1965): 194–205. Print.

Whelan, Feargal. "*A Dirty Low-Down Low-Church Protestant High-Brow*: The Shape of Protestantism in Samuel Beckett's Work." *Emerging Perspectives* 1.1 (Autumn, 2010): 4–15. Print.

———. "Samuel Beckett and the Irish Protestant Imagination." Diss. University College Dublin, 2014. Print.

White, James L. and James H. Cones. *Black Man Emerging: Facing the Past and Seizing a Future in America*. New York: Routledge, 1999. Print.

Wills, Clair. *That Neutral Island: A Cultural History of Ireland During the Second World War*. London: Faber, 2008. Print.

Woloch, Alex. *The One vs. the Many: Minor Characters and the Space of the Protagonist in the Novel*. Princeton: Princeton University Press, 2003. Print.

Woodruff, Philip. *The Men Who Ruled India, Volume 2: The Guardians*. London: Cape, 1954. Print.

Woolf, Virginia. *The Diary of Virginia Woolf, Volume 4*. Ed. Anne Olivier Bell, with Andrew McNellie. New York: Harcourt, 1982. Print.

Woulfe, Patrick. *Irish Names and Surnames*. Dublin: Gill, 1922. Print.

Yeats, W. B. *The Collected Letters of W. B. Yeats, Volume III, 1901–1904*. Ed. John Kelly and Ronald Schuchard. Oxford: Clarendon, 1994. Print.

———. *The Collected Works of W. B. Yeats, Volume I: The Poems*. Ed. Richard J. Finneran. New York: Scribner, 1997. Print.

———. *The Collected Works of W. B. Yeats, Volume III: Autobiographies*. Ed. William H. O'Donnell and Douglas N. Archibald. New York: Scribner, 1999. Print.

———. *The Letters of W.B. Yeats*. Ed. Allan Wade. London: Hart-Davis, 1954. Print.

———. *Memoirs*. Ed. Denis Donoghue. London: Papermac/Macmillan, 1988. Print.

———. *Purgatory*. In *Eleven Plays of William Butler Yeats*. Ed. A. Norman Jeffares. New York: Macmillan, 1964. 197–206. Print.

Archival Materials

Copy deed of release (AR/add/52/22) among the Shaw Family Papers, housed at the Dublin City Archives in the Pearse Street Library, Dublin 2. An image of this deed can now be viewed online: "Reading Room: History & Heritage: Big Houses of Ireland: Shaws of Dublin: Estate Deeds." An Chomhairle Leabharlanna's *Allaboutireland.com*. n.d. Web. February 23, 2015.

The Siobhán McKenna, An Taibhdhearc, and digital Abbey Theatre archives housed at the Hardiman Library at the National University of Ireland, Galway.

Index

Lightning Source UK Ltd.
Milton Keynes UK
UKHW01f1844161018
330662UK00001B/64/P